A DETECTIVE SUPERINTENDENT
MATT DARNLEY INVESTIGATION

A DUTY OF
REVENGE

QUENTIN DOWSE

Matador
9 Priory Business Park,
Wistow Road, Kibworth Beauchamp,
Leicestershire. LE8 0RX
Tel: 0116 279 2299
Email: books@troubador.co.uk
Web: www.troubador.co.uk/matador
Twitter: @matadorbooks

ISBN 978 1800462 434

British Library Cataloguing in Publication Data.
A catalogue record for this book is available from the British Library.

Printed and bound in Great Britain by 4edge Limited
Typeset in 12pt Adobe Garamond by Troubador Publishing Ltd, Leicester, UK

Matador is an imprint of Troubador Publishing Ltd

*To all those friends and colleagues
who played real parts in the story
of my thirty years of policing*

Foreword

Food for Thought

By the time any police officer has twelve months' service under their belts, they will have a handful of sad, funny, frightening or just downright crazy tales to tell. By the time they retire, they'll have hundreds – and they love to tell them. A large proportion of these tales extol the positive virtues of the central character as daring, astute, tough, cunning, funny – an amazing array of traits can help describe a "good copper". Other tales, however, get repeated because the main player was useless, frightened, cynical, thick, a drunk, a bully or bent.

The stories always start in the relatively small geographical area where "it happened" – in or near the local nick. The best stories spread more widely – throughout several stations, the division, the force and further. They are recirculated over and over again – literally for years, subtly changing as things are added, new words said or even different people appear. Fiction built on fact. A few stories become part of local police folklore and their main characters legends, helping create a local policing culture. Ask any copper who has moved around stations and departments how many different cultures they have had to adapt to.

Then we come to a second set of stories.

These are played out in the endless diet of high-octane cop shows on TV, and in films and books. Many officers can't bear to watch their TV counterparts, or if they do, ruin the experience for their families with a running critique of the shows' plot holes and endless comments such as – "That would never happen." The stereotypical modern TV cop, far removed from *Dixon of Dock Green,* may tarnish their own image of their chosen career – fashioned by that local folklore and culture. A few others actually identify with and mimic their TV heroes. Whatever the effect on serving officers, there is little doubt that this drip-feed of fictional crime, criminals and cops fuels a wider cultural view of policing.

Finally, there's a third set.

Stories that can only be told by the people who actually played a part and who must promise to "tell the truth, the whole truth and nothing but the truth". The storytellers are even cross-examined to ensure accuracy. A story recorded word for word, backed up by sworn documentary evidence and scientific fact.

These stories appear in the newspapers, on the radio and TV news, with some even ending up as documentaries or films. For the most controversial, only a public inquiry can be seen to get to the "whole truth". Think of the Yorkshire Ripper, Brady and Hindley, Fred and Rosemary West – an endless list of true crimes, with a cast of real characters etched into the nation's subconscious.

These stories help shape the nation's view of our police officers and their forces. Who hasn't formed a view of The Met through the murder of Stephen Lawrence, or of South Yorkshire through the Hillsborough Disaster? But even under this intense scrutiny, we are always left with question marks. What really happened? Where is the body? Who gave the order? Why didn't she speak up sooner? Was the "confession" lawfully obtained? Whose fault was it?

In reality, is it even possible to answer all of the questions? Where do the answers lie?

In any well-investigated, serious and complex crime, there will genuinely be some unanswerable questions. Not every conundrum can be explained. But sometimes the truth is deliberately hidden. Dodgy deals and sordid secrets do exist. Those "secret" parts of major crimes are told – but only in hushed tones amongst trusted friends.

True justice can only be delivered within the rule of law and in my experience nearly always is. But this story is about revenge – justice taken, not delivered. As you will see, even the main characters involved never knew "the truth, the whole truth and nothing but the truth". Only I did.

Matt Darnley
Detective Superintendent (Retired)

One

Spitting did not come naturally to Anne Beedham. Her initial idea had been to try a head-butt, but even in her panic she'd worked out that would hurt her more than her attacker. Spitting was the only form of attack left, as she couldn't move her arms or legs. Her spittle landing on the only part of the man's face that was visible, his eyes, gave her a momentary sense of satisfaction, but the stinging slap that followed jolted her back to reality. Anne Beedham was a suburban, middle-class wife and mother, and being struck was as alien to her as spitting, but within the last hour she had found herself in a world she had only ever seen on the TV or films.

The man wiped his eyes with his free arm and then resumed where he had left off before she had decided she had had enough of being a placid victim. Pushing her back against the desk, he roughly thrust his right hand beneath the hem of her skirt and between her thighs. In doing so, he lowered his gaze to check out the action, allowing a now enraged Anne to sink her teeth into his right cheek and channel all her anger into trying to bite through it. Her jaws locked and the man howled as she flung her arm around his neck and pulled him closer, determined he would not escape her already aching jaws. Just for a moment, despite his size and strength, Anne had him overpowered and was on the verge of tearing half his face off.

Through her fury and his screams of pain she heard footsteps pounding up the stairs before a second masked man burst into the room. Anne growled like a cornered animal and ground her teeth yet more tightly, encouraging further screams of rage and pain, and watched the tall, powerfully built man she had already identified as the leader of the gang take stock of the situation. He pulled a handgun from the pocket of his blue overalls as he strode across the small office towards them and then viciously grabbed a handful of Anne's dark hair. Instinct made her bite even harder.

Then came a command in a tone that was incongruously calm and polite in such a situation: 'Let go... Now.'

The barrel of the handgun was then placed gently against her temple. The refined delivery of the instruction made the implications of not obeying all the more menacing.

The man with the well-chewed cheek howled again as Anne delivered her final effort to make her teeth meet before letting go. For the second time in ten seconds she spat – a mixture of the man's blood and wet fibres from his balaclava. He staggered unsteadily away from her, clutching his face, growling with his pain and anger, while keeping his eyes on the man with the gun. Anne was similarly transfixed, seeing the armed man as her saviour and seeking a message from the narrowed dark eyes staring through the slits in his olive-green balaclava. He waved the gun to indicate that she should sit in the padded leather chair behind the desk. She did as instructed, continuing to dare to look him in the eyes, scarcely able to believe how defiant she felt. Now judging her to be compliant, he turned to his injured accomplice and brutally thrust the muzzle of the gun into his injured cheek.

'Stay here. Do not touch her again,' he commanded in the same calm, cultured voice. He then strode from the room.

The injured man cringed like a whipped dog, leaning heavily against the wood-panelled wall of the office, cradling his damaged face in his gloved hand.

'Not so tough now, are you?' she sneered at her captor. 'He's got you shit-scared.'

Emboldened by the adrenaline that coursed through her, Anne felt anger more than fright, although her head and her heart were pounding. For the last hour she had been terrified, but now she felt inexplicably aggressive, with every emotion, nerve and sinew seemingly on high alert.

Reacting to her scorn, the man moved towards her, clearly aching to teach her a lesson, but rather than cringe away Anne felt herself bristle with rage, ready for "fight" not "flight". But the man stopped short, glaring at her from the other side of the desk, still nursing his damaged face. She knew he would obey the man with the gun. For the time being, she was safe.

He flopped down in the hard chair that the manager of the Hardstone Building Society kept especially for his staff, when they made it past his secretary and into his office. Anne was one of the nineteen employees that all worked at its branch situated in Wednesday Market, Beverley. For her to be sitting behind the desk and in the chair of its unpopular manager, Noel Priestley, was a further novel experience. Her emotions unravelled further as she imagined the pompous little git's reaction to the robbery and her "role" in it – she wanted to laugh out loud.

Footsteps mounting the stairs dragged her back to reality, and her earlier saviour, accompanied by a third masked man, entered the office. Was it only an hour ago they had led her from her home at gunpoint, leaving her husband and son bound and gagged, before using her keys to disarm the alarm and enter the building society? He was now carrying a navy blue holdall with the gun in his other hand. The third man came around the desk and took hold of Anne's upper arm, pulling her to her feet, while the gunman motioned to Anne's attacker to leave the office. Without a word, the four of them descended the stairs and left the building by a rear door, into a small staff car park. A heavy drizzle driven by an icy cold wind quickly soaked through Anne's thin blouse as they walked silently towards a BMW parked in a dark corner, hiding it from the casual glance of any passerby. Anne was pushed into the rear seat and then joined by the gunman, while her attacker, still subdued and nursing his injury, climbed into the front passenger seat. The third man did the driving, pulling silently onto Lord Roberts Road and through the quiet rain-soaked streets of the market town. Within minutes, they had passed the racecourse and were heading along the A1079 towards York.

Anne no longer felt aggressive and angry. She was shivering uncontrollably, her mind a blur of panic and dread, convinced the men were now intending to kill her – dispose of the witness – after doing God knows what else to her. She knew she would never see her son and husband again and prayed they would be safe. When, about ten minutes after leaving Beverley, the car pulled into a long, dark lay-by hidden from the road by a deep stand of trees, Anne was so traumatised she could only stammer, 'Please… no… please.'

The gunman reached down into her footwell and removed her shoes before leaning across and opening her door. He motioned her with the gun to get out of the car. Still expecting to be shot, she did as she was told and then just stood with her back to the still-open door. The door slammed shut followed by the powerful purr of the BMW and the crunch of loose gravel as it sped away.

For ten seconds, Anne Beedham did not move. Then she looked up into the sky, feeling the cold drizzle on her face. She laughed out loud as she felt the warm urine dribble down her thighs and then warming her bare feet. She hitched up her skirt and began to run. Ignoring the abrading pain of the lay-by's gravel, she soon gained the smoother tarmac surface of the A1079 and at a steady jog headed back towards Beverley.

*

An Hour Earlier

Janice Cooper had always found the guest bedroom at her neat bungalow in the village of Atwick, near the East Yorkshire seaside town of Hornsea, to be cold. It had been added as a loft extension a few years earlier, but the builders had never warned her how cold such rooms could get, particularly facing eastwards towards the North Sea coast less than a mile away across the flat exposed farmland. It was ironic that not a single guest had ever stayed in the room, but tonight she had unwillingly become its first ever occupant, and it now seemed highly likely that she was going to die in it.

As her chest heaved with the effort of trying to keep breathing, her mind escaped to those summers back in the 1950s when her parents had taken her and her younger brother to stay at the Fresh Fields Caravan Park on the clifftops between Hornsea and Atwick, to escape the industrial grime of her native Barnsley. As her lungs burned, her mind raced forward through the years to when she eventually realised one half of her childhood dream – a bungalow near the sea. A new job at the Hardstone Building Society in Beverley, only about ten miles from the rapidly eroding but still beautiful east coast, had been the opportunity. Proudly settling into her new home at the age of thirty-five, she'd reluctantly accepted the fact that the complementary half of her dream would never be realised. Janice had never even had a steady boyfriend, let alone an offer of marriage. Janice's work colleagues were her only real friends. They admired her stoic yet cheerful disposition, while at the same time at a loss to understand why she hadn't attracted a man – after all, she wasn't unattractive, albeit being what they would kindly describe as "homely and comfortable". Several seemingly suitable customers had been steered, sometimes less than tactfully, towards asking her out, and despite several dates, not one had asked twice.

Janice wriggled in the hard kitchen chair, trying to relieve the cramp in her arms and shoulders. She remembered how she had gradually shrugged off the disappointment of having no one with whom to share her dreams and taken comfort in the knowledge that when the extra bedroom was finished, Mum and Dad would come to stay. She hoped that her brother and his wife and their three children would also be regular visitors. Those dreams had also shattered when her dad died of a heart attack just three weeks after the bedroom was finished and Mum had slipped effortlessly into the role of professional widow, refusing to be happy and viewing a holiday by the sea as somehow unseemly. Her brother and his family had visited her a few times after Dad died but they never stayed the night. Janice eventually accepted that his wife viewed her spinster sister-in-law and her seaside retreat as both boring and embarrassing, and only came under sufferance.

Janice wondered why, in this cruel situation, she was now allowing herself to admit how lonely and unfulfilled her life had become, constantly hiding her sadness beneath a facade of outward jollity and practicality, which her work colleagues, totally unbeknown to her, so often discussed and admired. Now faced with death, the walls she had built to protect herself suddenly crumbled, releasing the tears she thought she'd forgotten how to shed. She choked at the irony that it would be this long denied weakness that would kill her.

She felt her tears start to flow. The tape binding her wrists tightened the more she struggled to get comfortable, and her tears turned to sobs. Her sobs became frantic gasps for air and became shallower and shallower as she struggled to breathe. The thick woollen sock cruelly stuffed into her mouth and held in place by a length of broad black tape only allowed her to breathe through her nose. Not a problem for most, but as a chronic asthmatic, Janice had started to panic the moment the man forced open her mouth and rammed in the sock. Years of managing her condition enabled her to calm down when she felt sure the three men had left her house, taking with them the keys for the building society's safe. She told herself not to panic. Panic would be fatal. But as the minutes dragged on and she grew colder and sadder, she began to wonder just how long she must sit immobile, bound, gagged and unable to breathe properly. The rain hammered onto the bedroom window driven by an onshore wind, forcing a cold draught through the cheap double-glazing, ruffling the thin net curtains, penetrating her cotton nightie and further chilling her body. Despite Janice's best efforts to block them out, her thoughts continued to drift into the past, dredging up uncomfortable memories and emotions. After what seemed like hours since the men had forced their way into her house, those emotions brought the tears, which sparked the panic she had fought so hard to quell. That panic and the tears brought on an asthma attack that only her inhaler could now stem. Janice Cooper slowly began to suffocate. As an almost welcome haze of unconsciousness slid over her, she wondered if whoever found her body would be kind enough to lay her on the unused double bed atop the weekly laundered but also unused Laura Ashley quilt.

Constable Peter Granger had a lot on his mind. Married for only three months, he was convinced that his wife, PC Amy Granger, was already having an affair with her sergeant, Dave Knaggs, some fifteen years her senior. In fact, from what he had recently gleaned, albeit from a dubious source – overheard gossip between Betty the cleaner and Frank the civilian property officer – she had been in this relationship for the four years she had been on Knaggs' shift. This was longer than he had even known her. According to Betty, Amy was a hot arse who couldn't keep her knickers on, and she'd only married that nice PC Granger because his dad had just died and left him a house and a handsome cash sum. Apparently the affair was particularly active when her young husband was on nights. The actual eavesdropper, PC Lynne Stubbs, had relayed this verbatim conversation to him two nights previously while they shared a patrol car for a few hours of the shift. Peter had been dubious about Lynne's motives in disclosing this shocking news from the outset. Known as the "station bike", Lynne had tried to ensnare him when he was a naïve new probationer only two years earlier, and he had tactfully rebuffed her in favour of Amy. Her probity as a witness had suffered a further setback when within ten minutes of breaking the news of his wife's infidelity she had offered him a blow job as a means of comfort!

Not wanting to believe it, Pete had spent the last two nights at work in an agony of doubt, unable to dispel the image of his Amy at this very moment getting shagged by Knaggs. In their new bed. In their brand-new, detached, four-bedroom Barratt show home. He had to find out the truth.

He resolved to do it now, while it was quiet. The radio was dead, the drizzle and the cold wind having quietened Beverley even earlier than usual. He'd venture off his car beat, nip home and catch them. He'd not worked out what he would do if he caught them – but Amy was always nagging him to be more spontaneous.

'Control to PC Granger, PC Granger, are you receiving?' the radio demanded.

'Bollocks,' he swore. Sod's law. He intended to ignore the message and wait until they called someone else.

'Control to PC Granger, PC Granger.'

Despite himself, he reached for his radio – a Pavlovian response after four years of police service.

'PC Granger receiving. Go ahead.'

'PC Granger, straight away to the phone box on the A1079 in Bishop Burton village. A Mrs Anne Beedham is waiting for you there. She reports being taken from her home in Dunswell at gunpoint and being forced to help rob the Hardstone Building Society, where she works. More information to follow.'

Already driving at speed towards the location, PC Peter Granger forgot his personal problems. Guns and robbery? In Beverley?

'On my way. Do we know if the offenders are still in the area?'

'She reports her three attackers have driven off in a dark BMW 5 series towards York. You are safe to approach.'

The criminal use of a firearm in these parts was as rare as rocking-horse shit, and on a rainy night in December, nothing much was happening anywhere. So this radio message woke up every keen copper who even had a sniff of getting in on the action.

As Pete Granger sped towards Bishop Burton, he heard another officer being dispatched, to the home of the woman he was en route to meet. The officer was told he would there find her husband and son bound and gagged in an upstairs front bedroom. An ambulance was also en route. Traffic units patrolling near the A1079 were directed to search for a dark BMW 5 series containing three armed men. With no audible sign of irony, the controller explained that at least one of the men was carrying a handgun and that these unarmed officers should take care. It still amazed him how most police officers rushed towards anything that was remotely exciting – even if dangerous. The nearest of the two armed response units covering the force was deployed, but it was currently in East Hull, miles away from ever being able to confront the BMW before unarmed officers, if it should be sighted.

The next call directed a Hornsea-based officer, PC Harry Willis, to The Bungalow, Cliff Lane, Atwick in the same urgent but quietly controlled tone.

'PC Willis, we are told we have another female victim at this address. Janice Cooper, forty-five years. Our information is that she is severely asthmatic and may be bound and gagged. We are organising an ambulance and another unit is en route from Bridlington.'

Granger imagined the collective groan as units heard that "Windy" Willis was being sent on such an urgent task. In his mid-forties and massively overweight, Willis was the classic uniform carrier, off work sick more than he attended – and bloody useless when he did.

'PC Willis to control, I was out of my car on foot, so it will take me fifteen, that's one five, fifteen minutes. How do we know the armed men haven't gone back there?'

Everyone listening knew he would be spinning it out, hoping someone would get there before him. Out of the car? He never got out of the car – only to get fish and chips.

'PC Willis, attend as quickly as possible and effect immediate entry to the house. Do not wait for backup. The offenders were last seen heading towards York… now put your foot down!' Even the controller twenty miles away in Hull had got the measure of PC Willis.

*

Harry Willis rarely left the security of the streetlights of Hornsea when he was working nights – and he did his utmost to avoid night shifts. In the job for twenty-five years but frightened by its demands, he longed for his pension that was still five years away. Following an acrimonious divorce and painful separation from his two teenage children, he had fallen into depression, taking long periods of sickness. He'd piled on the weight and lost all interest in police work, and life in general. He took every opportunity to take as much time off sick as possible – especially on nights – using the classic skiver's excuses of back pain, upset stomach and flu. His supervisors were closely monitoring his sickness, so not every set of nights could be avoided. So here he was, alone, at almost three in the morning, driving through drizzle and a coastal fog in the pitch-black towards God knows what. He just hoped that the ambulance crew would get there first, and to help make that happen, he drove at barely thirty miles an hour down the deserted country roads.

Harry knew where he was going. He'd been to the bungalow before. About two months previously, Janice Cooper had reported a suspicious caller, efficiently recording his car number and description. By the time Harry had arrived, the man had long gone, but over a cup of tea she had passed the information over to Harry, even though she could see he was completely disinterested. He'd spent about an hour with Janice chatting over a cup of tea, recognising the similarities in their lonely lives but at the same time envious of her outward optimism and friendly nature. Harry had momentarily felt ashamed of his own gloom and mean-spirited nature, which he knew his work colleagues despised and ridiculed behind his back. By the time he left the bungalow, that envy had turned to dislike for the jolly outgoing spinster and he had stereotyped her as a nervous nosey parker, not worthy of his help. He made no further enquiries about the man and the car, writing the incident off as a non-event and including only a vague description of the man on the incident log.

However, whatever else he was, PC Willis was not stupid and as he drove towards the bungalow, his mind made the potential connection between the suspicious man and tonight's obviously serious events, and he began to worry. She was just the type to mention the man and his car – and he'd taken no action. He slowed down further and tried to think, but Atwick was only a five-minute drive and all too quickly he was outside the bungalow.

Harry knew he couldn't just sit there, so switching on his torch he stepped out into the mist and drizzle and approached the house, frightened by the dark, the isolation and what he might find – and how he may well be in deep shit. He'd been told to force an entry if necessary but knew his fat backside would not pass through any of the double glazed windows, even if he smashed one, so he tried the back door. Trembling with apprehension, he shook the handle, fully expecting it to be secure but the door opened, almost causing him to fall into the opening. The house was in darkness and totally silent. He shone his torch through the doorway to reveal a small, neat kitchen. Now almost desperate to hear the ambulance approaching, he stood still and listened. Silence.

'PC 1471 Willis to control, I'm at the scene and the house is insecure. I am about to go in.'

Still afraid but rationalising that there was probably no one in the bungalow but a bound and gagged middle-aged woman, PC Willis transferred his torch to his left hand and took his ASP from its belt pouch and with a swift downward flick of his wrist extended the weapon. Peering into the kitchen, he spotted a light switch within reach. A fluorescent tube fizzed and flickered overhead before starkly illuminating the room, making Harry brave enough to shout.

'Hello. Anyone there? This is the police and I'm coming in.'

With that, he stepped over the threshold, ASP raised as if he were the SAS about to storm an enemy stronghold.

Having committed himself to action, he moved quickly through the kitchen, finding himself in a narrow hallway off which he first found a small bathroom wedged beneath the stairs. Empty. He moved further into the house, knocking down two switches that lit up the hall and the upstairs landing. Quick glances into the front room and two downstairs bedrooms left only the upstairs to check. He cautiously climbed the stairs. As his head became level with the upstairs landing floor, he looked to his right between the spindles of the banister and through an open door into the only room. A bright security light from outside diffused through the thin curtains, creating a silhouette of what Harry had been led to expect. Janice Cooper was sitting on a dining chair, directly facing the open door. Her head and shoulders were slumped so far forward towards her knees that without her restraining bonds, she would have fallen forward off the chair. Harry exhaled his pent-up breath in an involuntary gesture of relief as he realised not only that he was in no danger but also that his failure to investigate Mrs Cooper's suspicious caller would not now be exposed, as the woman was clearly dead.

Well practised at watching his own back while avoiding work, his immediate thoughts were about how he would be able to look good by suggesting the suspicious caller could be connected to tonight's events. There would be no Mrs Cooper to throw a spanner in the works. He gave not one passing thought to either the fate of the poor woman, how his developing plan might actually damage any future investigation, or even consider that if the two events were actually connected, he had failed in his duties to record an accurate description of the suspect or his car.

Feeling much more confident, he moved on up the stairs and into the bedroom and put on the light, taking in the tape used to bind Janice Cooper to the chair. Even a lazy copper has seen plenty of dead bodies in twenty-five years' service and a good proportion are in strange, suspicious and downright weird scenarios, so Harry was unmoved by the presence of the body. He felt at the neck for a pulse to confirm life extinct, as it wouldn't be the first time a copper had been in the presence of a "body" only to find it was no such thing – and it wasn't the last – Harry felt a weak but definite pulse.

Ten years of trying to avoid police work were forgotten and PC Willis went into autopilot. He tore the tape from Janice's mouth and moved to clear her airway, finding the sock and throwing it to the floor. He scrambled for the Swiss Army knife on his equipment belt and cut through the tape, actually thinking about the forensic potential of fingerprints, hairs and fibres from the criminals adhering to the tape. He laid her gently on the bed, tilted back her head and began mouth-to-mouth resuscitation.

By the time two ambulance staff were running up the stairs, Janice had regained consciousness, and as they carried her out of the house, PC Harry Willis sat on the bed, grinning. He felt better about himself than he had done for years.

Two

10:30 That Same Morning

'This is a fantastic opportunity, Darnley. We cannot afford to let it pass. A middle-aged uniformed police officer saving the life of a similarly aged female in the dead of night. It's community policing in action,' Chief Constable Miles Crabbe enthused.

Community policing – the Chief was on his usual soapbox and once again I marvelled at how his enthusiasm never waned, even though he must know that I was thinking he was talking crap. But he was invigorated by his own credo, his bug-like eyes wide and his Adam's apple bobbing up and down in time with the nods of his head. Crabbe was a firm believer that enthusiasm was like the clap – highly contagious – and if he voiced his ludicrous ideas often enough and with appropriate gusto, all his cynical, and in the main, more realistic and practical, workforce would catch a dose. The problem was, I really liked the bloke and would have hated to upset him, although most of his senior officers agreed that he was so intelligent, so far removed from reality and so wrapped up in his own vision of modern policing that he was probably impervious to insult.

'The actual crime is less important, we can do far more for the reputation of Humberside Police through this human-interest story than we can by detecting the crime and apprehending the villains… unfortunately,' he added as an afterthought

'Absolutely, sir. I'll get the press office on it straight away… but I wanted to talk to you about setting up an incident room and getting it on the HOLMES system.'

His enthusiasm evaporated in an instant and he sat back in his chair with a look that a father would give his naughty son with whom he is regularly disappointed. I'd seen the look dozens of times before and had expected it, so I ploughed on, talking rapidly to avoid the interruption I knew was coming.

'There's a good chance that last night's job could be linked to the Post Office raid carried out in Bridlington in September. Last night's was slightly different in that they tied the families up and left them, rather than leaving one of the gang to guard them.'

Such crimes are indeed very rare and known as tiger kidnaps, involving short-term hostage taking, often of family members of someone who has access to cash or other valuables.

'I can't believe the jobs aren't connected… we need a thorough investigation. Robberies and kidnaps like these are as rare as hen's teeth nationally… and that's two in four months in the bloody East Riding. And the level of violence used last night makes the crime even more worrying. As you rightly point out, sir, the woman at Atwick nearly died, and the other employee taken to the building society was close to being raped by one of the mad bastards.'

'Yes quite… but I'd like you to do the press interviews, not the press office.'

He was bloody ignoring me.

'Get the PC from Hornsea… what's his name… Walters… Witters… and the woman he saved on the TV with you. Don't think we need an incident room. A standard divisional investigation will suffice. No one died. We don't know the cases are linked and I want most of the CID out on the streets in uniform in the run-up to Christmas.'

Same old bloody rigmarole – Bobbies on the beat in fluorescent jackets – he was obsessed. However, I had fought this battle several times now and had figured out a winning strategy, but it galled me each time I had to appear to toe his party line, when what I really wanted was a damn good argument.

'Excellent idea, sir, but you should front it, or the local chief superintendent. Get the uniform on the TV and in the papers. Otherwise, it smacks of the CID being in charge… not an image we wish to portray.'

'Quite right, Darnley… spot on… glad you can see that we need to break down the media-led myth of the CID being the brains in policing. I've no truck with elitism.'

He gave a couple of blinks, couple of nods, and then just stared at me, grinning, oblivious to the fact that he had just rubbished the bulk of my twenty-eight-year career. I recognised the abrupt halt to the conversation, accompanied by the stare and grin as my dismissal, but I continued with my well-used strategy.

'You're right about the incident room as well, sir. We need the troops out on high visibility patrol. I guess we won't get another robbery with a kidnap in our area. Richer pickings in West Yorkshire and softer targets in North Yorks. I suggest that when you hold your press conference, you should reassure the public that they're unlikely to strike a third time here.'

'Mmm… that could sound complacent rather than reassuring.' Eyes now narrowed and head still. This meant progress.

'Not at all… if nothing else happens. You front the story and give your personal reassurance as to how unusual such crimes are in this area. How gun crime is a big-city phenomenon and kidnapping is only the stuff of TV drama. Emphasise the fact that the lady only survived because our brave officer was out and about on uniformed night patrol. The press are bound to ask if the job at Brid is linked, but I would say not at this stage and then we can keep our fingers crossed we don't get another job. You're spot on, sir. The chances of another job happening here… and it going horribly wrong… and someone actually getting shot are miniscule.'

Optimistic enthusiasm was now tempered by self-preservation. Nobody gets to the top job in policing without keeping him or herself out of the shit. He slowly leaned even further back in his chair and looked at the ceiling, hands brought together on his chest in a position of prayer, his neck stretched taut with his Adam's apple like a misshapen marble, stationary on an impossible incline.

Having suggested how easily he could drop himself in the shit, I shifted to how he might improve his national standing as a Chief.

'I'd better contact the National Crime Faculty to let them know we're *not* setting up an incident room. I know they're keen to visit forces investigating such crimes, looking for best practice. Pity. Could have got us some national kudos.'

This was absolute bullshit. I had no desire to have that bunch of ivory towered know-alls sticking their noses into one of my cases. But he'd never know. My guess was he wouldn't be able to resist the potential brownie points.

'Right. Invite the Crime Faculty up here, Superintendent. Let's get Chief Superintendent Sharples at Beverley to front the press. He deserves his moment of glory, with his staff. He can give *his* personal reassurance and also explain how we are setting up an incident room to ensure we add to the national intelligence picture.'

Mission accomplished.

*

Within an hour, I had arranged for the Major Incident Room (MIR) at Driffield to be designated for the job and set the wheels in motion for an incident team to be assembled. The small market town of Driffield was ideally situated, being midway between Beverley and Bridlington.

On my way to Driffield, I called in at the nick at Beverley, as the officers dealing with Anne Beedham had completed their initial enquiries and thought I should meet her. As the Senior Investigating Officer, it was not my usual practice to meet witnesses, leaving that to the officers on my team. I justified this as enabling me to keep a more objective overview of the incident, preventing the clouded judgement that I knew could occur by my personal involvement in the emotion inevitably surrounding every crime. However, it was custom and practice for the SIO to always meet a murder victim's family, or indeed anyone at the heart of a case that may have been traumatised, badly injured or courageous, for example. The fact that all the lads had raved about how gorgeous Anne Beedham was, had absolutely nothing to do with it.

Although she looked shattered, her eyes shone fiercely with what I guessed was a mixture of relief and excitement at still being alive. I had seen a similar look in the eyes of officers who had been in highly tense and dangerous situations and come out the other side. I also knew that the shock would hit her soon.

I walked to the side of the desk behind which she was seated and held out my hand. 'Mrs Beedham, pleased to meet you. I'm Detective Superintendent Matt Darnley, the officer in charge of this investigation.'

She stood up and shook my hand, looking directly and challengingly into my eyes. 'You better catch the bastards 'cos they'll kill somebody… the one that had a go at me was evil and they never gave a thought to poor old Janice. I heard one of your lot on the radio crowing about how you'd saved her life, but these things shouldn't be happening round here. Bloody police are useless.'

She was extremely angry, which was bringing a flush to her cheeks and a dark fire to her eyes, which made her look extremely attractive, despite her outfit of a baggy white forensic suit, unkempt hair and ruined make-up. The anger infused her with an energy that made her tremble as she clung on to my hand.

'We'll get them, and your bravery in biting the one who attacked you has put us well on the trail. His blood was all over your blouse and that'll get us his DNA. We'll find him, don't you worry.'

I realised I was still holding her hand and returning her stare, but now her anger and emotion and my words of comfort had turned the situation into one of embarrassment – for me at least. She clearly knew the effect she was creating and using only her eyes she turned up the heat still further, until I looked away and dropped her hand. I turned somewhat embarrassedly towards DC Beatty, one of the officers that had dealt with her. He was grinning like an idiot and I bet itching to get out of the room to go and tell the team how the boss was acting like a horny schoolboy.

I tried to regain my composure. 'I just wanted to meet you and tell you what a brave lady you were and to let you know we'll keep you and your family and, of course, Ms Cooper up to date with the investigation. I think we intend to appoint PC Peter Granger, the young man who dealt with you last night, as your Family Liaison Officer, is that right, DC Beatty?'

'Yes, boss, he's just come back on duty.' He turned to Mrs Beedham. 'He's been to collect your husband and brought you some fresh clothes, then he'll run you both home.'

I explained it would be PC Granger's role to be the point of contact between her family and the inquiry, keeping them updated with progress and doing all he could to help them recover from their ordeal. We exchanged a few more pleasantries before DC Beatty took her to get changed, while I popped outside to meet her husband. He was not as I had imagined; small, skinny, a bit scruffy and a good bit older than her. As we shook hands, I could feel he was trembling. He looked a damn sight more traumatised than his wife. I asked after his son and how he was taking it.

'He's thirteen, with raging teenage hormones and an exciting story to tell his mates... and the lasses... at the minute, he's basking in the limelight and the gun gets bigger by the hour. But I know him and it'll hit him soon.'

'Kids are tough, he'll be okay but he may need to talk about it to someone. I've assigned the young PC who drove you here as your Family Liaison Officer.' I nodded towards the police car where I could see PC Granger waiting. 'Has he explained his role to you?'

'Yes, he's been great so far. Rory, that's my lad, seems to have taken to him.' He was about to continue but at that point his wife emerged from the back door of the nick with DC Beatty, and he broke away from me and embraced her fiercely. After about twenty seconds he let his wife go, clearly embarrassed at showing such emotion in front of others.

'I'll be in touch,' I smiled, as I shook hands with her again.

'I do hope so,' she responded, with a smirk that made it quite obvious what she actually meant.

'Your wife has been a very courageous lady, Mr Beedham, you should be proud of her,' I said to her husband as she walked towards the waiting police car, swinging her extremely shapely hips in an extremely tight skirt.

While he turned to shake my hand, his wife gave me a sly wink – quite literally behind her husband's back. She then turned to get into the car, saying a breezy 'Hello again,' to the young PC Granger, who blushed with pleasure.

Mrs Anne Beedham might as well have had *Beware – Dangerous Lady* tattooed on her forehead. Tempting – but risky. As things were to turn out, PC Granger never did figure that out – until too late.

*

I looked at my watch. I'd been at work about fourteen hours, having been called out from home just before 4am, as events unfolded. The incident was not yet fully staffed but most officers were still out and about carrying out the urgent enquiries necessary in those vital first twenty-four hours.

'Right, mate, I'm off, and don't you be too much longer. You can finish setting up tomorrow,' I shouted from the top of the stairs.

Detective Sergeant Tony Ride, the incident room office manager, was a devil for kicking the arse out of the overtime in the first few days of an incident, but he was a grafter, best office manager in the force, and he was trying to make sure we were ready for a full briefing at eight thirty in the morning.

The first day of setting up a major inquiry using HOLMES (Home Office Large Major Enquiry System) is always chaotic. Just finding a vacant incident room, enough IT equipment, securing the staff with the relevant experience and agreeing the necessary funding – basic organisation – is hard enough. Amidst that, the investigation itself has to tackle a plethora of immediate priorities. If a serious crime is not solved in the first twenty-four to forty-eight hours, you are usually in for the long haul, so early rapid organisation and progress is vital. In those initial hours, you have to maintain what I like to call "investigative velocity" – as rapidly as possible securing any evidence that is likely to disappear or weaken. So this means preserving, then examining, any crime scenes and securing associated forensic evidence, starting house-to-house enquiries around those scenes, getting written accounts from key witnesses and following up the immediate hot leads. In the middle of all this sits the office manager's job. Controlling and organising the information flow, allocating new tasks or "actions" according to priority and continually planning the next move so as to keep the inquiry moving forward.

'I'll give it another couple of hours, boss. We should have a full team here in the morning and I want everyone to have a tray full of actions. I don't want anyone hanging about after the briefing.'

'Great mate, but be on your way by eight. It'll be an even longer day tomorrow.'

'Aren't you going to watch *Look North* before you go, boss?'

He flicked on the TV, which was mounted on a metal bracket in the corner of the room, in perfect time to catch the unmistakable theme tune of our local BBC news. I watched as Harry Gration rattled off the overview of the evening's local stories. As usual, they ranged from serious crime and mass redundancies, to an art project in Grimsby and a skateboarding ferret in Scunthorpe. First up was our incident. A quick report from outside the Hardstone Building Society kicked the feature off, rapidly followed by Chief Superintendent Sharples outside Beverley's Sessions House Police Station smoothly delivering the Chief's message that we'd discussed earlier. The scene then switched to the old-fashioned, chintzy front room of Janice Cooper's bungalow, where the still obviously distressed victim of this latest outrageous crime to sully the rural idyll of East Yorkshire was being comforted by the hero of the hour, our very own PC Willis. I had never heard of Harry Willis before but by now had learnt of his reputation from officers attached to the incident. He sat in uniform next to the woman whose life he had saved, holding her hand and looking at her in a very caring manner as she outlined her ordeal between muted sobs. As her account reached a climax, she virtually flung herself into the arms of her saviour, throwing her right arm across Harry's ample midriff and dropping her head onto his chest. There she remained, her body heaving in a paroxysm of grief. As if briefed by Chief Constable Crabbe himself, our hero managed to combine solemn with caring and, while soothing the rescued damsel, he gave his own very modest account of his actions in the night.

'For fuck's sake,' laughed Ridey. 'He's got a terrible reputation has Harry Willis, and this performance won't help it any.'

I mimicked his laughter, while actually finding the little scene quite touching. 'Crabbe will think it's marvellous. His caring sharing service at its best.'

The report ended with a shot of Janice Cooper's bungalow, which showed viewers, and indeed myself, just how isolated it was.

'Bloody hell, we're not going to get any witnesses round there. How the hell did they find the place?'

I turned away from *Look North*'s next report and Ridey flicked the TV off as I sat back down behind my desk. How did they find Janice's house? Atwick itself is well out of the way if you don't know the area, and her bungalow looked to be down a grassy track well away from the village itself. As yet, I had not had chance to visit that scene, having spent the day initially with the Chief Constable, then meeting Anne Beedham at Beverley, before travelling on to Driffield and the incident room. The scene at Atwick was on my to-do list for tomorrow.

Tony rifled through one of his trays and pulled out a statement. 'It's pretty obvious they knew they needed two sets of keys and who had them. They'd done their homework. Beedham's house is easy to find… but this one?' He quickly leafed through the statement. 'Beedham claims they asked who had the safe keys and she gave them Janice's name, but she says they never asked where she lived. So they must have known.'

For the first time on the inquiry, I felt a quiver of excitement. 'Raise two actions before you leave tonight, Tony. The first is to get PC Granger to go over that specific point again with her. Let's be dead sure what they knew beforehand.'

'Are you sure, boss? He's a bit green. This could be crucial.'

'No, he's done a bloody good job so far and we've made him FLO. Brief him before he goes about how to handle her. We don't want her clamming up if she has told them Janice had the safe keys and where she lives and now feels bad and doesn't want to admit it. Judging by what we've just seen on the news, the address would be little use on its own. She'd have had to tell them how to find it. The second action is to get maps and aerial photographs showing the bungalow's isolation.'

DS Ride then showed me why I rate him so highly. 'I bet they'd been there before. I'll get all the incident logs checked to see if there are any reports of suspicious people in the general area. What do you think… go back three months for now?'

He again leafed through Anne's statement, reading quickly. 'In the background information, she states there are nineteen people working at the building society. How'd they know which two had the keys?'

'We can't answer all the questions tonight, mate, but you're right. Inside job? Someone's working with the robbers, or a case of loose talk. Or I guess they could just have watched the place and followed them home. We need to raise that discussion at tomorrow's briefing and put a small team on that aspect. Anyway, I'm off home. I'm knackered.'

As I walked down the stairs, I heard a phone ring back in the incident room and Tony shouted, 'Hang on, boss.' I paused, looked at my watch and thought briefly about home and a whisky but turned and headed back to the incident room. I perched on the edge of a desk listening as he asked a series of questions while making notes on a scrap of paper. Two minutes later, he covered the mouthpiece of the phone and sat back in his chair, wearing a huge grin.

'Now we've got a bloody body! Found half an hour ago by a chap walking his dog in a lay-by near Wilberfoss village on the A1079, about fifteen miles further towards York from where Anne Beedham was let out of the BMW. He's been shot in the back of the head. DI Baldwin from Bridlington is already up there, calling out the troops and asking for an SIO. The Command Centre know you're up here and are asking if you're happy to assess the scene and take it from there… or do you want the duty SIO calling out?'

Pound signs were flashing in Ridey's eyes. I could tell he was itching for me to say I'd go, and ask him to accompany me. We were only about twenty minutes away from Wilberfoss, so he knew I'd go.

'Come on then. Tell them we're attending. It's so close to our job it's got to be connected. I can't believe we've had two sets of nutters out with guns in one night in the sleepy East Riding.'

Tony pumped his clenched fist in triumph. As we left the nick, he was tunelessly singing "We're in the money", his mind definitely not on some poor bastard with a bullet in his brain.

Three

Detective Inspector Baldwin looked bloody frozen. Mind you, standing in the dark at the side of a busy road, with a bitter north wind howling through the trees and a dead body only a few feet away, is likely to chill anyone. Mally Baldwin had been a DI for about twenty years and had not spent a day in uniform since he was promoted to the job at the tender age of thirty, and apparently destined for the top. He was typical of many officers who threw themselves lock, stock and barrel into a CID role, forsaking family life and only living for the job. His early promise fizzled out, as he failed to spot that times had changed – being a good detective no longer assured promotion. But I knew he truly loved his job and in my book he was an astute DI, and as I would have expected, he had the scene cordoned off and the scenes of crime officer and a uniformed officer were busy erecting a tent around the body. He knew that we could not move a body with an apparent gunshot wound at night unless we were willing to miss potential forensic clues. The tent would protect the body and immediate scene for a closer examination in daylight by a forensic scientist and a Home Office pathologist. Mally had learnt years ago how normally mild-mannered scientists and pathologists could go ape-shit

27

if an interesting murder scene, unusual *modus operandi* – and thus a potential scientific paper – was cocked up by "the plod". The more we left well alone in such circumstances, the happier they were.

'I've had a quick look, boss, but left things untouched. The doctor's just declared life extinct and SOCO has taken a few photographs but retreated until daylight. PC Daines here has started a scene log and is taking a quick statement from the doctor.' He nodded towards a uniformed policewoman talking to another young female a few yards further into the tree-surrounded lay-by.

'It's an odd one, boss, looks like a fairly young bloke but I can't see his face 'cos he's on his front in long grass. He's stark naked and there's no sign of his clothes, but from his physique I'd say he was under thirty. There's an obvious single wound to the back of his head that I'm pretty sure is a gunshot. The body isn't hidden. A local chap walking his dog found him, when the dog wouldn't come away from the body.'

I, of course, wanted to have a look and not just out of morbid curiosity. Ask any SIO and they'll tell you that you can never fully appreciate a crime scene if you don't get to see the body in situ. But that wasn't the reason I was busting for a look. I reckoned I had a fair idea who our dead man was likely to be. I moved towards the blue and white police tape guarding the scene.

'Not telling granny how to suck eggs, boss, but there's nothing to see and there could be anything in that grass. It's not even worth you going to have a peek.'

The DI was right. I would do no good poking around in the dark and could mess up any forensics. But this granny wanted to get this particular egg sucked. Curiosity conquered professionalism. If I had to wait until tomorrow to check my hunch, I'd never get to bloody sleep – and as he said, I was the boss.

'You're dead right to tell me, Mally… but I need to check something. Record in the log that I entered the scene and looked at the body. Lend me your torch.'

His torch was virtually out of batteries and as dim as a half-starved glow-worm, but I bobbed under the tape and stepped carefully towards the body. Standing still, I tried to soak in the detail of the scene. There wasn't much to see. This was an execution – plain and simple. I bent forward and gently moved the long grass away from the corpse's head. Bingo. I could see the nasty bite mark on his cheek. She'd nearly ripped half his face off.

I ducked back under the tape, knowing the two men would be discussing what a knobhead I was for doing what I'd just done.

'Come on then, Ridey,' I said, rubbing my hands together, half to keep warm but also to help me keep calm. 'Who've we got here with a bullet in the brain?'

'How do I know? You've just had a look… did you recognise him? Must be connected to our job, I don't believe in coincidences.'

'Never seen him before in my life. Come on, mate. Work it out.'

Ridey walked off a few yards. 'Don't tell me, don't tell me… give me a minute.'

'Bloody hell, it's not charades,' laughed Mally Baldwin.

You could almost hear his grey matter grinding.

'Fuck me, it's the bloke she bit! You've seen the bite mark… but how did you know?'

I knew he'd work it out himself but I wanted to look like the ace detective – all SIOs have big egos that need regular nourishment.

'Same as you, mate. I don't believe in coincidences. While we were driving over here, I went through some possible scenarios and this was the only thing that made sense. Anne

Beedham got covered in his blood, so we get a DNA sample and quickly identify one of the villains. She says that the bloke who seemed to be in charge was really pissed off with the bloke she bit and threatened him with the gun. I reckon they've took him out the game to stop him leading us to them.'

Ridey fell silent, weighing up this scenario.

'Which is pretty damn calculating. They've executed him. I wouldn't mind being on this job, boss… any chance… need a DI?' Mally asked.

Before I could reply, Ridey continued, 'Christ. Who the hell are we dealing with? We don't get jobs like this in Humberside. Why not just try and get rid of the blood from her? Or why not bump her off?'

'That's what I find worrying. It looks like they've weighed up those options while travelling between Beverley and the first lay-by. Even if they'd taken all her clothes, they'd have missed some blood on her body, or in her hair. Not practical to keep hold of her until they could shower her down. They could have killed her and burnt the body, I suppose, but I reckon the boss man has made up his mind what he's going to do before they've let her out of the car. Fifteen minutes further up the road and they've literally destroyed the potential link to them and the job… as they say in the movies, "dead men don't talk". You're right, Mally, they are fucking calculating… and that's scary… they're good. They've even thought to take his clothes in case there was trace evidence on them.'

We were all quiet for a moment until Ridey said, 'His DNA is going to be on the database. They knew we'd get him. They shot him in case he blabbed.'

I'd already got there but let Ridey have his moment of glory. I was already thinking of the next day's efforts I'd need to put in with the Chief Constable to staff up the incident, which was now a murder inquiry, as well as a robbery and kidnap.

One thing was for sure: the Chief would now be bloody glad that it had been "his idea" to set up an incident room.

We were quiet for a moment, thinking things through.

'Another possibility why they didn't shoot Anne Beedham is that she is the source of their information. She's in on it,' I thought out loud.

'But this bloke attacked her, tried to rape her, and she's definitely bitten him. It doesn't make sense for her to be involved. It doesn't fit.' Ridey shook his head, dismissing the notion.

'Maybe he didn't even know she was involved. He just got carried away. A scenario with her involved resolves the questions about how they knew who had the keys. Another discussion for briefing tomorrow.'

There was little more I could actually do at the scene and I was dog-tired, but there was no way I could go home yet. I gave DI Baldwin a number of actions to complete using local staff and then told him to join the inquiry in the morning. I thanked the doctor, had a quick word with the policewoman left to guard the scene and confirmed arrangements with the Command Centre. I asked them to arrange for a Home Office pathologist and forensic scientist to meet me at Pocklington Police Station at seven thirty in the morning and for the policewoman to be brought a flask of coffee. Then it was back to the MIR. I needed to get my head in gear. The next day's priorities had shifted.

Ridey's raid on the force's overtime pot was further assured and as we drove back towards Driffield, I put the heater on full blast and asked, 'Well, mate, what do you reckon?'

'To be honest, boss, my head's spinning. It's been a hell of a day, one revelation after another. Once we get set up and start piecing today's events together, I reckon they'll have made loads of mistakes. There are plenty of lines of inquiry… but we're going to need some bloody staff. Crabbe's Christmas

plans for all the CID in uniform are looking a bit doubtful…
what a shame.'

'I hope you're not taking the piss out of our illustrious
leader,' I laughed. 'Seriously, though, they made a mistake
turning a kidnap and a robbery into a murder. The dead
bloke will have had mates and we'll let them know how he
died. Someone will know who he was running with and
they'll grass 'em up. Then we need to look at the staff at
the building society… especially our lovely Anne. I've got a
feeling about her… she's trouble.'

I felt confident the job would open up quickly, as there
were so many angles and opportunities for evidence, and I
was looking forward to the challenge ahead. If I had known
then how things would turn out, I'd have asked the Chief if I
could lead his Christmas high visibility campaign personally
– in an elf's outfit, never mind a uniform – and left this job
to some other sucker.

Four

The foreman of the jury looked slowly around the packed courtroom, puffing out his chest in a gesture of self-importance before slowly bringing his eyes back to focus on her Honour, Judge Jane Sanderson.

'Not guilty.'

'What the… ' gasped DS Gavin Braggs.

DC Jo Young sat back sharply. 'Rubbish.'

I looked across the crowded courtroom to the dock where the defendant, Sean Grantmore, was now wildly punching the air and grinning like a demented schoolboy at his adoring family and friends. He suddenly stopped his celebrations as if remembering his manners and turned solemnly towards the victim in the case and gave her a lascivious wink. The object of his gratuitous show of derision slumped forward in her seat and thrust her hands deep into the roots of her long dark hair in a caricature of despair.

Lisa Holland had just turned seventeen and barely started her A-levels when she had met Grantmore in Spiders nightclub in Cleveland Street, Hull. He had given her a lift home and then raped her as payment for his petrol costs. In his book, this was a good deal – cheaper

33

than a taxi – and the lucky virgin got to sample one of Hull's superstuds.

A commotion behind me diverted my attention from Lisa's anguish and I saw a man I recognised as her father clambering from his seat in the row behind me and over the back of the bench on which I and my two police colleagues were seated. He roughly pushed his way between DS Braggs and a man sitting next to him, then vaulted the low wooden divide separating the public gallery from the main body of the court. Looking back, one of us should have made a grab for him, and slowed if not halted his progress, but I think my subconscious had registered where he was heading – and was quite content to see him make it. He hurtled forward, a pent-up ball of fury intent on instant retribution, barrelling Grantmore's defence barrister aside. The loud exhalation of the skinny barrister's breath served to galvanise Grantmore, who began to climb out of the back of the dock towards the now open arms of his mother, the infamous Tracey Grantmore.

Sean had managed to get one leg over the back of the dock when my hero of the moment launched himself head first towards the six-foot-high dock by using the court usher's chair as a springboard. He landed squarely on his target's back, and every male in the room gave a sharp intake of breath, as the four-inch-wide beech-veneered dock edging became the resting place for Grantmore's bollocks.

Meanwhile, the furious father's forward momentum ensured he rolled off Grantmore's back and on into the public gallery and the open arms of Tracey Grantmore. Tracey, and her other two sons, who were either side of her, then disappeared from view behind the dock along with the human missile, and a ferocious scrap ensued.

Less than twenty seconds had elapsed since the verdict had been announced and it was only the desperate banging of the judge's gavel that snapped me out of my inaction.

My two colleagues had been similarly transfixed and it was only when I poked DS Braggs in his ribs that he burst into action with DC Young hot on his heels. As befits my rank, I remained seated and began to mentally prepare my response to the forthcoming inquiry about how three police officers failed to prevent a man who had been sitting behind them, carrying out very appropriate summary justice on the "innocent" man his daughter had accused of rape.

The details of how Russ Holland was subdued and arrested, Grantmore removed by ambulance and order restored in Hull Crown Court are unimportant, but my subsequent response to what I had just witnessed would lead to the most challenging months of a most challenging career.

*

'Come in, Detective Superintendent.'

Her Honour the Judge, wig removed to reveal what I guess you'd call "wig hair" – a matted and flattened bleached blonde tangle – was sitting behind the leather-topped desk in a most un-judge like posture – leaning back in her chair with her bare feet on the corner of the desk, revealing a pair of calves that would have looked more at home supporting a billiard table.

'What a cock up, Darnley! Not only did the arsehole get off, but also the victim's dad manages to emasculate him in front of judge and jury while three bloody coppers sit watching. If that wasn't enough, there was a reporter from the *Hull Daily Mail* in court.'

I should explain at this point that Crown Court judges do not normally present themselves in such a fashion, make derogatory comments about jury decisions or describe defendants as arseholes in conversations with police officers – whatever their rank. However, Jane Sanderson and I go back, as a chivalrous man like myself would say. Crown Court judges have all been lowly junior barristers, just as detective superintendents have been beat coppers. The passage of time – and wives and husbands – had long cooled the ardour we once shared – but not our friendship, built in the combat zone known as the Criminal Justice System.

'Sorry, Jane, but I was that gobsmacked at the verdict, I just didn't react quickly enough, but neither did young Braggs and he loves a good scrap. To be honest, I was pretty impressed with Mr Holland. I hope it takes a month for Grantmore's knackers to drop back into place. We'll be okay with the *Mail*'s reporter, he seems a good lad… I've had a word.'

Jane pulled her feet off the desk, stood and walked to a grey metal filing cabinet. 'Drink?'

'Not for me, thanks. I've got a briefing to do at six back up at Driffield.'

'Is that the robbery at the building society in Beverley… and the shooting? I presume they are connected, despite your very guarded media snippets so far?'

'Definitely. We're working on the theory that the dead chap was basically executed because the woman who they kidnapped bit him and got covered in his blood. His DNA could lead us to the rest of them. We've also found out that they'd done some very careful preparatory work. The building society rotates key holders pretty regularly. One worker has the door and alarm keys with a second having the safe keys. We already believe they'd sussed out one of their addresses a few weeks earlier by calling and asking if they wanted their drive repaired. The woman who nearly died while bound and gagged reported the caller as suspicious at the time—'

'I saw her on the TV with the copper who saved her. Shit, she was lucky. You nearly had a double murder,' interrupted Jane, pouring herself a large whisky.

'Yeah, you wouldn't believe it but our hero copper was the one she reported the suspicious caller to back in October. He's bloody useless and didn't bother to do much with the information, not even write it down, but luckily she's come up with a brief description of the bloke, and she had written down his car make and number on the back of her telephone directory and still had it. But then our luck ran out, as the car's been sold on through the auctions and we're having trouble backtracking to the owner at the time, but it's early days yet.'

'Do you know who the dead bloke is yet?'

'Yeah, one of the DCs on the incident recognised him as a local toerag off the Bransholme estate called David Emmerson, who, according to his form, was completely out of his depth. We can't find anyone willing to identify him as yet, no family locally and now suddenly no mates. They're all shit-scared. But we've confirmed his ID with fingerprints. The DNA will confirm his link to the job but we'll be waiting a bit for those results, so we're looking at likely associates, but up to now, none of his local mates are up to a job like this.'

'Getting all the support from the Chief Constable that you need? I'm seeing him tomorrow at the Criminal Justice Forum in Leeds and I just love winding him up about public confidence levels and that stuff he spouts on about.'

'Aye, have a go at him for me about how vital it is for public reassurance to solve serious crimes. He'll rattle on about community bloody policing, reflective jackets, Bobbies on bikes and community consultation until the cows come home... but major crime is just old hat now. Anyway, that's enough of me on my soapbox, I'd better get back to the incident room. I only popped into court to catch the Grantmore verdict. I wasn't involved in the case but I've wanted to see that bastard get sorted for ages.'

'Yeah... what were the bloody jury thinking?' Jane downed her double whisky in one gulp.

'Like poor Lisa Holland, they were conned. I knew there were weaknesses in the case, but I didn't think a jury would believe his two mates, claiming she was drunk and acting provocatively.'

'They stuck to their story in the witness box and of course she never reported the rape straight away… waited until after she told her dad in the morning.'

'The jury swallowed Grantmore's act… good-looking, blue-eyed Jack the Lad, with the gift of the gab and an eye for the ladies. They believed him… and his two bent mates… not her.'

'But to wink at her like that after the verdict, just like she claimed he'd done in the club and after the rape. What a bastard. Anyway, what are we going to do with Mr Holland? He's still downstairs, cooling off in a cell. You're going to have to charge him with assault.'

I didn't respond but my face told her that was not my intention.

'Darnley, you will be charging Russ Holland with assault. An assault committed in front of a judge and jury, three coppers and the press. Not to mention the victim's family and friends – and Smythson his barrister. Even you can detect that one.'

'I'm going to have him cautioned. He fits the bill… never been in trouble before and not likely to be in the future.'

She raised her eyebrows in surprise and poured another double. 'But Grantmore will complain for sure. And what about Smythson? Poor little bugger has probably only just started breathing normally again. He was flapping about on the floor like a landed fish.' Despite herself, she laughed.

'Grantmore won't complain. He'll know he's been bloody lucky and want to keep a low profile. As for Smythson, I've already had a quick chat and he's too embarrassed to complain. He just wants his moment of ignominy to be forgotten. No, in my book, the Hollands have suffered enough. We've not seen justice delivered today and I'm damned if I'm going to add to their misery.'

Jane nodded her reluctant agreement. 'Poor girl, not enough to be raped at her age by a thug like Grantmore, but having had the courage to come forward and report it, knowing he'd claim consent, and then a jury believe him. Sometimes I hate the jury system.'

'Aye. You can't blame her dad. Many men would react the same way. I'll go downstairs and arrange his transfer to Central, get him cautioned and on his way home. Don't worry, the press will be fine, and Grantmore won't create waves but if he does, I'll personally take the flak.'

Jane drained her whisky, put down the glass and rubbed her hands through her hair in a belated effort to fluff out her "wig hair".

'You're right, Matt. The family's had enough. Just let me know if the shit's going to fly… and I'll send it your way. Let's face it, you dinosaur, it won't hurt you. With this Chief, your career's peaked.'

Five

Thirty minutes later, I was back at Queens Gardens Police Station, or Central as both the public and the force knew it. I ran up the stairs to my office on the third floor, tossed my coat onto the spare chair in the corner and dumped my briefcase amongst the untidy piles of papers on my desk. It was already dark as I looked out onto the public gardens that gave the police station its name, my mind trying to compartmentalise the events of the afternoon and leave them behind so I could prepare for the briefing later that evening.

From beat copper to detective superintendent, I had always felt empathy with the victims of the crimes I dealt with, particularly those who were weak or vulnerable and thus more likely to experience long-term mental anguish alongside what was often physical pain. Lisa Holland, her dad and the rest of her family would never get over what happened to her, however loving they were and however tough she might be. Despite that empathy, I tried never to get "involved" with the individuals concerned, as along that route lay mental anguish of my own. Instead, I allowed myself to feel aggrieved on their behalf and use my time and effort in getting revenge or retribution for them. As a professional, I should describe my goal as justice. Maybe for crimes like theft or damage, justice fits the bill. But a personal attack like this one? Surely justice needed to deliver some tangible revenge. Justice. Revenge. A dichotomy? Different words, with different definitions, evoking different feelings – but are they the same?

Lisa Holland didn't receive justice. The delivery mechanism ran its course – but failed – so her father took a small measure of revenge. Can justice only be given? Or does it sometimes have to be taken?

I'd wrestled with such dilemmas ever since I'd joined the police at nineteen, and was none the wiser after twenty-eight years. My interest in the concept had been spawned by my first sergeant, a blunt Yorkshireman, whose guiding mantra was "do right or do nowt". His beliefs guided his methods. Do the right thing morally – if the law allowed. If the law didn't facilitate it, his morals would not allow him to take a lawful course of action that was likely to result in consequences that did not support the right outcome as he saw it. Over my service, I have come to realise that police work, like life – like justice – is rarely black or white, but shades of grey. Furthermore, how the police are allowed and enabled to achieve justice through the law has changed and shifted over time, like the sands on an exposed beach.

Sean Grantmore had escaped justice. The court case should have delivered it, as the evidence had been legally gathered and well presented. There was no way now I could help the Hollands gain revenge, but I was planning to do "right by doing nowt". Grantmore was scum – owning a number of brothels fronting as massage parlours and in that role had gathered previous convictions for several physical and indecent assaults. I thus had no qualms about flouting procedure and not charging Lisa's father. My first sergeant, now in his eighties and long-retired, would have been proud of me.

I was dragged from my somewhat sanctimonious and depressing thoughts by a knock on my door.

'Got a problem, boss.' DS Braggs walked into the office without ceremony and joined me at the window. 'He's as good as gold, admits assaulting Grantmore, but he won't accept a caution. Says he wants to be charged so he can tell his story in court.'

I had anticipated that Holland was so wound up that he might take that approach, and I didn't want to get Braggs involved in my breach of police procedure. On its own, an assault that necessitated a trip to the hospital in an ambulance, as it had done in Grantmore's case, should have led to a charge and a court appearance. Throw in the witnesses of judge, jury and three coppers and there was no doubt a caution was inappropriate. Furthermore, a caution had to be accepted by the accused and proved by their signature, as it is essentially a finding of guilt.

'Don't worry, Gav, you get off home. I'll sort it out.'

He dug his hands into the pockets of his suit trousers and stuck his chin out. I was in for an argument.

'Gavin, go home. I'm not charging Holland. He'd get a conviction he can well do without.'

'I don't agree…'

'Go home.'

Still with his hands in his pockets and with his chin stuck out like a belligerent schoolboy, he stomped out of the office, knowing further discussion was not an option.

*

The Police and Criminal Evidence Act of 1984, or PACE as it is commonly known, is often referred to as a watershed in modern policing, and for coppers like me who actually learnt their trade before then, it had certainly proved to be a massive shift in the balance of power between delivering justice and the rights of the suspect. Yet here we are today, years later, with every TV detective carrying on like we're still in the seventies. I tell you, it pisses me off – and spoils all the cop shows for loads of officers and their families, as the legal mastermind on the couch rubbishes the storyline accompanied by a lecture on PACE. We watch as the TV detective cuts massive legal corners with barely a murmur from the custody sergeant. In the real world, most custody sergeants want to reach their pension and follow PACE rigidly, protecting their prisoners like a lion protects its cubs. Everything, and I mean everything, is recorded on the electronic custody sheet. Video and audio recording in custody suites renders any actions or words that could be interpreted as contrary to PACE as likely to ruin any prosecution. The vast majority of pre-PACE coppers just rolled over, left the police force and joined the police "service". The small minority of those who wished to remain on the force either got caught big style and were "retired", or after some smaller misdemeanour begrudgingly toed the line. An even smaller minority just got ever more careful and crafty.

Custody Sergeant Howard Mulligan had opted for the service approach, and like many career-long uniformed officers, he was no fan of the CID, viewing us as arrogant, vain, elitist, lazy, womanising pissheads. Add to that his views, shared by many, that any officer above the rank of inspector must have got there through brown-nosing and were, as a group, over-educated tossers who had never experienced real police work, then detective superintendents were about as welcome in his custody suite as moths in your wardrobe. He was the custody sergeant that evening. The one I now had to convince to see things my way. Fortunately, I had no problem with Howard Mulligan.

As a newly promoted inspector, I had attended the scene of a violent domestic incident when a young and inexperienced PC Mulligan had requested urgent assistance. I arrived to a veritable bloodbath. A drunken man had slashed his wife across the cheek with a Stanley knife as a permanent reminder not to flirt with other men, an action he claimed to have witnessed in the local pub earlier that evening. He had drunkenly explained his thought processes to the young PC, while still clutching the bloodstained Stanley knife, with his sobbing and bleeding wife watching on. Trust me, this is a fairly average type of incident a beat copper regularly faces, and as a new recruit from a stable middle-class home, Howard Mulligan found himself frightened, disconcerted and angry.

As the drunken husband continued to justify his actions, young PC Mulligan snapped, head-butting the man and breaking his nose. This was the point at which I entered the scene. The man was arrested and charged with wounding but obviously wanted to complain that he too had been assaulted. At three in the morning, I was the most senior officer on duty, so it was with me he raised his complaint.

PC Mulligan was distraught, ashamed at his lack of control and unprofessionalism and couldn't stop saying so when I took him into my office. He knew he had committed a crime and feared the sack and made no effort to justify his actions. After he had unburdened himself, I let him read the statement I had taken from the injured wife. With some coaching from me, she had agreed that her husband had waved the Stanley knife in a threatening manner at the calm young officer and he had had little choice in view of their close proximity but to defend himself with a single head-butt. Mulligan still failed to grasp the lifeline I had thrown him, as he was so traumatised. It took me some minutes to convince him that this was exactly what had happened. I then formally cautioned him and together with the duty sergeant, we interviewed him for the assault the man alleged.

As tutored, he responded to give a complete and legal defence to an assault – that of proportionate self-defence. Six months later in Crown Court at the man's trial, Mulligan described his act of self-defence and the judge commended the young constable for his honesty and his courage. Mulligan was forever grateful and when he got promoted a few years later, when PACE had been enacted, I got a tame custody sergeant. We had never spoken about that night since. Originally, he had been all too keen to show his gratitude by covering up minor PACE infringements, but as my career progressed and the villains and crimes I dealt with became more serious, I knew he was becoming progressively out of his depth – and also growing to hate my guts. But hey-ho, there you go; shouldn't go nutting prisoners and getting into the clutches of Matt Darnley.

I rang the custody suite. 'Evening, Sergeant. Detective Superintendent Darnley here. Don't reply until you have heard what I have said… remember… that tape is running.'

I paused and could hear his breathing quicken.

I looked at my watch – it was 5.10pm. 'Record on the custody record that Holland was formally cautioned by me at 5.15pm and then formally release him. Leave the custody suite as if you were escorting him to the front exit of the nick but bring him up here. Straight up to my office. Don't explain to him. He'll just be pleased to be on his way home. I know you want to know how I am going to cover this one but you'll have to trust me. Make that entry and it covers you, and I'll take care of the rest.'

I hung up, knowing they'd soon appear.

I checked my watch again. I needed to get this matter sorted and get to the briefing at Driffield by six. I mused again on the course of action I was about to take, the rules I was about to flout and likely repercussions if I was found out. I was doing the right thing.

I was standing at my window looking down on Queens Gardens, watching folks making their way home from work, thinking that I still had to persuade Crabbe to give me additional staffing for the incident, when Mulligan ushered Holland into the room.

'Thank you, Sergeant, the paperwork I need to complete will be done before you go off at eleven. Come in, Mr Holland. I'm Detective Superintendent Darnley. We've never met but DS Braggs and DC Young are members of my team. I was in court this afternoon for the verdict and I wanted to speak to you before you leave.'

Before Holland could respond, Mulligan stepped forward in front of him and through gritted teeth hissed, 'I've had enough of this. This is the last time.'

With a friendly smile, I beckoned a clearly angry yet distressed Mulligan forward and whispered in his ear, 'You will have had enough when I say you've had enough. It'll be sorted with my head on the block if it goes wrong, not yours.'

Still smiling at Mr Holland, I guided the sergeant out of the office and offered my hand to Lisa's dad. 'I am so sorry about the verdict. I wanted you to know that we all believed your daughter and I hope that makes some difference to you and your family.'

Holland just stood staring at me, his gaunt face expressionless. I felt extremely uncomfortable and would have preferred open grief, anger, disgust or indeed any of the emotions I would have expected, but I now felt at a loss as to what to do or say next. All I wanted was to persuade him to sign a caution form and get him out of the nick and myself to the briefing. Rules dictated that a caution must involve a tape-recorded admission of guilt, but I knew he'd never go for that in his state of mind and I didn't blame him. I knew that the chances of the custody record ever being cross-referenced with an admission on tape and matched up to the caution form was negligible.

After about ten seconds, Holland moved to the window and looked out at the scene below. 'It's ruined my daughter's life, this whole experience. She barely leaves the house and when she does, she returns in pieces. That bastard must pay for that... he will pay.'

'Lisa was brave to come forward, to stand in court and face him. She's not a quitter. She'll get better, give it time.' I realised as I said it I sounded trite and condescending, and was not surprised when Holland erupted.

'I know that... don't lecture me about my own daughter... but he can't get away with it. I'm her father. It's my job to protect her... always. Her mother's dead... there's only me. I couldn't protect her that night or today in court, but by God, I can make recompense and I'll have him.'

I put my hands on his shoulders, hoping I could calm him and try and reason with him, but he shrugged me off, squaring up to me with his fists clenched, albeit held low at his sides. He looked me square in the eyes with undisguised malevolence. I feared he was about to attack me and stepped back and away from him, my thighs backing into my desk, so that I was trapped. He followed and grabbed my upper arms with such strength and ferocity that I was unable to move as he thrust his face close to mine and almost growled.

'The man's an animal, a dangerous fucking animal...'

He suddenly seemed to realise where he was and what he was doing. He released his grip, stepped back and then seemed to collapse inwardly, his shoulders slumped and his fists relaxed.

'Sorry, it's not your fault. Gavin and Jo were great... it's the system. We used the system and it's failed us. Oh, just let me go home.' He was close to tears now.

Although my instincts were to try and smooth things over, I knew this was not the time, so I moved over to my desk, picked up my pen and said, 'Come on, let's get you home. Just sign this release form.'

I was banking on the fact he would be too distraught to read it and sure enough he just grabbed the pen and dragged a line across the caution form where I had indicated. Good enough for my purposes. When I filled in the form and sent it for filing along with the detected crime report for the assault on Grantmore, the paper and computer records would all match and the Holland case would be officially closed.

Before he could ask any further questions, I put my arm across his shoulders and guided him out of the office and along the CID corridor. As we made our way downstairs, he remained quiet, lost in his own thoughts, but as we neared the front foyer of the station, he stopped and turned towards me, his icy blue eyes again locking onto mine.

'How can you do your job knowing that an animal like Grantmore can just rub your nose in his shit? Did you see him wink at Lisa, when he got off? Rubbing her nose in it too. Well, he's not going to do that to me. Dangerous animals need caging… or rendering harmless…'

He turned, wrenched open the door to the street and walked rapidly away. I stood there thinking, *Darnley, you may well have dropped a bollock.*

If only I'd known.

Six

Busy days, however, soon dispelled the worry that my altruistic, albeit slightly dodgy dealings with Russ Holland would come back to bite me on the arse. As well as the Emmerson murder and robbery, I was still SIO on a domestic murder that had taken place in October. It had reached a crescendo of activity as we amassed the evidence to arrest and charge Oliver Daggett for beating his wife to death with a cast-iron lamp stand, when he discovered her affair with his business partner. His alibi of a business trip, and finding her body when he came home, although a fairly obvious lie, had taken us several weeks to dismantle. This was Daggett's first foray into crime, and his efforts to cover his tracks, although impressive, had proved ultimately inadequate.

Two or three days after I had seen Holland storm out of Central, I had all but forgotten about him and his poor daughter. The evening after Grantmore's acquittal, the *Hull Daily Mail* had carried the story of the court case – and how he had got his swollen knackers. The young reporter had sacrificed short-term glory for my promise of bigger and better stories and his piece was sympathetic to the Hollands, leaving the reader in little doubt as to how fortunate Grantmore was to be acquitted. As I had hoped, Grantmore had also kept a low profile and had been "unavailable for comment". I rang the reporter, Richard Wilde, as promised and gave him some steamy "off-the-record" inside stories about the murdered Sonia Daggett's love affair with her husband's business partner, Chris Knowles – who also happened to be a very prominent local councillor. Sonia hadn't deserved to die but neither did Chris Knowles deserve to take full control of D & K Engineering, so a bit of public embarrassment for the pompous arse fitted nicely with my idea of getting justice done – and got young Wilde owing me a favour in the future.

On the Saturday morning after we had charged Daggett, I'd had a much-needed lie-in before popping into the incident room at Driffield. I intended to work for just a few hours to catch up with my reading on that job – which was getting nowhere fast. I parked my Honda Accord in the rear yard of Driffield nick, which on a Saturday morning was virtually empty, and made my way to the incident room, and within forty-five minutes I was wading through a whole tray load of statements trying to catch up with the finer detail of the crimes. My efforts to try and persuade the Chief to give me additional staffing had failed, despite my usually successful manipulations. I guess his desire to put on the additional Christmas uniform pantomime had overridden his earlier worries. So with not quite enough staff, the necessity of me reading every statement and considering every angle became even more vital. I also had several statements from the Daggett murder with me, as despite the charge, there were still several inconsistencies that were nagging at me.

Once again, unlike on the telly, it's often after the murder charge is laid that the detailed work really begins. Okay, we all go to the pub straight after the charge, but unless you want some clever barrister pulling your case to bits, you then make sure the job is watertight. In my experience, it doesn't even pay to relax after the conviction, as very few murderers just give in gracefully and sit in their cell making matchstick models. Appeals are almost automatic and the science of hindsight is then applied to your investigation in a second concerted effort to rubbish it. Equally, the ace TV detectives never seem to have to balance being SIO on two non-linked murder enquiries at once. On the telly, just the boss and his trusty sidekick find the serial killer in an hour – or less if there are adverts. In reality, the bulk of the effort is in the mundane piecing together of the known facts to make a coherent and thus convincing sequence of events, which will initially convince the Crown Prosecution Service there is a realistic prospect of a conviction. Then there's a judge and jury. I can tell you, switching your mind from one set of names, dates, times, witnesses, suspect and evidence to an entirely different case is not easy.

My main task this Saturday morning, I had decided, was to examine the issue of whether someone at the building society had given the robbers inside information about how the key system worked. We suspected the robbers might have sussed out Janice Cooper's house a few weeks earlier, and they had known to go to Anne Beedham's house. How? The action of solving this little riddle by interviewing all staff members at the society had been given to DI Mally Baldwin. He and two DCs had completed the action without coming to a definitive solution. I read the statements provided by the staff and DI Baldwin's covering report and conclusions. I had worked several major enquiries with Mally and trusted his judgement, as he was thorough and competent. I could see he had done all that was possible at this stage of the inquiry, but I was not content that the conclusions he had drawn were correct.

He felt confident Beedham was not involved. She had grown extremely angry at the suggestion, to the point that PC

Granger, her FLO, had to persuade her not to make a formal complaint, explaining why the suggestion had to be put to her. Once again, I was impressed by this young lad's skills with so little experience. Her righteous anger had impressed the DI as honest, and he rationalised that she would not have put her husband and son in such danger. Furthermore, he argued, if involved, how had the attack by Emmerson been allowed to happen? He'd also ruled out Janice Cooper, for obvious reasons – her near death and the earlier reporting of the suspicious man, and his Vauxhall Vectra. All other members of staff had been spoken to and none had any connections with Emmerson, nor given the DI and his small team reason for suspicion. Ten of them were so junior that they were not trusted with the keys and did not know the system used, although they could easily have sussed it out.

The only loose end was the manager, Noel Priestley. A brief initial interview about the crime had taken place on the first day of the inquiry, but the idea of an inside leak had not been covered. Unfortunately, the next day, he had collapsed at work and ended up in hospital for three days. Stress had apparently triggered a minor heart attack. DI Baldwin had spoken to his wife, requesting he be able to speak to Mr Priestley at home in order to complete his enquiries. Mrs Priestley had refused point-blank, quoting the doctor's instructions that he should remain stress-free. In short, Mally could not totally rule out employee involvement but concluded it was unlikely. His theory was that the robbers had watched the society, seen Anne Beedham and Janice Cooper, and no doubt the other key holders, lock up and followed them home. Perhaps Cooper's house had demanded a second visit, as it was so isolated and hard to find. Having decided on the date for the robbery, they realised Anne was locking up that week, so she was the first port of call and she'd named Janice Cooper?

It was plausible but I wasn't convinced. It was too neat and tidy and few criminals are that patient and thorough. Despite the DI's confidence, I still did not rule out Beedham. I couldn't see it being Cooper. I wanted a comprehensive interview completed with Noel Priestley, as his views of his staff would be invaluable. Consequently, I did not sign off the action as complete but added my thoughts and requested DI Baldwin discuss the matter with me.

So involved was I in my analysis that I didn't hear a uniformed sergeant enter my office through the open door until he politely coughed to alert me.

'Excuse me, sir, but we've a chap at the front desk who's insisting he talks to you immediately.'

This was the last thing I needed. I had deliberately come in on a Saturday to get a bit of peace and quiet and plough through this paperwork. Ten days into the inquiry, the early frenetic pace had slowed a little and the overtime reduced so now half the team were off at the weekend. I'd banked on there being only one or two about in the incident room, with the others out on enquiries. So, with the benefit of hindsight, I didn't respond positively to what was about to unfold.

'What about?'

'Says he's got information about a rape, sir. Something about someone who was acquitted at Hull Crown Court earlier this week? But he won't talk to me.'

Grantmore. My interest was aroused – but hell, I had other matters of a more pressing nature.

'Call someone in off the incident to deal with him, but tell them that I've specifically assigned them to the task.'

He left to do my bidding and without further thought, I returned to my reading. About an hour and a half later, I was again disturbed, this time by young Pete Granger.

'Excuse me, sir, but I've been speaking to Mr Morley and I think you might want to hear what he has to say.'

I'd forgotten all about the earlier interruption. 'Who?'

'They called me in, sir, to talk to a Mr Graham Morley. He came here from Hull to try and speak to you about the Grantmore rape. I've been talking to him for the last hour and I really think you need to see him.'

The lad looked so keen and excited that I tossed the statement I'd been reading back into my tray and said, 'Wheel him in then.'

'Before I do, are there any developments on our job, boss?' he asked. 'I had Friday off and with there not being a briefing today and hardly anybody about, I've lost the plot a bit.'

'Not a breakthrough yet, I'm afraid, but an interesting little development. We've recovered a twenty-pound note that came from the building society cash. Remember, it had only been delivered that day and it was new money, so we circulated the serial numbers. Well, one of the twenties was banked up in Newcastle, as part of the takings from a local pub. Serious local villains use the pub, so I've sent a couple of lads up there to explore a potential north-east connection. Maybe we'll find a link to Emmerson.'

'Anne... sorry... Mrs Beedham is really cut up about Emmerson. She reckons she feels responsible for his death. She knows that it was her biting him and the blood that led to the others shooting him. Crazy, I know, but it's all affected her badly.' He sounded quite emotional.

I studied him thoughtfully for a moment. He was a good-looking lad, still with the remnants of acne, so he can't have been much more than twenty-two at most. He was too young in service to be on a major incident really and had only just completed his FLO training, but I'd been impressed with the statements he'd taken from Anne Beedham and her family and they were happy with him, and so I'd swung his attachment with his divisional commander. He'd been sceptical, saying the lad was having marriage problems and his mind might not be on the job. I'd kept him in uniform intending to use him for the many jobs on the inquiry that didn't always need a detective. His trousers had a sharp crease and his boots shone, so in my book the lad "had the makings". However, I could tell from what he'd just said that Anne Beedham and her family had clearly got under his skin. Maybe he was too green to be that close to the family's trauma. I made a mental note to find out a bit more about his personal problems and maybe think about withdrawing him. I didn't want someone as young in service cracking up just because I'd taken a shine to him, but this was not the time to explore his vulnerabilities.

'So what's this chap at the counter want?'

'He's got some evidence in the Grantmore rape case.'

Intriguing. 'And what do you know about that case?'

'I realise he's probably too late because the trial's over, but from what I know about Sean Grantmore, I thought you'd want to have every bit of intelligence on him we can get.'

I was impressed that he knew about the case, and even more that he had heard of Grantmore, who operated in Hull while he policed the East Riding. He got bonus points for recognising the investigator's insatiable need for intelligence.

'Bring him up. We'll have a word with him together.'

I could see he was excited at the prospect and clearly chuffed to be asked by a detective superintendent. He was back within five minutes, accompanied by a thin, bespectacled young man. His age was almost impossible to determine due to his shockingly old-fashioned haircut and clothes. Our Mr Morley had a huge beaked nose upon which rested the most enormous round tortoiseshell spectacles, and a complexion that suggested he rarely saw daylight. His beige corduroy trousers were worn bald on the thighs and were three inches too short. His open maroon-coloured anorak revealed a hand-knitted, multi-coloured zip-up jumper. This bloke was at the back of the queue when God handed out looks – and when the jumble sale opened in 1972. I had a mental image of him having arrived out here in Driffield in either a Reliant Robin or astride a ladies' shopper moped – you know the type?

My new young partner introduced me to his witness, showed him to a chair, closed the door to the office and perched on the corner of my desk, as if we'd been working together for ten years.

'Fetch another chair, Constable,' indicating he should collect one from the briefing room. I didn't want him too cocky too soon.

He returned pushing a wheeled office chair, his acne even more inflamed by all the excitement. It was soon about to get worse. I leaned towards Mr Morley, invading his space.

'What the hell do you mean by coming in here several days after an important trial has bloody finished and telling us you've got evidence?'

Granger almost fell off his chair in surprise at what he must have regarded as an unusual stance to take with someone trying to help us. Mr Morley, however, just blinked at me from behind his huge glasses. His appearance had convinced me that he was one of the usual fruitcakes that like to try and get involved in high-profile cases, and my intention was to piss him off double-quick so I could get back to my beloved paperwork. Granger had already fallen off my "one to watch" list, as an inability to identify time-wasters – before they actually waste it – is a rapid route to the Traffic Branch or Community Affairs – not the CID.

Morley shuffled uncomfortably in his seat but calmly returned my stare.

'You don't intimidate me, Inspector. I have been bullied by experts. I have proof that Sean Grantmore raped that girl. What do you say to that?'

'Two things, Mr Morley. It's Detective Superintendent Darnley, and as I said before, why tell me now... after the case has concluded?'

However, he had aroused my curiosity and his steady gaze in the face of my intimidation had made me think I may have underestimated him. So I decided to back-pedal.

'I hope you'll understand I had to take that forceful tone with you, Mr Morley, as all too often we receive salacious information surrounding rape cases, but I can see by your response that you have confidence in your information. What do you mean you have proof?'

Morley sat forward and pushed his huge glasses back up his nose with his right forefinger and looked conspiratorially at Granger. Then he took a hand-held tape recorder from his anorak pocket, placed it on the desk, pressed "Play" and sat back.

A disembodied mechanical voice came from the small machine. *Message left at 1.47pm on Friday 17 April 1998.*

This was followed by a second voice I easily recognised as Sean Grantmore's.

'Daz? It's Granto. Ring me back straight away. We need to get our stories straight for last night. That lass is reckoning I raped her. Ring me straight back... the cops are looking for me.'

I started to ask questions but Granger held up his hand to silence me and indicated I should continue to listen. There were a couple of clicks and then the voice I now realised was an answerphone recording gave another time and date followed by a voice I did not recognise.

'Granto. It's Daz. I've spoken to Tommo and he'll say the same. She was pissed and gagging for it. So send the coppers to us once they lock you up.'

Again, Granger held up his hand, letting me know there was more to come.

This last call was two days after the first messages and again it was Grantmore.

'Daz, my old pal, meet me in the Cheese as soon as you get this. I got bail and no charge as yet. It's her word against mine… and yours.' Grantmore gave a hearty laugh. *'Bring Tommo. I owe you both a drink.'*

Morley leaned into the desk and switched off the machine, a triumphant look upon his face. Granger was also looking very pleased with himself. As for me – I was just confused. I looked at Granger, demanding an explanation.

'The first message you heard was left by Grantmore on the mobile phone of a man called Daryl Jenkins. I've checked the crime report relating to Lisa Holland and she reported the rape at ten o'clock, about eight hours after the offence took place and about four hours before Grantmore left the message. So it obviously refers to her. It sounds like he rang his mate once he knew we were looking for him.'

I still hadn't grasped where these messages had come from – this was long before phone hacking was in the news. Not used to being slow on the uptake but now apparently being left behind by a spotty plod and a retro nerd, I reverted to the Darnley everyone knows and loves – grumpy and aggressive.

'Get on with it, man. I haven't got all day. Where has this recording come from? I can see the significance.'

Morley looked at me as though I was an idiot. 'I accessed Grantmore's and Jenkins's mobile telephone answerphones and recorded those messages. They prove that Grantmore concocted his defence with his two friends. Tommo is Jamie Alan Thompson by the way.'

I just sat gobsmacked.

Granger chivalrously leapt into the hiatus.

'Mr Morley has followed the case, sir, and he tells me that both Jenkins and Thompson gave evidence at Grantmore's trial that Lisa Holland was drunk when in Spiders and was being openly promiscuous towards several men, themselves included. Surely these tapes show an offence of perverting the course of justice and help to illustrate Grantmore's guilt?'

I didn't know where to start, although the mists were beginning to clear somewhat.

'Play them to me again,' I commanded.

Morley did so.

'Tell me, Mr Morley, how did you gain access to these voicemails?' Despite myself, I was intrigued.

The young man proudly puffed out his chest – or what passed as a chest – and somewhat verbosely explained. It was all about PIN code combinations, probability and prediction. Mumbo-jumbo that left me baffled.

Seeing my confusion, Granger helped out: 'Mr Morley works in IT, sir... he's a bit of a whizz at this sort of stuff.'

Clearly as proud as punch to be centre stage, Morley announced, 'Nothing to someone like me with patience, purpose and persistence.'

And there lay my next question. Why did he have such patience, purpose and persistence?

'Why did you do this?'

'I hate Grantmore... and Jenkins for that matter. Both of them used to bully me at school to the point where I tried to kill myself when I was fourteen. They literally ruined my life. I've never got over it.'

His voice cracking with emotion, he continued: 'Over the last few years, I started to see things in the paper about Grantmore; court appearances, prison sentences and heard how he was a drug dealer and controlled prostitutes and I started to try and find out more about him... I... I just thought I could get my own back... get him into trouble and in prison for longer. It sounds stupid now... telling it to you... but I know loads about him.'

PC Granger rose from his chair and put a comforting arm across Mr Morley's shoulder and handed him a lever arch file that he was holding. 'Let's show the boss your dossier.'

Morley opened the file on his knees and turned it towards me, inviting me to look. He slowly turned the pages and I saw carefully annotated pages of notes, newspaper cuttings and photographs. The file was about four inches thick and had clearly been put together with a great deal of attention to detail.

I sat and thought for a moment, trying to assimilate all that I had heard. The recordings would have been dynamite in court, showing collusion between the defendant and his two key witnesses. As Granger had said, the recordings strongly suggested a crime of perverting the course of justice and cast severe doubts upon Grantmore's version of events. But they were of little use now in getting justice for Lisa Holland. Back in 1998, once a court had acquitted someone of a crime, there was no way of having a "second bite at the cherry". What was known as double jeopardy was enshrined in English Common Law, until the Criminal Justice Act 2003 for the first time allowed a second trial if substantial new evidence emerged. It was this change in the law that allowed the second trial and conviction of Gary Dobson in 2012 for the murder of Stephen Lawrence after his acquittal for that same offence in 1996. Sure enough, a charge for perverting the course of justice was still possible – as that was apparently what they had done – successfully. But no way was it possible with this evidence – it had been illegally obtained and was thus inadmissible. As my mind worked through what Morley had sat on for eight months, I could feel my anger building.

'Come on then, supercop, how the hell are we going to use this evidence?'

The final word was loaded with sarcasm.

'Surely that's your domain?' Granger immediately responded with a confidence that both astounded and angered me further.

'The interception of communications – which is what this represents – requires the police to obtain a Home Secretary's warrant. To get one, we'd have needed some evidence about what we would be likely to find. A man with an axe to grind has obtained these tapes illegally. Your pal here needs arresting and charging under the Interception of Communications Act 1985,' I boomed.

Morley looked terrified. Granger looked angry.

'He's just done his best. He didn't know... did you, Graham?'

'I did actually... and thought long and hard about coming here, knowing I could be in trouble, but I just wanted to do what I could for that poor girl.' He made a last effort at being defiant.

I stood up and again leaned into his personal space, my face only inches from his.

'Bullshit. You just want revenge on Grantmore and his cronies. You're not interested in justice for Lisa Holland. I might have been more inclined to believe your motives if you'd brought this to us before the trial. We couldn't have actually used the tapes but we would have known for sure they'd concocted the story. Imagine what we might have done to discredit their evidence if we'd known that before court.'

'I resent that tone of voice, Inspector. I cannot be expected to understand the rules of the Criminal Justice System. I have done my duty by coming here today.'

The cloying stink of righteous indignation hung in the room.

'Bollocks! You were clearly a spineless wimp as a school kid, letting a bully like Grantmore piss all over you, then you pratt about like Miss Marple and still haven't got the actual balls to get even when you get the chance… You've sat on this for eight months and now it's useless. A young girl's life has been ruined by Grantmore… by far worse than bloody playground bullying. You could have helped put that right. Get him out of here before I charge him.'

I got up and flung open the door, shaking my head in disgust at Morley as he gathered up his file, while Granger waited in the corridor with a look of thunder on his face, clearly directed at me.

Morley stopped as he left the room and looked at me, and I could see there were tears in his eyes.

'You don't understand…' he almost whimpered.

Granger tried one last approach.

'Sir. You really need to examine the file Mr Morley has assembled…'

I stalked into the corridor towards the young officer and poked my finger into his chest.

'I thought you were better than this. I'm bloody disappointed. I don't give a shit what's in his file… probably more illegally obtained crap… now get him out of here before I lock him up.'

I stomped back into my office, slammed the door and dropped heavily into my chair.

'Bastard, bastard, bastard!' I hissed in sheer frustration, realising one was for Grantmore, one for Morley – and the other for me, as I hated losing my temper.

I sat pondering what might have been. Staring into space, thinking of Lisa's anguish and her father's cold fury. I had literally only seen Lisa Holland for those few minutes in court and then her dad for the time it took to wangle his caution. So why had this case got to me when others, often far more distressing, hadn't? The reality was that sometimes playing the cool, dispassionate and objective cop just didn't work.

I confess that I barely gave a second thought to what my duty should have been as regards Morley's illegal phone hacking. He had committed serious offences, and thinking back now, twenty-odd years after the event, he must have done it lots of times. He hadn't just struck lucky on those three messages. I should have done something about it, but I had bigger fish to fry and he seemed such an insignificant wimp of a man, I did not anticipate any comebacks. Even worse, I did not think for one moment about the poor man's battered self-esteem and how I had further damaged it – something I would truly come to regret.

After about twenty minutes of this navel-gazing there was a knock on my office door. It was Granger. By now, I had calmed down and was regretting that I had taken my frustrations out on him and so was pleased he had returned. Although I did not intend to apologise – not my style with a junior officer – I did want to clear the air.

'Come in, sit down,' I offered.

'I'd rather not, thank you. I just wanted to say that I feel that my position on your inquiry is now untenable. I do not think I can continue to work for you and request I be returned to divisional duties.' He stood there, almost at attention, looking me directly in the eye.

Talk about knocked off track. This kid continued to surprise me. I was now angry again. Who the hell did he think he was?

'PC Granger, I decide where you work. Not you. You'll stay on the incident and learn your trade. You will do as I tell you. Do I make myself clear?'

There was a lengthy pause. 'Yes... sir.'

'Forget about Mr Graham bloody Morley... I don't want to hear any more about him and his tapes, and neither does anyone else. Now get back to work.'

He turned on his heel and left without another word, slamming the door.

'Bastard!' Now the reference was just for me.

I felt an absolute prick for letting myself down in front of him earlier by losing my temper and acting as the stereotypical senior detective – arrogant and egotistical. Even more uncomfortably, I also realised that he was witness to my neglect of duty over Morley's actions. It was a unique experience for me to be in the same position into which I had manoeuvred other officers, so that I could manipulate them to my own ends. I didn't like the feeling. I felt a moment of worry that he might decide to report the matter, particularly if my earlier misdemeanour over Holland's phony caution were also revealed in the course of an internal disciplinary inquiry.

After a few more minutes thinking things through, I decided it would be wise to get him back onside. He was clearly ambitious and would surely welcome support from a man in my position. I was still pissed off that a spotty kid barely out of school had got the black on me, but my arrogance and ego also concluded that with a bit of nurturing he could be almost as good a copper as me. Despite his cock-up with Morley, he was still "one to watch" and a potential member of what I knew the troops called "Darnley's Clan". I resolved that I'd find the chance to win him over. As for Mr Morley, I barely gave him a second thought.

For the second time in the space of five days, I had made another serious error of judgement.

Seven

A totally naked Sean Grantmore strained against the handcuffs. Both wrists and his left ankle were already secured to three corners of the specially constructed dominatrix table, kept in room three at Nicole's massage parlour on Witham, barely half a mile from Queens Gardens Police Station. Nestled between a second-hand car dealership and a cheap furniture shop, Nicole's was the second of Grantmore's parlours. As the boss, he regularly sampled the merchandise – particularly any new lines. Katia, a very shapely Romanian girl wearing a short, tight white masseuse's tunic and a pair of red killer heels was currently struggling to complete his immobilisation by handcuffing his right ankle to the bed. Sean had almost given in trying to thwart her efforts by kicking out with his right leg, as she was valiantly hanging onto the loose end of the handcuff, and the harder he kicked, the tighter the end around his ankle was getting. With a final pull that felt like it was going to slice his foot off, Katia snapped the handcuff in place.

This new girl had fascinated him from the moment he first saw her a week ago, when he'd called in to collect the takings from Janine, who ran Nicole's, and she'd introduced her as the latest recruit. The girl, in her early twenties, seemed brighter and more self-confident than most of the girls Nicole's "employed", and had shot him a look of defiance when Janine explained he was the boss. He decided there and then that he would teach her some respect the first chance he had, and her explicit teasing since their first meeting had served only to fuel that decision. Earlier that morning, he had rung Janine and told her to keep Katia free. Grantmore liked to frighten the girls in his employ and although he would never admit it to himself, he could only become aroused when his conquests were afraid. However, this girl had been such an expert seductress that Grantmore found himself going along with her in a state of excitement he had rarely before experienced, even though she was in total control and he had not even touched her. That state had lasted until the first set of handcuffs had rasped shut on his ankle and he had begun to feel vulnerable.

Before he had chance to think through his predicament, Katia had grabbed his exposed genitals and viciously squeezed, ramming his own socks into his mouth as he opened it to scream. She reached under the elevated table and pulled a length of wide adhesive tape from the base, where she had previously hidden it, and secured the socks by sticking it over his mouth. As her employer and non-paying customer, he now desperately wanted to end this excursion into what he still presumed was Katia's speciality – the world of sadomasochism. Or at least reverse the roles. He tried to shout for help but all that emerged was a barely audible "Ggggnhhhhhh". He was now just terrified about what was going to happen next – sex was the last thing on his mind. How could punters pay for this?

Suddenly Katia slapped him across the face with surprising strength and then spat in his face. Grantmore's fear ratcheted up a notch as it slowly dawned on him that this was not a sex game. The girl was truly angry – and in complete control. She then disappeared from his view and he could hear her moving about behind him. With his eyes shut like a kid lost in a nightmare, he felt the terror rising as bile in his throat, his fear growing along with the wait. But then he felt gentle fingers stroking his cheek and he tentatively opened his eyes. Gone was the tight white tunic, replaced with a baggy grey Gap hoodie. She was holding his wallet and with a theatrical flourish she removed the fat wad of notes that he used to flash around to impress. She tossed the empty wallet aside and stuffed the cash into the pocket of her jeans before moving out of his very limited eyeline.

'Bye, you nasty, worthless piece of shit,' she taunted – in a broad cockney accent.

Grantmore raised his head and strained to look down past his feet. He watched as she pulled up the venetian blinds on the sash window, then raised the lower half and stuck her head and shoulders outside and whistled softly. He then heard footsteps running nimbly up the metal fire escape that led from a platform below the window down to an enclosed yard at the rear of the premises. Katia began to climb out of the window as Grantmore saw a tall hooded figure appear on the platform. A bulky brown envelope was passed to Katia, who quickly inspected its contents then turned and blew a kiss to Grantmore before disappearing from sight down the fire escape. The hooded figure climbed into the room and stood staring at Grantmore through a Tony Blair mask. It was obviously a man, with a slim but athletic build.

Grantmore began to struggle against his bindings but there was no slack, and he succeeded only in causing the handcuffs to bite painfully into his wrists and ankles. Only his flaccid penis managed any form of free movement, serving to increase his terror and shame.

The man reached into the pocket of his black Adidas sweatshirt and Grantmore saw he was wearing yellow washing up gloves. He removed a syringe from his pocket and uncapped the needle, placing the orange cap back in his pocket. He moved next to Grantmore and held the syringe close to his head, depressing the plunger slightly, squirting small drops of colourless liquid onto his cheek. Grantmore moaned in sheer terror and then urinated as he smelled bleach. He screwed his eyes tightly shut in an effort to block out what was happening.

The man did not hesitate but stabbed the needle through Grantmore's right eyelid and into his eyeball before carefully depressing the plunger. Grantmore emitted an almost silent scream of agony through his gag and began to shake his head violently from side to side, succeeding only in snapping the needle off in his eye. His attacker was left holding the syringe, which he returned to his pocket. He then took out a plastic modelling knife and waited silently and patiently until his victim ceased the wild thrashing of his head. He then calmly took a tight hold of Grantmore's chin and with two long strokes of the knife cut an X across the same eye. He then pocketed the knife.

Through the intense burn of his pain, Grantmore felt a hand press something to his chest, before hearing his attacker climb out of the window and rattle away down the fire escape.

Eight

11:00 That Same Morning

'For pity's sake, fucking get me off here!' screamed Grantmore.

Detective Superintendent David Kingston stood looking down at the brutalised and bloodstained Grantmore, who remained shackled to the four corners of the table. A Special Course graduate from Bramshill Police College, Kingston had shot through the ranks and was now at least two promotions above his competence, yet still four below his aching ambition to be a Chief Constable. The man carried a sad mix of ambition and uselessness that rendered him decidedly unpleasant. He was currently shitting himself in an agony of indecision, desperate not to allow the two junior officers who had requested a senior detective attend the scene, to see that he was unsure what to do next – while dying to ask them. Meanwhile, they were relishing his discomfort almost as much as they were Grantmore's.

Janine, used to hearing the anguish of Grantmore's "conquests", had eventually come to investigate the silence. With no way of releasing him, she called the police. The attending uniformed officer had quickly assessed the scene, torn off the gag, removed the socks from Grantmore's mouth and then called out the CID, an ambulance and the fire brigade. The medics had arrived first but were thwarted by the handcuffs. The bemused female crew could only stand aside while the three firemen took a closer look and sent the rookie back outside to get the bolt croppers. He'd returned with two more crew members eager for a look at what would turn out to be the topic of much fire station hilarity. Janine, as gloriously happy as she could ever recall, joined the merry throng to cover her employer's embarrassment with a pink fluffy towel. The assembled audience expanded further with the arrival of Detective Sergeant Hudson and Detective Constable Jo Young. It hadn't taken the deductive powers of Sherlock Holmes for her to immediately spot the significance of Grantmore's injury, and the cardboard note taped to his chest confirmed it. She immediately advised her DS to ask for Darnley to attend but he was off-duty and Kingston, who was "on call", had been sent over from nearby Central. Jo Young quickly briefed him about the obvious suspect.

'Shall we chop him loose?' asked a fireman, flexing the bolt croppers.

'SOCO need photographs first, boss. This is a major crime scene,' said a delighted Jo Young, knowing full well that this ridiculous statement would not only prolong Grantmore's pain and humiliation but increase Kingston's indecision.

With a sideways wink at the DC, her DS chipped in. 'There might be some DNA on them cuffs, sir. We need 'em swabbing before they're cut off.'

'Hospital must be the priority, Superintendent,' said the ambulance driver, clearly pushing for a positive decision.

'For fuck's sake, get me out of here,' screamed Grantmore, his head thrashing from side to side.

Janine stepped forward. "We have a Polaroid in the salon.' Hardly able to suppress her mirth, she trotted off to fetch it.

Even Kingston could figure out that the imperative was to get Grantmore cut free and into the ambulance and that was what he ordered, as soon as DC Young had taken a couple of snaps with the Polaroid, insisting to her bemused boss that they would have to do in lieu of SOCO photographs. The photographs, although somewhat blurred, probably due to Grantmore's unwillingness to lie still and pose, clearly showed the attacker's message. Printed in red felt tip pen on a piece of plain grey card, roughly torn from some form of packaging, was the message –

*

'Sorry to disturb you at home, boss, but we've got a job on I knew you'd want to know about.' Jo Young described the crime scene that she had just left.

'If it hadn't have been me called to the job, it may have taken a little longer to link it to Holland, but as soon as I told Kingston about the rape case and what happened in court he was like a dog with two tails. He's already sent two arrest teams out, one for Russ Holland... fair enough, the link is obvious... but the other team's gone for Lisa. He reckons it could have been her... and if not, she'll be useful as a lever to get her dad talking. What a bastard.'

My immediate reaction was one of self-preservation. I had bent the rules over Holland and this incident and subsequent investigation was bound to uncover it. Holland had to be arrested and questioned, so his attack on Grantmore in court would all be presented as part of a chain of behaviour culminating in what was a vicious attack. If he was charged,

I was highly likely to get called to give evidence and it would be professionally damaging that I had not only made a serious error of judgement in cautioning him but had also circumvented the correct procedure.

'Thanks for letting me know, Jo. Are they bringing them into Central?'

'Kingston's at Central waiting for Russ Holland, but he's sent Linda Swales and myself to interview Lisa at Priory Road. I've told Kingston that I think he's bang out of order having Lisa locked up and Linda agrees. I was her Victim Liaison Officer for four months and I know her. There's no way she could have done that to Grantmore. She's damaged enough by the rape without this.'

'Okay, you and Linda go easy with Lisa. You know her and I trust your judgement that she'll have had nothing to do with it. But keep her talking, while I go into Central and speak to Kingston. Thanks again.'

From what Jo had told me, it was obvious that Russ Holland had extracted the revenge he'd threatened. Half of me had to admire a man who could avenge his beloved daughter in such dramatic fashion. The other half was pissed off that in doing so he'd dropped me in the shit.

Forty-five minutes later, I was walking down the corridor towards the office that Kingston occupied next to mine. I was about to walk in when I heard him in conversation.

'Yes, ma'am, it's looking good. We found the Adidas top Grantmore described at Holland's house along with a bottle of bleach under his sink. And of course we have the attack in the Crown Court in front of dozens of witnesses... you probably read about that in the *Mail*?'

He paused, obviously listening to the other side of what I now surmised was a telephone conversation.

'Actually, no, he wasn't charged. I've been in touch with the custody suite who have checked his custody record and believe it or not… Superintendent Darnley cautioned him.'

My little secret was out.

After another pause, he continued with obvious glee.

'Yes, I agree. A caution was totally inappropriate. The man should have been charged. This is going to be a very high-profile case. Such an unusual and cruel scenario will attract much press interest… even nationally, I suspect. When I charge Holland with this attack, Darnley's ill-judged decision is bound to come out and it will reflect badly on the force. But between you and me, ma'am, Darnley enjoys bucking the system… he thinks he's a law unto himself.'

Again he went quiet.

'Exactly, ma'am. Grantmore will now discover Darnley cautioned him and try and sue the force.' He was so enjoying this.

Again he listened, this time for a while longer, before continuing in what was a much more subdued manner.

'I thought it was a good tactic to arrest the girl, ma'am. I thought it might put some pressure on her father to admit his crime.'

I realised he must be talking to Jane Greenhall, one of the force's two assistant chief constables. He was obviously just letting her know what a clever chap he was, so quickly netting his prisoners and – as a bonus – what a liability I was. But from the abrupt change in his tone and the way he was now backtracking, I guessed the ACC was not happy with his decision to arrest Lisa Holland. I heard him hang up.

I quietly stepped down the corridor, went into my office, closed the door and rang the custody suite at Priory asking for Jo Young. As luck would have it, she was about to start the interview with Lisa Holland and I just had time to explain what I wanted her to do and why. I then returned to Kingston's office and rapped on the still open door before walking in.

'Afternoon, Dave,' I smiled, knowing damn well he preferred David. 'I hear you've got a bit of a job on'

For the first time I could recall since he had been posted into the CID about five months ago, for career development purposes, he looked genuinely pleased to see me. He immediately began to recount the incident, stressing how he had made the immediate connection to the rape of Lisa Holland and her father's attack in court and how, acting decisively, he had ordered immediate arrests and a search of their home. On occasion, the tactic of arresting a relative in order to apply pressure to a chief suspect is legitimate and I agreed with him that the suspicion to justify such action was present in this case as, in principle, Lisa could have been the attacker. She had the motive and the attacker was masked, albeit I knew from Jo Young that Grantmore had described a man. So in these particular circumstances, he was on very dodgy ground, particularly in light of Lisa's vulnerability. From the telephone conversation I had overheard, I reckoned that was what the ACC was also worried about. Imagine the fallout on the force if it went wrong. An already traumatised rape victim, further damaged by her attacker's acquittal – and then we go and lock her up – without evidence.

Still unsure if the plan I had been hatching since Jo Young had tipped me off was built on safe ground, I explored further.

'Apart from the obvious, what evidence have you got against him?'

'Well, there's plenty of potential forensics. We've got the handwritten note that was stuck on Grantmore's chest... so we might get a handwriting match from Holland... or Lisa. We might find the cardboard packaging that matches the torn piece the message is on. SOCO are going over the room where it happened so there are obviously possibilities there. We're swabbing Holland's hands for traces of bleach and we might find the modelling knife he used with Grantmore's blood on it. Then there's the syringe… so I'm hopeful.'

He didn't look as confident as he sounded but ploughed on: 'We've already found a newly-opened bottle of bleach under his sink and an Adidas top in a cupboard of his bedroom that matches the one Grantmore describes.'

I nodded enthusiastically. 'If you get some of those forensics back you're laughing. If you don't, the Adidas top and the bleach mean nothing… circumstantial… everyone has got bleach under their sink and even I've got an Adidas top… they don't really add much to the motive and the attack in court. Your best bet would be to trace the girl who cuffed him. She's obviously involved. Any ideas who she is?'

'She only started there a few days earlier, pretending she was an illegal from the Eastern Bloc, so no questions were asked. I reckon she was deliberately put there by Holland to set this up.'

'Prove that and you've cracked it. So how are enquiries going to identify her?'

I was starting to sweat a bit now as there were clearly plenty of ways this could all fall to Holland, and I was looking at trouble.

'Christ, I haven't even started that line of inquiry yet. How do you keep all the plates spinning?'

I could see he was already feeling the pressure. Since he'd joined the CID, he hadn't run a major incident, so I thought I'd turn up the heat.

'Don't worry, mate, let's draw up a plan of action. First thing, have you updated the top corridor? This is a job that could blow up in the force's face because of what happened in court.'

Since he had already discovered I had cautioned Holland, I decided to pretend I had never tried to hide it. 'You ought to know I cautioned Holland for the attack in court… so that'll add to any bad publicity… he might even try and sue.' I shook my head in self-recrimination.

He pretended to look surprised.

I ploughed on. 'Secondly, arresting the victim in that same case was a brave decision, Dave, and I can see your reasoning, but if anything goes wrong there… well… you've really stuck your neck out. Does Grantmore say it could have been a woman?'

Kingston was shrinking before my very eyes. He never answered and I knew Grantmore knew his attacker was a man. He loosened his tie and undid the top button of his shirt. Blimey, he never did that – I almost felt bad but kept going.

'So update the top corridor… then start a policy book and get one of them to sign it… then you're covered. Have you alerted Priory to put Lisa on suicide watch when they put her in a cell? She's obviously very vulnerable… that's why you decided to use her as a lever in the first place.'

I sat back, shaking my head, and feigned a worried look. 'Brave decision, Dave, arresting her. Bold tactic. Not sure I'd have had the bottle.'

He couldn't take his eyes off me, waiting for my next piece of advice. He was hooked.

'I made a mistake at the start of this job by cautioning Holland. We now have to make sure, for the reputation of the force, that you don't compound it. Oh and by the way, how's Grantmore? In severe pain, I hope.'

He visibly slumped as he saw his next rank fading into the distance.

'I've already briefed the ACC and to be honest she was anxious that I'd arrested Lisa. She saw the same dangers you brought up. As for Grantmore, he's going to lose his eye and he's gone into severe shock but he'll survive.'

Come on, Darnley, final push, he's nearly over the edge.

'Well, just be careful. It doesn't pay to piss Jane off... she can bear a grudge. Bloody hell, Dave, you've copped a right dodgy job here... bit of a make-or-break case. Good experience for you, though.'

I paused. Gauged his reaction – that should do it!

By now, the Chief's insignia he envisioned on his own epaulettes had, for the time being, disappeared and I knew he was on the verge of asking me exactly what I wanted him to ask me, when bugger me, the phone on his desk rang, breaking the spell.

'Kingston', he barked into the phone.

I watched as the colour drained from his face.

'But is she okay?'

Followed by, 'Is the ambulance there yet?'

Then the plea. 'Ring me straight back.'

In my head, I punched the air in triumph. Good girl, Jo, you've come up trumps again. But of course I maintained an outward air of concern.

'What's up, Dave?'

Head in hands, his carefully coiffured greying locks now dishevelled, Kingston looked like he was about to cry for his nanny, something that I had no doubt he had at one time done regularly.

'Shit, shit, shit! Lisa Holland has had some sort of fit during interview and is unconscious. They're waiting for an ambulance.'

'Better let the ACC know straight away, particularly as she wasn't happy anyway. Better she hears it from you first.'

I was loving this.

'I think I'll wait until the ambulance gets there. They might not have to take her to hospital... it might not be too bad.'

Indecision was written all over his face. It was my duty to help him decide.

'Or she might die on the custody suite floor... tell her now.'

I picked up the phone handset and handed it to him.

He took the phone from my hand but placed it back in the cradle. He stood up and walked to the window and looked out, clearly thinking things through. For the life of me, I couldn't think of anything else to say that might make him react how I hoped he would, so I just kept quiet and joined him at the window, as if in silent but comradely support. After about thirty seconds, he let out a heavy sigh that marked a decision made.

'You're right. Would you mind leaving the room, Matt? I'd rather do this alone.'

I was jubilant. 'I'll be next door when you're done.'

I walked to the door and then stopped as if I'd just had an idea. 'Tell you what, Dave, in light of these unfortunate circumstances, but only if you want... I'll take over the inquiry. I'm familiar with the original rape case, was present in court when Holland attacked Grantmore, and I made the mistake cautioning him, so maybe I should clear up the mess. Suggest it to the ACC... but only if it suits you.'

I returned to my office, confident he'd use my offered escape route and try and swing the job on me. I was equally sure the ACC would accept. The last thing the force would want was a scandal if anything happened to Lisa, and the ACC knew I was far more capable of handling such a case than Kingston. More importantly, and somewhat uncomfortably, I also knew that if things did go wrong they would much prefer to sacrifice me than him. After all, he was destined to be one of them, while I was fast becoming an anachronism in modern policing and often a thorn in their sides.

The beauty of it was that I knew nothing was wrong with Lisa Holland. There was no danger of a comeback from that direction. The fact that I'd cautioned Holland was now known but once in charge of the inquiry, I could make sure how I'd fiddled the paperwork remained hidden.

Knowing that Jo was no longer busy interviewing, I rang her mobile. She answered on the first ring. 'How's that then, boss? Worth a G 'n' T tonight, I think.'

'As ever, Young, your timing was perfect. Are you free to speak?'

'I spoke to Lisa just before we went into interview and told her to trust me but to pretend to collapse ten minutes in. I got to know her really well when we were investigating Grantmore, and she could see I was disgusted about her being arrested, so she didn't even ask any questions. You should have been there, boss... I was nearly convinced by her performance. It's really upset Linda. She obviously believes Lisa's had a fit because of the stress, and she's shitting herself, but adamant she was only following Kingston's orders to lock her up... and intends to say so.'

At this point, Jo told me the ambulance had just arrived and Lisa had "come round" and was refusing to go to hospital. I told her to ask the custody sergeant to release her without charge, on my instructions, and insist she went to hospital and accompany her. I arranged to meet Jo later to buy her a drink and explain what was happening. I made a mental note to try and get the hugely competent and likeable DC Young onto the Emmerson murder inquiry. I needed officers like her on my team.

Before long, a very dejected Kingston was back from licking arse in the top corridor. I had indeed been asked to take on the investigation and within minutes the ACC rang me to discuss matters. I now asked Kingston to leave me to take the call.

I was contrite about my decision to caution Holland and expressed my desire to make amends by investigating the attack on Grantmore. I was very surprised to pick up the impression that she didn't want me to try too hard to solve the case. Her rationale of course was that my failure to prosecute Holland for the attack in court could now leave the force exposed if Grantmore tried to sue for this latest attack. That would not be an option if it could not be proved it was indeed Holland that had blinded him. I guessed the fact that the Hollands were a decent family and Grantmore a low-life thug, helped her to justify her thinking. Of course, she voiced none of this, but I knew we were on the same wavelength. She was also keen that the press did not get hold of the fact that we had arrested Lisa Holland, and adamant that I update her as soon as I knew how she was. I took the opportunity to lay it on thick about what an ill-considered decision it was to arrest her and how I would do all I could to keep the lid on Kingston's *faux pas*. I reassured her I'd get an overview of where we were and call her back.

Firstly, I debriefed the officers who had arrested and interviewed Russ Holland. They were convinced he had attacked Grantmore – as was I – although after two hours of interview, he had not uttered a single word. Enquiries with Janine at the massage parlour had failed to identify the girl beyond the name she had given. She had walked in off the street looking for work and said she was from Romania – or was it Bulgaria – or Estonia? Needless to say, Grantmore's HR policies were somewhat lax and she had neither been asked for, nor provided, any proof of identity. The search of Holland's home had failed to reveal the knife, any syringes, or even washing up gloves, the remnants of the cardboard used for the note, or a red felt tip pen. The Adidas top had been bagged to send to the forensic laboratory to see if it had traces of Grantmore's blood, although there were certainly no visible signs. We concluded that the bleach under the sink was of no use. How many sinks in Hull have a bottle of Domestos beneath them?

I doubted the scene of the attack would render any evidence. The attacker had worn gloves, and considering what the room was actually used for, the chance of identifying and then eliminating any fingerprints was improbable. Enquiries had also failed to find any witnesses nearby. It already looked likely that we'd only have his very obvious motive, the attack in court and the note – quite a compelling story – but not even a circumstantial case without something linking him to the events at Nicole's. I appreciated that just a sighting of him, or even his car in the area at the relevant time, could help build that circumstantial case, but I knew that even I would have the devil's own job of building a case – even if my heart had been in it.

When I reported back to the ACC, she seemed as relieved as I pretended not to be. The icing on the cake was when she rather indiscreetly let slip that DI Swales had made a formal complaint about Kingston's order to arrest Lisa. Finally, she instructed me to visit the Hollands and apologise for the error of judgement in arresting Lisa and in doing so assess the likelihood of them complaining.

I did not want to meet Russ Holland again, keen just to let sleeping dogs lie, but had no choice but to call round at their home after he was released. He answered the door and curtly invited me in. Both he and Lisa were extremely quiet and obviously did not even want to discuss events. Lisa was a bright girl and must have known her father had carried out this vicious attack on her rapist, and so it was pretty obvious why neither wanted to say much. If that was the case, it seemed unlikely that either of them would then go on to make a fuss about their arrests. They didn't even mention Lisa's collapse, trip in an ambulance and brief sojourn in A&E, but he did ask me to thank DC Young for all her support. I thought it best not to reveal that Jo had been following my instructions. As quickly and sensitively as I could, I offered the appropriate words of apology about the arrest of Lisa and her collapse and informed them that I would be the officer investigating the attack on Grantmore. Neither made any meaningful response and I was glad to get out of the house so quickly – and without having to witness Mr Holland's unsettling anger again.

As I drove back to Central, I had to face the fact that I did not want to unearth the evidence to prove Russ Holland had maimed Grantmore. I felt comfortable admitting to myself that it was through self-interest, and slightly less comfortable justifying it from the ACC's standpoint of protecting the force's reputation and preventing Grantmore suing. But deep down, I knew neither of these reasons were what was driving me. The idea that Holland had extracted revenge – taken justice when none had been delivered – gave me a contented buzz of satisfaction. Following my old sergeant's maxim of "doing right or doing nowt" over his caution had left me with no feelings of guilt. But would this? Could I really go this far? Failing to try my upmost to detect a serious crime was a whole new ball game.

Nine

'Right, gentlemen, let's move on. Mr Jones, please update the meeting on the current state of major enquiries in the force.'

ACC (Operations) Paul Jones selected a paper from his loose-leaf file, snapping the clips noisily as he did so, while other members of Strategy Team sorted through their papers for copies of the same report that had been circulated earlier. Before the meeting, Crabbe had told the ambitious young ACC that he expected his support in reducing the number of officers engaged on the force's several major enquiries. Within minutes, it had been agreed to end the five-month-old investigation into a fatal stabbing in Grimsby, despite reasoned arguments from the SIO set out in the report. Objections from the Head of CID, Detective Chief Superintendent "Wizz" Wilson, an old-school detective who Crabbe regarded as long past his sell-by date, were ignored.

Crabbe looked challengingly around his most senior officers. 'Moving quickly on... let's look at Darnley's cases.'

They all scanned the comprehensive yet succinct report prepared by Detective Superintendent Matt Darnley. Firstly, he had outlined the successful conclusion of the murder of Sonia Daggett with the charging of her husband and recommended that the incident room at Hessle Police Station be closed by the end of the month. Crabbe smiled contentedly.

All attention then focussed on what were currently the force's two most high-profile major crime enquiries. Both Darnley's – and both undetected.

Major Inquiry Status Report

Detective Superintendent M. Darnley
27 January 1999

Murder of David Emmerson / Tiger Kidnap & Robbery at Hardstone Building Society on 10 December 1998.

Status: Undetected.
Strategy Team are familiar with the facts of this case from last month's report.

Ongoing main lines of inquiry
1. *Trace Vauxhall Vectra, N348 JAT, seen at scene of False Imprisonment at Atwick, 10 weeks prior to the crime. The as yet unknown driver of this vehicle, a tall white male, aged approximately 35 years may have been involved in the offence.*
2. *Trace BMW 5 series car, believed R (1997) registration plate and dark in colour used by offenders.*
3. *Trace, interview and eliminate associates of deceased David Emmerson.*

4. Investigate links to Newcastle area where five separate £20 notes stolen from the building society have been recovered.

5. A small number of outstanding forensic results are awaited from all scenes, although to date all results have been negative. Ballistic results on bullet recovered from Emmerson's body are still awaited.

6. House-to-house enquiries around all scenes now complete.

7. Explore links to Bridlington Post Office Tiger Kidnap in September 1998.

Investigation Summary. *A serious and unusual crime for Humberside that I believe is linked to the similar crime at Bridlington in September last year. There are no concrete leads other than the recovered money and the as yet untraced Vauxhall car. However, the incident has already recorded 1,210 statements. 2,312 actions have been completed, 400 are currently being investigated and there are 700 actions raised and awaiting allocation. There remain several potential forensic hits. The inquiry remains "live" and I am confident it will be detected. The incident team is based at Driffield and consists of myself, 2 detective inspectors, 4 detective sergeants, 12 detective constables and 3 civilian indexers. 2 uniformed FLOs are attached part time. Team now working normal hours with overtime only allocated for necessary actions.*

Recommendation: *MIR at Driffield continues with same staffing until next month's report.*

False Imprisonment and GBH to Sean Grantmore on 16 January 1999.

Status: Undetected

Prolific/target local criminal Grantmore was handcuffed naked to a massage table in one of his own massage parlours by a female only known as Katia, ostensibly in preparation for a consensual sex act. The female was newly employed at the parlour and initially believed to be an Eastern European illegal immigrant. Her true nationality and identity remain unknown. While he was so restrained, the female facilitated entry into the room of an unidentified male, who passed her a bulky brown envelope we are presuming to be cash. The man then injected bleach into Grantmore's right eye before disfiguring the area of that eye with an X-shape cut, utilising a modelling knife. The assailant left a note on Grantmore's chest, which stated, "Wink now you bastard". The assailant fled the scene. Grantmore has lost the sight of the eye and is badly disfigured.

The chief suspect is Russell Holland, 47 years. Grantmore was acquitted of the rape of Holland's 17-year-old daughter Lisa at Hull Crown Court on 15 December 1998 and upon the jury returning its verdict, Russell Holland attacked Grantmore in the dock. As you are aware, I took the decision to caution Holland for this assault, him being a man of previous good character.

In her evidence, Lisa referred to Grantmore winking as part of his chat-up technique, and he gave her a very obvious wink upon his acquittal. This was picked up on by the press.

Holland and his daughter were arrested and interviewed. Neither admits any involvement and to date no evidence – other than the obvious motive and note – has been found to link them to it. I have personally spoken to both Lisa Holland and Russ Holland since their arrest and interviews. I have apologised to them both for the arrest of Lisa, which I consider to have been ill-judged. Mr Holland remains extremely angry towards Grantmore as a result of his acquittal on the rape charges. You will recall that he provided no responses whatsoever in interview. Forensic results have proved negative and there are very few useful lines of inquiry remaining.

My own view of this crime is that a criminal rival has attacked Grantmore, using the well-reported rape acquittal as a smokescreen. I honestly cannot see a middle-aged man with no previous convictions capable of such a well-planned and executed, vicious attack, however angry he may be.

Recommendation: *Although a serious and unusual crime, I agreed to run this as a divisional incident, using only divisional staff. The inquiry should continue, but I estimate all useful lines of inquiry will be completed by the end of this month.*

Matt Darnley
Detective Superintendent

'Two very unusual crimes,' said the Chief. 'Is this Grantmore business going to blow over, Paul?'

'I think so. As Darnley says, there's no evidence against the Hollands other than the obvious motive, and he seems convinced of the criminal rival theory. It's very unlike Darnley to admit he's not hopeful in detecting major crime, but I suggest this crime will be wrapped up in drugs, people trafficking and prostitution. I suggest we just let it run its natural course. He's only using a DI, a DS and two DCs.'

'We should leave the Driffield incident at full strength too, sir,' chipped in DCS Wilson. 'The National Criminal Intelligence Service is really interested in this job, particularly the tiger kidnap element, the potential links to the other robbery at Bridlington and it involving the murder of one of their own gang.'

'I've already had all this glory-boys stuff from Darnley. He's had almost two months and got nowhere, so I'm cutting the staff from next Monday.'

The Chief looked around the table at his fellow ACPO officers, his four Divisional Commanders and Head of CID as if to challenge anyone to disagree.

'With respect, sir, I disagree,' Chief Superintendent Sharples from C Division volunteered. 'I'm having weekly meetings with Matt and he's doing a thorough job and we should let him keep the staff a while longer. We can't allow undetected crimes like this in the East Riding.' Provocatively, he continued, 'Sorting out serious crime is far more reassuring for the public than coppers on the beat.'

'With your division's poor detection rate, I'd have thought you'd have wanted your staff back on normal duties, let alone high-visibility patrol,' said Jones. He turned to the Chief. 'I agree, sir. We need to scale the inquiry down now.'

None of the other divisional commanders demurred, all keen to get their staff back.

'Agreed then. Paul, get hold of Darnley this afternoon and negotiate a scaled-down team… it's up to you what size of team you leave him with… and no overtime from here on in, unless it's for arrests. And Mr Sharples, the policy of this force is to focus its primary effort upon high-visibility foot patrol. I need my divisional commanders to be four-square behind that policy... do I make myself clear?'

'You have no need to remind me of the policy of the force, sir. But surely the purpose of Strategy Team is for all members to speak their minds, express their views and in that way maintain a healthy balance in force policies.'

Sharples folded his arms and held Crabbe's icy stare, while maintaining a most amiable expression that was intended to rile him further. However, his defiant composure rapidly evaporated when Paul Jones interjected.

'So, Chief Superintendent Sharples, how do your views about public reassurance and balanced policies reconcile with the recent behaviour of three of your officers at Beverley?'

Sharples knew exactly what was coming, but he had no idea that the ACC knew anything about the events of the previous night. Clearly, neither did anyone else seated around the table. The embarrassed paper shuffling that had accompanied Sharples' exchange with the Chief suddenly ceased, and all eyes flitted from the almost exultant Paul Jones to the deflated Divisional Commander of the East Riding.

'I trust you are aware of the brawl between an on-duty uniformed sergeant and an off-duty young constable in Saturday Market Place last night?' Jones asked.

The ACC looked smugly at the Chief for approval and continued. 'A sergeant who, I might add, is in his early forties and carrying on a sordid affair with a married twenty-five-year-old police officer on his own shift. His attacker was the policewoman's cuckolded husband.'

He sat back, triumphant.

However, Sharples had decided that it was now "shit or bust" and he jumped to his feet and leaning forward on the table, he spoke directly to the Chief Constable.

'Your ACC bringing up a confidential matter that should be left to me and my staff to deal with is typical of his somewhat archaic management style and is totally inappropriate at Strategy Team. I am aware of the incident, have spoken to Professional Standards Branch, and the matter is in hand.'

Paul Jones now rose from the table, doing his best to look authoritative and dignified. 'How dare you question—'

'Sit down, Paul.' The Chief interrupted in a calm but commanding tone. 'My office, please, Mr Sharples. You can tell me about this matter in private… which is how I would have expected to have been informed. Ask Sally to make us a cup of tea,' he added pleasantly, gathering his papers and rising from the table. 'Paul, get hold of Superintendent Darnley and sort out the staffing on the Emmerson incident. Then see me in my office straight after lunch.'

He strode from the room followed by Sharples.

The ACC looked around at his fellow officers, clearly hoping for words of support but found none, most studiously ignoring him, busying themselves collecting up papers or chatting with each other. Only his fellow ACC (Personnel and Support) Jane Greenhall met his gaze, shaking her head with a look of pity mixed with disdain. The ACC (Operations) job was as good as hers – Jones was welcome to Personnel and Support.

Ten

That Same Day

Thirty miles away from the rarefied air in Strategy Team, in Driffield, I was waiting for the call that I knew would come when that meeting ended. Part of my duty as an SIO was to regularly brief the divisional commander in whose division the crime had taken place. Martin Sharples was entirely supportive and also seriously interested in detecting the crime. Earlier that week, we had surmised that Crabbe would want to cut staffing levels, and Martin agreed he would try his best to keep the full team on the job, but we knew that unless the inquiry kicked into life before Strategy Team met, we had no chance.

As I read another pile of entirely necessary but entirely unhelpful statements, my mobile rang. Expecting it to be ACC Jones, I let it ring without answering it, childishly making him try a landline. When it rang again, I pulled it from my pocket, seeing a number I didn't recognise. When I answered with my rank and name, a strident female voice began a tirade of abuse.

After about thirty seconds of foul-mouthed invective, I realised that the caller was Anne Beedham, who I had not seen since she climbed into the back of PC Peter Granger's police car, in that tight skirt, on the day of her ordeal. It seemed that wasn't the only place into which she had climbed with my young FLO.

In graphic detail, she recounted how they had been having an affair almost since that very day but that he had now decided to end things and patch things up with his wife. Having correctly identified Mrs Beedham from the outset as trouble – sexy as hell – but trouble, my intuition was confirmed.

'He's been shagging me in his uniform... on duty... in my bed when my old man's been at work. It's in my diary... so I can prove it... I want him sacked!'

Talk about a woman scorned.

After ten minutes, I had calmed her down and made an appointment to see her the following afternoon. There was no way I was going there on my own and was thankful I'd managed to wangle Jo Young onto the inquiry, swapping her for a DC from Central who was required at court for a two-week trial. I reassured Mrs Beedham that I would take the matter seriously, as indeed I would have to do, as this was taking your responsibilities for looking after family members several steps too far and putting the whole investigation in jeopardy. What the hell was I going to do with Granger? Yet again in our very short relationship, I re-assessed the young cop's abilities.

Ten seconds after I had hung up on Anne Beedham, my mobile rang again. I recognised Martin Sharples' number and guessed he was about to tip me off about Crabbe's decision but was surprised when he too started to talk about PC Granger. In disappointed tones, he explained how last night young Peter had assaulted a sergeant who was having an affair with his wife and unfortunately for Martin, all three were officers based at Beverley, and thus under his command.

'To make matters worse, the daft young bugger did it in the middle of Beverley at pub chucking-out time and then legged it like some bloody yob, and we haven't tracked him down yet,' bemoaned Sharples. 'It's a bloody shame, he's a good lad and I know you've been pleased with him on your inquiry. Between you and me, his wife's a right slag and the sergeant he smacked is an idle waster… and he's the lass's sergeant, so he's in the shit as well.'

It was obvious he would have to face disciplinary charges and be suspended. I was about to add my tale of woe about Mrs Beedham's allegations but something made me hold my tongue. While Martin went on glumly to tell me about my team being reduced in numbers, and to expect a call from Jones, my mind was focussed upon PC Granger's predicament. The lad was looking at the sack without much doubt, but surely a bloke who has shagged another chap's wife deserves a thump? Especially when he's her senior officer. Here was someone else who deserved a caution. That old revenge versus justice debate again. But could I say the same for his indiscretions with Mrs Beedham? I thought back to my meeting with her and determined that she was probably the predator and he wouldn't have stood a bloody chance – a rabbit versus a fox. The clincher was when I asked myself what I'd have done at his age in the self-same circumstances. So, as Chief Superintendent Sharples asked me to find PC Granger and send him directly to his office, I decided to keep Anne Beedham's outrage to myself – at least for the time being.

'Thanks for trying with Strategy Team, mate. I appreciate it. I can still manage… we just need a break. It'll come. I'll get Granger over to you as soon as I can.'

I ended the call and immediately my phone rang for a third time. It was the man himself.

'Afternoon, sir. Are you at Driffield, or in your office at Central? I need to see you urgently.'

'I bet you do. I'm in the incident room.'

'Oh… I guess you've heard about last night? I was going to tell you but something more important has come up. I know they'll suspend me but you need to see and hear this before anyone else does.'

He seemed almost breathless, and very excited – and not at all worried.

'Get your arse in here. I think there's even more than that you need to tell me. I've had your girlfriend on the phone.'

'She's not my girlfriend, sir, we're married. We're going to patch it up after this. She's realised that Knaggs was just using her… she loves me.'

What did I say. He knows fuck all about women.

'In here now!' I shouted, and cut the call.

*

It was about forty-five minutes before he appeared, during which time I'd tried to figure out why I was even contemplating doing anything other than just washing my hands of him. I just couldn't weigh him up. One minute showing great promise, and the next – a ruddy car crash.

I had come to no conclusions when he strode purposefully into my office and without saying a word dropped a blurred and grainy photograph on my desk. It showed a back view of a man wearing a black Adidas sweatshirt and faded jeans climbing a metal fire escape at the back of a two-storey building. He dropped a second photograph, showing the man at the top of the fire escape, clearly wearing some type of mask. By now, I knew what the photos were showing. A third photo was dropped. I wasn't too surprised to see a female figure climbing out of the window at the top of the fire escape being greeted by Tony Blair. The next showed a bulky package exchanging hands.

I looked up expectantly – he had one photo left. The final instalment. Talk about dramatic effect. The young bugger had clearly planned this moment for maximum impact. He dropped it and as clear as day in the alley below the fire escape, wearing the black Adidas sweatshirt and just about to pull a plastic mask into place, was Russ Holland.

I was speechless.

'You didn't really want this crime detecting, did you?' As cool as you like. 'This one, however, will be of far more interest.'

He reached into his briefcase and withdrew yet another photograph. He looked silently triumphant and then repeated his nonchalant drop onto my desk.

I immediately recognised the location as outside the Silver Cod pub on Anlaby Road in Hull. Although it was dark, the streetlights illuminated a tall, well-built male climbing out of a dark-coloured Vauxhall Vectra, as if about to meet another man standing by the front wing of the car. It was snowing heavily. It took me a few seconds to grasp the significance of the photograph – it was the vehicle recorded by Janice Cooper, after she had had the suspicious caller some weeks before she was attacked. The registration number was discernible, but identifying either man from the grainy photograph was a different matter. But I realised that there must be more to come.

Triumphantly, PC Granger mouthed just one word: 'Grantmore!'

My office door was wide open and there were only two others present in the incident room. They were taking no notice of our exchange, but I guessed we were about to embark upon a conversation we would both want to keep between ourselves. I rose from my desk, picked up the photographs and my car keys and shepherded him out of the building and into my car. I set off into the countryside towards Bridlington.

We rode in silence. My mind was in overdrive, with dozens of questions that as yet I could not even frame. The sudden rush of information just would not compute, so I kept quiet and tried to calm down. Unnervingly, Granger sat alongside me staring straight ahead, seemingly as cool as the proverbial cucumber. After five minutes, I pulled into the car park of the King's Head at Nafferton and turned off the ignition. I took off my suit jacket and handed it to him, indicating he should take off his tie and thus disguise his uniformed state.

Having only spoken to ask what he wanted to drink, we found ourselves sat at a small round table in a quiet corner of what turned out to be an empty public bar, each with a pint of bitter. I took a drink, placed the pint back on the table, sat back in the chair and in a voice that did not betray my own anxiety said, 'Go on then.'

Leaving his untouched drink on the table, he leaned forward and in a hushed, emotional, yet strangely conspiratorial tone, he began at the place I was the least interested in – his failing marriage. It was clear that he was treating this occasion as some form of confessional. Perhaps it was the chance to tell an older and wiser man and gauge my views. Whatever had sparked this need to unburden himself I decided to just let him get it off his chest. He took me through how he had met his wife, his falling in love, his misgivings based upon her reputation, his colleagues' and even his dying father's warnings. Then the rumours, the confrontation, her confession and on into how his temper snapped when he saw them together on patrol the previous night while he was out having a pint with a few mates. He drew to a close by necking a good half of his pint and acknowledging that his actions would get him the sack but he didn't care, as he had forgiven Amy and they were going to try and make a go of the marriage.

I then added to his woes by describing Anne Beedham's phone call. To be fair, he coughed up straight away and with typical male bravado and a degree of engaging humour described how Anne Beedham had seduced him the day after her ordeal, when I had sent him back to clarify whether or not she had told the robbers where Janice Cooper lived. Despite the seriousness of his predicament, like most blokes, he couldn't help but impart some of the more lurid details of how this married woman, who must have been about twenty years his senior, had behaved. Their relationship had continued in a rather wanton fashion until this morning when, in a fit of remorse, he told her that he wanted to end the affair and win back the heart of his wife. She went ballistic. Having completed this bizarre episode of male bonding, I began to explain that shagging a victim for whom you were acting as an FLO was almost certainly going to get him the sack in itself – even without the fact that he had also thumped a uniformed police sergeant in full public view. By this point, we had both drained our pints and I was keen to move the conversation on. In my mind, I was now facing an ex-PC Granger. He'd be history by this evening, suspended until his dismissal following a disciplinary hearing – or even a court appearance. I doubted the patched-up marriage would last long under the pressure of no job and the big black stain on his curriculum vitae that most decent employers would avoid like the plague. My thoughts were purely on personal survival but due to his control of the conversation thus far, I had been unable to marshal my thoughts and still hadn't figured out the provenance of the photos or what exactly they meant. I was just trying to figure out how to play the young man when he, all too calmly, asked me if I fancied another pint.

While he was at the bar, I nipped outside and rang Martin Sharples, who of course was waiting in his office back in Beverley to suspend my young colleague. Without going into too much detail, I asked him to trust me and reassured him that the lad was with me and involved in important developments in the inquiry. I assured him that he would not be out of my sight until he went off duty that evening and I would personally accompany the officer to his office at ten o'clock the next morning.

'Matt, what are you up to? You know I trust you, but I also know what a devious bastard you are and I don't want him in any more trouble than he is already. I've discussed with Professional Standards how I'd like to proceed with this and I'm confident I can save his job, so don't you go messing that up. But okay. My office at ten in the morning.'

After making the call, I remained outside, trying to think. I needed to get back in control. Granger was playing me and I didn't know where this was leading. I tried to shrug off these doubts. I was an experienced detective superintendent, well versed in manipulating people and getting things done my way. He was a spotty-faced rookie and obviously bright, but no match for Matt Darnley. My confidence a little restored, I nipped for a quick pee then rejoined him in the bar, intending to get back in the driving seat. Looking back, I had seriously underestimated him and thus had no clear plan of action. He, on the other hand, as I was about to find out, had done his ruddy homework.

*

Two hours later, I'd dropped him back off in Driffield and I headed home, with a lot of thinking to do before we met Martin Sharples the next morning. Over that second pint, I learnt what an extremely ambitious and ruthless young man Peter Granger was. I was dumfounded as he explained the photographs were courtesy of the bespectacled nerd I had so disgracefully dismissed back in December. Graham

Morley's personal surveillance of his arch-enemy Grantmore had continued unabated since then – at Granger's direction. Although serving under my command on the incident, he had not told me, or any of his supervisors, that he had tasked Morley to continue to gather information about Grantmore, assuring him of his ability to eventually assist him to exact his revenge. Usually while off duty, he assured me, he had been meeting and briefing Morley and going through his extensive archives of over five years' of his amateur, but quite skilful, surveillance. He had found evidence in those files to link Grantmore to two or three already recorded serious crimes and to others that were not even reported. The young sleuth had put together his own file showing the potential of Morley's efforts, his intention being to approach me when he felt the time was right and impress me with his investigative acumen. He then planned to get me to help turn Morley's amateur sleuthing into hard evidence, followed by a high-profile arrest and convictions. In this way, he envisaged securing a mentor at my level, entry into the CID and onward and upward. As I say, this kid was ambitious.

Halfway through his account, I'd asked, 'Why me? You were disgusted with my behaviour towards Morley. Surely you could have taken this to anyone. Grantmore's head on a plate would be an offer few senior detectives would refuse.'

He gave me the obvious answer, which I'd been too slow or too complacent to cotton on to.

'For a start, you'd have had no choice but to listen and help me. I can prove that you neglected to fully question Mr Morley back in December. If you had, you'd have seen what I've seen in his files. Even back then, we could have had Grantmore arrested, charged and remanded for two serious assaults... Graham had the evidence. If you'd done that, Grantmore wouldn't have ended up being mutilated by Holland, as he would have been in prison on remand.

It's common knowledge that you cautioned Holland after his attack on Grantmore in court, and if it came out he did in fact go on to blind him... which these photos prove... Grantmore would surely sue the force and you'd be disgraced.'

My arse was now twitching.

'What I don't understand is why Morley has sat on all of this. If he wanted revenge, why didn't he come to the police as soon as he got something on him?'

'To be frank, although he followed Grantmore around, photographed him and listened to his voicemail, he more often than not didn't know what he'd got. I was able to link it to crimes or incidents recorded and it became obvious. Secondly, he's still terrified of Grantmore and it took him tremendous courage to come in on the day he saw us. Then you just blew him out of the water.'

The lad was right; I'd badly misjudged Morley and failed in my duty. If this series of events was revealed, I'd face serious disciplinary charges, but more importantly, my reputation would be shot to pieces. I'm ashamed to say that it wasn't until that night, when I couldn't sleep, worrying about how to save my own neck, that I gave a first thought to the victims in the cases Granger outlined – a badly injured prostitute he had paid someone to assault for trying to escape his clutches, and a rival drug dealer whose leg he had broken in a brutal attack with a wheel brace. Nor for that matter to poor old Morley.

I was now feeling well and truly on the ropes and unsure as to how this was all going to pan out. 'So what do you want now?'

For the first time he looked unsure of himself, even embarrassed.

'As I said, I just wanted to show you what I'd found out and impress you. I want to get on... and you'd have had to help me.'

The mists cleared.

'But today you're in the shit… so you want to trade?'

'I came to you this afternoon because I knew my attack on Sergeant Knaggs was likely to get me fired. I intended to ask you to speak up for me and help me keep my job… if you'd have refused, I'd have threatened to bring the Morley files out into the open.'

'Blackmail.' I let that sink in. 'Believe it or not, I'd have done that anyway, as I think would your own chief superintendent. But you now have the added problem of the lovely Mrs Beedham, already emotionally damaged by her ordeal, then cruelly used by the police officer meant to protect her. I doubt Martin Sharples is going to remain on your side when he knows that. In fact, the force could never condone that behaviour, even if they can accept the provocation over the assault on Knaggs. You're dead meat.'

I was beginning to see a glimmer of hope.

'Then so are you, sir. I think this is what is called a Mexican stand-off.'

I most definitely would not want to play this lad at poker, as he did not look in the least bit worried. His moment of embarrassment had passed.

At this point, I realised the only slight edge I had was that he did not know that Anne Beedham had not yet made any sort of official complaint. As far as I knew, there was just the three of us who knew that the force's FLO policy – and indeed the sexy Anne – had been abused. Still playing it by ear, with no thought-through battle plan, I tried to take back control.

'Okay, for now we seem to be in something of an impasse, but I think you're overestimating your hand. You are looking at the sack and possibly a criminal charge of assault, while I'm just facing professional embarrassment. Which one of us is the force going to support? There's no way your little escapades can be hidden away. Fuck me, you smacked the sergeant in front of witnesses, several of 'em being coppers, and Mrs Beedham's bravery has been all over the media. They're not going to let a mere constable get away with trying to blackmail a senior officer.'

Before he could respond, I then added, 'And what about the Grantmore pictures? How are you going to explain sitting on evidence about two current serious investigations?'

'I haven't sat on them. There are literally hundreds of photos in his files and I'd seen the one at the Silver Cod several times but just never spotted its significance until today, when I recognised the reg. number. Morley has dated it in his files and the snow helps date it… it was taken quite a while after Janice Cooper had her suspicious caller. He of course only took the photo as he was watching Grantmore, when the car drew up. I know you could never formally identify him from the photo, it's too blurred. But when you know it's him, I think you can tell. One thing's for sure, though, show Grantmore and he'll know it's him and he'll think he's identified. Morley has notes that go with all the photos.'

All thoughts of his predicament were momentarily absent. He was excited about finding this photograph, recognising its significance and being responsible for the first positive breakthrough on the murder.

I pressed on. 'You've sat on that evidence until it's suited you.'

'Actually, sir, the photo was in the file that you had a chance to examine when he brought it in. Had you bothered to look, no doubt you would have spotted its significance immediately.'

He made no effort to hide his sarcasm and I realised he once again had the upper hand.

'But what about the shots on the fire escape? They were over two weeks ago. Once you saw them, you would have realised exactly what they represented… the whole bloody force knows about the attack on Grantmore. You've kept them to yourself.'

He shook his head. 'Morley hates Grantmore. He wants Holland to get away with it. He never showed me the photographs until this morning, when I spotted the significance of the one with the car. They weren't in the file… he didn't want me to see them.'

'So what changed his mind?'

'I honestly don't know. I went to his house this morning knowing that I had to use the evidence he'd gathered and I'd already assessed… today… to show you before the shit hit the fan over Knaggs. When I just leafed through the files again and spotted the significance of that car, I explained to him how it linked Grantmore to the kidnap, robbery and murder and that this was probably what we needed to sort him out for good. He just got up, went to a cupboard and took out the photos of Holland taken on the day Grantmore was attacked. I guess he realised things were getting serious and coming to a head.'

'But how did he know Holland was about to attack Grantmore? Why was he there?'

'He didn't know. He hangs about his house and his businesses and sometimes just follows him, taking his photos in the hope he catches something worthwhile. He's just obsessed. It's really sad. He was in the back alley, saw something strange was happening and took the photos. Just luck.'

At this point, we both seemed to run out of steam and fell silent. There was a lot to think about. We finished our drinks and by the time we got back in my car and started back towards Driffield, it was dark. My mind was racing, figuring out how to play the scenario I now faced, and I guess he was in a similar frame of mind.

Twice he asked me, 'What are you going to do, sir?' Both times, I ignored the question, marvelling at how his police conditioning made him unthinkingly continue to call me sir while actually in the act of threatening me. I was asking myself the same question – what was I going to do? About him, about Beedham, about Holland, about Morley's evidence, about Grantmore – and deciding on a course of action before ten o'clock in the morning when we both had to meet Martin Sharples?

We pulled up outside the nick and I sensed he was going to ask me yet again what I intended to do.

'Don't ask me again. I need time to think. Stay away from Morley and Beedham and meet me in Burgess' Café in Beverley at eight thirty in the morning. We have to see Mr Sharples at ten. Let's just let things settle. Nothing's going to change tonight.'

Everything was set to change that night.

Eleven

Nineteen-year-old Ryan Harrod should not even have been at his parents' home in Ponteland, a quiet village to the north-west of Newcastle. He should have been thirty miles away in the Scotia Quay Halls of Residence at Sunderland University but had made an unannounced dash home to see his mum on her forty-fifth birthday. So he should not have been the one responding to the hammering on the door in the early hours – confronting the three armed and masked men who pushed him backwards and followed him into the hall.

'He shouldn't be here,' snarled the smallest of the three intruders.

He waved the handgun around wildly, using it to indicate where the family should sit, once Ryan was back in the living room and had been joined by his mum and dad.

When two of the intruders left the house with Ryan's dad, heading for the family-run post office about a mile away in the village centre, their armed colleague should have only been standing guard over a terrified forty-five-year-old postmistress. Now he also had to control her handsome, six-foot-three rugby-playing son, who was built like the proverbial brick shithouse.

Ryan should have sat quietly next to his mother as instructed and should not have weighed up the option of suddenly diving over the coffee table that separated them and their captor and ripping his head off. He should not have considered the odds of the gun being a replica. He should not have concluded he could overpower their guard.

He should have been a chess player, not a rugby prop forward. He should not have been angry and outraged. He should have been calm and cowardly.

But Ryan was what he was.

Totally unexpectedly in the eyes of both his mum and the gunman, he threw himself across the room with an almighty yell and closed his strong hands around the neck of the gunman while smashing his forehead down with bone-crunching ferocity on his nose. Blinded by the pain of his broken nose, the battered intruder instinctively pulled the trigger, blowing a hole in Ryan's guts.

The gunman should not have had to shoot Ryan.

Ryan should not have died in front of his screaming mother on her birthday.

Twelve

That Same Morning

As a rule, as soon as my head hits the pillow, sleep rapidly follows. But not last night. I lay on my back plotting and scheming – something I usually did in work time. I ran through the various scenarios I was presented with, looking for a way forward that could protect my job and reputation and get Granger back under control. I had no luck laying in the dark, so at about 4am, I got up and sat at the kitchen table with a strong coffee and tried to work it out with a pen and paper. Most definitely not my usual style – I like to fly by the seat of my pants and rely on gut instinct or intuition, call it what you will. After an hour, I gave up and resolved to meet Granger and play it by ear – it usually worked, so why change the habits of a lifetime?

I went for a run, then showered and shaved, put on my sharpest suit and headed for Burgess' Café in Beverley, feeling remarkably calm. I was chewing on a toasted teacake accompanied by yet another strong black coffee when Granger strolled in, looking remarkably fresh. He ordered tea and toast then joined me at the battered pine table in the front window looking out onto Beverley's only remaining medieval arched entrance, known as North Bar. For a while, we were quiet, both obviously weighing up our options.

He broke first.

'Sleep well, boss?' he asked nonchalantly, chewing on his toast.

I nearly choked on my teacake. Talk about cool. It had been my intention to keep quiet until he started things moving, thinking he'd have spent a sleepless night worrying about a criminal record, the sack and a long stand in the dole queue. Instead, he seemed to be playing me at my own game and I was immediately on the back foot.

'Fine. You?'

'Liar. You've been awake all night… just like me… trying to figure out what to do now.'

'Got any ideas?'

'North Sea Ferries to Rotterdam, escape onto the continent until it all dies down?'

A definite light-hearted response, so I just thought *"bollocks"* – and took a leap of faith.

'What I do know is we can't continue to try and shaft each other. We've got to work together. We've got each other over the proverbial barrel and unless we start doing some smart thinking, we're both fucked. You'll be suspended, charged with assault and sacked. Your next career is going to be a pretty shit one after that… nobody wants to employ a sacked copper. I'll probably keep my job but my reputation will be shot and I'll end up in charge of fucking traffic or the pissing dogs 'n' horses.'

He did not respond.

'You know, I've been impressed with how you handled Anne Beedham…' I stopped, looked at him and laughed at my unintended pun. He broke into a wry smile. I was encouraged and ploughed on.

'Professionally, I mean. That's why I kept you on the inquiry despite your length of service… you know that. I've told you. And I was wrong about Morley. You've made good out of my cock-up and come up with an excellent lead for the inquiry. And, while I'm being honest... I have to admit you've got the drop on me. You are an intelligent, crafty young bastard and I can tell you have a copper's nose. If we work together and trust each other, I think we can both get out of this mess... what do you say?'

He was sat forward, elbows on the table, cradling his drink in both hands, deep in thought. Before he could respond, my mobile rang. The display showed it was Tony Ride.

'Are you on your way in, boss?' he asked.

'I'll be in about eleven. I've got to see Chief Superintendent Sharples in Beverley at ten. Why, what's up?'

'We've been contacted by Northumbria about a job they had last night in Ponteland near Newcastle. Another tiger kidnap and a robbery at a post office. They shot and killed the postmaster's nineteen-year-old son. They were alerted to our job by NCIS... too early to tell if they're linked but we should have more by the time you get in.'

'Bloody hell, it's close to where we recovered the money from the building society. Coincidences again? Find out as much as you can before I get there. See you as soon as I can.'

I briefly outlined to Granger what I'd been told and expressed my view that this was almost bound to be the same team. The stakes had now been raised considerably and the potential Grantmore connection he had unearthed was in reality our one and only tangible, workable lead.

'Come on, this is why we're coppers. A nineteen-year-old lad's been murdered. That's got to be our priority now. Listen to me and we can sort out our problems and detect the job... but you've got to trust me.'

He sat back and sipped at his drink. Now I kept quiet.

'Okay, let's start afresh. So have you got any proposals?' he asked, a touch too sarcastically.

'Yeah. The first thing is, you've got to stop being such a clever little shit. It's no use carrying on like this, strutting about trying to prove you've got the biggest dick. Accept I'm the boss, have more experience than you, and I'm meant to tell you what to do. Then you do it.' I paused. 'Then we both just might emerge from this cock-up relatively unscathed.'

'Go on then, tell me what to do.'

'Right. First thing is that you keep quiet while we go see Mr Sharples and I get him to convince Professional Standards not to suspend you. I intend to show him the photograph at the Silver Cod, explain the significance and tell him that you have cultivated an important informant who will only talk to you and I need you on the inquiry. When we add the job last night where the young lad was killed, he'll agree... I know him.'

The lad looked hopeful but doubtful at the same time.

'You belting that sergeant won't go away, but if we can detect these jobs with information that you have gained through good police work, me and Martin Sharples can speak up very powerfully on your behalf... and maybe save your job. It's the best chance you'll get.'

I had no intention of telling him that Anne Beedham's complaint was still just between her and me. Extra bargaining power.

'You'd do that?'

He now looked almost grateful.

'As you've pointed out, you've got the black on me over the attack on Grantmore. I'm looking after myself... but in doing so, I have to look after you. We use Morley to get to Grantmore. We agree to leave Holland and that'll keep Morley sweet.'

I had no intention of telling him the full details of how I had misread Holland, faked his caution and then manipulated Kingston and the ACC. If Morley's photos of Holland came out, I was well and truly shafted. He literally only knew the half of it. But I could see how I could still make all that go away.

'Give me the photos of Holland at Grantmore's place but tell Morley you've destroyed them and told no one about them. He hates Grantmore. Holland's probably his hero.'

'But Holland mutilated Grantmore and now we can prove it. You're just looking after your own skin.'

'Too true... and as I said... I'll look after yours.'

I took a deep breath and another leap of faith.

'Look, Grantmore's a dangerous arsehole. He got exactly what he deserved. You and I... and Morley... know for sure that Grantmore raped Lisa Holland and got off. The evidence of Lisa plus those answerphone messages is enough for me. Her dad just dispensed the justice she deserved... the justice we, and the courts, failed to deliver. Let's leave it alone and get Grantmore and whoever killed Emmerson... and maybe this kid up north.'

He reached a decision – and then into his briefcase and sorted through a few documents before handing me the photographs.

He sat back, seemingly content. But that lasted only seconds. 'But... shit... there's still Anne Beedham...'

'Forget her for now. One step at a time.'

'But...'

'Not now. Leave that with me... trust me.' My tone made it obvious I did not intend to discuss that problem any further at this point.

He sat back, deflated and deep in thought.

My priority was definitely to save my own skin, but I was suddenly struck by the realisation that I also really wanted to keep him out of the shit. I wanted to help him. Why?

I bought us another round of coffees and then explained to PC Granger, who was now acting like a constable again, how we would proceed from here.

By eleven o'clock, we were both in the incident room with PC Granger's suspension – at least temporarily – suspended. Martin Sharples had taken a practical approach, as I knew he would, and was far keener on detecting serious crime on his patch than seeking retribution on a young copper who had only done what both of us may have done at his age in the same circumstances. A brief conversation with his counterpart (and friend) in Professional Standards won a temporary reprieve, but the top corridor would ultimately have to be convinced. My priority now was to inject investigative velocity and propel us ahead of the problems snapping at our heels.

I instructed DS Ride to get all the team in for a briefing at one o'clock and then took Jo Young aside. Jo had worked on several major incidents I had commanded and I knew that she had the same absolute trust in me that I had in her. I told her about Anne Beedham's complaint about Pete Granger, and although her eyebrows raised as her eyes widened, she made no comment. I told her that I had arranged for us to see Beedham at 2pm that day to record her complaint but due to developments in the case, I would not be able to make the appointment, so I wanted her to deliver a message. My gut reaction about Anne Beedham was that she was angry at being rejected – not hurt at being used. She wasn't outraged at our young FLO abusing his position, just pissed off that he had been the one to call a halt. I would have bet my pension that if someone more "suitable" had made a play for her, young Granger would have been chucked out of her bed without a second thought. It was based on that hunch that I instructed DC Young.

'I want you to apologise that I am unable to attend due to urgent developments in the case. I appreciate that at the minute you don't know what they are, but you will after the briefing. I want you to act as if you are just a messenger and a very pissed-off one at that, and that you clearly haven't got a clue about why she and I need to meet. I want you to let her read this note... but do not leave it with her... actually tell her that I want it back.'

I handed her the typewritten note and she read it out.

'Sorry, Anne, but due to urgent developments, I cannot keep our appointment. Rest assured I am taking your complaint very seriously. Please contact me on 07854 252347 (private mobile), so we can arrange something, although it will be a couple of days. Sorry to let you down but I will explain when we meet.'

She handed me the note back, shaking her head in mock disgust and I sealed it into a blank envelope.

'Am I reading her right? Will that last sentence intrigue her? I'm just trying to buy some time while I figure out how to look after young Granger.'

'I reckon if I act a tad jealous and seem interested to know what's in the note, she'll be well and truly hooked,' she laughed, clearly looking forward to this somewhat irregular errand.

'But, Jo, if asked, you never delivered a note. You just cancelled our meeting, as I was busy.'

Jo Young is one of the smartest coppers I've ever worked with and can read people and get them onside better than most. I knew she wouldn't fail me on this occasion.

'Note. What note?' she grinned.

As she left the nick, I grabbed Ridey and showed him the photograph of Grantmore and the car at the Silver Cod.

Ten minutes after Jo had left the nick, he was heading for the photo lab at Beverley Police Station.

I then took Pete Granger into one of the interview rooms and put the finishing touches to the young man's introduction to noble cause corruption as the media like to call it, or – as I prefer – getting justice done.

*

At one o'clock, I faced my assembled team. The room was buzzing with anticipation. The inquiry was now almost two months old and had entered a stage that had become dull and routine – a process-driven trudge. I had learnt the hard way on previous long-running enquiries that by and large, coppers have the attention span of goldfish. We were at the point where some of my team would start to switch off and begin to yearn for a new incident, new excitement and new chances for personal glory – as well as more bloody overtime. So for me to call for an urgent briefing mid-week was a clear signal that something was about to break.

I knew the next hour was when I would either rev up the team to work longer and harder and more confidently towards a result, or lose them altogether with what they viewed as just another phony lead that would fizzle out. Without doubt detailed regular briefings are one of the necessary components of a major investigation, vital for keeping a team up to date, sharing information, debating potential lines of inquiry, dissecting witness testimony and planning the future direction of the case. For me, it was all that and more. A vital ritual, but something I had practised hard in choreographing whenever necessary to build tension, anticipation, outrage, anger, sorrow or whatever emotion would inject passion and energy into the team. That afternoon, the sequence of my disclosures was designed for such impact.

I intended to portray the photograph of Grantmore with our suspect vehicle as the break the inquiry deserved – no doubts or worries – the shit or bust lead. Grantmore was to be the key to unlock the case. At this stage, I did not want to debate contrary arguments from the team that it could all be coincidence. I needed them to believe that we were going to nail Grantmore and our murdering robbers.

'Good afternoon, ladies and gents. Hope you've all got a drink.' I looked around. Most nursed a mug and had pens and notebooks poised.

I nodded to Ridey, who stuck the photograph on the whiteboard behind me. Now blown up to A3 size, it was easy to see in the small incident room.

Most clocked the car number straight away, sparking a murmur of discussion.

'Come on then. Who are these two?'

The photograph's clarity had not improved by being enlarged and in truth would never be useable in evidence to identify either of the two men.

'No way you can ever identify anyone from that,' said a young DC from Bridlington.

'But what can we get from it?' I asked.

'It's the Silver Cod, so it puts the car in Hull. Also, it's snowing hard and it snowed like that a couple of weeks before our job,' volunteered Jo.

'With what do we associate the Silver Cod?' I asked expectantly.

'Great beer and... and football,' someone chipped in. 'Before and after each Hull City game, supporters gather there.'

Graham Beatty stood up and walked nearer to the photograph, paused and then turned around to face the rest.

'The big guy getting out of the car is wearing a Sunderland scarf. It's the fucking north-east connection,

115

the recovered money and the job last night where the young lad got shot.'

A buzz of excitement.

'And guess what date the Sunderland cup game was?'

My strategy was working. The room was alive with the sound of brain synapses firing.

I paused for dramatic effect but Tony Ride, an avid Hull City supporter, already had his Tigers diary out.

'Saturday, 28th of November, and it snowed like hell... and we lost 2-1.'

Each turned to their partner and the room was enveloped in a hubbub of speculation and excitement. I let it continue for thirty seconds – this is what I wanted and the investigation needed.

'Okay. That car is connected to our job. We assume for now that these two are involved in our job. Who are they?'

I looked round as if the answer was obvious. Nobody spoke and the euphoria dropped a notch.

'The one waiting by the car is Sean Grantmore.'

Perfectly on cue.

All eyes turned to the only uniformed officer in the room. The talk all morning had been about how the hell PC Granger was still at work after smacking a uniformed sergeant. That titbit of gossip had arrived in the incident room the previous day and had been quickly confirmed. Granger's street cred had shot up immediately, as Knaggs was not a popular man.

'Where's this photo come from?' asked one of the HOLMES indexers.

The question I did not want to answer and had not yet figured out how to explain.

'Our young uniformed colleague here has got himself an informant. The informant took the picture and he has told PC Granger it's Grantmore.'

Another pause for dramatic effect.

'It bloody well is,' said DC Beatty. 'I've had loads of dealings with him and now you've said it's him, I can recognise him. It'd never stand up in court, though.'

A couple more muttered their agreement and claimed to recognise him. I felt the first stirrings that the photograph may truly be the key to the case.

'Tactics then, folks. How do we proceed?' I asked.

Although I knew exactly what we were going to do, I wanted them involved in coming to the same conclusion – thus having a stake in the outcome.

'We only got the photo yesterday and later on today I will get the informant formally registered and hopefully get more info, but I want to move on this now. Tony, have we had any more information from the CID in Newcastle about the murder of the young lad last night?'

'Nothing fresh, but they have recovered the bullet at the post-mortem, so we might get a match with ours from Emmerson. They also used a BMW, just like on our job. I briefed everyone on the details we do have this morning, so everyone's up to speed. With this photo as well, it's got to be connected, boss.'

'PC Granger, tell us what else you've found out, please.'

I beckoned the lad to step forward.

The experienced detectives would hate that this young uniformed copper had cultivated an informant and obtained the photograph and now – they were presuming – another nugget of information. They liked the lad and already admired him for chinning Knaggs – they'd really have loved him if he'd told them how he'd been shagging Anne Beedham. But now I wanted them to start getting pissed off. I wanted them fired up for action.

PC Granger faced the team and looked suitably cocky, as I'd instructed.

'When I saw the photograph and my informant told

me it was Grantmore, I did some digging on the Criminal Intelligence System. He is a known associate of David Emmerson. He has acted as "muscle" at Nicole's and Cleopatra's for Grantmore.'

More excited mutterings.

DC Beatty asked, 'Why has the snout taken this photo?'

I knew that awkward question would be asked but used Granger's information about Emmerson and Grantmore's association to deflect it.

'Never mind about that. How have we missed the Grantmore and Emmerson connection? I thought we were working through Emmerson's associates.'

Ridey banged the keys on his computer. 'We haven't missed it. We created over a hundred actions on associates and we've focussed upon those with firearms and robbery markers for interviewing. Grantmore doesn't fit that profile, so he wasn't interviewed. DS Naylor wrote the action off without speaking to Grantmore, based on that intelligence.'

'I suppose that's fair enough,' I mused. However, I shot a look at Naylor, which clearly suggested he had made a mistake. He looked around his colleagues for some support but none came.

Truth was, I didn't rate Naylor and he was not popular. He'd been on a few of my enquiries and was one of several detectives that seemed to rotate from one major inquiry to another, as their local bosses didn't rate them either, so constantly offloaded them whenever the chance arose. He, on the other hand, had a high opinion of himself, just seeing his experience on major crime enquiries as proof of his worth.

At any rate, my deflection had worked. No one re-raised the issue of why the informant had taken the photograph. But this would only be a temporary reprieve. So I gave a stalling explanation.

'I don't want to discuss the whys and wherefores until the informant is formally registered. All I can share at the moment is the photo and the fact... I stress... fact... that the man next to the car is Grantmore. You know everything that's relevant for now. The date the car was in Hull, the Sunderland scarf and the Emmerson connection are enough for me. Grantmore's involved and is the key to the job. I want him locked up this afternoon.'

As I'd earlier agreed with him, Tony Ride played devil's advocate. 'But it's all circumstantial, boss. He'll never cough. Grantmore's been locked up more times than the Beatles were number one. He'll say nowt and there's nothing to hold him on.'

'We're going to do this the old-fashioned way. Rattle his cage, shake him up, and see what falls out. Let him know we know... and then see what happens.'

'But, boss, he's not even in the bloody car,' Ridey continued.

'And we're not even going to use the photo in interview. I'm hanging on to that for later. We use the connection to the car and Emmerson, that's all. We tell him we've got information he had connections to that car and we know he employed Emmerson. See what shakes out. He'll admit nothing... but he'll know we know.'

I looked around as if to challenge any dissent but saw none. Everyone wanted some action, to get the job moving. To make something happen.

But then DI Baldwin, always careful and thoughtful, raised a valid point. 'Are we discussing this with Northumbria, boss? If the jobs are connected... and I'd bet they are... we could be treading on their toes. What evidence have they got? Any suspects?'

'Excellent point, Mally, and thanks for raising it. I have discussed our intended action with their SIO, Tom Corrigan, and at this stage of their inquiry, he's happy for us to proceed.'

The team looked relieved that the DI's objection wasn't going to halt the action.

'DS Naylor and DC Beatty, I want you to interview him. We'll discuss an interview strategy after the briefing.'

As was my intention, Naylor visibly brightened at being chosen to do the interview. It got him back onside and showed I'd forgiven him his lapse. To be fair, he couldn't do any damage, as the interview was something of a paper exercise, intended only to rattle Grantmore and hopefully lever out further information. Beatty was a good interviewer and would make sure all that needed saying – and no more – was said.

I turned to DI Baldwin. 'Mally, organise search and arrest teams, find him and bring him in. I want his home and both massage parlours searching... thoroughly. We're looking for cash, the gun, anything that links him to the Hardstone Building Society, the Vauxhall Vectra, Anne Beedham, Janice Cooper, links to the north-east, Ponteland... you know the score. Let's see if we can get him in custody this evening.'

Chairs scraped back. Officers moved quickly towards Mally Baldwin to volunteer.

Investigative velocity.

Thirteen

I sat in the greasy spoon café, nursing as opposed to drinking a cup of lousy instant coffee as I watched the entrance to Cleopatra's Exotic Massage on Spring Bank, close to Hull City centre. Yesterday's arrest and interview of Grantmore had gone as well as could be expected and more or less as I had planned. He had admitted nothing, laughed at our lack of evidence and been released about three hours after he'd arrived, full of righteous indignation at our "fishing trip". The searches at his home and the massage parlours had revealed nothing. After the interview, DS Naylor had expressed his doubts to me that Grantmore was connected to our job, as he had not seemed in the slightest bit worried that we had connected him to Emmerson and were alleging he had access to the car. I later heard that Naylor had since been criticising my tactics to anyone that would listen, saying if we were sure he had used the Vauxhall, we should have waited for the informant to come up with something more concrete, but as it was, we'd shown our hand. Also having failed to get anywhere in interview, he deployed the face-saving explanation that the suspect was innocent. When I had to cut staff, he'd be gone.

I hadn't expected him to get anywhere in interview. I knew we had nothing concrete to put to Grantmore, and what we had was hardly on a firm evidential base. Half the team would be thinking we had overplayed our hand by arresting him – in essence, agreeing with Naylor. Others like Ridey and Jo Young would be guessing I had something else up my sleeve and the arrest was just a means to an end. The arguing and discussion between the two groups would ignite everyone's curiosity and maintain that investigative velocity – but only for a short time. I now had to make something happen and had set wheels in motion last night after his release and was now about to grease those wheels. As far as the team were concerned, I was at HQ on other business.

As I sipped at the manky coffee out of an equally manky mug, I spotted Grantmore stride into view. He was heading towards Cleopatra's, the flagship of his seedy empire, from the direction of the city centre, wearing his signature black leather bomber jacket, black jeans and Rockport boots. He pressed the intercom set in the wall at the side of the garish pink door, stooped to speak and was quickly admitted. I waited ten minutes and then crossed the road, pressed the intercom and looked directly into the CCTV camera set above it.

A bored-sounding female voice with a strong Hull accent responded.

'Hello, love, have you got an appointment?'

'Oh, I didn't know I needed one.'

I tried to sound like a man whose sexual hopes were dashed.

'Hang on, love, don't worry. I'll fit you in.'

The door buzzed and I pushed it open to reveal a dingy four-foot-square stairwell. The same female shouted from upstairs, 'Come up, luvvie.'

I trotted up the stairs, which were carpeted in a pink shag pile that had seen much better days, and emerged into the reception area that was your stereotypical tart's parlour. I was taken aback by the appearance of the receptionist who'd have looked more at home on a Tesco checkout than fronting a quasi-brothel. Spotting my surprise, she quite politely put me out of my apparent misery.

'Morning, love, don't worry. You won't be getting me... I manage the businesses not do the business. The name's Pauline. Take a seat. Lulu won't be long.' I looked around the room at the slightly cleaner pink carpet, purple and black wallpaper and old battered black leather sofa, strewn with well-thumbed copies of *Mayfair, Fiesta, Knave* and other sundry contemporary classics of the porno-mag genre.

She pointed me towards the battered leather sofa that was overloaded with – you've guessed it – pink fluffy cushions. No way was I sitting there. I confirmed that there were only two doors leading from the office, the one leading to "Paradise Parlour" was ajar and the room beyond seemed empty, but judging from the sounds coming from behind the door of the "Kontiki Room", it most certainly wasn't. I tried to imagine the sheer desperation of a man waiting out here while contemplating a sexual act with who I assumed was Lulu and being able to hear his "sloppy seconds" actually being prepared! The moans from behind the closed door were reaching a stomach-churning crescendo, so I thought now was a good time to say hello to Grantmore, who I now knew I was going to find in a somewhat less than welcoming mood. Exactly as I had hoped.

'Sounds like she's nearly done to me.'

I smiled genially, flipped open my wallet to reveal my warrant card. 'Stay out here.'

As I opened the door, Pauline muttered, 'Black bastard,' and I saw I had timed my liaison with Sean Grantmore to perfection.

'Morning, Sean. Hard at it already, I see,' I sung out cheerfully, as if greeting an old mate down on the allotment.

Delicacy prevents me from describing the scene that confronted me but needless to say, Sean and Lulu were well beyond the point of no return – but on seeing me, return they did. There followed grunts and squeals, some wild flapping of limbs, leaps for towels and dressing gowns and no doubt a rapid cooling of ardour.

'Darnley, you bastard, what the fuck do you think you're doing bursting in here?'

'Sean, who is this pervert? You fucking sicko,' screamed Lulu as she clutched a bright pink fluffy towel to her chest.

'Morning, love... Lulu, I presume. Police raid. Step outside, would you, and keep Pauline company.'

I again flashed my warrant card and indicated she should leave. She picked up her discarded clothing from a chair and with my second 'Black bastard' of the morning, stalked from the room, slamming the door behind her.

Grantmore had meanwhile covered his embarrassment by slipping on what was obviously Lulu's pink silk kimono – yes, everything was pink. He stood desperately trying to cover his embarrassment by standing with his hands across his crotch, while trying – but failing hopelessly – to look aggressive. His one good eye glared from an extremely red and sweaty face and the jagged, still livid, scars that marked his ruined eye stood out in vivid and horrific relief, just as I am sure his attacker had intended. He must have been desperate to get dressed and save face, but I had no intention of showing such courtesy. In his place, I would have calmly removed the kimono and slowly got dressed in an effort to show I wasn't intimidated, but for all his violence and bullying I knew he was a coward and that I had, and would now keep, the upper hand.

'Fuck me, Sean, you look a right state. God, your eye's a real mess... real shame. Thought of trying an eye patch? Sorry to barge in but I needed a word about yesterday.

"No comment" isn't going to work, so I'm here to give you another chance.'

'Fuck you, Darnley, you aren't gonna get away with this… I know where you live.'

I stepped towards him and feigned a thump to his face, which made him raise his hands to protect himself, allowing me to grab his bollocks through the thin kimono, which thankfully remained in place preventing actual bodily contact. I squeezed. Hard. I actually chuckled to myself, thinking how poor old Grantmore's nuts had really taken some punishment these last few months.

'Big mistake, Sean. This was going to be a civilised discussion but you've just blown it.'

I squeezed for emphasis. He grunted in reply.

Using my grip to steer him, I forced him backwards and with a final twist and tweak released him, pushing him back into a chair that had his clothing strewn across it. I stepped back so as to be able to repel any retaliation. None came. His hands again covered his crotch as he groaned and rocked with his head bowed.

'Bloody hell, Sean, I can see your bald patch from this angle. Life isn't going your way lately, is it? And I'm here to make sure it gets a whole lot worse… unless you wise up pretty smartish.'

I grabbed him by the front of his hair and roughly pulled his head back and thrust the photograph that Morley had taken outside the Silver Cod into his line of vision – or should I say half vision?

He stopped rocking – and groaning. I knew he knew I knew.

From the moment Grantmore had threatened me – and as I interpreted it, my family – I had stepped out of character, relying on violence as opposed to wit and wiles. I concentrated on calming down. I let go of his hair and waited while he composed himself, then told him to get dressed. Leaving the door slightly ajar, I joined his two employees, who together questioned my ancestry, sexuality, dress sense, choice of aftershave and anything else they could think of, in the most colourful language. Once dressed, their boss came into the reception area and immediately made an effort to reassert his position.

'Shut up, Lulu. Get back in there and get ready for your ten o'clock.'

He followed me downstairs across the road and back into the café. I motioned him to take a seat while I bought two more chipped white mugs of crap coffee then joined him at the table he had selected in the darkest recess of the place. No way did he want to be seen in public, hobnobbing with the filth.

I placed the photograph on the table. I said nothing. He stole one quick glance at the photo. He sipped his coffee, trying to look cool, but he had to use two hands to stop the mug shaking, so I knew I had him. Neither of us had spoken since we'd left the massage parlour and I didn't want to be the first. But neither did he.

After a good five minutes of coffee-slurping on his part with not even a grimace at the taste, nor as much as a further glance at the photo, I was beginning to get bored – but confident I was onto a winner; otherwise, he would have walked out. I was about to lose the "who's going to speak first?" contest when a chap at the next table got up to leave and tossed his newspaper onto the table as he bid farewell to the guy behind the counter. We both instinctively glanced across as the *Sun* newspaper landed with a slap. Under the banner headline **SLAUGHTERED: Mum appeals to robbers** was the handsome face of the young man murdered in Northumbria, Ryan Harrod. I couldn't believe my luck. I looked Grantmore in the eye, fascinated by how his empty eye socket was twitching, and nodded towards the headline.

'Darnley, what the fuck do you want from me?'

I just tapped the photo I had brought with my finger.

'That's you. Who's the other guy?'

'That's not me.'

'Stick to that crap then... but let's see what this other chap thinks when this photograph appears in the national press with an appeal for the identity of the two men... in connection with the murder of Ryan Harrod,' nodding towards the *Sun* and its headline.

'You're full of shit, Darnley. No paper's gonna run that. You can't tell who either one of them blokes are. There is no connection and you know it.'

He came across super confident but his empty eye socket was now jerking madly – his days as a poker player were definitely over.

'Listen. Carefully. You are going to get one chance. I am now going to tell you what you already know. At the end of this, you will agree to help me. If you refuse, I am pretty sure you will be a dead man before the week is out.'

He snorted in derision.

'The car in this photo was used to visit a house in Atwick, from where a gang from the north-east got the keys to rob the Hardstone Building Society in Beverley. One of your old mates David Emmerson was on that job, and the gang shot him when he fucked up by leaving his DNA on the victim at the building society. That same gang killed that young lad the night before last, up in the north-east.'

'Bullshit, Darnley.'

'This photo was taken barely two weeks before the job. The other bloke was at the Silver Cod for the football, Hull v Sunderland, on the 28th of November last year. That bloke is in that gang. A gang that shot one of its own when he fucked up. You fucked up, Sean. This photo shows you with the car and a gang member. No one will identify that man from this photo, but I'll make sure he gets to see it and he'll know it's him – just like you know it's you. Then you're dead because he'll know you can lead us to him.'

'You can't link me to that car, to that robbery or the murders, and you know it.'

'I know that. You know that.' I again tapped the photo. 'But he doesn't. He'll just think that the idiot he used in Hull and had to shoot has an idiot mate who has now dropped him in the shit. The article in the paper will say the police are seeking the identity of both men in connection with the murders. So he will think we don't know who you are... but he does... and he will not risk you grassing him up.'

I then formed a gun with my right hand and shot him in the forehead.

He jumped up, knocking over his chair, and then leaned forward, both hands on the table, and stuck his face close to mine.

'Bollocks! You don't frighten me, Darnley. You're bluffing. The paper wouldn't print it and you wouldn't dare do that... and that's not me for a start.'

'You just said that in the wrong order, Sean. If that's not you, whether I'm bluffing or not is irrelevant. You have just confirmed it is you... so sit back down and let me save your life.'

But Sean is not the brightest one-eyed massage parlour operator in Hull, and he hadn't grasped the significance of what he'd said. He stormed out of the café and crossed Spring Bank. Outside Cleopatra's, he paused and looked back.

'Come on, Sean, you know I've got you. Come back.'

But the penny still hadn't dropped and he disappeared through the pink door.

Well, my initial plan hadn't worked – yet. Maybe he just needed a bit more persuasion. Part two of my plan was now necessary and it involved sticking my ever-extending neck out even further. But I knew I was on the right track.

Fourteen

16:15 That Same Afternoon

The two men sat huddled together in a corner of the pub, their heads almost touching as they engaged in what was clearly a serious and tense conversation. Both nursed pints of dark beer, as did the majority of the other totally male patrons of the Brown Cow in Pennywell, a suburb of Sunderland. For a Wednesday afternoon, the pub was busier than one would expect but also quieter. No music played, there was no rowdy banter or laughter and all of the men were either alone or in pairs. This was a drinker's pub. Although most of the customers knew or recognised each other, no one knew the two in the corner.

'Please, Paul, he's got kids, for fuck's sake. We've known him for years and he's never let us down. He's a mate.'

The man speaking was smaller, stockier and older than his companion, and spoke with a broad Geordie accent that was brimming with obvious emotion.

The tall, well-built younger man took a swallow of his beer and responded in a calm and cultured voice without any trace of accent.

'Well, he's let us down now… and become a liability. He's as panicked as a bolted horse and in our game, panicking leads to mistakes. We cannot afford mistakes.'

'The gun's gone. In the sea. They'll never find it. He swears he left no blood at the house for the cops to use. There's no way they'll get back to him.'

'Just like that idiot Emmerson... he bled. The kid nutted him and broke his nose. That means DNA... evidence. They'll get him and charge him with murder. He'll do a deal and grass us up because he's got nothing to lose. I should have shot him on the night, like I did that liability from Hull.'

'He swears he left no blood at the scene... he cleaned up, and you know he'd never grass,' pleaded the older man, his drink forgotten.

'Look, Mick. You saw him... he was covered in blood. He pulled the trigger but we all go down for murder if he talks. The bullet that killed the kid will match the one in Emmerson's head and they'll know the jobs are linked. They'll end up asking questions up here again. If they get a DNA hit on Billy, they'll be all over me and you like a rash. They'll find out we're mates and were in the army together. If he talks, we're done.'

Mick shook his head in denial before taking a long drink from his pint.

Paul remained calm. 'Tomorrow, we all go out fishing on your boat. Tell him we need to talk. He goes the same way as the gun.'

'Why would they come to us? Only Billy's got a record. One assault... years ago. We've got no criminal records and you're a businessman for God's sake and I'm a fisherman. The cops won't link us to the robberies just 'cos we know each other. Billy would never grass.'

'No, he won't grass. He won't get chance. I'll meet you both at your boat at half six in the morning. And Mick... be there... and make sure he's there too.'

Mick sat back in his chair, creating space between himself

and his younger companion. 'Are you threatening me as well, Paul?'

'We all survived Bosnia because I was in charge and you and Billy followed orders. We agreed when we started this we'd have to adopt the same principles if we hoped to succeed. Billy messed up... so Billy has to pay. Just don't mess up, Mick.'

'But you messed up with getting Emmerson involved... If we'd stuck with just us three, that wouldn't have happened.'

Paul calmly placed his glass on the battered surface of the circular table and sat back upright on his chair. Mick mirrored the movement and for a few tense seconds they just stared at each other – until Mick bottled it and looked away.

His point made, Paul pointed his forefinger at Mick and through gritted teeth hissed, 'And I put it right. Billy wasn't available and we needed some help to make it work in an area we didn't know, and Emmerson fulfilled his purpose. One more job then we pack in. Near Hull again, well away from here. I'll get back onto my local contact down there.'

He downed the rest of his pint, stood up and stared hard at Mick.

'Your boat. Half six. Both of you be there.'

Then he turned and walked out of the pub.

Mick sat for a moment staring out of the window before draining his pint and muttering to himself, 'Aye and you should have got rid of the gun after Emmerson... you clever bastard.'

He rose and followed his old major out of the pub.

Fifteen

The Next Day
Thursday, 4ᵗʰ February 1999

At 11.30am on a Thursday, the newsroom at the *Hull Daily Mail* was almost empty. Tonight's edition was agreed and reporters were out and about chasing up the odd loose end, or working on future stories. On the horns of a dilemma, Richard Wilde sat nervously chewing his nails in between sips of lukewarm coffee. Ever-increasing computerisation, the changing face of advertising and the rise of the internet meant that throughout the country, journalists were being shed like leaves in an autumn wind as local newspapers closed, downsized or went weekly. Nobody even wrapped fish and chips up in newspaper nowadays. Only that morning, the editor had announced likely redundancies and Richard had been sure he'd received a sympathetic smile that seemed to say "hard luck". It was bound to be last in, first out and he'd only been with the *Mail* for just over a year, his first job straight from his degree in Journalism. He knew that the seedy backstory fed to him by Detective Superintendent Darnley about the Sonia Daggett murder had impressed the crime editor but he doubted that alone would save his skin.

Ever since the incident in court when he'd witnessed the attack on Grantmore and was leaned on by Darnley, the young reporter had wrestled with his conscience. The "you scratch my back and I'll scratch yours" arrangement Darnley had promised never featured in his university training, but he had already recognised that other reporters traded ethics for stories. But last night Darnley had approached him with something in an altogether different league – and he was shitting himself. It was one thing to be facing redundancy, but quite another to be contemplating the sack and having to change careers.

So Richard was trying to weigh up the pros and cons of doing Darnley's bidding. His hand would stray to the desk phone when his logic told him that no one would ever find out and he'd get the scoop to save his job. Then he'd put his fingers back into his mouth and savage another nail, as his heart overruled his head and he saw the unethical – and job-threatening – nature of Darnley's request.

Decision suddenly made, he picked up the phone and tapped out the number Darnley had given him during their brief meeting early yesterday morning at the café at Hull Railway Station. However, before the call even connected, he hung up again, stood up, pulled his jacket from the back of his chair and left the building. Ten minutes later, he had found a telephone box that worked, and redialled.

*

An Hour Earlier

'Paul… great to hear from you,' Grantmore lied, his mouth suddenly going dry and his hands sweating so that his mobile almost slipped from his fingers. He had only just joined Lulu on the massage couch and was angry when his mobile had rung. Recognising Paul Frame's number, his ardour and anger rapidly turned to fear and he couldn't stop himself from answering it.

'I'll keep this brief. I want another job setting up similar to the last one.'

As usual, Frame's gentle, polished tone chilled Grantmore far more than the rough, profanity-laden accents of the villains he usually associated with.

'Look, Paul, I'm really grateful for the work you've put my way and for the loan for the business but to be frank...'

'Sean, I don't want to hear any buts. Emmerson was a but and Billy's become a but. You don't want to become a but.'

He paused to let the veiled threat sink in.

'Tell you what, set this one up and on the word of an officer and a gentleman, this is the last time... and I'll forget the last twenty grand of the loan. That can be your cut this time, with an extra five for your trouble.'

Grantmore hardly heard the offer as he contemplated telling Paul that the police were all over him. He should tell him to quit the country. But he realised that was as good as telling him he'd cocked up just like Emmerson and, by the sound of things, Billy too. He was also desperate to know if the murder of the young lad in Northumbria was also Frame's work. When he'd left Darnley in the café yesterday, he'd sent one of the girls out to buy a newspaper and read the full article. Was it connected like Darnley had said? It easily could have been – but was Darnley just bluffing? He needed to know just how deep he was getting – but how the hell could he ask? He needed time to think.

'That's a good offer, Paul... you're on. But, look, I'm with somebody. I'll ring you back later today for some details. Shall I use this number?'

'No, I'll ring you. Tomorrow morning about eleven. Be available on this number and then we need to meet up to discuss details.'

The line went dead.

One hundred and twenty miles to the north-east, Paul Frame threw his mobile into the sea from the stern of Mick Keegan's trawler. He felt no more or less sorry about wasting a decent mobile than he had done an hour ago when he ended a fifteen-year friendship with Billy Pike. He too had entered the cold North Sea from the stern of *The Blaydon Races,* wrapped in a heavy-duty builder's sack weighed down with rubble. Extreme caution and a lack of emotion had kept Frame alive in Bosnia and served him well in his short but successful criminal career. Mobiles were easily replaceable and so were careless associates. One more robbery and then he'd get out of the country. Another old army pal was making a mint working out of South Africa, hiring out mercenaries, and was always suggesting he try something similar. He'd done his homework and had secured the three of them jobs with a Nigerian businessman. He'd worried Billy might not want to join them – but that was now all sorted. A bit of sun and fun was beckoning and he'd make sure there were no loose ends to spoil it. He watched Mick as he changed course for the fish landing docks. Mick had hardly spoken to him since they'd met in the pub yesterday but had followed instructions and made sure an unsuspecting Billy had met them on board. While Paul had engaged Billy in conversation, Mick had smashed him over the head with a mallet and helped prepare his make-do coffin. Paul knew that Mick was a vicious bastard and he'd now have to watch his own back until after the last job. Mick, he knew, would be asking himself when it was his turn to die – when might he too become a "loose end" that needed tying off?

He'd also need to work out how to make sure Billy's young and attractive wife, Debbie, didn't make waves. Billy had only managed to pull such a woman using the money from the robberies, and he suspected she'd easily swap horses if a sweeter life beckoned. She was a "bit of a gal" and had given Frame the come-on in the past, so he was planning to have some fun with her – and keep her sweet – before he left for Africa.

After mulling over that scenario for a pleasant minute or two, his thoughts turned to Grantmore. He'd run into him a couple of years ago over a few drinks in a pub in Hull, while watching his beloved Sunderland on the TV, and in subsequent meetings had learnt he ran a few massage parlours and prostitutes and acted as a criminal fixer for gangs all over the north. Frame's haulage business, which he had started when he left the army, had never really given him the life he felt he deserved after serving Queen and Country for twenty years, and he had persuaded his two ex-army pals to put their training to good use – crime. By the time he met Grantmore, they had already pulled off a handful of robberies well away from Tyneside, keeping them well separated by time and geography, and hadn't been too greedy. As their expertise grew, so did the proceeds and although firearms had been brandished, they'd never fired a shot and none of the robbery victims had even been hurt. However, always an ambitious man, Frame had begun to dream of the big one before giving up crime for a life of luxury in sunnier climes.

Frame came from a privileged background with a private school and university education. Despite that and his Sandhurst officer training, a successful army career and rising to the rank of major, he found himself strangely impressed by Sean Grantmore. Although the man was an ill-educated braggart and bully, Frame recognised a certain criminal cunning and saw his wide network of criminal contacts, hard man persona, illegal know-how and small but successful empire as evidence of a man who had made good.

Slowly but surely, they developed a criminal association, starting with the robbery of a filling station near Sleaford in Lincolnshire. As the number of joint crimes grew and their association deepened, Frame began to see Grantmore for what he really was and realised that he needed to gain the upper hand – become the "officer" in the relationship – the one in charge – just as he was with Billy and Mick. His chance came when he lent Grantmore some money to help him open his third massage parlour. During the months he was under investigation, bailed and on trial for the rape of Lisa Holland, Grantmore's businesses suffered and he fell behind with his payments to Frame. Subtly, Frame made him realise he was unhappy and drip-fed details of his military career, which had involved an expertise in black operations with his two current criminal associates. Slowly but surely, their roles reversed until the career criminal became overawed and afraid of the man he had initially seen as an amateur in *his* game. Then Frame deliberately compressed the loan repayment schedule for a couple of months, making clear the implications of not paying but eventually offering a now terrified Grantmore a way out – setting up bigger, better and more lucrative crimes – which involved more risk for Grantmore. He relaxed repayments as Grantmore fed him information to facilitate the Bridlington and then Beverley robberies.

He blamed Grantmore for recommending Emmerson and kicked himself for allowing his initial impressions of Grantmore to cloud his judgement and weaken his defences. Grantmore had to go the same way as Billy. With two murder hunts on his tail, too many people could lead the police to him. He knew Grantmore had many enemies, so when he turned up dead there would be more suspects than the police could shake a stick at, and he doubted they would work too hard to find the killers. When someone had half-blinded him only a few weeks ago and the police had failed to charge the obvious suspect, he knew that eliminating Grantmore was not going to be too much of a problem. But only after the final job.

*

Grantmore's heart had only just stopped hammering after Frame's call when his mobile rang again. He roughly pushed Lulu away and reached down onto the floor for the phone. With his heart already starting to race, he stabbed the answer button, fully expecting to hear Frame's voice again.

Instead, a rather timid male asked, 'Is that Sean Grantmore?'

'Why... who the fuck wants him?' Just glad it wasn't Frame again.

'I wanted to ask Mr Grantmore some questions about a murder that took place in Ponteland near Newcastle recently.'

Ridiculously, Richard Wilde felt exposed and vulnerable in the telephone box on Ferensway. He pulled the collar of his jacket higher, trying to shield his face, and turned in towards the phone's cradle. Not really understanding the implications of the instructions Darnley had given him, Wilde quickly rehearsed the next step in his head.

'Who the hell is this? Is this the fucking press? Did Darnley put you up to this?' Grantmore screamed hysterically.

Wilde almost shit himself when Grantmore used Darnley's name – and guessed it was the press. His initial reaction was to hang up but somehow his reporter's curiosity took over. Darnley had claimed he had a photograph that somehow implicated Grantmore in the murder, and his promise of a scoop when the full story broke drove him on against his better instincts.

'Yes, this is the press and I assume from your response you know exactly what I am talking about. Would you care to comment?'

He held his breath. He hadn't yet even mentioned the photograph. All he could hear was Grantmore's laboured breathing – a clear indication of his fear – and in that instant, Wilde knew Darnley was on the right track. He also realised that he had not revealed his identity or even his newspaper. Emboldened, he ploughed on.

'We have come into possession of a photograph that we have reason to believe is you...'

He paused, holding his breath again and dared to hope.

Again, there was quiet, so he added, 'We are planning to publish the photograph...'

There was a long sigh at the other end.

'Tell Darnley to meet me in the Molescroft in Beverley at seven tonight.'

The line went dead.

Richard Wilde pushed open the phone box door like he was leaving a Wild West saloon after a gunfight. He set off briskly towards the office, his heart pumping, blood surging and his mind whirring.

He hadn't compromised himself. The young reporter realised that Darnley would think he now had greater control over him, with a man like Grantmore thinking he had crossed him. He hadn't even had to pass on the request for a meeting. As far as Darnley would know, he had done exactly as he was asked and got the result he wanted. Could he turn this situation around to his own advantage? Get out of Darnley's grip? Get a better story?

He had to think. But he had to pass on the message to meet Grantmore in the pub at seven o'clock. He checked his watch, only three thirty. He decided to keep Darnley waiting and make out when he rung him that he'd had a hell of a job in getting Grantmore to meet him. It was only a small step in trying to get back in control – but it was a start.

As he walked back to the newsroom, he reviewed what he knew. He'd researched the murder in Ponteland and Darnley had told him that Grantmore knew who had done it and that he had a photograph that somehow helped prove it. He quickened his step. He needed to find out more about Grantmore, the death of this young lad Ryan Harrod, and figure out how he could capitalise on the knowledge he now had. He needed to investigate. The rest of his journey was occupied with dreams of the call to join the *Telegraph* or the *Times* – Richard Wilde, Investigative Journalist. He'd always known he would make it.

*

18:45 That Night

I drove one-handed down Lairgate in Beverley as I undid the top button of my shirt and pulled my tie loose. I was going to be a bit early arriving for what was bound to be another confrontational meeting with Grantmore, but I intended to claim the territory. Wilde had rung me about fifteen minutes beforehand, keen to let me know how hard he'd worked to get Grantmore to meet me. Fortunately, I'd been at Police HQ on Priory Road, updating the new ACC (Ops), Jane Greenhall, with my heavily sanitised version of progress with the case, so I was within twenty minutes' drive of the pub. My tame newshound had sounded anxious. Worried that Grantmore knew who he was and that he was doing my "dirty work" as he put it. He'd tried to push me into giving him more information, saying his job was on the line due to redundancies and he needed a story as his reward for helping me. To be honest, I felt sorry for him and promised he'd get the story when it broke, but there was nothing I could give him for now. But he was no mug and now knew Grantmore was somehow connected to the murder of Ryan Harrod in Northumberland. I surmised he'd have made the link to my investigation of the Beverley robbery and the murder of Emmerson. So I warned him off from digging around Grantmore. In truth, I was a little worried about the position I'd put him in. He was young and green and Grantmore was a dangerous bastard who wouldn't think twice about getting at me by shafting Wilde with his bosses – or worse. Conversely, he was an ambitious young journalist and I didn't want him telling his bosses what he had got from me. Shit. Just more complications I had to try and wrestle with, in what was fast becoming a minefield of potential disasters.

I dragged my mind back to the job in hand as I decided to park my car at Sessions House, the local Beverley nick, as I didn't want Grantmore clocking my private car. I walked up Molescroft Road towards the pub to find only a handful of elderly folks enjoying the local pub grub. I'd realised why Grantmore had suggested this place, as no one he knew was ever likely to clock him associating with the law in here. I bought a pint of bitter and a bag of crisps then took up a position tucked away behind the side bar, where I guessed he'd feel more comfortable, as we'd be well out of sight. To be fair, I shouldn't have been having a one-to-one meeting with a known criminal, so I was also keen on remaining incognito.

Just after seven, he strolled in, looking far more relaxed than I'd expected. He didn't seem in a rush to get out of sight and actually nodded a pleasant enough "evening" to the four old fogies sitting to the left of the door enjoying their steak and ale pies and fish and chips. He may have wanted to be inconspicuous but in middle-class Beverley, in a pub full of nosey pensioners, he stuck out like – well – a one-eyed, scar-faced thug. I beckoned him over, as the two women in the party he had acknowledged turned to their men-folk clearly in a state of high excitement. Poor old Sean recognised that he had made something of a mistake meeting me here and tucked his head further into the upturned collar of his leather jacket. He dodged quickly around the main bar into the small side room with only two tables that I'd claimed for our meeting. I wanted him onside and not his usual confrontational self, so I slid along the bench seat, letting him have the most discrete corner in the whole pub.

'What you having, Sean?'

I stood and took the two steps to the small bar as he settled himself in, looking nervously around, unsettled by the interest he had piqued by merely walking into the place.

'Large whisky. No ice.'

The barmaid was unoccupied so within a couple of minutes I had paid for the drink and sat back down. Sean sat slouched on the bench, his arms folded across his chest and his shoulders buried deep in the folds of his jacket, trying his best to look bored. He took the drink and downed half of it in one macho swallow. His eyes locked onto mine in a defiant stare that was almost a caricature of a hard case.

I gave a low chuckle and then took a leisurely sip of my beer.

'Drop the act, Sean. I've got you by the bollocks… only proverbially this time… and you know it… or else you wouldn't be here. You know what I want. His name and as much as you know about the jobs.'

'You must think I'm stupid, Darnley. I'm saying fuck all to you even in a pub. You could be wired up… or had the place bugged before I got here.'

I laughed. 'You've been watching too much telly, Sean. But if you're worried about it, let's go somewhere else. You decide.'

I turned towards him and raised my arms as if offering him the chance to frisk me.

'I don't trust you, Darnley. Let's move tables.'

He got up and moved to a table that was in a busier area.

I laughed to myself at him thinking I could have bugged our conversation. I had moved too far down an unethical path to have even tried to obtain the necessary surveillance authority. However, his actions just further confirmed to me his involvement. He knew something.

After a couple of minutes more of the hard-man silence, he kicked discussions off.

'Okay, I don't want your tame reporter putting that photo in the paper, so I'll give you something, but I want full immunity before I say a thing. Like you said, the bastard will kill me if that photo appears in the paper, but if I give you him… and his gang… I want immunity, or else I'm dead anyway.'

I had anticipated this. There was no way I, or anyone else, could offer Grantmore immunity for his part, whatever that part was, in the robbery at the building society and murder of Emmerson. These were far too serious a set of crimes to let anyone walk away. I didn't know if, or how, he might be involved in the murder of Ryan Harrod, but that further tied my hands, as another force was involved. In a perfect world, I needed him to tell me who the man in the photograph was, who his accomplices were and as much about their crimes as he could. He would then admit his part, plead guilty and then give evidence against them, with the prospect of a lighter sentence. I knew all that was as likely as Hull winning the FA Cup, but I always like to be optimistic, so I explained all this as he finished his drink.

When I'd given him the "official offer", he just laughed.

'Yeah, then when I come out I can go and do charity work in a homeless hostel. So what's the real deal?'

The truth was, I didn't have one beyond that official line and I knew all along he'd never take it. All I could do was try and build the pressure.

'Take it or leave it. If you leave it, you'll be rearrested and questioned again, then that photograph of you and the bloke in the Sunderland scarf of whom you are so scared will appear in the national press. Keeping up so far? Next, I'll release you with a press conference to follow, explaining how since your arrest, the focus of the inquiry has shifted to the north-east. He will of course then think you've grassed him up for a deal. Then I'll put you under surveillance until he comes to bump you off, and catch him... hopefully, before he's succeeded.'

All of this was just a threat – pure fantasy.

Although I was convinced that the photo was the only key we had to the case, it was unusable other than to exert this pressure on him to reveal the north-east connection. Of course he didn't know that, but he was no mug, having been through the wringer of the Criminal Justice System countless times – as his response showed.

'Fuck you, Darnley. I'm a businessman and I don't do anything for nothing. You can't prove anything against me or else you'd charge me. That photo is not clear enough to say it's me. I'm stood near a car – big bloody deal. It's all circumstantial and you know it. Without me talking, you've got nothing.'

He finished the last of his whisky and shoved the empty glass towards me.

I stood at the bar waiting for the drinks, frustrated that the pressure that I was undoubtedly applying was not going to deliver the result I needed. I took the drinks back to the table and, unable to conjure up any new tactic, I wasted ten minutes merely reiterating my threat to expose him as a grass to try and turn up the pressure. He didn't even speak. He was not going to succumb. Eventually, he held up his hand to silence me.

'Now I think I should buy you a drink. Another pint... or something stronger?'

I handed him my pint glass and watched as he leaned on

the bar flirting with the barmaid as cool as you like. I felt the control slipping away from me again.

While I drank my pint, he made me a proposal.

'I'm not giving you any names but I've been asked to set up another job. I'll do it and then tip you off, when and where. You catch them on the job. They end up in the nick… and I stay out. I still owe the bastard twenty grand from fifty he loaned me and this way I keep the money… and my life.'

My mind raced. In tightly controlled and authorised circumstances, this was an actual tactical option. Even with the police in full control, this was still a high-risk strategy and only ever used when no other course was possible. It could never be sanctioned in these circumstances – with a criminal dictating the terms.

Maybe not legal – but possible?

'As I said, Darnley, I'm a businessman. I've got where I am by taking risks. This would be a big risk for me but I'm willing to take it… but have you got the balls?'

There was no further discussion. We both agreed to sleep on it but set ourselves a twenty-four-hour deadline. I walked slowly back towards Sessions House, my mind in turmoil, seeking an alternative solution to the one Grantmore was offering. Being manipulated by a villain was a bitter pill for me to swallow, especially since I had always had him marked down as just a vicious thug of low intelligence. I realised I had underestimated his criminal cunning and would have to work hard to regain control of a situation that would see me move from a copper who was prepared to bend the rules, to one who was now contemplating ripping them up completely. I was heading for another sleepless night.

Unbeknown to me, things were moving rapidly, and not for the first time in this case, circumstances were yet again about to change. My plotting and scheming could not keep up with events.

Sixteen

Richard Wilde was knackered. He too had spent a sleepless night wrestling with his conscience, his emotions and his plans. He showered at 6am then drove into Hull and checked in at the newsroom before stationing himself in the same café opposite Cleopatra's that Darnley had used two days earlier. Like Darnley, he watched for Grantmore, his mind still churning through all the scenarios that had kept him awake. Grantmore was in some way involved in the murder of the young man up north, and it wasn't too far a stretch to figure out that that crime must be connected to the murder of Emmerson following a similar robbery in Beverley. Wilde didn't want Darnley's titbits. This was real investigative journalism – what he'd dreamed of when he was at university. His plan, if you could call it a plan, was to follow Grantmore, see who he met and just hope something developed.

He'd read the *Guardian* from cover to cover and by 9.30am there was still no sign of his quarry, when his attention was drawn to another customer who had entered the café about twenty minutes earlier, polished off scrambled eggs on toast and was now just sitting staring across Spring

Bank. It was the Canon camera with telephoto lens that the man constantly fiddled with that had piqued his interest. Richard coveted the camera and was about to engage the man in conversation about its qualities, purely to fill the time, when the man suddenly raised his camera, adjusted the lens and fired off three or four shots through the café window. Following the camera's angle, Richard was gobsmacked to see that Grantmore was the subject of the man's photography. He watched as his target waited at the door of his business before being buzzed inside. The man lowered his camera and left it on the table while he ordered another pot of tea before continuing what clearly seemed to be the same vigil as Richard's.

The journalist was intrigued. Could the other bloke be a copper maintaining surveillance? His rudimentary knowledge of such practices made him quickly rule that out. He didn't appear to have a radio. Certainly, no earpiece was evident and he had written nothing down in a surveillance log that Richard knew was essential. Having discounted that option, he mused that the man was perfectly suited to such a role, as he would never have been identified as such. His age was indeterminate, anywhere between thirty and fifty, and he looked like a skinny relic from the 1970s. He sipped his mug of tea as if it was in a fine china cup, with his little finger sticking out as if at afternoon tea with the gentry, not in a greasy spoon in Hull. Wilde weighed up his options.

He had just decided to approach him in the guise of talking about his camera when the little man suddenly jumped up, grabbed his anorak from the back of his chair, picked up his camera and rushed out onto Spring Bank, heading towards Ferensway. Then Richard spotted Grantmore walking in the same direction on the opposite side of the road. The man was clearly following Grantmore. Without a thought to the whys and wherefores, Richard joined the hunt. Now this was journalism.

Twenty minutes later, now on Witham, he saw Grantmore enter his other emporium of delight, Nicole's. Grantmore's "shadow" had positioned himself in the entrance to a narrow alleyway about thirty yards away from Nicole's entrance but on the opposite side of the road. Richard hung back, pretending to look at cars for sale on one of the used car showroom forecourts that cluster along Witham. He watched as the little man moved deeper into the alley entrance and seemed to settle down for another wait.

After fifteen minutes of looking at cars and realising that the salesman hassling him was not going to "leave him to browse", he approached the alley entrance with no clear idea of his tactics and confronted the diminutive observer.

'Why are you following Sean Grantmore?'

Startled, and reacting purely on the instinct that Wilde must be one of Grantmore's thugs, the man thrust the expensive camera with its long lens straight into Richard's nose, causing a nasty gash. Since the camera's strap was round his neck, his head followed the trajectory of the camera resulting in his forehead smashing into the back of it. There ensued considerable moaning, groaning, bleeding and struggling, with the reporter eventually ending up sitting on the prostrate cameraman, who lay face down on the footpath outside the Poundstretcher store, adjacent to the alley.

Now thoroughly pissed off, and with all semblance of professionalism abandoned, the much stronger reporter dragged Grantmore's stalker to his feet and out of sight of Nicole's. Once safely round the corner into Holborn Street, he sat him on a low wall and took a seat next to him. While Richard dabbed at his still bleeding nose with the sleeve of his shirt, the little cameraman stared up at him.

Both men just sat. Panting, bleeding and sizing each other up but with all aggression dissipated.

'Well… why were you following Sean Grantmore?'

This time, Graham Morley answered his question and half an hour later, the two men were back in the café on Spring Bank, sharing a pot of tea and still talking.

*

13:30 That Afternoon

I made my way into the tearooms at Wolds Village, a newly refurbished set of old farm buildings close to the village of Bainton and about three miles from Driffield. When who I now thought of as my tame reporter had rung me in a state of high excitement, demanding we meet immediately, I had thought of this place as discreet and out of the way – and I knew the coffee was good. He'd demanded that I come into Hull but I insisted he came to me – keeping the upper hand.

He was already waiting for me, nursing a coffee. As he saw me, he left his seat and approached the counter and ordered me a drink. I made myself comfortable at the table he had just vacated, on top of which lay his notebook and pen. He walked to the table carrying my coffee, set it down and resumed his seat, looking around as if expecting to see someone else approaching – and clearly nervous. He also sported a sticking plaster across the bridge of his obviously swollen nose.

'What the hell's happened to you?' I indicated his injury. 'What's all this about… and why the urgency?'

I noticed his hands were shaking slightly as he nervously fiddled with his pen and scanned the café.

'Calm down, Richard. What the hell's the matter?'

Using my best fatherly tone, I adopted my "you can trust me, I'm a copper" look and put my hand out to squeeze and still the arm that was still twiddling the pen.

'I know it was Russ Holland who maimed Grantmore… and I know you can prove it.' He sat upright and back in his chair, further away from me, and pulled his arm out of my grip. 'Don't deny it. You know it was Holland who poked his eye out, or whatever he did, and you've shoved it under the carpet.'

'Have you got me here just to threaten me? You know nothing.'

'Look, I need to do my duty, not as a reporter but as a citizen, and I need you to do the right thing now and protect Grantmore. I know he's a thug but the police have a duty to protect everyone. If you don't, I'll go to your superiors and tell them you can prove Russ Holland maimed Grantmore.'

'What do you mean, do the right thing now and protect him?' I was puzzled about what the hell was driving this conversation.

'I know you think he's involved in those murders. That's why you've used me, but now *he's* going to be murdered and I won't be involved in letting that happen. You've got me involved in something that's way over my head… now you've got to get me out.'

He slumped down in his chair, defeated and clearly shit-scared.

At this point, I just thought he had figured out that my tactics of pressurising Grantmore into grassing on his accomplices would put Grantmore in danger. He was having second thoughts about his role in helping me, and possible repercussions if Grantmore rolled over. But what was all this about Russ Holland?

'Grow up… you're in it up to your neck. You rang Grantmore and then passed on his request for a meeting to me. You want to stay on the Hull rag all your life, that's fine by me, but if you want to be a real crime reporter you have to get your hands dirty. Your chosen profession is mired in shit. Press tactics are far murkier than mine. Stick with me and I'll make sure you get a great story that'll have the nationals gasping.'

Plenty of stick followed by a bit of carrot. I sat back, waiting for his rapid u-turn, a smug grin on my face.

'Fuck you, Darnley. You've got a witness who saw Russ Holland at the crime scene. You could have stopped him after he blinded Grantmore... but now he's going to kill him and I want no part of it.'

The kid was almost shouting, and a couple of old dears sharing a pot of tea and scones a couple of tables away turned to see what was going on.

My mouth went dry – he knew about Morley? I stood up, took hold of his arm, pulled him to his feet and guided him out of the café. He came, unresisting.

'Let's continue this in my car... and keep your voice down.'

It took him about five minutes to calm down before he began to tell me the story of his confrontation with Morley and what he had learnt from him. My reading of the situation had been way off. He knew about Morley's obsession with Grantmore and even how he'd first met me when he'd brought in the answerphone tapes after Grantmore's acquittal for rape. He now understood the provenance of the photograph of Grantmore with the Vauxhall that I had persuaded him to threaten to publish. When he came to tell the tale of Morley seeing Holland and the woman on the fire escape at Nicole's, I could feel my heart pounding in my chest and my over-worked brain turning to mush. It was not until he had completed his account that I registered his last comment – that unfortunately Morley had not photographed the event?

I saw a glimmer of hope. 'Hang on, you've lost me. Tell me again what Morley told you about Russ Holland attacking and blinding Grantmore.'

'He's told me he's already told you. You know Holland did it but you've done nothing. He was hanging about near Nicole's that day and saw Holland climb the fire escape, meet a women who climbed out of the window, hand her a package and then climb in the window she'd come out of. Trouble was, he didn't have his camera... it was in for repair.'

Why Morley had made the decision not to fully disclose to Wilde I didn't know, but it gave me room for manoeuvre – fingers crossed.

'I suppose he didn't tell you that he has refused to give evidence about what he saw? I can't do a thing without evidence. This is just the same as when he had the answerphone tapes. He's spineless. I haven't ignored what he's said... you know that Holland has been arrested based upon the attack you and I witnessed in court. He denies the attack at Nicole's and there is no other evidence. I'm not ignoring it... I'm biding my time... I'll get him.'

Some of the anger dissipated from the young man's face and he seemed to slump further into his seat. He conceded that Morley had told him that he was glad that Holland had maimed Grantmore. He saw it as justice, not vengeance. So he could understand why he wouldn't give evidence.

'But why has he told you all this?' I was still confused.

'Because things have changed. He's convinced that Holland now intends to kill Grantmore, and even he can't just stand by and see that happen.'

He explained how Morley had told him he had continued his observations on his enemy, still intent upon gathering evidence of his wrongdoings. The previous night, while he'd been hanging about near Grantmore's home, he'd seen

Holland enter his rear garden and check doors and windows. Morley had recognised the man's agitation and anger and was convinced he would soon attack Grantmore again, and what more could he do to harm him beyond what he had already done? Morley was convinced Holland now intended to kill his daughter's rapist.

'Richard, you've done the right thing to tell me this. I can see why Morley has not told us... he's frightened of his own shadow.'

'You've got to arrest and question Holland. You can't allow him to go ahead and actually kill Grantmore. I can't just sit on this. I want out.'

He reached into his jacket pocket and pulled out a folded sheet of paper, which he handed to me.

'There's more. He's no ordinary vengeful father. Look at this.'

It was a photocopy of an archived article from the *London Evening Standard* dated October 1982, with the headline **'Local Army Hero Honoured'** above a formal head and shoulders photograph of a young man in the uniform of an army captain. I quickly scanned the article but a section had been highlighted with a yellow marker pen:

...without a thought for his own safety, 30-year-old Ralph Harrison of Walthamstow, a captain in 3rd Battalion of the Parachute Regiment, who had already been in combat for over 15 hours, charged a machine-gun post...

There followed heart-warming words of praise from Harrison's mother and his commanding officer.

Walthamstow's Ralph Harrison was now Hull's Russ Holland. It was unmistakable. The years had hardly altered his features.

I sat there, stunned. The direct attack on Grantmore in court, his manner at Queens Gardens when he spoke of eliminating vermin, the planting of the girl Katia into

Nicole's and the calculating way he had literally branded the object of his hatred. These were obvious hallmarks of a man trained for action.

'He was a bloody Para… he's trained to kill and he's stalking Grantmore.' He was then clearly struck by another bombshell: 'And I'm grassing him up… but I've got to… and you've got to protect me.'

He snatched back the article and stared hard at the photograph, as if trying to make sure it was really true.

'How the hell have you found this out? He's obviously had a change of identity.' My mind was racing, the implications spiralling and colliding in a frenzy of apprehension.

'It's Morley, he's fanatical about the whole saga. He's blaming himself for Grantmore getting off the rape of Holland's daughter, glad Holland wreaked revenge but uneasy that he knows he did it and you've not nicked him for it. He's told me about the other photograph he got that's enabled you to link Grantmore to the murders and the northeast. He's desperate you get him this time but he's wracked with guilt about it all. You've met him… he's a sad and lonely man but he's a genius with a computer and at searching the internet. He must be spending every waking hour on this… he's obsessed.'

I looked again at the press clipping. Shit. Shit. Shit.

Events were now out of control. So much had happened so quickly, my mind could not assimilate all the nuances of my predicament. After our meeting in the pub, I'd spent yet another sleepless night, followed by a morning in the incident room, supposedly reading statements and signing off actions but actually churning over my limited options. Since the arrest of Grantmore three days earlier, the incident had settled into a disappointing lull. I knew I was failing to give any investigative direction and the team were getting restless – losing heart. I had to make up my mind as to how to move forward or pretty soon the top corridor would pick something up on the force jungle drums and I'd start to be asked awkward questions. At the moment, the new ACC (Ops) had been fobbed off that Grantmore's arrest had been down to informant information and was just a fishing trip and so far the team were keeping tight-lipped about the photograph. But that situation wouldn't last. Northumbria had no exciting developments, with their major incident still getting up to speed with lots to do but no leads.

And now the whole saga of Holland wounding Grantmore was back to haunt me – but now with a fucking journalist aware of the truth.

It was not the moment to figure out how to proceed. The priority was getting Wilde calmed down – even if not fully back onside. I spent the next half-hour reassuring him that he'd done the right thing and there was no way I would not be tackling Holland and continuing to try and get Morley to commit to giving evidence. I could sense that the very act of unburdening himself had helped. Perhaps he now saw that matters were in official hands. I repeatedly thanked him for warning me about Holland and also promised him that he would get the scoop when the cases were resolved – which I repeatedly assured him they would be.

I decided to call it a day. I was mentally exhausted. It was the weekend and we were now at the stage where only a skeleton staff were keeping the incident ticking over until Monday. I was aware the twenty-four-hour deadline Grantmore and I had agreed was fast approaching, but I was in no state to make any decisions. I prayed he wouldn't contact me.

I needed time to think.

Surely nothing else could go wrong?

Seventeen

Cheryl tenderly spread more baby oil across the broad shoulders of her ten-thirty appointment and sensually yet firmly began to massage it in, occasionally leaning forward to gently rub her naked breasts on his warm skin. Normally by this stage in a "massage", the punter was keen to roll over and get on with the "extras", but this guy seemed about to nod off. Cheryl would usually relish the prospect of an easy half-hour with no sex involved, but the rent was due and she was skint, so she bent lower, whispering in what she thought was her sexy voice, 'Is that making you feel good, luvvie? Do you want me to do your chest now?'

There was no response. She carried on for another five minutes, with increasingly less enthusiasm. She may as well have been polishing a car bonnet. She finished with a gentle slap on the man's shoulders. 'That's your lot, sunshine.'

There was no attempt at the sexy voice. Again, there was no response. The man just lay still, breathing steadily with his eyes closed.

'Come on, love, time's up. Put your clothes on. Me eleven o'clock'll be joining us in a minute if you don't move.'

Cheryl slipped into her pink beautician's smock, beginning to feel slightly uneasy about how this was going. She chuckled, trying to lighten the situation while giving the man a gentle nudge. There was still no response.

Shrugging her shoulders, she left the naked man lying there, his well-toned body glistening under the harsh glare of the very unsexy strip light above the massage table. Leaving the room, she quietly closed the door behind her and entered the reception area, quickly explaining the situation to her mate Pauline. Cheryl's eleven o'clock customer couldn't help hearing what was said and slowly rose from the scruffy leather sofa where he had been impatiently and excitedly waiting his turn and scuttled off down the stairs. As the local ward councillor, the last thing he wanted was to be involved in an incident in the local knocking shop.

'That's more cash down the pissin' drain,' grumbled Cheryl, watching her next customer scarper.

'I reckon we've got a nutter. Where's Grantmore when you need him?' Pauline reached for the phone and dialled the sister establishment on Witham and was soon explaining their predicament to the boss.

*

Fifteen minutes later, an agitated Grantmore bounded up the stairs to find Pauline and Cheryl sitting side by side on the sofa, nestled amongst the pink fluffy cushions enjoying a cup of tea. He looked at them expectantly.

'He's gone then?'

Pauline was well used to her boss's temper and was hardly fazed by his rants and threats after almost seven years in his employment, so she'd persuaded Cheryl they should make best use of this unexpected lull in trade and enjoy a nice cuppa.

'Nope, he's still there. Not moved a muscle.' She slurped on her tea. 'And don't go mad at us. You always say any trouble and we should fetch you... so we 'ave.'

Their boss was feeling extremely stressed. He had heard no more from Paul Frame and it was now 11am, so he was likely to call at any minute. He strode purposefully to the door and without entering, flung it open. The girls leaned forward to look into the room through the gap between Grantmore and the doorjamb, but all they could see were the soles of the man's feet hanging over the end of the massage table, toes pointing towards the pink shag pile. He still hadn't moved.

Thinking the man had died mid-massage, Grantmore groaned at the thought of all the questions the bloody police would ask. So his immediate reaction was not to wade in aggressively as he normally would with a troublesome punter – of which there were many. He entered the room and repeated what Cheryl had done about half an hour earlier – he gave the man a gentle nudge on the shoulder.

'You okay, mate?'

After a five-second pause, the man steadily pushed his head and torso off the massage table and then swung himself into a sitting position facing Grantmore, who instinctively stepped back, catching the backs of his legs against the couch, causing him to flop back clumsily into it. The girls on the landing were also caught unawares and jerked backwards, with Cheryl smacking her head into Pauline's, causing her to spill her tea into her lap and yelp.

The customer glanced to his right at the sound and firmly but politely asked the girls to close the door. Cheryl jumped up and did as she was told. Her last sight before doing so was of Grantmore slouched on the sofa, with his mouth hung open and his one working eye wide with shock. She beckoned Pauline and both listened at the door.

The man remained sitting on the massage table, seemingly unembarrassed by his nakedness, and looked down at Grantmore, who remained slumped in the couch staring up at Paul Frame.

'Morning, Sean. Thought I'd come down for a chat rather than ring. I always think a personal call is better. I can look you in the eye... no offence mate... and make sure you get the message.'

He bounced lightly off the table and stood in front of Grantmore, his six-foot-three-inch, broad-shouldered nakedness adding to the intimidating nature of the unexpected meeting.

'Brought you a little something just to make sure you don't let me down. You sounded slightly apprehensive about working for me yesterday when we spoke.'

He padded around the head of the table and briefly bent over the chair where he had left his clothes. When Frame turned and walked back to him, Grantmore saw that he was holding a handgun, his arm slack so that the gun pointed unthreateningly towards the floor. Grantmore stared at the gun, convinced he was about to be executed yet unable to move or speak.

Frame positioned himself directly in front of Grantmore, who remained slumped on the worn coach, his eye transfixed by the gun. He hadn't noticed that in Frame's left hand, there was a fat brown envelope and when the gang boss tossed it into his lap, he jerked upright with shock.

'Five grand... as promised. Count it while I get dressed.'

He tossed the gun onto the couch next to Grantmore, walked back to his clothes, and began dressing with his back turned.

Grantmore looked into the envelope and saw the money, looked at the gun, looked at the money, back at the gun and then at Frame's broad muscled back. He quietly put the envelope down on the floor, quickly picked up the gun and curled his finger around the trigger. He didn't want any more of Frame's cash or any more involvement in his crimes, however lucrative they'd been. There was no way he was going to die in his own premises. He was in charge here.

'Heavy, isn't it?'

Grantmore almost pulled the trigger; he was that startled. Frame hadn't even turned round but was standing looking out onto Spring Bank while buttoning up his shirt, Grantmore's reflection visible in the window.

'Very noisy too and actually not that accurate even at this range… unless of course you're trained.' He bent to pull on his jeans.

Grantmore's resolve evaporated and he gently placed the gun back on the sofa. 'I … I was… I was just feeling its weight. I've never used a gun.'

'Then you definitely shouldn't point one at someone's back'.

Frame fastened his belt, picked up his shoes and socks and walked over to the sofa. He picked up the gun and handed it back to Grantmore, before sitting next to him and starting to put on his socks and shoes.

Grantmore let the gun lie in his lap, his hands useless. The realisation that Frame, by this bizarre intimidation, now held full sway over him chilled him to the core. Used to being the intimidator himself, the truth of his situation was all the more frightening. The ruined socket of his missing eye began to itch uncontrollably and he tenderly rubbed his knuckle into it, trying to lessen the feeling but at the same time giving himself something to do. He didn't know how to react to Frame, what to say or do.

His shoes tied, Frame again stood up, picked up the gun from Grantmore's lap and pushed it into the rear of his trousers beneath the hem of his smart tweed jacket.

'Five grand, Sean. For the last job, like I promised. And

we'll forget the rest of your loan. Now let's go get a drink and discuss what you're going to do to earn it.'

He opened the door and walked into the reception area, where Pauline and Cheryl had just had time to get sat back on the sofa. He gave them a jaunty salute of goodbye. 'Ladies. Come on, Sean. Look sharp.'

As Frame trotted lightly down the stairs, Grantmore pushed himself out of the couch, across the landing, past his two employees and without a word followed him. He could only think of the expression "dead man walking".

Eighteen

Sean Grantmore was not a man used to feeling afraid. He was accustomed to stirring up that emotion in others – and enjoying the power it gave him.

When he'd first met Frame, he'd regarded the public schoolboy turned criminal as a toffee-nosed joke but inexplicably grew to be more and more proud to share his criminal know-how with him. Little by little, as he revealed his army background and own expertise, Frame had exerted subtle intimidation until their respective positions were reversed. Grantmore grew to feel like the hired hand of a professional criminal. He found himself following Frame's orders and getting involved in a type of crime that, even before the murder of Emmerson, could attract a life sentence. Owing Frame a large amount of money freaked him out further, and the threats he had made today were no longer even veiled.

Then there was Holland. Initially, his acquittal of the rape had boosted his confidence and enhanced his local reputation, but he knew that it must have been his victim's father that had disfigured and blinded him. Having Russ Holland still walking the streets of Hull was terrifying – the man was bloody deranged. What might he do next? He had resolved to strike back against Russ Holland and had even contemplated involving Frame but realised that would put him even deeper in his debt.

Now he had Darnley threatening to expose him as a grass.

Upon leaving the massage parlour, Frame had walked him casually along Spring Bank to the Polar Bear where over a pint he had explained the type of job he wanted Grantmore to set up next. To further complicate matters, Frame had instructed him to find them a driver for the job. Someone who would follow orders, keep their hands to themselves and keep their mouths shut – unlike Emmerson. Frame left him in no doubt as to what would happen to him if he refused to cooperate by referring to Emmerson in his usual calm manner, which made the implied threat all the more menacing. He told him that this was to be his last crime, after which he would leave the country. He knew Frame's purpose in disclosing his intention to quit was to reassure him that after this last job his debt was paid and he was off the hook. What it actually did was convince him that he'd be dead before Frame had even packed his bags. He doubted that any driver he supplied would live to tell the tale either.

Frame left the pub after an hour, telling Grantmore he wanted to move things forward and he had ten days to find a new target and a driver. After he'd left, Sean sat and seethed. Terrified but angry. Frustrated and ashamed. Was Darnley his only way out? How could he use him to free himself from Frame and not end up looking over his shoulder for the rest of his life?

He knew he needed to transfer his gut-wrenching fear onto someone else. He needed a woman. He stood, drained his pint and strode from the pub, meeting the gaze of those lunchtime drinkers who knew who he was and were keen to nod their acknowledgments to one of Hull's hard men. Just being recognised in this manner boosted his self-esteem a notch and spurred him on to boost it further, in the way he so often did.

He hailed a taxi and three or four minutes later, opposite Nicole's, he peeled a twenty-pound note off his usual wedge of cash and shoved it into the cabby's hand, telling him to keep the change. He was now buzzing with anticipation. Only yesterday, Janine had brought in a young girl from Withernsea, needing to work in one of his parlours to feed her heroin habit – bit skinny because of the drugs but pretty enough to keep the middle-aged punters happy. He planned to use her to replace Marilyn, who was well past her sell-by date. Well, she certainly would be by the time he'd finished with her. No point taking his anger out on the fresh stock; plenty of time for the new girl when she'd settled in. He laughed to himself, proud of his business sense and with his fear now submerged beneath a thin veneer of anger and lust.

As he stepped out of the taxi, a strange noise intruded into his reverie. It stopped but then started again as he strode across the road towards Nicole's. Reaching the footpath outside his premises, he glanced back to where the taxi was just pulling away and caught a brief glimpse of a figure retreating rapidly into the mouth of an alleyway, close to where he had alighted from the taxi. The person disappeared but pointing towards him and clearly visible was the large zoom lens of a camera. Someone was taking photos of him – that's what he'd heard. He checked the road and strode rapidly across towards the alleyway. The camera lens withdrew slowly into the shadows as he drew closer.

Behind the camera, Graham Morley began to shake, and backed further into the gloom of the alleyway. Still viewing the world through his Canon, he unthinkingly continued to capture the unfolding events.

Grantmore's fear, frustration, anger and shame also clouded his judgement. All thoughts of taking it out on Marilyn were instantly forgotten. His emotions funnelled towards the bastard who was taking photographs of him. Adrenaline ruled his actions. No pause to think and reason; he just knew it must be connected to the arrogant bastard who had put him into this state of high anxiety. Anger gained supremacy over his other emotions. He'd show Frame. No one pushes Sean Grantmore around. Fear was forgotten and retribution was due.

Through the camera, Morley saw Grantmore enter the alley and move towards him with that sense of purpose displayed in his face and his movements. He kept firing off shots as he retreated but made no attempt to try and escape. It was as if he'd always known this moment had to come and he wished only to record it. His mind was as blank as Grantmore's. As his back came up against a wall where the alley turned at right angles, he stopped and lowered the camera.

His pursuer also stopped and looked at the insignificant weasel of a man that he knew Frame must have sent to try and spook him further. With a bellow of rage, he rushed at the much smaller man and with a sideswipe knocked the camera out of his hands. It swung on its strap over Morley's left shoulder and clattered against the alley wall. He then thumped a petrified Morley hard in the stomach and as he doubled over in pain, he drove his right knee up into his face, grabbing him at the same time and flinging him to the left, deeper into the alley behind the shops and thus out of sight of potential witnesses.

Morley landed hard on all fours, his camera swinging and scraping on the ground. Grantmore kicked him forward, flat onto the floor and Morley's chest collided solidly with the camera, breaking a couple of his ribs on his left side. He instinctively rolled onto his undamaged right side and came to rest leaning with his back against the wall of the alley, looking up at the man who had for so long haunted his thoughts.

Grantmore kicked him hard in the stomach and when he curled to protect himself, he stamped down on him, inflicting further damage to his chest, and followed with a vicious kick to his face. Still wedged against the wall, Morley watched as Grantmore bent his knees and leaned in close.

'Tell Frame he can fuck off. No one pushes Sean Grantmore around. Did you get that, you puny little runt.'

He rose and again kicked out into the bloody pulp of Morley's face and gave a final stamp on his head before spitting between his eyes. 'Got it? Tell the bastard to fuck off.'

He roughly pulled the expensive camera from around Morley's neck and then walked off, swinging it by his side.

Morley's bitter last thought before he passed out was that Grantmore didn't even know who he was.

Still seething with rage, Grantmore strode across to his business. He was buzzed inside by Marilyn and gained the sanctity of his office. By sheer fluke, there were no witnesses to what had just occurred, and Marilyn was too busy painting her nails to spot his bloodstained boots and shirt. She never even looked up, oblivious to his flushed face, agitation, still pulsing anger and the camera – blissfully unaware of how close she had been to falling foul of his violence that she had suffered so often in the past.

He fell into his office chair, chest heaving with emotion as adrenaline coursed through his body. He pulled a bottle of Jim Beam from his desk drawer and with a shaking hand swallowed straight from the bottle. The alcohol calmed him, and his judgement slowly ebbed back into his consciousness. What the fuck had he done? Two hours ago, he had thought he was a dead man walking – now he'd just dug his own grave.

Remorse never entered his head. The possibility that the attack may have been witnessed was not considered. His total focus was on his deepening predicament as the realisation slowly dawned that as soon as Frame knew he'd attacked his hired hand, he'd come for him. Further slugs of whisky followed, slowly dulling his rampant fear until he realised what he had to do. The man must not report back. Then Frame would have no reason to think he had crossed him – just another unreliable gang member going missing.

He had to finish the bloke off.

He knew that he'd left him unconscious and badly injured. Only about ten minutes had passed. He had to act quickly. No time to think. He shoved Morley's Canon into the back of a filing cabinet – he'd get rid of it later. Then he entered the small cloakroom that adjoined his office, washed his face and hands, wiped his boots with the towel and changed his shirt. He shoved the bloodstained shirt and soiled towel into the same cabinet. He breathed deeply to calm himself while staring at his reflection in the mirror, telling himself to act and take the initiative. Just minutes later, fully psyched-up, he was back in the alley, this time taking more effort to slip in unnoticed. Marilyn had hardly glanced up from her manicure. He stood over Morley's inert form and prodded him in the chest with his foot to confirm that he was still unconscious and unlikely to rouse. Where the hell could he hide him? There was no way he could move him far in the middle of the day. He moved further into the alley and pushed through a six-foot-high gate that opened into the back yard of a kebab shop that only opened in the evenings. A large green industrial-sized waste skip was all that occupied a surprisingly clean and tidy yard. He pushed back the lid and was dismayed to find it almost full, until he realised there'd be enough room to hide the body beneath the rubbish. He could return that night and sort out a more permanent disposal. Returning to the alley, he grabbed Morley's ankles and dragged him into the yard, closing the gate behind him while confirming he was not overlooked.

His confidence returning, he looked down at what he now regarded as little more than a nuisance. If Grantmore would ever have recognised Graham Morley from their school days, he certainly couldn't now. His face was just a distorted bloodstained mush. He stepped close to Morley's head and raised his right leg above his face, ready to stamp and finish him off. He paused and considered finding another weapon, as this would clearly mean having to get rid of an expensive and fairly new pair of boots. Then he saw that both boots were already stained with smeared blood, despite his efforts with the towel. He shrugged and started stamping.

Grantmore had committed many acts of violence and it was more by luck than judgement that he had never killed anyone before. He had given people worse beatings than he had given Morley in the alleyway, and they'd lived. So he had never considered that Morley was already dead before this final onslaught. He was just wasting energy.

Nineteen

Marjorie Priestley was a very fastidious woman and expected her husband Noel to comply with the house rules she had imposed during their thirty-eight-year marriage. So when she awoke that morning at 8.30am and went downstairs for her breakfast, she expected, as usual, to find her husband's breakfast pots neatly stacked next to the sink, not still on the table. Marjorie stood in the kitchen doorway surveying a half-eaten bowl of cereal and an almost full mug of tea on the table, sitting on the placemats she insisted Noel always use. She tutted her displeasure and surveyed the kitchen for other transgressions. Noel's failures to follow her rules were rare and although she never even acknowledged it to herself, this was a disappointment. Noel acting out of character was something she could get her teeth into. Something to berate and belittle him about. A minor frisson of excitement in her dull and dry-as-dust marriage. When she spotted the cereal packet on the worktop instead of in the cupboard and the tea towel alongside it, not neatly spread on the towel rail, she tutted again and started to plan her errant husband's reception when he returned home after work from the building society.

Sweeping up the bowl and mug as she strode into her domain, she felt a draught from the back door and to her absolute amazement saw that it was slightly ajar. She pulled her quilted pale blue nylon housecoat more tightly across her skinny frame, pulled the door fully open and peered out into the back garden, which was covered in a thick white frost. Surely Noel had left for work? It was his first day back after a minor heart attack brought on by stress after the robbery at the building society in December. He was always gone by 8.00am, convinced of the absolute necessity of him being at his office desk by 8.30am so that as the staff at the building society arrived for work they would see him there and recognise he was in charge; keener and more dedicated than them and thus indispensable. Marjorie never ever got up when he did, nor prepared his breakfast nor joined him for the first meal of the day. She would lie awake in bed, listening to him shower and shave in the en-suite and dream of the day she would wake up and he'd be gone. She'd long ago worked out that him leaving her, or vice versa, was no good, as along that route there was no life insurance payout, no half of his generous pension and the big detached house would have to be sold and shared. Why, oh why did his recent heart attack have to be minor? Just her bloody luck. But he had gone back to work today despite his doctor's advice. Maybe he'd drop dead at his desk – this week if at all possible! Each and every morning, she dreamed about how wonderful life would be without the pompous little bastard.

How dare he leave the door open in the winter? That was one of his rules. How often did he rattle on about the energy bills? Telling her to wear a jumper when she asked for the heating on. As his retirement approached, he would endlessly reiterate how they would need to tighten their belts and she should get used to it now. She knew he would receive a handsome pension, and his shrewd investments and years of his parsimony meant they were already very comfortable and would continue to be so. The only luxuries allowed in the Priestley household were those required for show. A new car – for him – every year. An annual holiday – chosen by him – selected to allow him to lord it over his staff.

'Noel. Noel. What are you doing?' she shouted out into the garden.

She assumed that there was a problem with the new Volvo and he had left the door open while in and out to the garage. She realised she had the opportunity to admonish him now – why wait until tonight?

'Noel. You've left the back door wide open.'

She pulled her anorak on over her housecoat, slipped her feet into her gardening shoes and still tutting, trotted round the back of the house to the double detached garage. She expected to see the Volvo on the drive and Noel defrosting the windows or something and, although very cold, she was burning with the thrill of berating him for his tardiness in the kitchen, and especially for the open door.

As she opened the side gate alongside the garage, which gave access to the front drive, she could hear the idling engine of the car. Ensuring her face bore a suitable scowl of indignation, she burst onto the drive ready to start her day with points scored over her pious, penny-pinching, pompous pillock of a husband.

But the car wasn't there and neither was Noel. The double garage doors were closed and when she tried them, locked. She could, however, hear the car engine from inside. She walked back through the gate and tried the side door of the garage, finding it unlocked. The garage was in darkness so she turned on the fluorescent strip light and quickly took in the scene. Her husband was sitting slumped in the driver's seat of his two-month-old metallic gold Volvo, which was full of thick white clouds of exhaust fumes. A hosepipe ran from the exhaust pipe into the front passenger side window.

Marjorie's anger rapidly dissipated. She was transfixed in the doorway of the garage, her hand still on the light switch as her mind assimilated what she was seeing. Then she burst into immediate action.

She switched off the light and shut the garage door, quietly closed the side gate and returned to the kitchen. She tidied away Noel's pots, put the kettle on and sat and looked at the kitchen clock, working out the optimum time she should leave before going to the garage and finding her husband dead – and presumably finding the note explaining why he had decided to kill himself.

*

Just as Marjorie's kettle boiled, Janice Cooper collected her post off the front doormat at her bungalow in Atwick, carried it through to the kitchen and placed it on the tray that she had just prepared with breakfast. She climbed the stairs carefully, balancing the tea and toast on the tray and calling, 'Sit up, lazy bones, here it comes.'

Constable 1471 Harry Willis stretched luxuriously under the Laura Ashley quilt. The same quilt upon which he and Janice had first "embraced" as he saved her life. He pulled himself up into a seated position, plumped up the matching pillows and smiled broadly as Janice entered the bedroom.

'Morning, gorgeous,' he grinned.

'Granary, real butter and marmalade... just as you like it,' beamed Janice as she placed the tray on Harry's lap before tenderly kissing his forehead.

It was only about ten short weeks since Harry had found Janice bound and gagged in this very room. In those weeks, Harry had told Janice, at least a hundred times, that she had saved his life just as surely as he had hers. In the days following his rescue, the force press liaison officer had literally pushed the two of them into each other's arms – staging good-news stories at the demand of the Chief, who was beside himself with delight at the success of his idea. Janice and Harry had needed little encouragement. Harry initially loved the idea of being a hero, ignoring the jibes of his colleagues and concentrating instead on the plaudits from his neighbours, the milkman, at the newspaper shop, the Co-op – all those who'd seen him on the news. He soon grew to enjoy hugging this plump, homely woman with such an indomitable spirit. Expecting her to be physically and mentally shattered by her ordeal, Harry had been amazed to see her shrug it off, overcome by an overwhelming gratitude to have survived. Janice was the best therapy he could have ever had. If a middle-aged woman who had always been alone could possess the strength of character to overcome such an awful experience, surely he could shake off his years of despondency and uselessness.

For Janice, it was much simpler. This man had saved her for a purpose. It was obvious. It was meant to be. He was *the one*. She knew the initial hugs were stage-managed and he was only doing what he was told by his bosses. But she hugged him for longer than was strictly necessary and he soon began to squeeze back in equal measure. As Christmas approached, they had their first night out and agreed they were officially dating. By mid-January, he had moved in. Janice had decided to exorcise the demons of her ordeal and her former lonely existence by declaring the upstairs "guest" bedroom as *their* bedroom. It gave her immense pleasure to think that this lovely man made that cold, inhospitable room the warmest in the house.

She climbed into bed beside Harry and they shared the pot of tea and toast, while she opened the post. Suddenly with a gasp her hand flew to her mouth and she thrust the letter she'd just read into his lap.

Harry saw it was a handwritten letter on the headed notepaper of the Hardstone Building Society.

7 February 1999

Dear Janice,

I cannot live with the shame of what I have put you and Anne through. It is my fault that those evil criminals knew you two had the keys. It is my failure to institute adequate security precautions that led them to your door and you having to suffer as you did. Anne is quite rightly seeking compensation from the Society and I know the Board will agree, pay her and see that the fault lies entirely with me. After such a long career with the Society, I cannot face the humiliation that will surely follow my censure. I know I am not popular at work or within the wider organisation and would be unable to bear the glee with which many will greet my disgrace. I have sent you this letter as I feel you alone at the Society do not judge me and may feel some sorrow at the misfortunes I have suffered in this affair. I needed a sympathetic audience for this message.

The police will need to see it.

Please try and forgive me.

Yours Faithfully
Noel Priestley
Manager

Harry's somewhat inadequate police brain took in the first class stamp on the envelope and the previous day's date at the head of the letter.

'That's nice of him, Janice. He clearly likes you. Okay, it's taken him a couple of months to say so but at least he's said sorry. He's ruddy upset about it all, though. I reckon he's going to resign.'

He turned to smile at his bedfellow, who still had her hand over her mouth and was shaking her head violently at a now somewhat bemused Harry.

'It's a suicide note,' she groaned.

Harry rapidly reread it.

'It's not… is it?'

'He could never say such things and face Anne and me again. I know him. I think he's killed himself… or is planning to.'

'But it's more like a business letter. It's so formal.'

Janice jumped out of bed. She had just noticed the date on the letter.

'Quick. Ring the police. Alert somebody.'

For the second time in those few short weeks, Harry leapt into action.

*

On this occasion, however, the newly decisive and confident PC Harry Willis was too late.

I had just arrived at Driffield with the resolve to contact Grantmore. Our agreed twenty-four-hour deadline was long passed. I hadn't rung him, as I was still trying to figure out how to proceed without agreeing to his proposal. I was surprised that he hadn't got in touch, demanding an answer, but assumed it was pure brinksmanship. My second job was to get hold of Russ Holland and warn him off but for the life of me, I couldn't think of the best way to approach him, or anticipate how he'd react. My third priority was keeping the ambitious reporter onside, and finally there was Anne Beedham. What a bloody morning I was in for.

Before I could even get my coat off, Tony Ride burst into my office.

'We've got another body, boss,' he bluntly declared with a most inappropriate grin on his face.

My immediate and horrified reaction was that Holland had got Grantmore.

The DS, keen to keep centre stage, paused for dramatic effect, only adding to my tension.

After what seemed like an age, he announced, 'Noel Priestley.'

My relieved brain flicked rapidly through its filing cabinets. This incident now had a nominal index of over 2,000 people and I could never remember them all. But the outstanding action to re-interview the building society manager when he recovered, emerged from the morass.

'Suicide by hosepipe from the exhaust… in his garage. His missus found him about an hour ago,' Ridey blundered unfeelingly on.

My brain was now fully engaged. The cogs were whirring. 'So that's where our leak about the keys came from.'

I'd remembered DI Baldwin's report and the "loose end" of the manager. I had quickly added two and two and made ten.

'My thoughts exactly… but read the suicide note.'

I saw he was holding a sheet of paper, which he explained was a faxed copy of the original, which had been posted to Janice Cooper at her home address. The actual letter was in the hands of the officers investigating what would, at this moment, be classed as a suspicious death. They had soon realised the potential link to our job when they spoke to Mrs Priestley and had promptly faxed us a copy. It would be down to that investigation, a coroner and an inquest before a suicide could be formally determined.

'I've read the incident log and the post was delivered at about 7.45am this morning. Janice Cooper opened the letter at about 8.30am and… wait for it… PC Harry. Bloody. Windy. Willis rings it in at 8.35am. He just happened to be calling on Janice, checking on her welfare, according to his account. He's giving her one, boss… the old sod. Who'd have thought?'

Briefly acknowledging the likelihood of such a liaison, I focussed upon the content of the note. We then discussed its strange nature and likely implications. We agreed that he was most unlikely to have killed himself just because he had dropped a bollock with the security arrangements and concluded he was now our best bet for the inside leak. But why risk everything? A share of the proceeds? Or coercion? What was his connection to the robbers? Was the heart attack real? I instructed Tony to get hold of DI Baldwin and fast-track the actions necessary. This was surely another break and I wanted forward momentum.

Rereading the letter, it suddenly struck me how I could perhaps use it to resolve at least one of my dilemmas. This morning's lowest priority became my first. I grabbed my coat and after telling Tony I'd be in Beverley for an hour, I drove to the building society. It was obvious as I walked in and introduced myself that the news about their boss had not yet reached them, and now with the element of surprise, I asked to speak to Anne Beedham. A young lady from the counter rang her and then showed me into a small interview room usually reserved for customers seeking a mortgage.

It had clearly been Anne Beedham's tactic to try and discomfort me by keeping me waiting – or maybe she had just wanted to freshen up her hair and make-up. After about five minutes, she burst into the room. Full of anger and righteous indignation, she still managed to look damned attractive. Momentarily, I thought of Granger's escapades with envy.

'At last! Supercop actually finds time to speak to me. No pretty little messenger today then?'

She fixed me with an icy glare and remained standing; hands on her hips. In this small room, this meant she was only about three feet away, and her fresh spray of perfume was a bit too strong. It was obvious the outrage was an act and that my letter, delivered by DC Young, had worked; she was expecting me to eat humble pie and then sweet-talk her – and whatever else.

Well, I too can act. I looked shamefully at the floor and shook my head, as if about to embark on the first stage of my act of contrition. As I looked up, she took her hands off her hips and folded them purposefully under her bosom, using her hips to swing her weight from one foot to the other, the black stiletto-heeled shoe of the leading right foot softly tapping the carpeted floor in a gesture of annoyance and impatience. She looked bloody magnificent.

'Mrs Beedham, lovely to see you again and don't worry, we will discuss your relationship with PC Granger in a moment—'

She interrupted me angrily: 'Relationship! It was not a relationship! He was abusing his position. I want him sacked and if you—'

It was now my turn to interrupt. 'I could of course say it takes two to tango.'

I held up my hand to stem another outraged outburst and continued: 'Before we discuss PC Granger, I want to discuss some developments in the inquiry that concern you. It is important, so please just concentrate on this before we turn to Granger.' I motioned to her to take the other seat.

She was intrigued. Bit her tongue and did as I had bid.

'Are you in the process of seeking compensation from the building society for your ordeal?'

'I am indeed,' she replied indignantly, but looking puzzled at the direction of the conversation. 'Those bastards should never have known to have come to mine, or Janice's house for the keys. Your DI Baldwin even had the temerity to suggest I had something to do with it. My family and I have been traumatised and I think compensation is appropriate.'

'So you think it is the building society's fault?'

'Most certainly. Specifically Mr Priestley's fault. I told him that I was holding him personally responsible and surprise, surprise, he feigns a heart attack the very next day... and he's still off sick. I've worked here longer than he has and I know several of the board members. I've no doubt they will support my claim, as the security arrangements were pathetic... just like him.'

'Well, he has certainly taken personal responsibility.' I paused – purely for dramatic effect. 'He killed himself this morning.'

She just sat there, her eyes wide open with shock.

'I'm sorry to bring you such sad news but in view of the apparent motive behind his suicide and thus your potential role as a witness at his inquest, I thought you had a right to know as soon as possible.'

I leant across the small table and took both her hands in mine, giving them a comforting squeeze. 'He left a note and it spells out how badly he felt about what happened to you and Janice. He couldn't live with it.'

I took the folded note from out of my jacket pocket purely as a prop. I had no intention of showing her the letter, as it was clearly open to interpretation, but as soon as she saw it, she burst into tears.

'No. No, I don't want to see it.'

Needless to say, I did my duty and put a comforting arm around her and made all the right noises about how she shouldn't blame herself. I slipped in how his suicide, if indeed that was what the coroner's court determined, would surely help her compensation claim. When I asked if Janice was also seeking compensation, she sobbed even harder, then admitted that Janice felt no ill will towards the Society or Noel Priestley.

She asked a little about what would happen at the inquest and enquired after Mr Priestley's wife, and I could tell that she was already shelving the compensation claim. Her guilt would not allow her to continue. Once that point had been reached, I began to tackle the real reason for my visit.

'Anyway, Mrs Beedham, on to other matters. The police inquiry into poor Mr Priestley's death will continue and the inquest process will be a few months away yet. But what are we going to do about PC Granger? I can't believe how many casualties the robbery here has caused. It's a tragedy.'

'I can't think about that now. I'm too upset.'

'I'm sorry but I need to take some action *now*. I'll need a full statement, as there will be a disciplinary hearing and he'll most likely be sacked for taking advantage of you in this manner.' I shook my head, showing my distaste at his behaviour.

The next stage in my strategy was to ask if her husband knew about her fling with the young PC, as he was now bound to find out. Before I had to go that far, she stood up and with a touch of her old spirit said, 'Forget it. I've had enough. It was my fault as much as his... more. My God, what a mess. Tell him I'm sorry.' Then she broke down all over again.

Twenty minutes later, I left the building after informing a gathering of the staff of their boss's death. One of my problems was now behind me and I almost felt sorry for Anne Beedham. I drove back to Driffield wondering when and how to break the good news to young Granger.

Twenty

10:15 That Same Morning

The initial surge of satisfaction provided by exacting revenge had long since dissipated and Russ Holland was now consumed by the same feelings of anger, frustration and powerlessness as when his daughter first told him about being raped. He'd experienced the self-same pain when Grantmore was acquitted. The action necessary in planning and executing his attack on the man responsible had cooled those emotions. But the relief lasted only days and the same feelings soon bubbled up again.

They were raised to boiling point when he and Lisa were arrested.

His state of mind was damaged further when he realised that she was horrified to even contemplate that her father had committed such an act and he was thankful that he had never admitted it, even to her. When he was not charged, she seemed eager to believe his explanation that a criminal rival must have blinded Grantmore using the publicity surrounding the rape trial as a smokescreen. He'd argued that it was obvious that even Detective Superintendent Darnley and DC Young did not believe he was behind the attack.

In the days that followed their arrest, Lisa seemed to make great strides in her recovery. She was seeing a counsellor and was now refusing to allow herself to become a victim. She had gone back to her sixth-form studies and was slowly but surely regaining her confidence and previous *joie de vivre*.

There was no such improvement for Russ Holland. All the feelings now enveloping him he had experienced before, and he was terrified about sliding back into the long, dark months after the Falklands War. His daughter knew nothing about his life as a Para and his previous identity that Graham Morley had uncovered. She had been born to Russ Holland, the Hull-based self-employed electrician. Like so many war veterans, Holland had developed post-traumatic stress disorder shortly after being lauded for his act of bravery. When his wife, Caroline, found she was pregnant, they decided to relocate and start a new life, with new names, in Kingston upon Hull. The birth of Lisa, a pink and chubby bundle of joy, acted as the final antidote to the fear and horror he had endured, and lifted the terrors that gripped him. Caroline had been killed in a car crash when Lisa was only three, and Russ had never seen a reason to burden his beloved daughter with his past life. The responsibility of bringing his daughter up alone had somehow kept his demons at bay, but now they were fast encroaching into his life again and he couldn't extricate himself.

He was neglecting his successful business and losing money fast, as he sat for long hours, motionless, thinking, scheming and plotting. This time, his pink bundle of joy was unable to break the spell. He had tried to tell himself that Lisa was recovering, she was going to be okay, she was moving on. But nothing would work for him. In his heart, he knew that the only way of breaking this downward spiral was by exacting retribution. He craved revenge. He was not even sure if Grantmore's conviction for the rape would have secured that – but that chance was lost. He had believed that the symbolic destruction of his eye would have been enough but here he was, less than four weeks after his attack, back at square one. He wanted – needed – to kill him. Although it was obvious that Darnley had not pulled out all the stops to link him to the attack at Nicole's, he knew there would be no such grace if he killed him.

Desperate to find some way to alleviate his anguish, he had begun to watch Grantmore and learn his habits, haunts and acquaintances. He found it helped, and deep down knew it was the feeling of power, that at some point on one of his surveillances a perfect opportunity to kill him may present itself.

He had quickly identified Nicole's and Cleopatra's and then the new premises on Hessle Road he was developing for his third front for prostitution. He had tracked him to his home and assessed the layout of the house and gardens. He found he always used Lambert Taxis, had a gambling habit that he fed at Napoleon's Casino and used three pubs with distinct and separate circles of friends and acquaintances. Low-life criminals at the Earl de Grey on Waterhouse Lane close to the City centre, mates who supported Hull City at the Silver Cod on Anlaby Road and his non-criminal acquaintances at the Beech Tree, closer to his home.

On two occasions, he had come face-to-face with Grantmore and not once had the thug reacted. It was obvious that he did not remember him from their one and only meeting in Hull Crown Court. This angered him further. He needed Grantmore to know he was there. For him to recognise his suffering – and to know he was watching and waiting. He began to hatch a plan to confront the bastard and make sure he knew. That would be some form of mental release from his anguish, even if only temporarily.

He had no fears about Grantmore's reaction – he wanted one. He knew that for this tactic to work for him, he had to deliver the message face-to-face. But would Grantmore turn to the police? He couldn't risk their intervention again.

With a plan in his head for that confrontation, he was now on Hessle Road, across from the building that Grantmore was having renovated for his new business venture. Russ Holland was a self-employed electrician and in that capacity had a connection with many of the small building companies in and around Hull. He had learnt that J & S Renovations, a company he often worked with, were carrying out the conversions to the old shop that was soon to boast the name "Simone's Massage". As he watched, drinking a coffee from a nearby Greggs, he could see that Ken Johnson and Brian Standish were already there. Ken was unloading the van while Brian nipped across to Greggs. Holland knew from an overheard conversation between a boastful Grantmore and a young chap in the Beech Tree, a couple of nights ago, that Simone's was due to open in mid-April. He had also learnt that Grantmore did a site visit every Monday morning to discuss progress with Ken and Brian.

As he watched, he saw a Lambert's taxi pull up near the battered blue builder's van, and the focus of his hatred stepped from the rear and entered the building. He finished his drink while turning his face to the weak but bright wintry sun that shone from a perfectly blue sky and breathed steadily, pleased to feel the icy calm descend upon him just like when he was about to embark upon an operation in his old life. He tossed the paper cup into a nearby bin, crossed the busy road, pushed open the front door of the building and walked into what was clearly going to be the reception area of the new business.

The three men were engaged in conversation behind what would form the reception desk, with the plans of the renovation spread out before them. All three looked up as Holland entered.

Brian Standish walked from behind the counter, holding out his hand to shake Holland's, saying, 'Great timing, Russ. Mr Grantmore has only just arrived.'

'Hi, Russ. Hard luck, mate, you've just missed the bacon butties,' said Ken Johnson.

'Sean, this is Russ. He's come to have a look at doing the electrics on the job. He's popped by to give us a quote. Thought you might want to know who we're planning to subcontract it to.'

Holland was prepared for and had expected an immediate reaction from Grantmore, but it was obvious that he had not made the connection. By luck, Standish had not used his surname and he guessed the context of their meeting provided an initial camouflage.

Brian ushered Holland towards Grantmore as if they too should shake hands. He moved closer and faced Grantmore but did not offer his hand.

'Hello, Sean Grantmore.'

Grantmore looked perplexed at the man's strange use of his full name, direct glare and obvious reluctance to shake hands. There was still no recognition.

Brian and Ken were similarly confused at the electrician's manner. They only knew Russ Holland in his professional capacity and had no idea that he even had a daughter, let alone that they were renovating a building for her rapist. They knew exactly what they were building for Grantmore, and exactly who and what he was; but as far as they were concerned, he was just a paying customer.

'Are you happy for me to do this work for you, Mr Grantmore?'

'If the lads recommend you, I'm more than happy,' replied Grantmore, relieved that the bloke had got down to business.

'I always need work. If there's anything I can do for you at Nicole's or Cleopatra's... or for that matter at your home on Tranby Lane I'm your man. In actual fact, you could do with some extra security lighting at all three.'

Brian and Ken had moved slightly away while Grantmore and Holland chatted and were busy examining the next stage of the work.

Grantmore's brain synapses had started to fire. He had vaguely registered Holland's comments as meaning, "I know where you live". He was also processing the notion that he had met this man before, but a full interpretation of the situation had not yet fully formed.

'I heard about what happened to your face,' continued Holland in a friendly conversational tone. 'Do you know who did it? Must be a right nasty bastard. A nutcase.'

He moved forward and put his face closer to Grantmore's, invading his personal space as if to get a better look at the injury. 'Right fucking mess,' he concluded.

Grantmore began to react to what was obviously developing into a very strange confrontation. He put his hand on the electrician's chest and firmly pushed him back, out of his face. On the other side of the room, Brian and Ken became aware that the intended business meeting was developing into something altogether different and began to take an interest.

'I fucking know you...'

'I'm sure we can put all that behind us. Business is business after all. So no hard feelings between us then, Mr Grantmore,' smiled Russ Holland amiably.

Suddenly Grantmore made the connection.

'You fucking bastard,' he screamed, and launched himself at the man he was convinced had blinded him.

The two builders watched in amazement as Grantmore threw him to the ground, sat astride him and began raining blows to his face, causing blood to burst from Holland's nose. Before they could react, Grantmore jumped to his feet and kicked the prone and passive Holland several times to his body. He then stood back, panting, staring down at his victim who lay still.

Ken pulled out his mobile phone and punched in "999".

'You fucking bastard,' repeated Grantmore, breathing heavily, his fists clenched by his side. 'Who the fuck do you think you are, coming here?'

He launched a further kick, this time aimed at Holland's head.

The two builders would later describe to the police how Holland's hand shot out, grabbing Grantmore's inbound foot and twisting it so that Grantmore fell to the floor alongside him. They explained how, in fury, Grantmore once more sat astride the still prone Holland and began to throttle him. Their statements went on to outline how Holland never threw a punch or kick but in order only to protect himself, the electrician grabbed his attacker by the throat with his right hand and slowly forced him to his feet and against a wall. They were amazed that Grantmore seemed totally unable to continue his attack, turning limp and useless, while Holland was apparently effortlessly holding him firmly in place with one hand. They told how when Holland released the grip, Grantmore slid down the wall to sit slumped against it, panting for breath, only to resume his attack when he recovered. Again, Holland did not retaliate and the two builders had no choice but to restrain their employer while he struggled to get at Holland in a frenzy of shouting and swearing. It was only the sound of approaching police sirens that finally brought his aggression to a halt.

When a young PC walked into the room, the four men were now calm but the two builders were still hanging on to their captive, even though he had ceased to struggle. Russ Holland stood quietly trying to mop the blood away from his face with his handkerchief, although his nose was still bleeding heavily. Ken and Brian were both well-built and fit men and they had no trouble or qualms about manhandling Grantmore. Neither man was concerned about his criminal reputation as a hard man. They were Hull lads born-and-bred and moved in circles that would regard him as just a flash pimp and a bully. It was the nature and connections of the two builders that had led Holland to select them as the witnesses to his confrontation with Grantmore. He knew they would not be intimidated and would not be afraid to tell the truth about what happened. The phony tender to complete the electrics was a perfect opportunity to let Grantmore know he was watching him. That he was there. He wanted him scared, edgy and constantly looking over his shoulder.

He had not wanted or planned this police intervention and had been surprised at Grantmore's immediate violent reaction when he eventually recognised him. However, he had seen it as a possibility beforehand and had deliberately not fought back, using the choke hold not only to protect himself, but to illustrate to Grantmore how easy it would be to do him harm. Just doing something and evoking such an extreme reaction gave Holland some immediate relief. Grantmore was well and truly riled and he was sure that the two builders, who he had known for over ten years, would describe Grantmore as the aggressor and he would be unable to allege that Holland had in any way threatened or assaulted him.

Now that the police were involved, Russ thought he may as well gain another credible witness, so before the officer could even speak he held his arms outstretched, palms open in the universally accepted gesture of peace and reconciliation.

In a voice feigned to show his emotion at what had happened, he said, "Sean, there was no need for this, I just wanted the work. We have to move on.' He shook his head in dismay and went back to trying to stem the blood from his nose.

As he had hoped, Grantmore again went berserk, struggling against his captors and screaming blue murder. Ken and Brian renewed their efforts to hang on to the bloke who was, for a couple of months at least, paying their wages. How he was going to react to their restraint was weighing heavily on both their minds. Would they keep the contract? Ken, who was the "brains" in the partnership, decided that the cops were here now and unilaterally decided to let go. Brian was caught unawares and Grantmore pulled violently free only to crash into the officer, knocking him over into a filthy pile of brick and plaster rubble, his helmet dislodging and going skittering across the dirty concrete floor. The collision stilled Grantmore, and Brian finally let his grip relax as they watched the officer rise to his feet and assess the damage to his uniform.

The sound of another approaching siren – or it could have been the sight of his ruined uniform – galvanised the copper into action. He flung his right arm around Grantmore's neck, pulled him into a headlock and threw him to the floor, lying heavily across his chest while maintaining his hold.

'You're under arrest for assault.'

At this point, whether that was for assault upon himself, or Holland, no one knew.

Twenty-One

I had returned from my meeting with Mrs Beedham to the incident room and imparted the good news to an elated PC Granger that he was now off the hook for his unprofessional amorous liaison. I did not, of course, reveal how I had achieved this unexpected result; just that I had put myself at some risk in so doing. I told him that DC Young was taking over as the FLO. By any view, this was a great result and he did seem extremely grateful. I just hoped he was now even more reluctant to use the leverage he had over me around Morley and Holland. Always the poker player, however, he didn't reciprocate and let me know that I was off the hook.

I'd started my Monday morning with four pressing problems. I'd resolved one – the least pressing. Now I had to make inroads into the other three. "Operation Look After Darnley" had to make progress.

Where to start?

I had an ambitious newspaper reporter literally sitting on a career-making scoop – a Falkland's War hero living under a false identity mutilates the man acquitted of his daughter's rape, and a top cop fails to act on eyewitness testimony. He even had a follow-up story with the ex-Para now stalking the victim to finish him off. Thank God he didn't know about Morley's photographs. Although I thought he'd swallowed my lie about Morley refusing to give evidence, I couldn't imagine him sitting on the story for long. My promise to feed him stories he must now have seen as just minor titbits.

My first priority in trying to stop him exposing this saga was to stem Russ Holland's bloodlust. I had to warn Holland off and convince Wilde that Grantmore was safe. The longer I could stall Wilde, the harder it would be for him to ever use the story, as it would seem like he had colluded with me – which of course he had.

But let alone Wilde; how long could I rely on Morley's hatred of Grantmore and Granger's gratitude to me, for neither of them to expose my failings?

Self-preservation was undoubtedly my overriding priority, but the murder of the young man in the north-east and the potential links to my inquiry had increased the pressure not only on me as the SIO, but also on the force for progress. Due to the rarity of tiger kidnap offences, the National Criminal Intelligence Service (NCIS) had arranged to send officers to both incident rooms to make sure enquiries were effectively coordinated. Our arrest of Grantmore six days earlier, on the day Harrod was murdered, had sparked the interest of our ACPO team, who because of those added national pressures were pushing me ever harder for updates – and more detail. I now had little choice but to reveal the source of the photograph outside the Silver Cod, used to justify Grantmore's arrest, as I honestly believed, from Grantmore's reactions, that it was the key to opening up the two enquiries. I had to persuade Morley to step forward as a witness and explain why and when he had taken the photograph. In this way, the identification of Grantmore with the Vectra and the as yet unknown driver could enter the official evidence chain. This route obviously risked exposing my initial failings with

Morley, but I considered I could ride that lack of judgement – as long as the full story about the evidence in his files didn't come out. I was now pretty sure Granger would back me up. I'd considered meeting Morley personally, apologising for my earlier mistakes and seeking his cooperation but judged that Granger would have more success. Even if he did, I still had to hope that Morley's hatred of Grantmore would continue to override his public duty in relation to the photographs proving Holland mutilated him.

Having thus secured the witness introducing the photograph, I then intended to be open with NCIS and ACPO about Grantmore's arrest being an attempt to try and pressure him to inform on the man driving the Vectra, and who I was now assuming were his criminal associates from the north-east. I had also determined that I would admit "off-the-record" conversations with him – albeit somewhat sanitised versions – in which I had "threatened" to release the photo to the media to increase that pressure, and he had already clearly implied his involvement.

Although some of my fellow investigators and senior officers might feel my methods somewhat out-dated and ethically dubious, I doubted they would have a better idea. I expected them to discuss holding an identity parade for Janice Cooper to look at Grantmore, but from her brief description of the man with the car, it sounded much more like the tall, well-built man wearing the Sunderland scarf. It wasn't Grantmore, who was a good six inches smaller, and we'd also ruled out Emmerson. The reality was that there was no hard evidence to link Grantmore to the actual crimes and no easy legal and ethical way forward. The only suggestion I could make was to continue to exert any pressure we could summon to make him grass. Get that photo in the paper. They'd never agree.

What I had concluded was that I needed to get hold of Grantmore – today – and tell him our negotiations were at an end – from here on in, it was by the book. I couldn't afford to stick my neck out any further with this review of the inquiry approaching.

The bit I couldn't figure out was how to stop Russ Holland. I was toying with the idea of letting him know I knew his true identity, showing him the photographs Morley had taken and warning him off any further reprisals. I had even considered telling him I was close to linking Grantmore to the robberies and murders and he would soon get the sentence he deserved, so he had no reason for his personal vendetta. But in my heart, I knew he no longer trusted the legal process and was a complete loose cannon. I would be telling him too much for little practical purpose.

But I had to warn him off and reassure Wilde. How?

Not for the first time did I wish I had never gone to Hull Crown Court on that day, hoping to witness Grantmore get sent down for rape. I wished I'd never set eyes on Russ Holland – or whoever the hell he really was.

The small NCIS team were due in Humberside on Wednesday so I had two days to prepare. I resolved to have a final run through my plans, ensuring I had spotted all the pitfalls, loopholes and threats, while I ate my sandwiches. Then pitfalls, loopholes and threats or not, I would have to act.

*

I had no sooner bitten into my cheese and tomato sandwich than DS Ride again appeared at my office door. The bloke always seemed to be the one to deliver the "bombshells" – and this was his second of the day.

'Just had Detective Superintendent Kingston on the phone, boss. He asks that you ring him straight away. He sounded rather smug – smugger than bloody normal.

Apparently Sean Grantmore is in custody at Central on suspicion of an assault.'

Great. This at least saved me the bother of trying to track him down, and maybe a final chance to get him to grass the north-east gang before the forthcoming review. But Kingston's interest worried me.

'Who has he smacked this time? One of his girls?'

'Nope. Bit more interesting than that. Try again.'

'Stop pissing about, Sergeant. I'm not in the mood.'

'Sorry, boss,' he grinned, not looking the least bit sorry. 'He's smacked that bloke Holland... you know, the main suspect for blinding him... one of your rare failures... although no one thinks you tried too hard. Oh, and he's locked up as well for harassing Grantmore.'

My heart sank as my blood pressure rose.

Although Tony had not been involved in the investigation of the attack on Grantmore, most coppers based in and around Hull had heard the story of his acquittal for the rape, and then the attack on him a few weeks later. The manner of the attack was highly unusual and probably one of the all time top ten Hull black humour stories. General opinion was that Russ Holland must have done it – and should receive the Freedom of the City of Hull for his contribution to community life. Most of the discussions I'd heard, or had reported to me, judged that I had not tried too hard to detect the crime. Suited my ego. If only they knew. I was still bloody anxious that no one else did know, so I rang Kingston immediately after closing my office door.

Without exchange of pleasantries, Kingston explained what had happened at the building site on Hessle Road and how both men had been arrested. He took great delight in explaining how Grantmore was demanding to speak to me – privately – and threatening to go to the press about how I had failed to protect him from the man who had obviously blinded him and was still harassing him. The slimy bastard let me know that he had already briefed the ACC (Ops) about this latest incident due to the high level of media interest in the rape acquittal and subsequent attack on the "innocent" man. He concluded the conversation with a barely disguised threat.

'I know you manipulated me to get that investigation, Darnley, but I don't know why... yet. I know for some reason... perhaps your famously twisted sense of justice... you buried it. Well, now it appears to have blown up in your face. I've just spoken to Grantmore and he's desperate to see you. Only you... and on your own. Why? I ask myself. I know your inquiry locked him up last week and he's on bail. You're up to something and it stinks. Let me tell you, I won't hesitate to drop you if I find out you're bent.'

'Fuck me, Dave, been speaking to a real criminal? Did you go into them cells all on your own? I'm shitting myself to think you're on my case. Go back to your office and write a policy or something.' I hung up.

Despite my bravado, I was now seriously worried. Kingston could hardly detect the smell of shit but was well capable of spreading it – into the nice sweet-smelling ACPO corridor. Not trusting him to have told me a full and accurate story, I rang the custody suite at Central and established that what had started out as a simple assault allegation had developed into Grantmore alleging Holland was stalking and harassing him. The fact that the whole incident had been witnessed by two men who were presently giving statements was concerning.

I gathered my papers, collected my jacket and coat and walked out into the incident room, explaining to Tony that I'd be at Central, and to ring me if anything happened.

'This anything to do with our job, boss... him asking for you, I mean?'

'Let's hope so, mate. Let's hope so.'

I looked around the room, thinking that perhaps I should take someone with me in case it came to a formal taped interview situation, as with my new resolve to play things straight I was reluctant to get into more "one-on-one/off-the-record" situations with Grantmore. But what might he disclose? Then I saw Pete Granger sitting in the corner, completing some of his actions. He knew my exposed position over Grantmore – and Holland. It made perfect sense for him to accompany me.

'PC Granger.' He looked up. 'Get your jacket. You're coming with me to Central. Our Mr Grantmore wishes to talk to me.'

The two experienced DCs in the room looked at each other, then at DS Ride, a quizzical expression on their faces. They may as well have said, *Why the fuck is he taking the woodentop?*

'Sorry, lads, but it was Pete that got us the photo of Grantmore and now here he is asking to talk to me… urgently. Seems logical… and fair… that he joins me. He knows the source and the detail of the information.'

I was right and they knew it – still pissed off, but accepting of the situation. Showing Granger I trusted him would hopefully further benefit my cause. I equally hoped the fact that Grantmore was in custody and wanting to talk to me would spread around the inquiry team and generate some badly needed enthusiasm.

As Granger and I drove out of Driffield towards Hull, I explained to him my new thinking and how I needed him to convince Morley to give a statement about how, and why, he took the photograph of Grantmore at the Silver Cod. I was reassured when he expressed the view that Morley would do it, as he felt so guilty about not coming forward earlier with the answerphone messages. He was similarly positive that he would be happy not to reveal the Holland photographs. If he thought Morley was happy to sit on those photographs, surely he was too? I felt this brief conversation and this morning's success with Anne Beedham had, hopefully, considerably reduced the risks I faced.

We then drove in silence. Pitfalls, loopholes and threats. Figuring out my tactics on the move. I now quite literally had a captive audience to deliver my messages to both men, and Granger ready and willing to sort out Morley. However, unlike on the telly, I was unable to just waltz in and have off-the-record conversations with them – PACE did not allow that. Kingston had said that Grantmore had refused to speak to the interviewing officers or anyone else until he had spoken to me. I suspected that he mainly wanted to rant and rave about getting Holland off his back, and why hadn't I charged him with blinding him? I was not anticipating any form of easy capitulation over grassing up the robbers – although I still hoped – but he would certainly want to discuss further his proposal to set them up. My intention was to speak to him in front of the custody sergeant on videotape and ask him what he wanted me for. I was pretty certain he would say very little while being recorded, and I would tell him that I could only speak to him off the record after he had been formally interviewed for the alleged assault on Holland. This would put my intended conversation with him on a firmer legal footing that NCIS and ACPO would accept.

As regards Holland, I could do nothing until he too had been interviewed and a decision made about whether to charge or release him. However, since Grantmore would definitely want him warning off, I again had a legitimate reason to deliver that warning, as I had been the investigating officer in Grantmore's injury. I would then be able to report back to Wilde that Holland had been arrested for harassing Grantmore and I had formally warned him off while he was in custody. Admittedly, Wilde and Granger still knew about the Holland photographs but I was beginning to feel a lot less vulnerable. But now there was bloody Kingston nosing around.

However, as I pulled into the rear yard of Queens Gardens from Dock Street, I dared to think that maybe things were at last going my way.

Twenty-Two

Later That Afternoon

Grantmore was used to passing time in a police cell. Being arrested and banged up was an occupational hazard. He knew whenever the local plod got the faintest whiff of a chance to arrest him, they took it. From that bastard Darnley to the newest recruit out to make their name, they all wanted his scalp on their belts. As long as the bulk of the arrests did not end up with a charge and a court appearance, he was content. His solicitor was on a retainer, paid handsomely for a rapid response to his calls. When arrested, he would always act confident and cocky but say absolutely nothing during interviews – not even "no comment" – that really pissed off the interviewers. His arrest for the rape of Lisa Holland had been a rare exception – his solicitor had told him exactly what to say. This was going to be another occasion when he would speak to his interrogators – to complain loudly that the police had failed to charge Holland for the attack at Nicole's and now the headcase was stalking him, intent on causing him more harm. He would claim self-defence.

Normally, anger got him through the time sitting alone in a cell. Anger at whoever had complained about him – usually one of his girls, or a weaker business rival. Anger at the arresting officer, who more often than not took the opportunity to handcuff him just a bit too tightly and made sure that plenty of people saw his temporary subjugation and humiliation. Even anger at the system that was never fair; but never anger at himself for getting caught.

This time, it was different. All he felt was fear.

He had demanded to speak to Darnley but the custody sergeant merely contacted the on-call SIO, which happened to be Kingston. When he appeared in the custody suite to ask why he wanted Darnley, Grantmore had recognised him as the bastard who had refused to allow him to be cut from the handcuffs in Nicole's, thereby prolonging his humiliation. He tried his best to intimidate the officer, who didn't seem comfortable in the cellblock, but the shame of that recollection just deepened his sense of foreboding.

Once alone in his cell, what bluff and bluster he had managed to summon up to save face rapidly evaporated. Now he was just shit-scared.

He had known all along that the person who had driven the bleach-filled syringe into his eye and then slashed his face must have been his accuser's father. In Grantmore's warped mind, Holland should have been able to accept his daughter had lied and that he was innocent – had not the jury declared him so? The circumstances of his initial attack in court showed the man was deranged, and then the planning and ferocity of his attack at Nicole's underlined his cunning and tenacity. This morning's events had done exactly what the ex-Para had intended; intimidated him even further by letting him know he hadn't finished with him.

But then there were the equally chilling, barely veiled threats from Frame. A man who had already murdered – or more accurately – executed, one accomplice.

His usual confidence in beating a potential criminal charge was shattered. He sensed he had no escape from being implicated in the Beverley robbery – a robbery that led to kidnap and murder. Darnley's persistence, he knew, would result in him informing on the gang to try and get a lighter sentence. His knowledge of the law meant he knew that he wouldn't face a murder charge but his role as a fixer in a crime with such serious outcomes still meant a lengthy sentence. And in prison, he was as good as dead.

On top of all this, he was now a murderer himself. He'd killed the man with the camera in a state of high passion, with no thought of limiting the evidential possibilities. Were there witnesses? There had been a lot of blood. Forensics? He had moved the body when he'd had time to calm down and was pretty sure no one would ever find it but in truth, he doubted he could escape justice.

He sat in his cell, filled with an overwhelming sense of doom.

When he was taken from his cell to see Darnley, he was almost relieved. Keen to start to negotiate a way out of this nightmare. When the slippery bastard pretended to be ignorant of why he needed to talk to him and insist he talk on videotape, his fears multiplied. After only minutes, he was back in his cell. Told he could not talk to Darnley until after his formal interview for the alleged assault upon Holland.

After what seemed like hours alone, he had eventually been interviewed and answered the questions put to him, claiming he had acted in self-defence, as this was the man he knew had blinded him and he was afraid of a second attack. Despite this, he had been charged with assault occasioning actual bodily harm and kept in custody to appear at court the next day. His solicitor had explained that Russ Holland had refused to make a written complaint about the injuries he'd suffered, but the police were using the evidence given by the two builders to prove the assault, as they were convinced that official action was needed to try and prevent what appeared to be some form of ongoing vendetta getting out of hand. However, his solicitor was of the opinion that as he, Grantmore, had no injuries and was painted by the two witnesses as the aggressor, Holland was likely to be released without charge.

As the warder returned him to his cell to await his meeting with Darnley, Grantmore could not stop shaking. For the first time in his adult life, he had no plan and no idea what he even wanted to happen next.

*

Waiting in interview room three at Queens Gardens Police Station with Pete Granger for the warder to bring in Grantmore, I was expecting his usual arrogance. I was amazed when he walked in. He looked smaller, bowed and beaten. Maybe, just maybe, this was the time to get him talking?

He took the only vacant chair, which was bolted to the floor on the opposite side of the bolted-down table and made no attempt at his usual defiance. He didn't speak and neither did I. I had already told Granger to keep quiet.

After about thirty seconds, I pointedly looked at my watch, and he released a torrent of abuse about how I had deliberately allowed Holland to walk away from the attack that blinded him. I let him have his say and waited until he had run out of steam.

'Yeah, yeah, yeah, Sean. So what do you want?' I asked in a sarcastic and bored manner.

'Who the fuck is this?' he asked, nodding at Granger. 'I'm saying nothing in front of any witnesses. This is between me and you.'

I had anticipated this response when I had asked Granger to accompany me, and had told him what to do. He got to his feet and moved towards the door and opened it. Grantmore sat back in his chair and for the first time since he entered the room, he began to look more like his cocky self. That was until I also stood and walked after my young colleague. I stopped in the open doorway.

'Before I go, I should just tell you that there is no deal on the table. That photograph of you and your mate from the north-east is going in the newspaper and on TV. It's all I've got and I've got to use it. We both know what it means. You are a dead man.'

Mentally crossing my fingers, I said to Granger, 'Get the warder, PC Granger. He doesn't want to speak, so it's back to the cells.'

I closed the door and waited outside in the corridor, hoping.

I was not disappointed.

'Darnley... you bastard. Come back.'

He was beaten.

Together we walked back in and resumed our seats. Grantmore was slumped forward, his head in his hands. Beaten.

'So who is the man in the photo?'

He sat up straight and back in his chair, clearly having reached a decision. He looked me straight in the eyes and let out a long sigh.

'Okay. I helped set up the robberies at Brid and Beverley. I put Emmerson in touch with the gang... as a driver and to supply the local knowledge. I took no part in either job and I had nothing to do with his murder. I was nowhere near. If I give you names, what happens to me?'

This was the first time he had made any unequivocal admissions about his role in these crimes, and PACE demands I should have cautioned him and arrested him for this offence, marched him back before the custody sergeant and then only proceed to ask further questions under tape-recording conditions with a solicitor present if he requested one. Grantmore knew all this as well as I did. I knew we both intended to ignore the law.

'That depends on what else you give me. The man in the photo, is he the main man? His name's a good start.'

He tilted back his head and looked at the wall above our heads, chewing on his lip, his damaged eye socket twitching like mad.

'Yeah. That's him.'

I glanced at Granger and was amazed that he was showing no reaction – at his length of service I'd have been punching the air.

'He wants me to set up another job and find him a driver. He's reckoning on doing it next week. I can give you the where and the when and you catch him on the job. He gets life and I'm safe… if I'm not in prison. You can deal on that surely… I've not killed anyone for fuck's sake.'

'So who is he and where is this job going to take place?' I was giving nothing until I heard more details.

'Kirkella or Swanland… somewhere west Hull way. I've already sussed out some targets. I've got a driver in mind and he'll pass me the details, as soon as it's planned… if I pay him enough. He's only the driver, so you can let him escape. If I've got you the gang… caught on the job… then I walk away?'

The more he explained his idea, the more excited he got and the more his empty eye socket twitched.

I laughed out loud. 'Bloody hell, Grantmore, this isn't the telly. This is real life. I can't trust you or some daft bastard like Emmerson to provide me accurate enough information to allow me to assemble a firearms operation to catch these bastards on the job. Dream on.'

'Come on, Darnley. It could work.' Desperation was in his plea.

'It's bollocks and you know it. I want a name and some evidence and I need them tonight. I have to stop this lot…

now… before someone else gets killed. You give me as much evidence as you've got so I can arrest and charge them before they hurt anyone else. Admit your minor part in the whole story and I'll ensure you get a suitably minor charge… and a good word to the judge.'

The old Grantmore struggled to the surface and he leant forward across the table, his damaged face jerking and throbbing like a separate being. 'And I end up stabbed in the prison showers as a grass. This bloke could fix that a piece of piss.'

'I guess it's the picture in the paper and on the telly then. *Tomorrow.* Think about how that will look. The very day after you spend a day and night in police custody… the day you appear in court. It'll be obvious you grassed in exchange for a deal. Especially when I fix it with the magistrate for you to get a conditional discharge…'

I stood up and Granger followed suit, leading the way out of the room. I paused at the door and looked back at Grantmore, who once more had his head in his hands. Beaten.

'Sean. Make your choice. It's either out there tomorrow, on your own, branded a grass with this man's picture in the paper. Or take your chances with me trying to do my best to help you, and with him locked up. The better the evidence you give me against him and his gang, the more likely he stays locked up. It's no contest. Think about it, Sean. I'll be back in a couple of hours.'

'Don't go, Darnley. Let's sort it out now… you're right,' he implored.

Beaten.

'See you in a couple of hours. Warder, please show Mr Grantmore back to his cell.'

Twenty-Three

One down. One to go. The officers investigating the incident at Simone's were of the view that there was insufficient evidence to charge Holland with any crime. He was the victim. Grantmore had injured him. The two witnesses, albeit somewhat reluctantly, fearing for their contract, had said so in sworn statements. Holland had cooperated fully; claiming he had found out the job with J & S Renovations was actually for Grantmore well after he had tendered for it. He'd thought long and hard about accepting once he knew but decided he had to move on, and that's why he had gone to the site to meet him – to offer the olive branch. The officers had told him that Grantmore was convinced that he had blinded him and was now stalking him with the intent to do far worse. He had calmly denied the attack at Nicole's, apologised for losing his temper in court and suggested that they contact me to confirm that I had thoroughly investigated the attack and proved it wasn't him. Cocky bastard.

The two experienced interviewers were of the view that everything he had said was utter bollocks. They believed that Holland had indeed stuck that syringe in Grantmore's eye and were both convinced that he was intent on continuing his quest for retribution. His little act in Simone's was just a well-thought-out attempt to wind his intended victim up. He'd never intended for Grantmore to be arrested and charged with an assault upon him, but he was now capitalising upon that outcome by refusing to give evidence against him, thus "on paper" at least, appearing to be genuine in his desire to move on.

And sure enough, the local DI and the Crown Prosecution Service agreed no charge would stick and he was due to be released. Granger and I were now waiting for him in the same interview room in which we had spoken to Grantmore. I was on a roll. I felt I now had Grantmore where I wanted him and now had the perfect opportunity to officially warn off Holland – which should satisfy Wilde. Furthermore, if Granger went along with this, knowing what he knew, the threat he posed to me was virtually eliminated. It was definitely all coming together.

There was a knock on the door and the warder showed Holland into the room, and he sat in the same chair previously occupied by his target. He looked content and at ease. The exact opposite of Grantmore. As I once again looked into those ice-cold blue eyes, my confidence of just seconds ago disappeared.

Pulling myself together, I introduced PC Granger and explained the reason for my speaking to him and issued a strongly worded warning about his future behaviour. He sat listening without interruption but when I'd finished, he decided to continue with the bullshit he had trotted out in interview. I had obviously anticipated this stance but for my peace of mind I needed to know he had truly got the message and this vendetta would now stop.

I leant forward, arms on the scratched desk. 'Quit the crap, Mr Holland. I know you blinded him. I just couldn't prove it. I know that today you were continuing your vendetta. I need to know you are taking my warning to stay away from Grantmore seriously. There is no tape running and you are not under caution.'

He smiled and shook his head. 'Who is this young fellow?' He nodded towards Granger. 'Why is he here, if you truly want to talk openly?'

Those eyes once again locked onto mine.

Looking back, I overcompensated for the deep unease he was creating in me. I had been naïve to think he'd just roll over, and ill-prepared for how to proceed if he didn't.

'This is PC Peter Granger. He uncovered the evidence that can prove you stuck that syringe in Grantmore's eye.'

Granger stiffened at my side. I hadn't told him that I might reveal what we knew and how. Because I hadn't planned to. It just came out in an effort to knock Holland off track.

Even as the words left my mouth, I had not formulated my next move.

Holland just shook his head and smiled.

I found myself reaching for my briefcase that was on the floor beside my chair and pulling out the envelope that Morley had originally given to Granger containing the photographs on the fire escape. I laid it on the table and folded my arms on top of it.

For the first time, a shadow of doubt crossed Holland's face. But he was good; it disappeared almost immediately and the smile reappeared as the eyes re-engaged.

'That the evidence then?' He actually chuckled.

'Yes. I couldn't prove it. But I can now.' I tapped the envelope. By now, my brain had engaged and those photos were not leaving the envelope.

Again, totally unplanned, I said to Granger, 'Go find us a hot drink, please. What do you prefer, Mr Holland?'

'Strong black coffee, please.'

Yet again, PC Granger impressed me by saying nothing, getting up and leaving the room.

Once he had left the room, I continued, still flying by the seat of my pants: 'I know you have no previous convictions, Mr Holland. You have no track record of violence.'

'None. As I say, my actions in court were totally out of character.'

'What about Ralph Harrison, the ex-Para? What's his track record like?'

He was good. He merely feigned a confused look.

'I'm a good copper, Mr Holland. I investigate stuff. I've investigated you. I know who you really are and what you were.'

I sat back, looking relaxed, with my fingers tapping on the blue envelope. Holland's eyes now literally boring into mine. If looks could kill.

I decided to change tack. 'When I came to see you after you and Lisa were arrested, I sensed that you knew I'd arranged for Lisa to fake her collapse. You know I stuck my neck out to caution you for the assault in Crown Court. You can trust me… I'm on your side.'

He said nothing.

'If I wanted to get you for blinding Grantmore, I could. Trust me on that too.'

'What do you want?'

'Having stuck my neck out twice for you, I now need you to end your quest for revenge… or I can't protect you anymore.'

He too must have decided to change tack. 'I don't need protection. He does.'

'If you don't back off, you will go to prison.'

I tapped the blue envelope again. I still had no intention of showing him the contents. I was banking on the fact that by being able to quote his true identity, he would surmise I wasn't bluffing.

He called my bluff. 'Show me.'

Oh well – shit or bust as they say. I pulled out the photographs and left them on the desk. They were still in the correct sequence. He picked them up and quickly scanned each one before placing them back on the desk on top of the envelope. He sat thinking for about thirty seconds.

'Who took them?'

'That's not important. They prove you did it.'

'But you've not used them. Why not? Either you are neglecting your duty in a most serious fashion... or... you can't use them in evidence.'

He paused, thinking.

'They're dodgy in some way... illegally obtained.'

I was shocked by how quickly he had worked that out. For the first time, I wondered exactly what his background in the Paras had been. He had a fascinating skill set.

'Arrived through the post this morning. Anonymous tip-off.' I had similar skills.

He awarded me a wry smile.

We both sat back, sizing each other up. I was wondering if I dared to trust him. Tell him more, to get him to trust me more.

The silence was ended in a way I did not expect. He suddenly shot forward in his chair and brought his clenched fists slamming down onto the desk. I shot bolt upright, instinctively trying to push the chair back to get out of his reach, forgetting it was bolted to the floor and ending up just looking, and feeling, stupid.

But he wasn't intent on violence; he was just emotionally fraught. He looked at me as if about to apologise and in a quiet and resigned voice said, 'I can't back off. I can't forgive him for what he did to Lisa and what it's done to me. He has to pay. So use the photos and charge me. When I get out of prison I'll start again.'

Now what? My turn to sit and think.

'If Grantmore had been convicted and sent to prison for what he did to Lisa, would you have been satisfied? Or would this lust for revenge have just continued when he got out? What would have been enough? Three years... five... ten?'

'If that jury had believed Lisa and convicted him and he'd gone to prison, I think I'd have accepted it. I don't know for sure but I think I would. But he didn't go to prison and he's laughing... he's not even sorry. I need retribution.'

'So an eye for an eye literally wasn't enough? You want him dead. Is that all that will satisfy you?'

'That's too easy for him. I want him wrecked. I want him frightened. I want him squirming. I never intended to get him arrested and charged this morning. I just wanted him to know I was out there, watching him. I just want him to suffer like he's made Lisa... and me... suffer.'

'What if I could get him a lengthy sentence for something else?'

Again, we both went quiet. I had certainly not intended to go this far, but I had to solve the Holland problem. I felt confident I could keep Granger and Morley quiet, and Wilde could be won over by Holland's agreement to leave Grantmore alone. I had little doubt now that Grantmore would give me the names and some evidence. I was nearly home and dry, so the extra risk was worth it.

'You agree to leave Grantmore alone for the next two weeks and I'll keep these photographs to myself. Within those two weeks, Grantmore will be charged with serious crimes that will get him a lengthy jail sentence. But if you continue to stalk him, you're likely to fuck all that up. But I need your word.'

'And I need more detail. You thought he'd go to prison for raping my daughter. Convince me and I'll agree.'

Although it never struck me at the time, I think I must have intuitively taken Russ Holland into my trust based upon his army record and his devotion to his daughter. I'd already revealed too much, but now I went further in a last-ditch effort to win him over. I explained how I knew Grantmore was involved in the robberies and murders and that I had manipulated him into a position where I was convinced he would grass up his accomplices – why he now had no choice. I emphasised how he too would go to prison for a lengthy period and spend it watching his back – exactly how Holland wanted him – frightened, exposed and anguished.

Once again, his intuitive understanding impressed me. 'You've done a deal with him to get him to grass.'

What exactly had he done in the Paras?

I explained how he was between a rock and a hard place and I was conning him. There would be no immunity, no words to the judge, no lighter sentence. I was in control.

'So you're asking me to trust you but in the same breath you're telling me that you're asking Grantmore to trust you, while intending to double-cross him?'

'He's a vicious thug. You're a wronged father. I think I've already exhibited whose side I'm on several times now.' I tapped the blue envelope. 'With these photographs especially.'

He sat quietly thinking.

I tried again, judging we were on the verge of agreement. I reiterated how his enemy would be exposed as a grass and spend years in prison – years looking over his shoulder.

'The thought of him in prison waiting for them to get even would be justice for Lisa. Not what I planned but as good as I'm going to get.'

He held out his hand to shake on it but suddenly pulled back.

'Hang on, though. All this depends on him giving you enough to charge them… and you having enough to charge him.'

I took the final step.

'Look, Russ, I need you onside now. Things are coming to a head. The gang have asked Grantmore to set up another job for next week and supply them with a local driver. I can't let that crime happen. Someone else could get killed. That young lad up in Ponteland… his mum and dad lost their son. I want your help… as a father yourself. Keep out of Grantmore's face. Let me do my job and use him to get to this lot before someone else gets hurt.'

He sat back. Thinking again. Then he told me more details about his army background and made me a proposition.

*

While the three of us drank our coffee, Granger played the part he now knew he was there to play – witness to the official warning. Holland's humble agreement to comply was as equally stage-managed. Granger then fetched the warder to arrange for Holland's release and to request Grantmore be brought back to the interview room.

While we waited, I made sure the young officer was securely onside. 'Look, Peter, I wanted you here with me today so that I have a witness about what Grantmore wanted to see me about. As far as our first chat with him goes, I need you to agree that all he did was rant about Holland and then test me out for a deal if he was to admit his part in our jobs. You didn't hear any admissions whatsoever. No grounds for a caution or arrest. You okay with that?'

'You know I am.'

'He's sweating now and that's why I've left him to think. I don't want him clamming up. These bastards will carry on and hurt someone else. I know him and he'll only open up if I'm alone with him. When I know he's going to give me what I need, I'll start with PACE, as if he's just opened up. So as far as you're concerned last time, when we were both in there, he said he'd only talk to me alone. That's best.'

'Best for me? Or best for you?'

'Both of us… if we are okay with each other now. Are we okay?'

'The longer this has gone on, the more I know that I'm guilty by association. If I'd told someone straight away about Morley and how you treated him, I'd have been on the side of the righteous. If I'd handed in the photos of Holland immediately, I'd have been fine… but now I don't think the argument that I was only obeying orders, or you were bullying me would wash, do you?'

I didn't respond. Just gave him a wry smile.

'The way you've sorted Beedham's complaint out and stalled my suspension, I realise that you'd have done your best for me all along, without my pathetic attempts to coerce you. While I was sitting outside just now, I was thinking I should say sorry.'

Again, I just smiled.

'My marriage isn't going to work. I can see that now. But I need this job and I need you to help me keep it. Will you speak up for me at my disciplinary hearing for smacking Knaggs?'

'I'll do more than that. I'm going to be telling them how it was your initiative that detected these jobs. There's no way they are going to want to get rid of you. Maybe post you to Scunthorpe or even Goole… but trust me, your job will be safe by the time I've done singing your praises.'

He smiled and I felt confident we had reached a point of mutual respect and understanding.

I reiterated what I wanted in the statement from Graham Morley so as to secure the evidence of the photograph at the

Silver Cod. We knew it would be upsetting for Morley to explain his background with Grantmore and thus why he had taken the photo, but it was essential. I also acknowledged that Granger would need to introduce in his own statement how we had both met Morley, how I'd messed up and why he had kept in touch with him to build intelligence on Grantmore and thus spotted the significance of the photograph.

'Build up your part. You really did break the case open. Grantmore has admitted the bloke in the photo is who we are after. But try and be diplomatic when you describe my original cock-up... please.'

He afforded himself a smug grin. 'And the photographs of Holland?'

'Make Morley understand that Grantmore is our target... not Holland. Tell him Grantmore will be going to prison for a long time... and he will be safe. I'm confident you can sell this to him.'

'But you're going to do a deal with him, aren't you?'

'There's not going to be a deal. You have to trust me.'

I was acutely aware that I was telling everyone to trust me, and even to me it was wearing a bit thin.

There was a knock on the door and the warder ushered Grantmore into the room. He still looked beaten. Granger left the room as Grantmore flopped heavily into his chair.

'Now where were we, Sean?' I began as soon as the warder had left us alone.

He just sat, slumped.

'Well, Sean, I have good news and bad news. What do you want to hear first?' I asked in my most cheery and friendly tone.

He remained silent and motionless. Beaten.

'Okay. Good news first... just to cheer you up. We're going to go with your plan... or at least a good part of it. I want you to set up the next job. If you do that and if you're telling the truth about your role, I'll keep your charges to a minimum and speak to the trial judge.'

There was no response.

'Now the bad news. I intend to arrest you on suspicion of robbery and get your admissions on tape.'

Now I had his attention. He pulled himself upright and looked a bit more like the old Grantmore. Angry.

So I carried on: 'This is what you're going to do to save your own life. You will admit to me now your role in the crimes. Keep it brief. Just enough for me to justify your arrest. Then I'll get two detectives off the incident to interview you formally. At that point, I want names and details of the man in the photograph and the rest of his gang. I want whereabouts of guns, the money, addresses, phone numbers, garages, lock-ups... you know the score. Where I'm going to find hard evidence.'

'There's no way I'm giving you a statement or saying any of this on tape. It's all got to be off the record.'

'I can't do that, Sean, and you know it.'

'I walk... without charges... or no deal.'

'Just think a minute, Sean. Say I agreed... which I can't... but you stick to that approach and then we arrest this lot and they drop you. Say you were there. You supplied the gun. You pulled the trigger. There's nothing to stop them.'

His bluster had disappeared. He was thinking. I paused a while to let it sink in.

'Then we'll have to arrest you and, of course, at that point you are going to look like a liar if you claim just to have set the jobs up... a jury would think "that's what he would say". It would be your word against theirs.'

'And remember, another force are involved... I can't control what the police up there decide to do. Stick with me. I'm offering to let you get in first... get your account down officially... it sounds more convincing. We'll formally alibi you for when the robberies and murders took place, so if they try and stick some of the shit to you, we'll know it's a lie from the outset. That'll make anything else they say look like lies. No guarantee, I accept, but…'

'I can prove I was nowhere near the murder of Emmerson. I've already got that covered. And I wasn't up north when that young kid got shot. I knew nowt about that 'til you showed me it in the papers.'

He was warming to my proposal.

'Just tell me now what you know. I'll make sure you get bail for this and the assault on Holland. There won't be a court appearance yet. I can argue that you are continuing to provide valuable intelligence about robberies and murders and I need you to be in contact with the suspects to gain more intelligence… and prevent another robbery and who knows what else.'

I paused. I was nearly convincing myself.

'Or we can just go right back to me putting the photo of you and the main man in the media and wait and see what happens. You'll just have to trust me.'

The truth was, he couldn't trust me. I was manipulating him into admitting his role, implicating his accomplices, and providing sworn evidence against them. I was arranging his prison time and probably his death warrant. But the reality was he had nowhere else to go. He was beaten.

He fell silent again. Slumped. Thinking. Until eventually: 'I've got no choice.'

All remnants of resolve deserted him at that moment and he started talking. First, naming the man in the photograph – Paul Frame. How Frame had coerced him into setting up the crimes, due to the fifty grand debt he'd first told me about in the Molescroft pub. Next, he named Michael Keegan and Billy Pike, telling me of their army background and how Frame had intimated he had killed Emmerson. As he spoke,

I could see why he was so malleable to my threats – he was already truly terrified of Frame.

What he told me was ample to justify the arrests of all three men – and himself – but he seemed either unable, or unwilling, to reveal any hard evidence. I pushed for information about the whereabouts of the cash or guns or anything he'd witnessed, but nothing came. My instinct was that he had little to tell beyond his part in setting the robberies up. I hoped he would reveal more under closer scrutiny, when formally interviewed. One thing was for sure: from what he'd said of Frame's planning and expertise, I seriously doubted we'd find any useable evidence if we locked them up now, based solely on his say-so. Then they'd walk.

I had to move on, so we quickly discussed his progress so far in identifying potential targets near Hull for Frame. He was expected to have completed that task later this week and the job was likely to happen the following week. He emphasised to me how Frame would always demand to meet the driver alone and then with that person and their local knowledge, carry out a reconnaissance of the potential targets, keeping the final choice secure from even Pike and Keegan, until the job happened. So he stressed how he would be unable to tell me the definitive target in advance.

I told him that my plan was for the job never to take place in any case. It was too risky. Then I dropped my next bombshell.

'No need to find a driver, Sean. I need the person we put into the gang to be trustworthy. Working for me… not you.'

He flung up his arms in horror. 'You mean an undercover cop? No fucking way. They'd give evidence behind screens and all that and everyone would know I'm a grass. I'd have everyone in the bloody prison after me, not just him and his crew.'

'Calm down, I'm not going to use a copper and they won't ever be giving evidence. Don't tell me a man in your trade has never heard of a participating informant? It's legal but they'll never go near a court, or give evidence, and their identity will be protected.'

I explained the basic principles to him and I could see his scepticism lessening as I told him how a judge would give their authority to keep their identity from the court.

'All I need you to do is to put my driver in contact with the gang, pretending he's your man. You won't even have to meet him. As I say, I don't want the robbery you set up to even take place. I can't let anyone else get hurt. And that's better for you. If we catch them actually committing a crime you set up, they'll know it was you or the driver that grassed. But if I can get them before the job because the driver unearths some evidence about the murders or robberies that have already taken place, it's safer all round… even for you.'

Not a very convincing argument – they'd still think it was him and the planted driver – but this was a war of attrition. I continued to explain the legal niceties around the use of participating informants, as I figured if we both kept talking and it all sounded legit, he'd fall for it.

He kept quiet. Thinking.

I then stressed that he could not tell his interviewers what we had agreed. All he must say was that he had told me that he suspected Frame was planning another job in the Hull area soon. That would explain why I would order his release after interview so that he could pass me details of the next job when he got them from Frame. I explained I could sell this plan to my superiors as protecting the public and potential victims.

I'd done all I could think of. I now just needed him to admit his part under caution and on tape.

I held the faint hope that he might tell his interviewers more than he'd told me, or Northumbria might have had a breakthrough. Maybe just the names of Frame, Keegan and

Pike might trigger rapid results, or at least the confidence to find hard evidence if we locked them up straight away. The last thing I wanted was for what we had just agreed to actually happen. I didn't want him setting up another job, let alone use an unofficial participating informant. That was just my "emergency" backstop that I prayed I wouldn't need. I didn't even want to have to let him have bail if at all possible, as with all the pressure on him there was a chance he could flee. But to be honest I gave that scenario little thought and judged it a risk worth taking. He was born and bred in Hull with his criminal empire in the city that I guessed he rarely left.

There were a thousand and one questions I still wanted to ask him. I still needed more details but I had to leave that to the formal taped interviews. As I walked him back to the custody suite, I reassessed my backup plan – my last resort. Was it viable? The planted driver would have several days to dig around and potentially find some additional evidence before another job even took place. If that didn't work, we could pull him out and still arrest the gang on what evidence we had. Was it worth a try? Worth the risk?

What I did know was that Frame intended to commit another crime. He would do that with or without Grantmore's help. Without Grantmore, we wouldn't know where or when it was and it was highly likely someone else would get hurt or even killed. So if we didn't have any evidence to make a speculative arrest stick, then the potential of my plan was obvious. It at least gave us a chance to find some before we struck – and before they did. We'd have more control. We'd know when and where they planned to strike – and could get in first.

In the custody suite, I formally arrested Grantmore and as he was led away to his cell, I began to feel energised, buoyed by the reaction I knew I'd get back at the incident room when I returned with the names of our suspects. I would be vindicated in my arrest of Grantmore as a fishing trip last week. Today's progress would re-energise the team. Investigative velocity would be restored.

I was still in the custody suite, on the phone with DS Ride discussing who I wanted to carry out the interview, when I became aware of the warder using the landline on his desk behind the counter. I gained the impression from the way he kept glancing at me that I was the topic of his conversation. I turned away and pretended to still be engaged on the phone, while I listened.

'Yes, sir, he's here now and has arrested Grantmore for robbery.' He paused, obviously listening, until, 'No, sir, he left just over an hour ago.' I guessed he must have been referring to Granger.

My hunch was that he was talking to Kingston. It made sense based upon his threat at lunchtime. It was obviously not just me who had snouts in the custody suite, and he would no doubt have a couple of his favourites on my inquiry. I'd have to watch my back, as although not the world's best detective, he had the authority to start to dig if he chose to do so, and if he dug in the correct places I was in bother.

It was late and I'd been at work since half seven and had only eaten a sandwich. I was tired and hungry – but wired. Things were happening and for the first time in weeks, I felt back in control. I rang Granger to check on progress but was disappointed to hear that so far he'd been unable to find Morley, who was not even answering his mobile. I told him to book off duty with DS Ride, update him and resume his search early the next day. I stressed the urgency of his mission.

My next call was to Richard Wilde.

Twenty-Four

Later That Same Evening

Pete Granger felt energised. Just glad to be concentrating on the work he loved after the trauma, doubts and worries of the last few weeks. He'd decided to ignore Darnley's instructions and pay one last visit to Morley's flat on Anlaby Road, before he booked off duty and went home, but as soon as he pulled up he could see he was wasting his time – the flat was in darkness. He wondered where he might be at this time on a Monday night. But then chuckled to think he could be outside Nicole's or Cleopatra's looking for his quarry, when Grantmore was safely tucked up where Morley wanted him – in a cell. He resolved to be back at the flat and talking to Morley before seven in the morning and thus able to update the briefing.

As he drove towards home, his thoughts turned to Amy and their continuing troubles. After things had come to a climax with his attack on Knaggs, she had admitted her affair but declared her undying love and become excessively loving and caring, which he found false and cloying. He realised as he drove that he was glad that she was on night shift and he would probably not even see her before she left. To make sure their paths didn't cross, he decided he would call in at his local, the Hop Pole, and have a well-deserved pint. The very fact that he had decided to do this convinced him that their marriage was over, and he resolved to bring matters to a head as soon as possible. As he pulled into the pub car park, his mobile rang.

Thinking it could only be Darnley, he answered it with, 'Hi, sir, he's still not in. I'll try again first thing in the morning.'

A voice he didn't recognise said, 'Who's not in, PC Granger?'

Immediately on his guard, he replied, 'Who is this?'

'This is Detective Superintendent Kingston. I asked you a question, Constable. Who is not in? And furthermore, to whom did you think you were talking?' The questions came as commands.

'I thought it was the incident room at Driffield, sir. I was trying to complete an action on my way home but the man isn't in.'

Granger had never met Kingston and only knew of him by reputation – a bully and a tosser. Like virtually every other officer in the force, he had laughed at the story of his indecision when Grantmore was found manacled to the bed with his eye ruined.

'Where are you, Officer?' demanded Kingston.

'Willerby, sir. Just about to go off duty.'

'I want you in my office here at Queens Gardens in twenty minutes.'

The line went dead.

He knew nothing about the current tensions between the two superintendents but rationalised that his only possible connection with Kingston was through Grantmore and Holland – and thus Darnley's ducking and diving. His "fight or flight" instincts were instantly alert.

He tried to ring Darnley but his mobile went straight to answerphone. He had little choice but to set off for Queens

Gardens, and arrived within the twenty minutes Kingston had demanded. He tried Darnley's phone again, this time leaving him a message about his summons to see his opposite number. A couple of minutes later he was on the top corridor, hoping he'd find Matt Darnley's office light was on, but the only office occupied at that time of night was Kingston's.

He knocked and waited. He was beginning to think he wasn't in his office when the command 'Enter' emanated from the room. He did as he was instructed and remained standing, looking at the senior detective, who was on the far side of his desk busily writing, with his head down over the pages. Granger thought it best to keep quiet. Even to anyone as inexperienced as he, it was all too obvious that Kingston was showing him who was "in charge".

After two or three minutes, Kingston ostentatiously replaced the cap on his Montblanc fountain pen, sat back in his high-backed office chair and fixed Granger with a hard stare, again clearly intended to intimidate. With a derisive flick of his hand, he directed Granger to the chair opposite him.

Granger gave him a confident smile and said, 'Evening, sir. You're working late,' as he sat upright in the much smaller hard-backed office chair. Although the intimidation tactics were working, he was determined not to show it.

Kingston tipped forward on the chair and came to rest with his arms on his desk, hands clasped together. 'Yes. And tell me why are you working at all?'

'Sir?'

'Why are you not suspended for assaulting Sergeant Knaggs? Because you damn well should be.'

Granger made no reply.

'Well?' demanded his interrogator.

'I thought you would know that better than I.' Granger knew he was being facetious but despite himself, he couldn't help wanting to wind up this pompous little man.

'Adopting some of your new mentor's attitudes, I see,' responded Kingston, apparently not wound up at all.

'Mentor, sir?' Granger continued to play dumb. Mainly because he didn't have a clue what this was about.

'Okay, Constable, let's play it your way. When you eventually face a disciplinary panel, you will be sacked. Detective Superintendent Darnley will not be able to help you one jot. You will be unemployed and virtually unemployable.'

Granger remained silent.

'I know that Darnley is in some way postponing your suspension, and my guess is that you are in some way involved in one of his schemes.'

Silence.

'He is damn well using you… you must see that?' stormed Kingston.

Silence.

'Furthermore, I know it is to do with Sean Grantmore and Russ Holland. Why else would a detective superintendent see both those men while they are in custody in the presence of a uniformed PC?'

The last three words were spoken with derision, as if a uniformed police constable was the equivalent of a Girl Guide in such a situation.

Silence.

'Well. What do you say for yourself?' now almost shouting, his face reddening with anger at what he saw as Granger's insolence.

'Sorry, sir, was there a question in there? I thought you were telling me something. I was intrigued.'

He knew he was really pushing his luck but he was damned if he was going to appear intimidated.

Clearly infuriated, Kingston rose to his feet and leaned forward on his desk.

'Look, Constable, I know all about you and your little slut of a wife. This force does not want people like you, or her... or the sergeant you assaulted for that matter. Unless you tell me what the hell you and Darnley are up to, I'll make it my personal mission to get you... and your wife... sacked. Is this getting through your thick skull?'

Granger was amazed. The man had clearly lost it. Intimidation coupled with insults. He decided he'd better tone down the insolence and appear to be intimidated – just to find out what the hell was going on.

'Sir. Tell me what you want from me... I'm sorry. I need to keep my job.' He looked suitably crestfallen.

Kingston realised that he was finally getting somewhere. He was used to bullying the more junior ranks. Accustomed to getting his own way. He saw it as his right – damn it, he'd been on the Police Special Course. He even looked down on those of his own rank who were less well educated than he – and, as far as he was concerned – that was all of them. But he was not a complete fool and grasped that this young man was not going to cave in as quickly as most did, so he changed his approach.

'Look, Constable, I know Detective Superintendent Darnley better than most. We work on the same corridor, we're the same rank and we do the same job... only I do it correctly. The man is a dinosaur, a throwback to the bloody seventies. His methods are extremely questionable... you must have heard the stories?'

Granger recognised the change of tone and approach and decided to appear more compliant. 'I don't know why you are telling me this, sir.'

'You do know why. From my enquiries about you, I know you are not stupid and I'd much prefer it if you didn't treat me as if I were. I know that Darnley has delayed your suspension, claiming that you have cultivated a vital informant in his current inquiry. I know about the photograph of Grantmore that Darnley is trying to hush up. It's not just Darnley that has informants in the force, you know.'

The last sentence was said with a pathetic attempt to impress. He then paused, as if unsure whether he should continue but clearly decided to plunge somewhat incautiously on.

'I know that all this has something to do with Russ Holland attacking and blinding Sean Grantmore. He has covered it up. And you are wrapped up in the middle of it somewhere... somehow.'

Granger opted for silence again.

'You are hoping that Darnley will speak up for you at your disciplinary hearing, probably supported by your own dim-witted divisional commander. Both of them are corrupt has-beens and have absolutely no chance in preventing your dismissal.'

Silence was again Granger's only choice.

'Darnley is bent. He is not trustworthy. He'll promise to help you but will just use you.'

The young man had worked out what was coming next. As his interlocutor had said, he wasn't stupid.

'What do you want from me, sir?'

Kingston sat back in his chair, smiling, looking smug.

'Tell me what Darnley is up to. Tell me what Grantmore wanted to see him for today... and what Holland has got to do with it. I know Darnley's bent... you give me the evidence to prove it and I guarantee you'll keep your job. I have real influence in this force... let me speak up for you at your hearing. I'll show how you were honest, upright and courageous enough to expose a corrupt senior officer... who is using you.'

For a ludicrous moment, Granger was actually amused. He now had two high-ranking detectives vying for the opportunity to help him. One wanting to sing his praises for solving serious crimes – the other for exposing corruption.

It slowly dawned on him that if he played his cards right, he could be shown to have solved the robberies and murders and also expose Darnley. Kingston had said that Darnley was using him. Would that mitigate his own part in Darnley's actions? If he got the statement from Morley and then Grantmore admitted his role in setting up the crimes and named the others involved, then his own role in solving the crimes was evidenced – he didn't need Darnley to speak up for him. For the moment he kept quiet, unsure what to say – or what to do. He desperately wanted to keep his job.

'Well, young man, what do you say?'

Detective Superintendent Kingston knew the young fool was going to tell him what he wanted to know. Shafting Darnley would give him immense pleasure and probably get him the next rank. Sticking up for a young PC who had thumped a sergeant and started to go native would get him nowhere. That was not going to happen.

'Come on, young man. You can trust me.'

Twenty-Five

The Next Day
Tuesday, 9ᵗʰ February 1999

At two thirty the next morning, Sean Grantmore walked out of Queens Gardens Police Station accompanied by his solicitor. Andrew Lynch had been advising Grantmore how to handle police arrests and interviews for several years and invariably that advice was to keep his mouth shut. Such advice had proved effective more times than not. The rape allegation by Lisa Holland had been a notable, and successful, exception. This interview had been different. Hearing Grantmore confess to his part in a kidnap and a robbery which had led to a murder was a novel experience – and totally contrary to his advice. When he also implicated three other men in those crimes and told how they were planning another, he knew that his client had struck some sort of deal with Detective Superintendent Darnley, well known in legal circles for his wheeler-dealer methods. Afterwards, Lynch had tried his hardest to get Grantmore to explain what the hell he was getting himself into but he had remained tight-lipped. His suspicions were confirmed when the prisoner was granted police bail for such serious crimes and the ABH charge on Holland was withdrawn pending further enquiries. He knew that Grantmore was digging himself a hole, and as they parted company on the steps of the police station, he made one last attempt to find out what was going on. A last attempt at damage limitation. Grantmore was still having none of it and he walked off to look for a taxi, leaving Lynch shaking his head in frustration.

After Darnley had left and he sat in his cell waiting to be interviewed, he desperately searched for a way out of his predicament. Darnley had instructed him to contact Frame as soon as he could after his release and arrange a meet with his "driver". He in turn had promised the detective the details of the targets by Wednesday evening. Darnley was anxious to move things forward quickly, getting his man into the gang and finding some concrete evidence that would mean the gang could be arrested before another crime took place. Grantmore knew Frame's methods. Darnley's hopes were futile.

Nonetheless, he was keen to comply. Doing Darnley's bidding gave him some breathing space, some time to get out of the mess he was in. Now he was out of the nick, he felt some of his old confidence returning and there was no way he was going to let Darnley put him away where he was almost certain to die at the hands of Frame's associates, or from some random attack on the prison's latest grass. There were no secrets in prison.

He went back over the interview in his mind during the taxi ride home.

The only evidence the cops actually had was that bloody photograph of him and Frame with the Vauxhall at the Silver Cod. They knew nothing else. So he had played down his role in setting up the robberies in Beverley and Bridlington. He claimed only to have identified the prospective targets and provided Emmerson as the driver. He described how he and Frame had met, the intimidation over the fifty grand loan, which had forced him through fear to help him. He explained how Frame had intimated it was he who had shot Emmerson and relayed the incident at Cleopatra's when Frame had the gun, as further evidence of coercion. He provided solid alibis for the time of the actual robberies at Bridlington and Beverley and Emmerson's and Harrod's murders. He denied knowing how the gang knew to target Anne Beedham and Janice Cooper but told them it was Frame who had visited the Atwick bungalow in the Vectra. The interviewers had obviously pressed him on these points but had nothing to refute his claims. What he did fully divulge was all he knew about Frame, Keegan and Pike. He wanted them behind bars.

Grantmore knew that Frame and the others would eventually tell a different tale when they were arrested. Exactly what was going to happen next, no one knew. Darnley had a plan – but so did Frame. And so did he. The possibilities were endless. He'd had to admit his part in the crimes in order to gain his temporary freedom, but it made sense to limit his exposure to eventual prosecution as much as he could.

Darnley's reassurances that Holland was off his back he took with a pinch of salt, just as he did all of the detective's promises. The only person he could trust was Sean Grantmore, and the one thing he knew for sure was that he was not going to spend one day in prison.

*

Peter Granger let himself out of his house at 6.30am, intent on finding Morley before the morning's briefing at Driffield. He was confident he could secure his cooperation as a witness and thereby enter into evidence how his work had got their first admission of guilt and driven a huge crack into the gang's defences. He didn't want to miss the briefing and the buzz of excitement, learn more about how Darnley proposed to formally progress the inquiry and of course bask in the limelight that was now bound to come his way.

He had hardly slept a wink worrying about his confrontation with Kingston and whether he had done the right thing. But he had now burnt his bridges and was committed to the course he had set with the young detective superintendent. He was even more worried about what Darnley was going to do when he heard what had happened. On top of all that, there was his marriage. Amy had left for her night shift before he had returned home and he had found several missed calls from her on his mobile, made while he had been busy with Kingston, along with a lengthy answerphone message in which she expressed her disappointment at missing him that evening. On entering the house, he found a handwritten note from her on the kitchen table in which she yet again swore her undying love and begged him for his forgiveness for her affair with Sergeant Knaggs. He left the house that morning knowing she would not be home until after he had left. He had no desire to see her.

As he drove down Willerby Road heading towards the city and Morley's flat, his mobile vibrated in his pocket. Expecting it to be Amy, he checked the screen, intending to ignore it, but it was Darnley. He had totally forgotten that he had left his boss the answerphone message the night before about Kingston wanting to see him. He was all too well aware that by mid-morning, the shit would hit the fan about what he had said to Kingston. He knew he had no choice but to tell Darnley – warn him. He owed him that much. But he'd planned to do it after the briefing, face-to-face. He declined the call and drove on. Within thirty seconds, Darnley had sent a text: *CALL ME WHEN YOU GET THIS – KINGSTON???* Again, he ignored it, hoping that Darnley would think he was still asleep.

Thirty minutes later, he had once again checked Morley's flat and found it empty. His concern grew when his mobile failed to even ring out. Clearly alerted by his knocking, a rather harassed-looking elderly gentleman peered from the door of a flat opposite Morley's. Granger showed him his warrant card and asked if he had seen his neighbour. He was invited into the man's neat and tidy flat, and his concerns multiplied. The old man firstly set out his credentials as a reliable witness – ex-military policeman; ex-Midland Bank manager; Treasurer, local Conservative Club; Secretary of St George's Road Bowls Club and active member of Neighbourhood Watch. He then categorically stated that something must have happened to young Morley. Apparently the two were mates and Graham had not called round since last Thursday evening to check that he was okay and have a cuppa. He never ever missed a night, unless he warned him he wouldn't be able to call. He had not clapped eyes on him since and had resolved to contact the police this very morning to express his worries. He assumed PC Granger was investigating Graham's disappearance. After trying to reassure the frail and elderly chap that his friend and neighbour was in all probability safe and well and that the police would track him down, he jumped back in his car and headed for Driffield. But his views now mirrored those of Morley's elderly friend – something had happened to him.

He arrived at Driffield just as the briefing was about to start and immediately sensed the change in atmosphere. The bare bones of Grantmore's confession and identification of the gang members had already spread through the team and everyone was keenly awaiting the full story from the boss. Several of the detectives gave him a congratulatory slap on the shoulder, or nodded a "well done" as he looked for an empty seat.

Jo Young passed him a cup of coffee and said, 'Great work, Peter. We've got the bastards now.'

Darnley came out of his office, symbolically rolling up his shirtsleeves. He motioned the young PC over to him and whispered, 'When I ask you to ring me, I expect you to do it immediately. As soon as the briefing is over, I want you in my office. I want to know what Kingston wanted. Have you found Morley?'

Granger shook his head. 'No and I'm worried.'

Darnley waited for the men and women before him to quieten down and then he took them in detail through the events of the previous day – or at least those parts he wanted them to know. He told them all about Graham Morley and how and why he had come to take the photograph of Grantmore and Frame. He was even open about how he had misjudged the potential of Morley and how Granger had kept talking to him, eventually discovering the incriminating photograph and recognising its evidential value. Once again, the young officer received appreciative nods from several of the others. He explained how Granger was now going to try and persuade Morley to give evidence and formally introduce the photograph into the evidence chain.

He then handed over to Jo Young and her partner who had interviewed Grantmore, and they described the full extent of his confession and how he had implicated Frame, Keegan and Pike, who he believed to be three ex-army pals, currently living somewhere in the north-east. The officers had researched the names on the Police National Computer and only Pike was recorded, but then only for a very minor assault years ago, before he joined the army.

The interviewers were sceptical that Grantmore had admitted his full part in the crimes, but things he had said could now be investigated and either confirmed or challenged in subsequent interviews. Would the alibis he had provided stack up? They still had the obvious link to Noel Priestley and his suicide to explore. Darnley had decided that they hadn't yet had chance to investigate Priestley's role and had instructed the interviewers not to ask Grantmore about it. Had the manager told Grantmore about the society's practice with the keys, or had that information gone directly to Frame? Grantmore could well have been the source that told Frame to go to Janice Cooper and Anne Beedham for the keys, even though at this stage he had denied it.

When DC Young revealed that Grantmore had said that Frame had implied to him, as a threat, that it was he who had murdered Emmerson, an additional wave of excitement rippled through the team. A double murder inquiry, crossing two forces, was something that few officers ever got to work on – and they now knew who'd done it. Overnight, the visit from NCIS and Northumbria Police, accompanied by their own ACC (OPS), had changed from an occasion they were dreading into one at which they'd have a chance to impress. An opportunity – not a threat.

When she then revealed that Grantmore had told them off the record that the gang were in the act of planning another job in Humberside and would commit the crime next week, the room really began to hum with excitement.

Darnley told them that he had spoken to the SIO in Northumbria and the names of Frame, Keegan and Pike meant nothing to their inquiry. They had few tangible leads and were now trying to discreetly locate the three men. He had also agreed that they should start enquiries with the army, again discreetly, so as not to alert the gang to their interest.

At this point, however, Darnley reined in some of the high-octane excitement and self-congratulation. He thanked PC Granger and the interviewing officers for their late-night efforts and for all the information they had gleaned from Grantmore.

'After two months, it's great news to have the suspects in our sights and *know* we will be successful. However, I have grave misgivings about how long we have got to gather sufficient evidence to make it worthwhile arresting Frame and his gang. A fishing expedition is no good at this stage... we need more than Grantmore's word. I'm worried about this next job they're planning... in our area. Someone else could get hurt and we cannot allow that to happen. That is why I arranged for Grantmore to get bail. I want him out there, trying to get us more information. I'll keep in touch with him. What I want to impress upon you all is the need for speed coupled with your usual due diligence. Tell your families that they aren't going to be seeing much of you for a while. It'll be twelve-hour days from today and only one rest day per week. Right... now let's determine the actions we need to raise, and prioritise them.'

As the assembled officers asked questions of the interviewers and the SIO, DS Ride and his HOLMES team made a list of all the actions and enquiries that would now need to be made to focus the last two months' work on Grantmore, Frame, Keegan and Pike. That focus and those specific actions were then refined and prioritised. An obvious immediate priority was to find Morley and secure his cooperation, and Granger was asked to describe what he had done so far, and he repeated the concerns of Morley's elderly neighbour.

As Granger sat and listened to the hum of activity and excitement, he realised the inquiry had spent two months searching for evidence, securing intelligence, information and even gossip. Blind alleys had been entered, cul-de-sacs explored, time-wasters interviewed, witnesses seen and re-seen, well over 1,000 statements taken and a nominal index of over 2,000 names created. A large majority of which was of no use now that they knew where to focus. It had been like trying to complete a jigsaw puzzle without a picture – and using pieces from the wrong jigsaw. But now it could be completed. Useless pieces could be ditched and the right ones searched for. He was also acutely aware of how he had been allowed to see more of the true picture than the others. He understood how Darnley had managed to gain the confession. He also knew that he did not intend to complete the puzzle in accordance with the rules. He had some shortcuts planned. But what?

As he listened to the conversations from the more experienced detectives in the room querying how PACE had been complied with, why Grantmore had been bailed and how further evidence might be obtained, he realised just how far out on a limb Darnley was.

Twenty-Six

That Same Morning

I returned to my office, happy with the way the briefing had gone and glad that my counterpart in Northumbria had agreed that once we had formally identified and located Frame and his mates, we would not rush to arrest them. I had explained to him how Grantmore was now working to deliver us further concrete information. He was keen to cooperate and looking forward to tomorrow's meeting. After the previous day's successes, I'd fallen into a deep and dreamless sleep and it wasn't until I switched my phone back on at about six thirty this morning, that I saw the missed calls from Granger and listened to his message. Kingston could be a big fly in the ointment.

I motioned Granger to the only other chair in my room. He sat looking extremely uncomfortable. His acne was flaring up, a sign I now recognised as stress. Without any request from me, he explained what Kingston had said. I didn't interrupt. I just sat and worried.

At the end of his tale, he fell into silence without telling me how he had responded. So I told him about Kingston's threat to me yesterday afternoon. His acne virtually pulsated and from the look on his face, I knew he wasn't going to give me good news.

'So what did you tell him?'

'I'm sorry, boss. You know what I'm like. I should have just said that I didn't know what he was talking about and left it at that… but I think I've been too clever… again.' He shook his head as if in shame.

'Fucking hell, Peter, just spit it out.'

'I didn't tell him anything… just that I had tape-recorded the conversation and was intending to report him for bullying and intimidation.' His eyes widened and he looked at me as if waiting for me to explode.

'And did you?'

'Did I what?'

'Tape him.'

'No. How could I? But he believed me… he wanted to search me. He went mental, threatened all sorts of stuff to me… to you… to Amy. He really lost it. He says he's going to see the Chief Constable today and tell him his suspicions about you… he's adamant you're bent… his words. He's going to get me suspended immediately.' He paused. 'I should have just denied what he was talking about. I'm sorry.'

Despite myself, I grinned at my young co-conspirator.

I asked him about the details of the threats and intimidation he thought Kingston had made and reassured myself he had told him nothing that the bastard could use against me. However, it was pretty obvious he was on my case – and thinking along the right lines. It was equally obvious that someone on my inquiry was feeding him information.

'You are a one-off. If you survive all this, you'll end up a bloody Chief Constable. I didn't get to your level of quick thinking… and let's be honest, deviousness, until I had about fifteen years in the job.'

He grinned back and in that instant I felt one hundred and ten per cent sure of his loyalty.

'I doubt he'll go to the Chief… he can't be sure you didn't

tape him... and without a doubt he overstepped the mark with a junior officer. He'll bottle it. But I wish we could make sure he does.'

We both fell into silence. Thinking.

'The fact that you have planted a fear about taping him and threatened to complain will stall him. You've put him on the back foot... for the time being. But we need something to distract him further until we get this sorted out.'

'I reckon I know who is Kingston's man on the inquiry. Could that help?'

He shuffled uncomfortably in his chair, clearly not happy at what he saw as his impending betrayal of a colleague. I allowed him time to wrestle with his conscience.

Eventually, he said, 'It's DS Naylor... I think. I heard him bad-mouthing you last week to DC Beatty after he'd interviewed Grantmore. He said the inquiry was a cock-up... and he needed to pass it on.'

'And he actually said it was to Kingston?'

'No... and at the time I was just pissed off at what he was saying and gave it no more thought, but last night Kingston implied someone on the inquiry was feeding him information. He knew about the photograph of Grantmore and said something about having informants. The two things just seem to add up...'

'So what's your thinking? How can we use Naylor?'

Why the hell was I asking him? I was the senior officer and manipulator-in-chief.

'Well, when he was slagging you off, he also talked about that job that was in the local papers and on *Look North* last week about the inquest on the cyclist. The one where all the shit's flying.'

I'd heard a bit about the case but had been too busy to absorb any details. I shrugged my shoulders to indicate he should continue.

'There was a chap found dead in a ditch next to a minor road near Pocklington, September or October time last year. His pushbike was on top of him. It was written off by traffic as a road accident, but no other vehicle was ever proved to be involved. The family have always said we never investigated it properly. There's been a lot of local media interest since the inquest, rubbishing the police investigation as inadequate, disinterested... you know, the usual stuff.'

My interest was aroused. 'Go on... where does Naylor fit in?'

'He was saying that he got sent to the scene when the rural bobby was suspicious about the cause and asked for CID. Well, at the inquest when he gave evidence, he was criticised for not taking the inquiry further, or alerting a more senior detective... and this is where it gets interesting.'

'I've not heard about this at all.'

'He was talking to DC Beatty... who I should say was not taking any part in slagging you off. He told him that he'd called Kingston who was duty senior detective... and he refused to come out. He claims Kingston told him to just call traffic.'

'Did Naylor tell the inquest about Kingston refusing to go to the scene?'

'No, he reckoned he was caught unawares with the line of questioning and didn't say anything. Probably scared to drop him in it. The inquest recorded an open verdict, strengthening the family's hand, who are now demanding further police investigations.'

I could sense he was warming to his tale being a potential answer to our dilemma, so I just let him continue.

'He told Beatty that after the inquest he asked Kingston what he was going to do about it and he totally denied he had taken a call from him. Naylor's incensed that Kingston's shafting him.'

'But his call to Kingston will be shown on the command and control log.' I was really getting interested.

'That's what Beatty said. But he didn't go through the Command Centre, just rang Kingston direct and when he wouldn't come, Naylor handed it over to traffic as he'd been told. I suppose he never dreamt it would come back to bite him and it'd be his word against a detective superintendent's.'

'Bugger. Pity it's not on the incident log.'

But he had more.

'Naylor told Beatty that when he rang him, Kingston got stroppy at being disturbed, saying there was no way he was trekking across the county for a bloody traffic accident… when he was out to dinner for his wedding anniversary at Oscar's Barn… you know, the posh place on the south bank.'

He looked at me, positively beaming.

'And I've checked… he was there in a party of four. The booking was made in his name.'

I felt ridiculously proud of him. A born detective.

'Bloody hell. With the family up in arms there'll have to be a reinvestigation, and whether Naylor's lying or Kingston's covering his own arse, the truth will come out. There'll be mobile phone records for a start. And if it was his anniversary on that evening… or even thereabouts… how could Naylor make that up?'

I was beginning to enjoy this scenario – and was already cooking up a plot.

'There's more, boss. Naylor implied that Kingston had some sort of hold over him and he told Beatty that he was pretty sure that all the shit would roll downhill and hit him. He knows there will be some sort of reinvestigation due to the fuss the family are making and he's shitting himself about it.'

'Did he say what Kingston's got on him?'

'No… do you want me to find out?'

Ten minutes later, PC Granger left my office to renew his quest to find Graham Morley. He left, I'd like to think, feeling pretty confident that any threats from Detective Superintendent Kingston were about to be neutralised. He also left trying to tell me how worried he was about being unable to find Graham Morley, but I was too preoccupied to listen.

He left me thinking I was not only about to enjoy myself – but also kill three birds with one stone.

*

When Richard Wilde had taken the call from Matt Darnley the previous night, reassuring him that Russ Holland had been warned off, he had been drunk. He had literally been drowning his sorrows. First thing Monday morning, another round of redundancies had been announced and one of the casualties was Richard's best mate. He had been a reporter about a year longer than Richard and having just emerged from his trainee role was due a substantial pay rise – but instead had got the boot. While trying his best to reassure his mate that he was good at his job and bound to get another soon, all Richard could really think was – me next. So when Darnley had rung with the news about Holland, the details hadn't actually registered in his drink-sodden brain.

But now he was in the newsroom, nursing a stinking hangover and trying desperately to recall exactly what Darnley had said. All had been sorted officially? All danger had passed? But Richard couldn't shake the notion that it didn't matter anyway as his career was knackered – his friend's future was his future – there wasn't one. At least not as a journalist. So what the hell did it matter?

Following the revelations from Morley and after confronting Darnley on Friday, he had spent the weekend in an agony of indecision. Going over and over what Morley had told him and how Darnley had appeared to have answers that lessened the impact of Morley's bombshells. Was he colluding with a corrupt senior police officer? What if Holland finished Grantmore off? He knew he'd sat on what he knew for too long and, even worse, continued to do the detective's bidding – his dirty work. The more he pondered, the more the message drummed into him from day one at the *Mail* haunted him.

'*You are junior reporters and if you get the merest sniff of something nationally newsworthy, intriguing, corrupt, dodgy, difficult, dangerous, etc., etc., etc., tell a senior member of staff immediately.*'

Morley's information about taking the photograph of Grantmore at the Silver Cod fitted that bill easily enough – it was about a murder. But that had developed into him having information that an ex-army hero, living under a false identity, had injected bleach into the eye of an infamous local gangster manacled to a bed in a whorehouse. Now that was news.

But still he'd told no one. Done nothing. Come Monday morning, he had determined that his only viable course of action was to say nothing and hope that the shit never did hit the fan and bollocks to journalistic ethics and standards. The more he thought about it, the more he concluded that Darnley had much more of a reason to make sure this never got out than he had. He had more to lose. And he seemed to be something of an expert at subterfuge, double-dealing and skulduggery. Having opted to keep his gob shut and his fingers crossed, the staff meeting was called and the additional redundancies announced. From that point on, his worries about Darnley, Holland, Morley and Grantmore slowly submerged in a sea of Carlsberg as he got pissed with his mate.

Now, on this Tuesday, his hangover was resulting in hopeless lethargy – *Who gives a shit? I'm finished anyway.* Staring unseeing at his computer screen where he was supposed to be writing an article about the current wave of shed burglaries in Holderness, he was suddenly jolted awake by the vibration of his mobile on his desk. He checked the screen and for a split second considered not taking the call. But he picked up the phone and left the room. For this, he needed privacy.

*

I'd decided to keep things light. I was convinced that my cub reporter was back onside after my reassuring call last night. So when he answered, I acted as if we'd never had the conversation last week and all was well with the world.

'Morning, Richard, how are you?'

There was silence on the other end.

'Richard?'

I could almost hear his brain whirring. I guessed everything wasn't "well with his world".

But then he responded in a tremulous stutter: 'But... but... but what exactly has changed... is Holland... has Morley...?'

I interrupted him. 'No time for that now... I told you, it's no longer a problem. It's sorted. Trust me.'

My God, how many times had I trotted out the "trust me" crap lately? But before ringing him, I had determined to act in a positive, controlled and confident manner, as I needed him to absorb my news and act exactly how I told him. I wanted him to be sure things were okay. Sure he could really trust me.

His next response was only slightly less pensive. 'But aren't you worried about what Morley told me?'

Clearly, more reassurance was needed.

'Richard, listen. As I explained last night, Holland is off Grantmore's back. I cannot afford to let him get to him and so I've sorted it... officially. In addition, I can't do anything with what Morley says about Holland attacking Grantmore, because he won't give evidence... and anyway, that's my problem not yours. You don't need to worry about that. Come on, Richard, it's sorted.'

There was no response, so I pressed on, sounding relaxed, confident and breezy. 'Now I'm ringing up to make your day... you are going to have a cracking Tuesday...'

Then Richard Wilde, budding crime reporter, decided to go with the flow – to trust me.

I told him what to do.

*

By 5pm that evening, Richard Wilde's fortunes seemed to have turned dramatically. He was now sitting with the crime editor and the newspaper's editor-in-chief – a man few employees at his level ever got to talk to, but here they were in the boardroom, each nursing a fine malt whisky.

Richard had immediately cottoned on to the context of Darnley's telephone call. He had been the reporter in Hull coroners' court when the family of fifty-four-year-old Keith Donavan had raised a right stink when the coroner returned an open verdict upon his death. He had witnessed the embarrassment of Detective Sergeant Naylor in the witness box, when berated by the family's legal representative for not treating the incident seriously. Following the inquest, he'd been tasked with investigating the surrounding circumstances of Donavan's mysterious death. He had already visited the ditch where he had been found, and spoken, albeit off the record to the local beat bobby who was first on the scene.

He had also met the family and was convinced that they had both the resources and the will to continue their "campaign for justice for Keith". The reporter could recognise the potential newsworthiness of the story. How on earth did Keith Donavan end up in a ditch with his bike on top of him? The cause of death was drowning – in just over a foot of water. Neither he nor his bike was damaged and although he had been drinking, he was not drunk.

Even from his limited experience, Richard knew that many aspects of what the police were asked to investigate were never fully explained – mysteries were common. But families always want to know why and often until they did, they looked for someone to blame. In this case, Humberside Police were in the firing line. Already the newspaper had run a short article on the mounting controversy, and the family were keen to start a campaign and had asked the paper to support it.

Now Darnley had inexplicably provided him with a whole new angle. An angle the family would seize upon and really use to stir the shit – and that would sell newspapers.

Clearly, Darnley had an axe to grind with his fellow detective superintendent.

The detective had not explained but implied it was a gesture of goodwill – an example of the tips he would continue to give him to further cement an ongoing professional relationship. It was essentially a bribe. Keep your mouth shut about Morley, Grantmore and Holland and you'll get more insider information. He decided to go with his gut – perhaps subterfuge, skulduggery and manipulation really were the way to career advancement. He'd go with the flow and ride this particular wave while he could.

Wilde was wise enough not to reveal his source to his boss, who was suitably impressed with not only the fact that this young lad seemed to regularly come up with crime-related scoops but also that he withstood his own and the crime editor's efforts to find out who his source was. Both were keen to know. The crime editor recalled the similar tip-off that young Wilde had gained on the Daggett murder before Christmas. He knew that Richard Wilde's job on the newspaper was as secure as it could be, even before this latest piece of excellent investigative journalism, but he had no intention of telling him. He believed in keeping his junior staff keen and hungry.

He had listened to Richard's account of how Detective Superintendent David Kingston, the high-flying, Special Course "blue-eyed boy" had probably dropped an almighty bollock. He was assured that the source was reliable and that he had personally rechecked the restaurant booking to confirm his source's veracity. He also revealed that he had Kingston's home address. While they planned their strategy, another reporter was dispatched to Oscar's Barn in an effort to find out if Kingston, who was on call and therefore to all intents and purposes on duty, was inebriated. A staff member who wished to remain anonymous confirmed that the whole party were pissed. With that little gem seen as the icing on the cake, the door-stepping that Darnley had asked Wilde to arrange was authorised. Accompanied by a more senior colleague, Richard had asked Kingston to comment on the allegation that he had refused to attend the scene of a potential murder, as he was too busy drunkenly celebrating his wedding anniversary at one of the region's top restaurants – when he was meant to be on call.

The doorstep confrontation had actually gone better than Wilde, the crime editor, or even Darnley could have hoped. The three journalists were celebrating that success.

The editor-in chief raised his glass to Richard. "You're going places, kid, if you keep this up. Well done. Well done. Why the hell he even said anything I don't get. If he hadn't run off at the mouth like he did, we'd have struggled to print anything.'

Richard could not help but bask in the glow of the top man's admiration. How things had changed in less than four hours. Darnley had gone from his nemesis to his saviour. He raised his glass towards his boss and blew his own trumpet a little more.

'He had refused to answer any questions and was busy ushering us off his property when I tried one last ploy. I intimated that the DS who was pilloried at the inquest by the family's solicitor was the person who had tipped us off about the celebration at Wintringham Fields. Then he just lost his temper... and his judgement.'

This was of course exactly what Darnley had told him to do. Imply that DS Naylor was the source of his information.

Wilde continued boasting. 'I must have just hit a nerve... it was a guess but there's obviously something about DS Naylor... he immediately began to cast aspersions on his ability, admitted that the DS had rung him about the body but never requested he attend the scene and had not accurately explained the circumstances.'

'So we have a neat and tidy... and verifiable account we can run with,' chuckled the editor-in-chief, 'family convinced it's a murder, Open verdict, an incompetent DS according to the detective superintendent, who himself is too busy having a posh dinner... and apparently well pissed... to visit a potential murder scene. We need a comment from the Chief Constable to round it off... then we run the family's campaign for justice. Fucking beautiful. This'll get national interest.'

'I have a little bit more', grinned Richard. 'Remember that case last month when Sean Grantmore was blinded? Kingston was taken off it because he buggered up the scene. Could we incorporate that into the story? I have checked what my source has told me and Kingston was definitely the first senior officer to attend the incident.'

'Oh, it just gets better. Our lazy, drunken senior detective is also incompetent. We can probably drip that in later… keep the story running a little longer.' The boss raised his whisky once more to his favourite young reporter and chucked in another "You will go far, young man".

The crime editor, however, was now lost in his own thoughts. Young Wilde was obviously getting his information from someone in Humberside Police who clearly wanted to shaft Detective Superintendent Kingston. From his experience, which was considerable, this had all the hallmarks of Matt Darnley. He recalled that it had indeed been Darnley he had interviewed about the attack on Grantmore last month and he had investigated the Daggett murder. So there were clear links. If Richard Wilde had somehow fallen into Darnley's clutches, he'd need to be very, very careful.

*

It was early evening and I had just put the finishing touches to my presentation for tomorrow morning's review. I was buzzing. Jane Greenhall had rung about an hour earlier to say that Crabbe was also intending to attend and had suggested we hold it in the incident room as opposed to Headquarters – to add an air of "authenticity". Even she couldn't resist a chuckle at Crabbe's choice of description. I was growing more confident that the review would go well, as the inquiry was looking set to progress rapidly. I was just keen to hear from Granger that Morley had provided a statement. Richard Wilde had contacted me immediately after his confrontation with Kingston, proud to be en route to debrief his editor-in-chief. He'd promised to ring me back after the meeting to let me know how the *Mail* proposed to handle the story.

It seemed like I had killed two of my birds.

There was a knock on the door and yet again the indomitable Detective Sergeant Ride came in with more news.

'Hey up, boss, something's afoot. I've just had Professional Standards on the blower telling me to let you know that DS Naylor has been suspended. Now. Forthwith. Do not pass go. Do not collect two hundred pounds. Superintendent Proctor wants you to ring him so he can explain.'

Bird number three dispatched!

I pretended to look surprised. 'Why? Do we know?'

'Well, they obviously didn't tell little old me... but a little bird tells me it's something to do with talking to the *Hull Mail*.'

'Bollocks... about our job? Not just when we are at a vital point?'

I hoped I was sounding convincing, as Ridey had an extremely well-tuned bullshit detector.

I hadn't expected anything to happen this quickly. Wilde had told me what had happened and how Kingston had lost his temper, and he was hoping that the story would appear in tomorrow's paper. I wondered if Kingston had taken the initiative, got in first and dropped Naylor.

'Cheers, Tony. I'll ring and find out what's going on. Have you heard anything from Pete Granger? Has he tracked Morley down yet?'

'I wanted to talk to you about that. He rang about an hour ago to say he's been to his flat again and then to his workplace... he works part-time for the Hull City Council in their IT department on Mondays, Tuesdays and Wednesdays, and he never turned up yesterday or today. Granger's really worried about him.'

'Damn. That old guy who lived in the same flats reckons he hasn't seen him since Thursday.'

I knew that Morley had spoken to Richard Wilde on Friday, so it seems he had not been about since then. I was also starting to get worried.

'Tell Pete to leave his number with the neighbour, at his work and with anyone else that might see him. Make sure they ring us as soon as he surfaces. When he's done that, get him back here to see me.'

When Ridey left, I sat and pondered about how I'd play tomorrow's review if we hadn't managed to track Morley down and obtain the statement. I needed to speak to Granger, so we could coordinate how we'd explain the photograph and Morley's role. But first I had to ring Superintendent Proctor before he went off duty. While I was looking up his number, another thought struck me. This morning, I had set out to merely knock Kingston off his stride – temporarily stall his desire to drop me in the shit by giving him something else to think about. It seemed from Wilde's earlier ebullient phone call that that objective had been well and truly delivered. Could I now go further?

Steve Proctor picked up immediately and after exchanging pleasantries, he launched into business explaining what I already knew about the inquest into Keith Donovan's death, the family's outrage and Naylor's alleged shortcomings. He explained that the family had this very afternoon made a formal complaint about the officer and about Humberside Police in general failing to adequately investigate the circumstances. He then went on to describe how Detective Superintendent Kingston within an hour of that complaint being made demanded to see ACC Paul Jones and described how he had been confronted at his own home by two *Hull Mail* reporters, using information that he alleged could only have come from Detective Sergeant Naylor. Jones had ordered Naylor's immediate suspension.

So Kingston had decided to get in first.

Already knowing the answers, I probed him for more detail about what the reporters knew and bit by bit the story of the anniversary dinner came out, along with Kingston's version of events – that Naylor had rung him but had not properly described the circumstances and had never actually asked him to attend the scene. How, of course, he would have done, if the DS had done his job properly. Kingston was also claiming that after his grilling at the inquest, Naylor had threatened him that if he didn't admit he had failed to attend and thus exonerate him, he would go to the press. I queried if that was true why Kingston had never done anything about such a threat from a junior officer. After all, this had supposedly taken place last week.

At this point, Steve Proctor asked me to hang on a moment, and I heard him get up and close his office door before he continued.

'Exactly. The whole thing fucking stinks. I've raised that already but everyone knows I hate the bastard, and think I'm just being vindictive.'

He sounded bloody vindictive.

Steve Proctor had been my fellow detective superintendent until Crabbe had decided that his career needed "developing" – to make way for Kingston's to be developed – in the CID. Steve had been a damn good detective, rising right through the ranks of CID in his thirty-two years police service and he had bitterly resented being what he saw as side-lined – put out to grass – for a "Bramshill flyer" on his way up the slippery pole to the top. He knew he'd never now get to be a detective chief superintendent and Head of CID, his ultimate and, to be fair, well-deserved final career goal. A sideways move to the Professional Standards Branch was in his view a way of nudging him into retirement and a humiliating end to his career.

It was all too easy to press his buttons.

'Look, Steve, we worked well as a team. We trusted each other and watched each other's backs. I can't stand Kingston and he's fucking useless, but apart from all that, I reckon you're dead right to smell a rat. If Naylor had really threatened him with going to the press, Kingston would have run crying to either his mentor Paul Jones or even the ruddy Chief.'

'I've said all this, but of course Paul Jones is overseeing the complaint and the inquiry into Naylor. Jones and Kingston are two peas out of the same pissing pod. Kingston's told him he never reported Naylor's threats, as he thought the man was just overwrought and he dealt with it himself... man to man. Didn't want to get him into bother. Like hell.'

'Just between you and me, I've got little time for Naylor but he just wouldn't dare not to try and call out a more senior detective to a suspicious death. He'd just want to pass the buck and watch his own back.' I paused for dramatic effect... 'And from what I've heard, he's Kingston's man, his snout... and Kingston has somehow got the black on him.'

'Can you find out what?'

'I'll do my best and be in touch. But this is just between me and you, okay?'

'Bloody hell, Matt, as you say, we've watched each other's backs enough times to trust each other. Come on, mate... I might even get my old job back.'

Twenty-Seven

That Same Evening
Tuesday, 9th February 1999

As Richard Wilde left the boardroom following what was probably the proudest moment of his fledgling career, one hundred miles away in Newcastle, Peter Frame sat up in bed and lit a cigarette. The woman beside him stretched luxuriously and with her sexiest smile asked him to light her one too. He did as he was asked, smiling back at the extremely attractive Debbie Pike, while mentally counting how long it had taken him to get Billy Pike's young widow into bed. His smile turned to a self-satisfied grin. It was just five days. Five days after he and Mick had dropped Billy into the cold North Sea from the stern of *The Blaydon Races*.

'What are you grinning at?' asked Debbie, poking him playfully in the ribs.

'Just thinking that you were even better in bed than I'd imagined… and wondering what the hell you see in Billy.'

He had almost said "saw".

'Money. Easy money. No more and no less.' She grinned too and drew hard on the fag.

After he and Mick had disposed of their bungling accomplice, Frame had grown perturbed that his wife had not contacted him, worried about his whereabouts. After five days, he had gone to suss out what the hell was going on and decided to ask her where the hell he was. Within half an hour, she had seduced him. The sex had been incredible and he was now confident that she wasn't suspicious about Billy's absence – and certainly wasn't concerned.

The truth was that Debbie suspected Billy was dead and that the man she had just slept with had killed him. If Frame had known what she was thinking she would have already met the same fate as her husband.

Debbie had known for some time that her husband, Frame and Keegan were committing crime. There was no other explanation for the change in Billy's fortunes. She had known Billy Pike a long time and him being flush with money was not due to hard work, a lottery win or the death of a long-lost relative – he had to be nicking it.

Billy had been one of the well-known local teenage tearaways when she was still at primary school. The sort of lad her mam and dad tried to steer her away from, but the type to which she was irresistibly drawn – the hard, bad lads. His conviction for an assault at a Newcastle United game, when he was about eighteen, only enhanced his appeal. By the time she was fourteen, he'd joined the army and left the area. She'd still see him about when he was home on leave and still fancied him, but their paths never crossed.

By the time she was twenty, she'd already had a kid to one bloke, who immediately cleared off, and within a year married another who turned out to be just as useless as the father of her young son. At twenty-three, she had two kids and was on her own in a council flat on the Cowgate estate, fulfilling the fears of her parents. When Billy Pike reappeared permanently in the area a few years ago, she had used her still effective feminine wiles to attract the ex-squaddie. She then basically used him as a meal ticket, in exchange for the odd night in her bed. Billy was infatuated by Debbie, who was about seven years his junior and far more attractive than any woman he had ever managed to bed without agreeing a price beforehand. Having actually met and got to know the object of her schoolgirl crush, she realised he was both boring and possessive. But he was generous. For those few years, Debbie enjoyed more creature comforts than she had for years and although she felt no affection for him, she continued to sponge off him while keeping him interested.

Then, over a period of two or three months, things changed. His gifts became more extravagant, he began to dress better and he purchased his rented flat. He told her about two of his old buddies from the army who had moved back to the Newcastle area, one of whom had his own haulage business and the other who rented a trawler. He had told her how he was working for both of them and making plenty of money, and his declarations of devotion became more earnest and regular – alongside his increasing generosity. This wasn't the high life but for Debbie Banks it was beyond what she'd ever experienced. Billy's pleas to marry him and move in became decidedly more attractive.

Debbie didn't even finish her schooling but she was smart and streetwise and had learnt through her experiences with her two previous feckless partners. She was no longer a mug where men were concerned. So before she committed to Billy Pike, she made it her business to find out all she could about Billy's new employers: Peter Frame and Mick Keegan.

Billy had never taken her out in either of the men's company but their paths had crossed a couple of times and she had been introduced to them both. She had blushed – a very rare reaction for Debbie – when Frame had overtly appraised her feminine charms. His height, good looks and dress sense were complemented by his velvety cultured voice and confidence. Billy had introduced him as his former senior officer and new employer. As he shook her hand with a warm, dry and firm grip, he looked directly into her eyes and told her what a lucky lady she was to have such a reliable and honest man as Billy Pike looking after her. Billy had virtually exploded with pride and later told her all about the university-educated senior officer, but despite her questioning remained vague about exactly what work he was doing for him. She was intrigued by Frame and why he was employing such a jerk as Billy.

When eventually they met Frame again in a city centre bar, he was with Billy's other ex-army colleague and employer, Mick Keegan. Frame was just as charming and even more attentive as he invited her and Billy to join them for a drink. He quite deliberately left his leg resting against hers beneath the table and as she rose to leave, gave her bare thigh a gentle squeeze. Keegan on the other hand barely passed the time of day, obviously not happy about Frame asking them to join them. As with Frame, she was unable to prise from Billy exactly what he did for Keegan, other than "this and that".

Over the next few months, Billy would stay more regularly at her house, and his efforts to persuade her to move in and marry him intensified, and her will to resist slowly weakened. When he bought a small house in a nicer area, she realised that although she'd never love Billy Pike, he would provide for her and the kids better than any of the other no-hopers she was likely to meet. Her only doubts now remained about how long this could last. She had spotted the pattern where Billy would disappear for several days at a time, saying that he was either driving for Frame, usually down south, or accompanying Keegan on a fishing trip. These absences would be prefaced by urgent meetings he had to attend and a string of phone calls on his newly acquired Nokia mobile, that all seemed to require privacy. Once away, he never contacted her but would return home in a much more animated state than was his normal demeanour, and his generosity would know no bounds. His reluctance to discuss where he had been, or what he had been doing, was obvious and it was at this point in their relationship, on the verge of agreeing to marry him, that she concluded he was committing crimes with his ex-army buddies and she needed to know more. She had no qualms whatsoever about living on the proceeds of crime, but she needed to be assured of her intended husband's future prospects. Was this ever-improving lifestyle likely to be long-lasting? A short-lived shot at a financially secure and comfortable marriage, quickly followed by a husband in prison was not in her plan. In the end, the fact that a well-educated ex-army officer was obviously in charge reassured her, and even Billy's tight-lipped stance on his job and where he had been, helped to convince her that things were being tightly run and her future was looking good. Eventually, all her misgivings dissipated and in August 1998 she married Billy and moved into his house.

Things had gone well for the first six months. Then in early February, Billy had returned from one of his trips away with a broken nose and in a state of obvious terror. He had crashed into the house, dashed upstairs and gone into the shower for what seemed like an age. When he eventually came downstairs, she could see he was trembling, unable to settle and clearly terrified. When she asked him what had happened, he would not communicate, leaving the house as quickly as he had entered it and was gone for hours. When he returned, he sat sullenly in front of the TV, refusing to open up.

Later that evening, when the local news carried the story of the murder of a young man in Ponteland during the course of a robbery the previous night, Billy began to cry. Debbie knew her brief period of married bliss was at an end. He allowed her to hold him in her arms and while he sobbed, the full story of how he had accidentally shot Ryan

Harrod poured out. Once he had started he couldn't stop, and he unloaded random details of the crimes he, Frame and Keegan had committed over the last few months. Debbie hushed and soothed him just like she would her kids until he fell asleep. Then she wrote as many of the details as she could recall in an old notebook and then hid it at the back of one of her drawers. She then sat thinking about what she should do. What was the best for her and the kids? She didn't want to leave this house. She didn't give a toss about Billy; he was now a lost cause. How could she use the information she had to best effect?

The next morning, she worked hard to reassure her husband that it was an accident. He wasn't a bad man. She would stand by him. It would all be all right. Bit by bit, slowly but surely, Billy calmed down. They didn't leave the house that day, other than to take and collect her son from school. They talked about how he would continue to work for Frame but be far more cautious and careful in future. Debbie gleaned how much cash they had netted – and what had been Billy's share. He described how Frame was the organiser – the leader – just as in the army, and how he recruited other gang members if they needed them.

At this point, he blurted out how Frame had killed one of the men they had hired. Billy had been ill with the flu and unable to take part in the job. She gathered that this had been a building society robbery somewhere near Hull that had taken place just before Christmas. Once Billy explained why Frame had shot the man, she knew that Billy would not be continuing his criminal career with Peter Frame. In fact, he'd be lucky to live. These latest "confessions" went into her notebook later that day.

Debbie was amazed that Billy had not even considered that he was destined to meet the same fate as the Hull thug. In fact, he kept repeating, almost as a mantra, 'Peter will sort all this out.' It was clear that the loyalty, allegiance and trust Major Peter Frame had imbued from his men in a war zone was just as strong here in Newcastle, when committing serious crime.

Even when Mick Keegan contacted Billy later that evening and commanded him to meet him and Frame at six thirty the following morning next to his trawler, Billy still didn't smell the rat that Debbie did. She spent the next few hours trying to wheedle more information out of him without any clear idea of why or how she might use it. She was resigned to the fact that just as in the past, all good things that came her way blew up in her face. But she was determined to salvage something from the wreckage that was her six-month-long marriage. Before they went to bed, she was pretty confident that she had enough information about their crimes to blackmail Frame and Keegan. She was equally sure that neither man would bend to such extortion, especially from a woman. But was there a reward? Without appreciating it, Debbie had followed the old adage that knowledge is power.

As she fell asleep, she had worked out that the odds of Billy surviving his meeting in the morning were slim. Frame had shot the other bloke from Hull for being the weak link and Billy had committed an even worse error. Consequently, five minutes after Billy left the house next morning, Debbie followed in a taxi, leaving the kids asleep and alone. She told the taxi to wait and keeping out of sight she saw Billy, Frame and Keegan talking on the dockside before they all boarded *The Blaydon Races* and cast off.

She never saw Billy again.

Keeping quiet about her husband's disappearance was difficult, but she rationalised that if asked, she'd say that he often worked away from home without contacting her. She banked on Frame turning up pretending to look for him, when she didn't raise the expected hue and cry – and when he did she'd be ready. She knew he was attracted to her, and guessed that he knew she'd reciprocate. At this stage, her only plan was to change horses mid-race. If Billy could no longer provide for her and the kids because Frame had killed him, then he should take on that responsibility. She was not daft enough to think this was a permanent solution to her predicament – just a satisfactory stopgap until she could figure out her next move. So when the dashing ex-officer rang, she offloaded the children on her mother and dressed in her best underwear. When he turned up at her door pretending concern about the absent Billy Pike, Debbie told him that she had thought he was at work with him or Keegan, but then became angry at her useless husband's unreliability when Frame explained he wasn't. She lied that Billy had often spoken about running away from his newfound responsibilities, realising quickly after their marriage that he was not cut out to be a surrogate father. Her rehearsals in front of the bathroom mirror at dissolving into tears about how the hell she and the kids would manage now, before subtly seducing him, seemed to have paid off. Frame, like most men, seemed to be putty in her expert sexual hands, and Debbie smugly believed that phase one of her plan was in the bag.

While they smoked their post-coital cigarette, Debbie worked on giving the impression she was slow on the uptake and trusting, anxious not to give Frame any clue that she suspected they were engaged in criminal enterprise. She was blatant about her sexual attraction to the posh ex-officer and her desire to provide him with all necessary creature comforts – if he was prepared to deliver hers. When Frame seemed to accept all she said and was all too eager to comply, Debbie felt herself relax a little. Maybe this could actually work out. If this man was as clever as he sounded, being the mistress of a successful criminal could be a sound lifestyle choice.

Frame for his part was happy to briefly enjoy Debbie's finely honed sexual skills. He knew she was just manipulating him for her own ends but for now it suited him – he wouldn't be around for long. He judged her to be a thick, cold-hearted, manipulative bitch and rationalised that a woman like her would have tried to blackmail him in some way, if she had any inkling about the trio's crimes or Billy's death. But Frame had never been involved with a woman like Debbie Pike before. He'd always moved in different circles. He saw her rough edges, lack of formal education and her willingness to marry Billy for money as a sign of low intelligence. He'd not recognised her cunning, callous nature and lack of heart.

For her part, she thought all men could be manipulated with sex – it had always worked in the past. Just as he had done, she had missed those same cold-hearted traits in him. Both had very seriously underestimated each other's survival instincts.

Each thinking the other was now under control, they enjoyed their cigarettes, both apparently in a state of post-sexual harmony and understanding.

In that mindset, Frame was not as careful as he should have been when his mobile rang and he recognised Keegan's number. He climbed out of bed and went into the adjoining bathroom, failing to register that Debbie had crept to the bedroom door and was listening.

'No problem. She just thinks he's cleared off,' he whispered. 'She's actually pleased to see the back of him and seems to be planning for me to take his place. Daft bitch. I'm going along with it for now to make sure she knows nothing.'

From this one short exchange, Debbie knew where she stood – and gained an immediate advantage. She was assuming the call had come from Keegan, as Billy had given her no reason to believe there was a fourth gang member.

'But we do have another problem,' Frame continued, 'my contact at Catterick has been in touch. Northumbria Police have asked for our army records.'

There was a lengthy silence while Frame listened.

'Don't panic. I've arranged for them to be mislaid for a couple of days. If they had anything solid, we'd have been arrested already... but they are clearly looking. So we'll bring the job forward and do the one we've selected up here, not the one in Hull. Keep out of the way now. We'll do it tomorrow night. I'll stay here the night... I'm sure the silly cow won't mind. Then we're out of here as planned.'

Silence.

'We still need a driver – we can't do the job up here without a third man. I'll ring Grantmore now and arrange to meet tomorrow morning, somewhere down there. Then he's probably going to need a trip on your boat too.'

Silence.

'No, leave it all on the boat for now. I'll ring you back after I've spoken to him. Give me a couple of hours... and, Mick; make sure that boat's secure.'

The loo flushed, giving Debbie time to get back into bed. Frame strode back into the bedroom and began to dress, with no effort at all to try and maintain the air of intimacy and romance they'd enjoyed before the phone call.

'Got to go, I'm afraid. Duty calls.' He bent and gave her a cursory kiss on the forehead. 'I won't be long... back before bedtime... if that's okay? I'll let myself out.'

With that he left.

Debbie was nothing if not a realist and knew her thoughts of just a few minutes ago of living off Frame's ill-gotten gains were dashed. He was clearly planning one last job and then planning to flee. She wasn't in his plans. Her mind switched to how she might still resurrect something from the situation. Frame had killed her golden goose and he now had to pay.

She fetched the notebook from her underwear drawer and added the latest information gleaned from listening to his conversation. That included the name Grantmore. She was now focussed upon either the blackmail approach or a police reward. Was revenge the only thing left to her? She resolved to grass up Frame and Keegan as her last resort.

But it was not until she actually wrote what she'd heard Frame say about making sure the boat was secure that she realised there was in all probability another option. After all, he would never suspect her – she was just a silly cow, a daft bitch. He'd see how daft.

Twenty-Eight

Still That Same Evening

I looked pointedly at my watch. It was ten past bloody nine and I was still in the incident room putting the finishing touches to my presentation for the morning. Pete Granger, however, did not take the hint.

'He's bloody disappeared, boss. There's something wrong... I know it. I can't help thinking he may have fallen foul of Grantmore.'

Although his absence was worrying, I confess I was more concerned about him providing the statement we needed than him having fallen into Grantmore's clutches. I pictured him at a stamp collectors' convention in Harrogate or a steam train rally in Pickering.

'Peter, you are right to be worried. I'm worried but there is nothing I can do right now. Tomorrow's review has to be my priority. I'm relying on you to tell them that you are one hundred and ten per cent confident he'll put all he knows into evidence. Do not even hint at his disappearance. After the review, we'll pull out all the stops to find him... we have to... we need him.'

I saw from his body language he had given up.

'Go home. Start again after the meeting... the meeting at which you have a big part to play... the meeting at which you bloody save your job… the meeting at which you emerge as the best detective… who never was a detective.' We both laughed and the tension eased.

When he left, he was smiling.

I saved my PowerPoint presentation, closed down my computer and was about to leave when Sean Grantmore rang. My mouth went dry as I answered my mobile.

'Sean. What you got for me?' I kept my voice flat and unemotional.

'Frame's just rung me. They want to meet my driver… or should I say yours… tomorrow morning at ten o'clock at Ferrybridge Services on the A1.' He sounded calm.

'Have you passed them details of the two possible jobs?'

'Not yet… he never asked for them either. I haven't finalised them yet anyway… it's not fucking easy. As soon as I've narrowed it down, you'll know.'

'Don't piss me about, Sean.'

'I'm not. He was keen to get the meeting set up with the driver but never asked me about the jobs. I dunno.'

'So he's still planning a job… or why else would he need the driver? Is there any way you can find out what the hell he's thinking?'

'Get your man in with him tomorrow and you'll find out. He was talking about next week before he did it, so he's gonna use your man as the local knowledge. He'll get back to me for the details… don't worry.'

I couldn't believe I had bloody Sean Grantmore reassuring me.

We went over the details of how Frame would approach the driver at Ferrybridge, and I ended the conversation by telling him to keep his mobile switched on and to get back to me with concrete information about the targets as soon as possible.

I had been praying that Northumbria would come up

with something evidentially concrete before I took the step of planting the driver – but now it was decision time.

The mere fact Frame still wanted the driver proved he was planning another job. Another crime where someone could get killed. With both the driver and Grantmore trying to find out more, we would have at least some element of control – a better chance of knowing where they might strike? A better chance of protecting another family? A better chance of uncovering some evidence of the crimes they had already committed?

I thought through the likely discussions at tomorrow's review. Most would favour the safe and obvious option of an immediate arrest of Frame and his gang based upon Grantmore's admissions. They'd argue we might unearth further evidence in house searches and interviews, etc. – which of course was possible but not guaranteed. I wanted to argue that the information we had, strongly suggested they were not planning another job for about a week and we should give Grantmore a chance to find us extra evidence and even their next target. I of course knew but could not reveal that I also had a driver with the gang, more than doubling that chance. I knew I'd get some backers for this approach but most, I guessed, would see it as too risky and even unethical.

Whatever the outcome tomorrow, if I didn't arrange for my driver to be at Ferrybridge in the morning, there'd be no choice – so decision time.

This was it then. All systems go. Shit or bust.

I rang Russ Holland.

Twenty-Nine

Debbie was woken by the sound of the toilet flushing just before 7am, and it took a couple of seconds for her mind to catch up with events. It was Peter Frame in her bathroom. She was instantly alert. He had returned the previous evening just before midnight as she watched television, walking in as if he owned the place. He'd virtually dragged her upstairs, and in what was an obvious state of high excitement edged with a hint of cruelty, he had insisted they shower together before roughly shagging her – that's how she'd describe it – up against the bathroom sink. Gone was the smooth and cultured seducer of only a few hours ago. As soon as he'd finished with her, he softened a little and took her to bed, where he quickly fell asleep. But she could not relax. She felt trapped, as if in a cage with a wild animal. It was only a few hours ago that she'd entertained the notion of being able to string him along as her new meal ticket. That option had totally evaporated.

She remained in bed, listening to him move about in the bathroom, before hearing him trot downstairs. She prayed that he'd just leave before the kids woke up. But a few minutes later, he returned to the bedroom, already fully dressed and carrying two mugs of tea. He smiled his gentle smile when he realised she was awake.

'Morning, gorgeous... tea?'

The feeling of being trapped with that wild animal flooded over Debbie again. He was acting as if their relationship was established. As if he lived there. As if he was in charge. Despite herself, she smiled back and raised herself up, plumping the pillows so that she could sit back and take the proffered mug of tea from him. His smile broadened as he appraised her nakedness and she instinctively knew it would not be a good idea to cover up. She told herself to keep playing the daft bitch – the silly cow who was compliant and under his control. It now felt like self-preservation. So she took the tea with a saucy grin and left her breasts on display. He plonked himself on the bed beside her and they sipped from the matching mugs, for all the world looking like a happy couple sharing the morning's wakening.

'Afraid I have to pop out shortly but I'll be back mid-afternoon.'

'Fine,' Debbie replied, unable to quickly think of a way of putting him off returning, so she just concentrated on the here and now and keeping him happy – to make sure he left.

'While I'm gone, you might have to do me a favour.'

She could tell he was mentally wrestling with something. He wanted to tell her something but didn't know if he should. She kept quiet and had begun to think he had decided to keep whatever it was to himself, when he continued.

'The police might come here looking for me while I'm out. I don't think they will, but if they do, you don't know me. Okay. Just put them off... you don't know me.'

Debbie played her part. 'But I do know you. And why would they come here?'

'You soft bitch,' he said gently. 'Pretend you don't if…
and it's a big if… the coppers come looking for me.'

'What have you done? Why are they looking for you?'
seemed to be the obvious questions he would expect.

'Never you mind.'

Now his impatience began to show and he turned and
took hold of her face and squeezed tightly, turning her head
to look directly into her eyes.

'Just do as I say… if the cops come knocking, you don't
know me. Then we'll be just fine, you and me.'

He let go of her face and winked at her, suddenly friendly
again.

'Peter Frame? No, never heard of him,' she giggled.

Daft bitch, silly cow – she could play the part. The
bastard.

'That's a good girl. Before I come back, I'll ring you
just to check. It'll be about four… so make sure you're in,'
delivered as an order.

'I'll be here, don't worry. Fancy a nice juicy steak for your
tea?'

'That would have been lovely, but I'll probably just be
in and straight out again. Tomorrow night would be great,
though… it's a date.'

He kissed her on the cheek, climbed off the bed and
with a cursory wave, he was gone. She heard the front door
slam.

She leapt out of bed and carefully looked through the
side of the closed curtains onto the street below. Frame
walked purposefully away from the house through the heavy
rain and climbed into the front passenger seat of a dark blue
Jaguar saloon parked about fifty yards away. The car pulled
away from the kerb and past her house, enabling her to
recognise the driver as Mick Keegan. While repeating the
car's registered number to herself, she withdrew the notebook

from her drawer and after the name Grantmore she'd written the day before, she recorded it.

Desperately trying to quash her mounting fear, Debbie set about getting her kids up, washed, dressed and fed. As she prepared to leave the house to drop her eldest son at school, she saw it was still raining heavily and both kids needed their boots, which were kept in the large walk-in cupboard next to the back door. She leaned into the cupboard, searching with her hand for the light switch hidden beneath layers of coats. She flicked it on. Nothing. She looked up at where there should have been a bare bulb hanging, but it was missing. She shoved the vacuum cleaner aside, moved the ironing board and groped amongst the other cupboard contents for the small brightly coloured boots. Her hand came up against an object that shouldn't have been there. On the floor at the very back of the dark cupboard Debbie felt the shape of a large canvas holdall. It wasn't hers. She dragged it out of the cupboard, bringing with it the kids' boots. She tossed the boots into the kitchen, instructing Josh to help his younger brother to put them on.

She knew it must be Frame's. He must have hidden it at the back of the cupboard and taken the light bulb out. With the holdall on the kitchen floor, she knelt and unzipped it. It was stuffed to capacity with what appeared to be clothing – rough navy-blue overalls. She pulled it open wider and saw a balaclava and several gloves. Wary about pulling anything out of the bag in case Frame saw that it had been interfered with, she carefully pushed her hand beneath the clothing. Along the edges of the base of the bag, she felt the unmistakeable shapes of two metal baseball bats and between them in a soft bag, another object that instinctively made her withdraw her hand as if it had burnt her. A handgun.

*

The Jaguar sped south on the A1 with Keegan utilising the cruise control so as not to exceed the speed limit. As soon as Frame had climbed into the car, he'd given his instructions, as if he was still the major and Keegan the corporal. He'd told him twice while they were still in the town that he was speeding and to slow down, and once they hit the motorway, he had, most unusually, lost his temper, swearing at the older man when he'd seen the speedometer nudge eighty-five. The last thing they needed now was to get pulled by the police for speeding, he had raged.

When he, Frame and Pike had met up again after their discharge from the army, Keegan had been all too grateful for his old senior officer taking charge but now he was heartily sick of it. As each day passed, he grew to hate Frame more and more, but the truth was, he was now too afraid to extricate himself from the relationship. He was scared shitless of Frame, worried that he was planning a similar fate for him as befell Billy Pike. He was perhaps even more afraid of going to prison. Last night, when Frame had told him how a still-serving army officer working in the personnel section at Catterick had tipped him off about Northumbria Police requesting their army records be located and set aside for the police to collect, he had immediately panicked. Although he and Frame were not due to meet that evening, he had demanded they did – he needed reassurance. However, Frame had been very guarded and seemed reluctant to meet up, telling Keegan everything was in hand and they should proceed as planned. When he had insisted, Frame had eventually agreed but gave him the name of a pub on an estate he'd never even been to, where they should meet.

While they sipped their first pint, Keegan began to feel reassured by his old boss's calm attitude – he wasn't panicking – everything must be under control. Frame confidently reiterated their plan. Ever since the job in Beverley – and the unplanned murder of Emmerson – the idea had been to do a couple more jobs and then leave the country. Frame had secured all three of them a lucrative contract in Nigeria providing security to a rich local businessman involved in the oil industry. With that and the money they'd made from the robberies, they would be sitting pretty. Frame had told the African that they were now only two, but the businessman was quite content, as it was always the ex-Sandhurst officer that had been the attraction – but he could afford the additional firepower. Keegan had no local ties left, had never been married, the trawler was only rented and his idea of earning his living fishing had turned out to be just a pipe dream. That was why Frame's inducement to give crime a try had been so appealing all those months ago. After they'd had a couple of pints, Keegan felt more relaxed. His major had kept him out of the shit in Bosnia and he'd do the same again now.

But here he was just a few hours later, once again on the edge of panic, and he couldn't help asking questions to which he already knew the answers.

'Why the fuck are we using this bloke Grantmore has supplied? What if he's as useless as Emmerson and lets us down?'

Frame inwardly groaned at the building anxiety in Keegan, and the building anger in himself, but he knew he had to calm the man down if everything was going to go to plan. He turned in his seat and looked at him. Trying to exude calm and confidence.

'The job needs three of us. He's just extra muscle. No brains required. He'll be fine.'

'Do we have to kill him?'

'We're already in line for three murder charges… what's one more? We get him to drive us back to the boat, with him thinking he's away free from there. I'll take care of it from there. More money for us.'

Keegan lapsed into silence, mulling it all over yet again.

'Listen, Mick, we've planned tonight's job well. It's tight. Getting on for a hundred grand, I reckon, to add to what we've already got. That will go a long way in Africa and you're going to be on forty grand a year... tax-free. We're laughing, my old buddy... laughing.'

'But bloody hell, Pete, they must be on to us... they ain't asked for our army records for fun.'

'No panic there. I've arranged with my contact at Catterick for them to be mislaid for a couple of days. I accept they're looking at us but we'll keep out of the way until we do the job tonight and we'll be out of the country straight after. Bob across to Holland, dropping our Yorkshire friend off en route and flights are booked from Schiphol. Next stop Africa.'

'But what if they're already coming for us... watching the boat... airports are warned...?

'Mick. We've been over this time and time again... we are home and dry.'

Frame turned away and looked ahead at the traffic, signalling that the conversation was over. He subconsciously tapped the false passport that sat in the chest pocket of his jacket. Well, his flight was booked anyway.

Thirty

09:50 That Same Morning

Yet again, I picked up my mobile and checked I hadn't missed a call from Russ Holland. He should be just about to meet Frame at Ferrybridge so why the hell was I expecting a call? He'd have nothing to tell me yet. Wishful thinking, I suppose. The need to have some answers before my interrogators started with their questions. I was hardly going to be in any position to take a call from him once the review got underway in a few minutes.

And I'd heard nothing from Granger about Morley. So no answers there either.

I had rehearsed the arguments I'd use to hopefully get everyone on board with using Grantmore and was as ready as I could be. But this case had thrown up surprise after surprise, and the potential pitfalls facing me were gnawing at the confidence I'd felt only a few hours ago. The successes I felt I'd achieved with the inexperienced copper and the trainee reporter paled into insignificance alongside the challenges remaining. Did I really have any control over the career criminal Grantmore? Could my deal with Holland really work? Where the hell was Morley?

I closed my eyes, took a few deep breaths and prayed for some good luck. As I stood up, intending to get a coffee before everyone arrived, there was a knock on the door and DC Beatty entered my office.

Without preamble, he said, 'You are going love this, boss. I've just taken a call from an anonymous female with a strong Geordie accent. She asked if there was a reward for information about the murder of Ryan Harrod... and... get this... the bloke from Hull that was shot just before Christmas.'

Both forces had agreed not to link the two crimes in the media, waiting for today's review to make that decision. So for this female caller to make the connection was extremely interesting. Her accent made it doubly so.

'I hope you said there is a reward.'

'I did, boss... but to be honest, I was thinking on my feet and reckon I was too slow... I think she twigged I was lying. But there's more. She said it's two ex-army mates and they're going to pull another job tonight.'

'Tonight. Shit. Two ex-army mates? Thought there were three? But bloody hell, this sounds really promising. She's not bullshitting. But another job tonight... shit. Anything else?'

He glanced down at notes he had made. 'She said the job isn't going be in Hull... but up here.'

My heart sank.

'Up here... and tonight?'

'Yeah. But where the hell is up here? Northumbria? Newcastle? Sunderland? She wouldn't give her name or a number but I begged her to ring back and my gut tells me she will. She sounded scared. I gave her my name and my mobile number.'

'See if we can trace the call... that's a start.'

I thanked him – but needed him gone so I could absorb this latest pitfall, but at the door he paused.

'DS Naylor isn't going to get to know I told you about Kingston finding out he was fiddling his expenses, is he?'

'Don't worry, mate. As far as Professional Standards are concerned, it was me that got that ball rolling. It's just another charge he's looking at and it's all rolled up in this mess with Kingston, the leaks to the press and the bloke dead in the ditch up near Pocklington. Your name won't feature, so don't worry.'

He looked reassured and left.

Damn. I had no time to process this latest twist. I could hear people arriving for the review. The anonymous caller sounded genuine; she'd connected the two crimes and knew about the army angle. So there was no way I could ignore what she'd said about another crime happening tonight – and not in Hull.

I rang Grantmore but there was no answer, so I left him a message demanding he contact me straight away.

I wanted to text Holland. Tell him to abandon. But he had impressed upon me that all contact must come from him. Only he would know if contact was safe at any given moment. But this was an emergency and my fingers hovered over the keys. But it was just too risky. He'd be with them.

I now knew that two, or was it three, possibly armed men were at this very moment at Ferrybridge Services where the A1 meets the M62 in West Yorkshire Police area – only about forty miles away from where I sat. We'd been told they were planning what I surmised would be another violent robbery – *today*. Doing nothing was not an option. I had no choice but to intervene now and try and have them arrested. The reality, however, was that all we had was names – and I could hardly give them Holland's. But I could see no alternative.

I would have to claim their whereabouts had come from Grantmore, so I picked up the phone and rang the Command Centre. A couple of minutes of rapid explanation from me and I left them organising an urgent firearms response between the two forces. They would keep me updated as events unfolded.

I just couldn't process all the implications.

There was no way now there could be a formal review – all my planning was in tatters. This was now a dangerous incident in action. Investigative velocity I didn't want.

I gathered my papers and walked out into the incident room to find the team all seated and Crabbe and ACC (O) Jane Greenhall just arriving. As I welcomed them, the contingents from NCIS and Northumbria also arrived and with the room packed and buzzing with excitement, I kicked things off with the bombshell from our anonymous caller followed up with the firearms intervention being organised between the two forces at Ferrybridge, initiated by a call from Grantmore. The Command Centre rang me back to confirm the operation was now live and there was a containment team due to arrive within five minutes.

We could do little but sit and await the outcome. My plans had been blown out of the water, with my presentation redundant and my mind unable to compute where the hell this went next. The only glimmer of light was that we just might arrest Frame and Keegan, without anyone else getting hurt and I could claim my arranging Grantmore bail had allowed him to tell us where they were – as I'd planned all along.

But Holland?

*

Debbie Pike sat slumped on her couch nursing a cold cup of tea in an agony of indecision. She had spotted the detective's lengthy pause when she had asked about a reward. There wasn't one. And that was all she had intended to ask about. So why the hell had she gone on to half-heartedly grass Frame and Keegan up? What good had she done by giving the coppers just a bit of the story? Her mouth had just run away with her. She was as good as dead – and God help the kids.

Before she'd rung up, she had searched through the holdall and realised it contained evidence to help convict the smooth-talking bastard and his surly mate – and probably Billy too, were he not dead. But what could she do with it? The one thing she did know was that Frame had told her that the police were likely to come calling and there was no way she wanted the holdall being found in her house so she had to dump it. But where?

Suddenly it was obvious. She'd guessed from the overheard conversation that the money from the robberies, or at least some of it, was stashed on board *The Blaydon Races*. So if she dumped the bag there and rang in anonymously again, the evidence to put Frame and Keegan away – and away from her – would be stacking up. Five minutes later, she was in a taxi clutching the heavy holdall. After dropping her youngest at her mother's, she was soon en route for the docks.

She observed the trawler from the same vantage point as when she had last seen Billy. It had only been six days ago but it felt like months, so much had happened. After a few minutes, the area around the trawler quietened and she was onboard. She pulled on some washing up gloves and then using Billy's keys, she entered the cabin and went below, having already decided to hide the bag in the crew's quarters, so as to make it more realistic when the police searched. There were no obvious hiding places, so she had little option but to shove it under one of the bunks. She dropped the bag on the floor and tried to force it under one of the lower bunks but the holdall was too fat. She knelt on the bag flattening it slightly and then shoved hard, but it still only went a short way under. She pulled the bag away and looked beneath the bunk to see if there was something in the way. Attached to the frame in the centre of the bunk, and hanging to within about three inches of the cabin floor, was a large wooden box. She could see that there was a bigger space for the holdall further along towards the head of the bunk, so she shoved again and this time it went in easily. She had to lie on the floor to push it right into the back of the space, up close to the bulkhead so it was well hidden. As she dragged herself out from under the bunk and regained her knees, she saw that there were now three twenty-pound notes on the cabin floor that she must have dragged out of the space with her. She quickly pocketed the sixty quid then looked to see if there was any more. The corner of a banknote was protruding from the top corner of the wooden box structure that had prevented her from secreting the bag initially. She pulled at the note, which slid out easily. She sat cross-legged on the floor and looked at her watch. She felt she had plenty of time.

She pulled up the mattress on the bunk and saw that the box was just sitting in the bunk's frame and looked like it could be lifted out. With a bit of a struggle, she soon had the box, which was about the size of a small suitcase, on the floor in front of her. She knew what she had found. She quickly checked the other three bunks in the room and each had a similar box – or as she now thought of them – moneyboxes.

She slid off the lid of the box she'd removed; amazed that it was not even locked. It was stuffed tight with banknotes. There must have been thousands of pounds in tens and twenties. She stuffed as much cash into the pockets of her anorak as would fit, then filled the pockets of her jeans and added extra inside her blouse, before spreading the remaining cash evenly around the box. She slid the lid back in place, replaced the box in the frame and dropped the mattress.

Five minutes later, Debbie was walking off the docks, her mind racing with a mixture of fear and excitement. She now had to make sure that Frame and Keegan went to prison for a long time, as he would know she'd planted the holdall – and robbed him. With two kids, she couldn't just take the money and run, but if she could hang on to it, there was enough to change her life – if she lived – and she'd have her revenge. She began to look for a phone box.

*

The Jag cruised north on the A1. Frame glanced across at Keegan, who was intent on his driving but seemingly very tense judging by the way his hands gripped the leather steering wheel. He dropped his eyes to the speedometer – just under seventy.

He turned in his seat to smile at the man in the back. 'Happy with our arrangement then, Steve? An extra five grand do you then?'

Russ Holland smiled back. 'You bet. Grantmore's gi' me two grand up front and promised another three when the job's done, so you've doubled my money... and just for a trip up the motorway.'

'And like him, you get the last three, when the job's done.'

Holland leaned forward, straining on the seatbelt, looking keen and excited.

'So what is the job then, Pete?'

'A bit more than just driving, I'm afraid. Hope that's okay? I'll explain it all when we get up there. Relax for now, enjoy the drive and you'll net ten grand for less than twenty-four hours away from home.'

'I'm cool, Pete. I'm cool. Grantmore told me you were planning a robbery but said in 'ull somewhere? Makes no matter to me we're off up north, but I got a right to know what I'm getting into. So what we robbin'?'

Frame saw Mick's hands squeezing and twisting at the steering wheel and recognised his anger and frustration were building. He too wanted to thump the middle-aged, low-life criminal who had done nothing but ask questions since they had met him at Ferrybridge.

Frame had been pleased that the driver Grantmore had supplied had already been standing at the agreed meeting place when they'd arrived a bit early. He wanted to be in and out quickly. The less time they spent where Grantmore knew they'd be, the better.

After they'd introduced each other, they had told him they were travelling back up north to do the job tonight and when Frame had offered him more money, he had readily agreed but started with the questions immediately. 'Is it a robbery? A bank? A building society? Will we be tooled up? Guns? Will I get a gun?' The bloke was like an excited kid, yet he was older than Frame or Keegan had expected. After letting him rattle on for a couple of minutes, Frame shut him up, explaining that he didn't need to know the details yet but all would be revealed. Eager to get going, Frame told him to move his car to a quiet corner of the large car park.

Holland did as he was instructed and for the few minutes he was out of sight, quickly tapped out a text to Darnley:

> Job is tonight up north somewhere – not Hull.
> No details yet.
> Just two met me – Frame & Keegan.
> Be in touch when I know more. Don't reply.

He pressed send but nothing happened. No signal. He deleted the text. He'd get another chance. He walked back to the dark blue Jag and climbed into the back seat.

Keegan suggested a coffee before the return journey but Frame just ignored the request with a command 'Drive'.

As soon as they had negotiated their way back onto the A1, Frame turned to Holland and demanded his mobile, holding his hand out to receive it. He thought about denying he had one but realised it was too risky.

'Why'd you want my phone?' asked Holland, looking offended.

'We haven't got caught because we don't take chances. I don't want you using your phone while you're with us.' Frame sounded calm – the voice of reason.

Holland, however, responded as he imagined they would expect. Angrily. 'Don't you fuckin' trust me?'

Frame just smiled and kept his voice level. Removing an envelope from his jacket pocket, he tossed it onto Holland's lap.

'We trust nobody. Let's call this a down payment for the phone. Two grand in there and you'll get another three when the job's done. That's on top of what Grantmore's giving you. I'm showing my trust, so you show yours… now give me the phone.'

Holland picked up the envelope and quickly flicked through the cash, smiling, playing his role of the thick, greedy low-level criminal. He handed his mobile to Frame, who quickly checked the call and text register and saw nothing untoward. He switched the phone off, buzzed down his window and threw the mobile into the hedge at the side of the road.

*

The earlier excited discussions, phone calls and updates within the incident room had now subsided. We were just waiting. The Command Centre had updated me with the West Yorkshire Police Firearms Commander's decision to stand down. There had been no trace of any likely armed suspects. No Frame, Keegan or Pike, nor indeed Russ Holland in or around Ferrybridge Services.

I didn't know whether to laugh or cry.

Had the meeting not taken place? Had Grantmore got it wrong? Was Holland with them or not?

We organised another round of drinks while everyone had toilet breaks and calmed down and began to assess where we went from here. To all intents and purposes, the review was both impossible and pointless – the urgent task now was to plan for a crime we had been told would take place tonight.

Detective Superintendent Tom Corrigan spoke to his Command Centre back in Newcastle, ordering that a firearms operation be set in motion. He explained that no addresses for Frame or Keegan had as yet been unearthed but they had one for Pike, although it was from several years ago from when he was prosecuted for assault. Up to this point, he and I had agreed not to approach that address, waiting to see what came from Grantmore and not wanting to alert Frame. But this address was all we had – and we had to make tracks.

I then gave my assembled audience a necessarily brief version about Grantmore's arrest and admissions, and how I had authorised his bail so that he could try and find out what the gang was planning next. I described how he had told me that Frame's intention was to target the affluent suburbs to the west of Hull, albeit next week, and that I had tasked him with providing me with specific targets. Despite the obvious suggestion that he was unreliable – look at the fiasco around Ferrybridge – we discussed the potential of such a crime still happening today, in Hull, despite what the female informant had said.

This prompted an inspector from NCIS to float the idea that Grantmore could be feeding me false information. Should we believe him? As a ruse to get bail, he had promised to get me information about Frame's next crime, but was now feeding me a line. Was not Ferrybridge proof?

I argued against that scenario, describing his fear of Frame and why, having admitted his role and then grassed him up, his best option of surviving was to get him and Keegan imprisoned. Tom Corrigan did his best to support me and suggested we had little to lose at this stage by leaving Grantmore to try and discover more. However, my own Chief Constable seized wholeheartedly upon the notion of "Dinosaur Darnley" cocking up, and suggested that Grantmore was already with the other three and ready to take part in whatever crime they'd planned. Ferrybridge was a smokescreen. He went on to cast doubts about my gullibility in believing him and my recklessness in granting him bail, when he had in effect admitted to being part of a crime that involved murder.

Someone suggested we could not ignore the possibility that all of them could be at one of Grantmore's addresses, and Jane Greenhall was tasked with setting up another firearms operation to manage searches of them all. Even if found alone, it was agreed Grantmore should be arrested. My side of our deal was now in tatters. If found, what would he say? My head was now the proverbial shed.

Despite Crabbe's insistence that he knew Grantmore was taking me for a mug, it was eventually agreed we should also establish a third firearms operation in and around Hull's western suburbs, just in case. This gave me a little comfort. We didn't know what we were looking for – just three or four men in a car, but if Hull were indeed still the target for tonight, surely a strong police presence would be enough to frighten Frame off?

There was now the clear potential of them being confronted by armed police. In Hull or somewhere in Northumbria. I just prayed Russ Holland would get the chance to contact me before that happened. Dare I contact him? He was going to need all the skills gleaned from the army. Could his counterinsurgency experience from nearly twenty years ago really help?

Thirty-One

12:30 That Same Day

Marilyn was just finishing off her favourite client when pandemonium broke out. She thought old Mr Roper, who came every Wednesday while his wife went shopping at Asda, would have a heart attack when the door to the treatment room was kicked open and three armed police officers in black combat gear stormed in.

'Foxtrot Tango One to Control. Nicole's is clear. No sign of target. All safe. Over,' rasped an officer into his helmet mike.

Simultaneously, teams at Cleopatra's and at Grantmore's home were reporting a similar lack of success.

Marilyn threw a fluffy pink towel over Albert Roper's bony shoulders and demanded, 'What the fuck are you lot doing here?'

Albert, having more fun than he'd had in ages, sat up with his skinny frame still glistening with baby oil.

'This ain't illegal. We're good friends. Why the bloody guns?' He sat there, naked, shiny and defiant.

The officers lowered their guns and removed their helmets, while Marilyn guided an animated Mr Roper into the vacant room next door to get dressed. Everyone was chuckling as she reassured him he could return next Wednesday – for a freebie. The team leader encouraged Marilyn to put her dressing gown on while he asked her a few questions about her employer. Enjoying the officer's obvious discomfort, she took her time.

'Reckon you've missed him, love. He's long gone. Came in here yesterday morning after you lot released him and emptied the safe. He's taken all the cash… and his passport… even left the bloody safe door open. He was in a right sweat.'

Bending excessively provocatively to remove her painful stilettos, she added, 'Is it owt to do with this?'

After slipping on a pair of fluffy slippers, she went through into the reception area and came back with a well-thumbed copy of the *Hull Mail*. She pointed out the article she wanted him to look at.

'Did Sean kill him?'

The officer quickly scanned the brief article, headlined **Local business leader found dead**, beneath which was a head and shoulders photograph of a Noel Priestley. None of it meant anything to the officer, who was specialist firearms response and not attached to the incident or to any division.

'Why do you think that?'

'He was a regular customer. Been coming for years… excuse the pun, love. Grantmore never chats to the customers but he always talked to him… and often in his office. I've heard them arguing recently. Is that why you're looking for him?'

After contacting the incident room with this information, he was told to take Marilyn straight to Central and within an hour she was dishing as much dirt as she could remember on the man who had abused her for over ten years, to an enthusiastic Jo Young. As she did so, search teams were going through Grantmore's home, Nicole's and Cleopatra's with the proverbial fine-tooth comb.

*

The Chief was torn between being delighted at his own investigative instincts being proved right and devastated that his force, via yours truly, had made such a cock-up and "let the good people of Humberside down". It certainly looked like Grantmore had done a runner – and I was a mug. Thoroughly enjoying battering my professional judgement, he continued his theme of Grantmore doing tonight's job with Frame and Keegan and then fleeing the country. He started ranting about roadblocks – and of course high-visibility jackets. At least he had those in place now around the area in West Hull, that he was sure I'd been conned into believing was the likely target. It was all I could do not to storm out and find somewhere just to think.

The obvious link between Noel Priestley and Grantmore just added to my humiliation. As motives for crime, sex and money were often the favourites, and it was now looking pretty likely that Grantmore had blackmailed him to get him access to the premises via Anne Beedham and Janice Cooper. Grantmore must have thought all his Christmases had come at once when he found out a building society manager was using his girls. Jo Young had unearthed more pieces of the jigsaw, having pinned Marilyn down to when she had heard them arguing. It had been just before Grantmore was attacked and blinded – just weeks after the robbery.

I was heartened that Tom Corrigan kept rigorously defending my thought processes in bailing Grantmore, and a surprisingly good proportion of the visitors from NCIS also supported me. To be frank, it was obvious this was more of a CID versus uniform scenario, but the point was well made about hindsight being a wonderful thing. I confess a little part of me still dared to hope Grantmore would ring me with something solid and I'd be proved right. A bigger part of me knew that my supporters would soon back-pedal if Holland ended up getting arrested with the gang. I kept willing him to ring me and resolved that if I had heard nothing in the next hour I would text or ring him, hoping he could somehow use his phone. I needed to get him out of there.

We had hardly absorbed the likelihood that Grantmore had fled when Northumbria informed Tom Corrigan that they now had a current address for Billy Pike and were en route with a firearms team. Officers had also been dispatched to Catterick to investigate the suspicious disappearance of the trio's files.

I was about to feign a heart attack – or bloody have one – when someone shouted from the back of the room asking everyone to be quiet. The room settled into a hush and we all looked towards the source of the request. DC Beatty was on the telephone, his right hand raised in a signal that showed it was he who had demanded silence.

We all listened intently to his one-sided conversation, which kicked off with, 'Thank you for ringing back, we really appreciate it.'

The anonymous caller.

When he replaced the phone on its cradle, the whole room looked at him, waiting for him to fill in the blanks.

'That was the same woman who rang earlier. As you must have heard, she has now named Frame and Keegan. She gave me their Christian names... Peter and Michael. Basically, she's claiming that Frame and Keegan are going to pull another job tonight, in Newcastle or nearby. She didn't mention Pike.'

He glanced at me sympathetically before continuing: 'She reckons they are being helped by a man from Hull who she thinks is called Grantmore. She didn't know where or what the job will be, and doesn't know how we can find them before they strike, but she does know that they are using a dark blue Jaguar saloon... and she's given me the number.'

He paused for dramatic effect and glanced down at his notes.

'Keegan has a trawler called *The Blaydon Races*, moored at North Shields. She claims that on that boat there is a gun and other stuff they've used in other crimes... and loads of cash. She's sure that they'll use the trawler after the job to escape the country. They plan to kill Grantmore when they get out to sea. That's about it.'

A series of questions followed, mainly about where exactly the crime would occur, where we could find the three men, and did she explain how she knew all this? Again, we set about trying to trace the call.

DC Beatty kept shaking his head. 'All she would say is that the information she has given is accurate. She sounded scared... but convincing.'

There was a clamour of voices as everyone began to discuss what they had just heard. The clear consensus of opinion, led by Crabbe, was that Grantmore was with them and actually on the job. I almost hoped he was – that could mean Russ Holland wasn't with them.

I could sense Tom Corrigan's support ebbing away, just as mine would have done were our roles reversed.

Thirty-Two

13:45 That Afternoon

Debbie left the telephone box shaking. She crossed the road to the Spar supermarket, where she worked on the checkout three mornings a week. As she crossed the unusually quiet shop floor, she waved to her mate who was sat looking bored behind her silent till. She walked quickly on, wanting to avoid a chat, and pushed through the swing doors at the rear of the store that led to the staff area. She nodded to one of the stockroom lads as he walked out of the kitchen and then she entered the small locker room, thankful to find it empty. As always, she tucked her long fingernails under the small air vents in the locker door and pulled it open. The lock had been knackered since the day she had been allocated the locker three years ago, and until today that had never bothered her. But she had to hide the money somewhere and the police were soon going to come knocking – Frame had said so – and Billy Pike had a record. As far as she was aware, no one had ever gone into her locker, so she hoped the cash would be safe, at least until she was able to think of somewhere safer to hide it. Praying no one would come in she pulled a Spar plastic bag out of the locker and quickly emptied her pockets of the cash before starting on the notes stuffed in her blouse. The bag filled quickly and she had to pull another from the locker, while shoving the full one to the back. As she hastily withdrew bundles of cash from around her body, she dropped a handful, which fluttered all over the floor. She pushed the second plastic bag into the locker and then fell to her knees reaching across the tiled floor and pulling the notes towards her into a pile. Before she had even finished picking them up, the locker room door swung open and in bowled the lad from the stockroom. He saw Debbie scrabbling on the floor with the small pile of cash and his eyes lit up in amusement.

'Come into money have ya, pet?'

He knelt alongside and picked up three or four of the notes that still lay on the floor and handed them to her with a quizzical look.

'Bingo last night. Two hundred and fifty quid.'

She pushed the notes into her pocket, stood up and closed the locker door, but with him there, she was unable to do anything further to satisfy herself that the money was safe.

'Looks like you've robbed the bloody tills, but if you take me out, pet, I'll not let on,' he chuckled.

'Yeah, when you've left school you might get lucky.'

She pushed past him with a saucy smile and left the locker room, then waved to her friend, now busy with a queue of customers as she left the store. As she gained the street, she let out a huge gasp of air, realising she had virtually held her breath while hiding the cash. When clear of her workplace, she took the cash she had dropped from her pocket and quickly counted it. Two hundred and eighty quid in twenties but the bundle looked so thin. Just how much had she hidden in her locker? Must be thousands – but how many thousands? She was dying to count it all – to find out just how sweet was her revenge for the loss of Billy. She quickly put the cash neatly in her purse. She couldn't help but worry that someone would go in her locker. Perhaps the lad from the stockroom. Did he believe her about the bingo win? As she walked, her breathing steadied and she rationalised that he wasn't the sharpest knife in the box, and for now the cash was safe. She forced herself to think about what the hell to do next. She knew the money was a whole lot safer than she was.

By the time she'd collected her youngest from her mother's and turned into her own street, she'd made some decisions. When Frame rang as he'd promised, she'd tell him the police had been round looking for him. That shouldn't come as any surprise as he'd brought it up. If he mentioned the holdall, she'd tell him that she thought the police were now watching the house. That'd keep him away. She felt proud of herself for working it out. Proud but still frightened.

As she rounded a bend in the road, close to her house, Debbie stopped in her tracks, and once again found herself holding her breath. She spun the pushchair round and walked back the way she had come. Outside her house were three marked police cars with a uniformed copper standing guard at her wide-open front door.

*

At exactly that same moment, the blue Jag turned into the street adjoining Debbie's. Frame had decided to collect the holdall and then go to another of his several girlfriends' homes where they would lie low until it was time to do the job. His sense of excitement at this final robbery had grown during the trip back up north and he was keen to get on with things. They had got back up to Newcastle more quickly than he had anticipated and although it was earlier than he had agreed with Debbie, he tried ringing her. There was no answer.

'Pull over, Mick,' he instructed.

Keegan knew they were heading for Billy's house and was amazed Frame was risking going anywhere near that bitch Debbie. He didn't trust her. Look how she'd run straight into the arms of Frame after Billy had "disappeared". He was so tightly wound. Frightened of what was going to happen tonight. Not frightened of the job. They'd planned that well and it would go off fine – as long as this dickhead Steve Long did as he was told. No, he was worried about what would happen after. He knew Frame needed him to skipper the boat, so he was at least safe until they got to Holland. But there was Long to be disposed of, and what did Frame really have in mind for him? He was itching to refuse to go anywhere near Billy's house but knew Frame was getting sick of his anxieties, so he pulled in as he was bid.

Frame sat quietly tapping his mobile against his chin, deep in thought.

In the back of the car, Holland leaned forward and stuck his head between the front seats, still playing his part. 'Where are we? What we stopped for?'

Keegan looked back at him and shook his head in disgust.

Frame ignored Holland's questions. He tried Debbie again but with the same result. He didn't want to hang about so decided to check out the house and use his own key if it all looked quiet. Although he was pretty sure her house was safe, as she and Billy hadn't lived there long, he knew the police had more chance of tracing Billy due to his previous conviction.

'Drive on, Mick. We need to go to Debbie's.'

'Bloody hell, Pete, why? For fuck's sake, Billy lived there... they might have the address. Let's just go to the boat.' Keegan finally exploded.

Holland picked up on the past tense – Billy *lived* there. With Debbie? He lodged the information in his memory banks.

Calmly, Frame swivelled in his seat to face the driver. 'I need to collect the gear. I don't want to go near the boat until we cast off tonight. Now drive.'

'Who are Debbie and Billy?' piped up Holland.

Again he was ignored and Keegan pulled the car back into the light traffic on the estate heading towards Debbie's home. The Jag approached the house from the opposite direction to that which Debbie had done only five minutes before, and just as for her the sight of the police activity came into view all of a sudden. They were within fifty yards of the police cars and travelling at about thirty miles an hour towards them and Keegan's automatic reaction was to brake hard. The big car came to a sudden halt, which drew the immediate attention of the copper on duty at the front door.

'Drive on. Drive on,' hissed Frame.

They could each see that the copper had registered them and the car. He reached for his radio and strode down the short garden path, across the pavement and scruffy grass verge until he was in front of the car. He raised his right hand in the classic stop signal and began walking towards the still stationary Jag.

'Go. Fucking go,' yelled Frame.

With a screech of rubber, the big car shot forward and with a sickening crunch, the front offside wing struck the police officer.

It had only been within the last half-hour or so that he, like all others on duty in the city, had received the radio message to be on the lookout for the dark blue Jaguar containing three men believed to be in the Newcastle area and planning an armed robbery. Although not privy to all the details, he did know that the house in front of which he was standing guard was being searched in connection with the crimes already perpetrated by this same gang. So quickly joining the dots had been pretty simple. What was less simple was how to react in those split seconds – and he made the wrong but instinctive choice. He had only had the chance to excitedly shout into his radio 'PC 987 to Control… urgent message,' when that instinct had kicked in. As he folded over the wing of the car before somersaulting in the air to land on his back on the road, he was strangely aware of his radio crackling away and asking him to 'Go ahead, 987'. As he looked at the strange position of his right leg, he felt no pain and was able to tell the control room exactly what his urgent message was all about.

As the powerful car shot past the three marked police cars, Holland looked back at the officer. He could see that he was alive and talking into his radio. He calmly reported what he had seen to Frame and Keegan but realised he had slipped out of role. How would Long have reacted?

'Fucking hell,' he laughed, 'you bastards don't mess about. He's gon' 'ave 'ell of a headache. But I reckon he'll 'ave got the car number.'

Concentrating on their escape, neither Frame nor Keegan noticed Debbie as they sped past her, still walking away from her home with the pushchair and with her back to them. The speed of the car would have attracted anyone's attention as it passed by on the narrow urban road, and she easily recognised it as the car she had seen Frame get into early that morning. She again made a mental note of the number and headed for the phone box at the end of the road.

'Head for the industrial estate, Mick, we'll have to dump the car,' Frame commanded.

Holland had been careful ever since entering the car at Ferrybridge not to leave his fingerprints in the vehicle, having used the sleeve of his jumper to both open and close the door. He needn't have worried, as within the next five minutes they'd pulled up in a remote corner of a small industrial estate and, using a can of petrol from the boot, Keegan had torched the car. The three of them walked briskly through a series of alleyways onto a busy arterial road and then boarded a bus, where they sat well apart. Within half an hour, they were sitting in the small kitchen of a house in a completely different part of the city.

Frame had introduced the other two men to his girlfriend Stella, a reasonably attractive woman of about forty. Stella had immediately busied herself making them a pot of tea. Keegan had no idea who Stella was and Holland had no idea where they were. Despite trying his best to keep track during their escape from the torched car and subsequent bus journey, he was now completely disorientated. He had been impressed how quickly and decisively Frame had responded to the incident, which, he had now gathered from the other men's conversations, had been outside Debbie's house – where clearly at one time Billy had lived. Billy Pike presumably – the third man – where was he?

He realised how little the two men had let slip. During the journey north they had hardly spoken to each other, let alone to him. He knew nothing about the planned crime. The only snippets he had picked up were that Keegan had a trawler and Frame a yard. Where the hell was Pike, the third man Darnley had led him to expect? With no mobile and now apparently in hiding at Stella's house, he couldn't see how he was going to get a message to Darnley. But he needed to. It was obvious from the police presence at Debbie's and the reaction of the officer they had run over, that the cops were aware of the blue Jag. How? Now they knew that three men had been in it. When he'd gone to meet Frame at Ferrybridge, just a few hours ago, Darnley had told him the job was going to be in Hull, probably next week. What had changed? He knew the crime was going to take place up here – presumably in Newcastle. What did the police know? What did Darnley know?

Despite his predicament, he remained icily calm and confident. He'd been in tricky situations before. Things had a way of working out. He wondered what Stella knew, if anything. She was obviously in thrall to the smooth-talking ex-army officer and seemingly not in the least concerned about why he had suddenly appeared on her doorstep with two mates. She handed out mugs of strong tea with a broad smile.

Frame pulled her to him and hugged her. 'Thanks, love, we've just got a bit of a problem with the coppers... you know how it is. Okay if we stay here for a bit? We'll be out your hair before bedtime.'

Stella looked blissfully unconcerned at this news, seemingly overjoyed to have him, and even his two mates, there.

'Course, darling. I'll have to nip out and get something for your tea, though. Not got enough in for four,' clearly as pleased as punch to have the company.

'You still got that holdall safe?' Frame asked.

'Of course,' she responded, smiling proudly.

'Good girl. Now just leave us for ten minutes while we have our tea. Get us a nice steak and all the trimmings,' as he pulled two twenty-pound notes out of his wallet.

As she moved out of the kitchen into the small front hallway and began to pull on her coat, Keegan leaned towards Frame and hissed, 'Bloody hell, Peter, who the hell is she? She shouldn't be going out... she could grass us up.'

In character, Holland loudly joined Keegan's objections. 'Yeah, how do we know we can trust her? We've just nearly bloody killed a copper for fuck's sake.'

He'd quickly decided to let Stella know they'd run over a police officer, hoping it might make her start to ask questions, and Frame or Keegan would have to respond. Something about tonight's plans might spill out. She heard exactly what he had intended and marched back into the kitchen with her coat only half on.

'Should have killed the black bastard as far as I'm concerned. Tell them you can trust me, Peter.'

Frame stood up beside her and helped her on with her coat, squeezing her shoulder in an expression of support before ushering her back into the hall and closing the door on her. As soon as he heard the front door slam, he opened the cupboard beneath the stairs, seconds later returning and dumping a navy blue holdall on the scuffed kitchen table. Without a word, he unloaded its contents. Three pairs of navy overalls, three navy balaclavas, three pairs of gloves, two baseball bats, a sawn-off shotgun and a box of cartridges. Clearly, there was only ever going to be three of them.

'Stella's sound. I've been seeing her for about six months and storing stuff here as well as on the *Blaydon* and at Debbie's. This gear will do us for tonight.'

Holland picked up on the name *Blaydon*, surmising it was the name of Keegan's trawler. He wanted to get them talking. He needed information. To get a reaction, he reached for the sawn-off and was surprised when Frame didn't stop him. He handled it knowing that he would look like he knew what he was doing, breaking it open and looking down the barrels. Seeing it was unloaded, he flicked it shut.

'Nice. Clean.'

He put it back on the table, wanting them to wonder how come he could handle the sawn-off so nonchalantly.

It was Keegan who asked the question. 'You've handled one of them before. Tell us when and why.'

Holland subtly altered his Steve Long persona. 'I've been around. I'm not one of Grantmore's hired hands. He's a mate and he asked me to do him a favour. Gun crime in Hull is as rare as rocking horse shit but I'm from Manchester and in the same line as Sean… massage parlours, girls, drugs… but over there you need a gun, so I know what I'm doing. And like Stella… you can trust me.'

Steve Long had raised his credibility a notch. Frame and Keegan exchanged glances and then Frame, much like he had done with Stella, squeezed his shoulder as a sign of solidarity.

'Then you are going to come in very handy tonight. I suggest we put our feet up now, and then enjoy a nice steak dinner during which Mick and I will fill you in about tonight's robbery. We'll be leaving here about eleven and by just after midnight, you will be heading south considerably better off.'

Frame began stuffing the kit back into the holdall.

An element of success. A robbery taking place between eleven and midnight, so it must be pretty close by, probably in Newcastle itself? They'd be using a sawn-off shotgun, baseball bats and masks. The picture was building. The trawler was called *Blaydon*, Frame had a yard and clearly the police already knew about the address of Debbie and Billy Pike and had presumably found the stuff Frame had stored there. He knew Stella's address. The potential sites for Darnley to eventually secure evidence were growing, but how could he alert him and prevent tonight's robbery?

'Heading back south after midnight. How's that gon' 'appen then?' Holland asked.

'We lost the Jag but I've got another motor ready to use tonight. You can take that when the job's done. Just dump it in the car park at Ferrybridge.'

'But what about you two?'

Frame grinned at Keegan.

'We'll be leaving by other means of transport. Won't be needing a car, so it's all yours.'

Keegan's boat? Another piece in the jigsaw.

But Keegan exploded: 'Another car, a second safe house, a second bloody girlfriend, another firearm… what else don't I know?'

Frame just smiled and quietly said, 'Remember Billy.'

Holland held his breath. This had been voiced as a clear threat.

Keegan visibly shrunk and almost whispered, 'After Billy, how can I ever trust you?'

Holland could see Frame was furious at Keegan, and decided to push things further, hoping for more revelations.

'Christ, if he don't know what's going on and I know sweet fuck-all, how the 'ell do we pull this off tonight?' He prodded Frame in the chest. 'I want some details… now.'

Frame grabbed the hand that had prodded him and in one fluid movement twisted it viciously up Holland's back, before forcing him face down onto the top of the holdall that still sat on the table. He continued to force the arm further towards Holland's shoulders while bending over and whispering in his ear.

'You'll find out when I'm ready to share it with you. I do not take risks and at this stage you are a risk. In less than eight hours, you will be ten grand richer and on your way home. Until then, just keep your mouth shut.'

He gave Holland's arm a final shove and then let go of him. Keegan looked as if he was about to continue with his objections but then decided against it. Holland straightened up, rubbing at his painful arm, concluding he too had best remain quiet. From their short exchange about Billy Pike, he now guessed that Frame had disposed of him. Presumably like Emmerson he had become a risk. No wonder Keegan was so wound up.

The small kitchen became claustrophobically quiet, each man apparently consumed by his own thoughts, sipping at their mugs of strong tea. After about ten minutes of silence, Frame pushed back his chair and went out into the small rear garden where he lit a cigarette. Keegan joined him and the two of them began to talk, and from their demeanour and glances towards the kitchen, it was obvious to Holland that he was the main topic of conversation. He used the opportunity to carefully wash the mugs they had each used, conscious that at some point he also needed to remove his fingerprints from the shotgun.

For the first time since he had met the two men, he began to feel uneasy. Frame was highly aggressive and seemingly ruthlessly efficient – in all likelihood a psychopath. It was patently obvious that Keegan no longer trusted him and was totally strung out – a time bomb waiting to explode. Holland looked at his watch – three thirty. In about eight hours, he was going to have to take part in an armed robbery with these two mad bastards, unless he could somehow get in touch with Darnley. He considered waiting for the opportunity to just clear out and let Darnley know what he knew. But if he disappeared, they'd do likewise and he didn't know their target so nothing would be gained. It wasn't hard for him to remember why he was there. Getting them meant getting Grantmore. Revenge.

He was lost in these thoughts when his eyes were drawn to a cheap-looking white handbag sitting on top of the breadbin. Frame had given Stella the cash to buy them a steak and she had obviously not taken her handbag with her. Could there be a mobile phone in there? But how the hell could he check it out? Next to the breadbin was the kettle and so without thinking too much about it, Holland walked to the kettle, picked it up and walked to the back door, which was ajar.

'Another cuppa, lads?'

Both men paused in their conversation but nodded in agreement.

Holland filled the kettle while looking out of the kitchen window above the sink, grinning amiably at the two men. He replaced the kettle and switched it on, and with his back to them, he rifled quickly through the handbag. He was in luck. He shoved the small red Nokia into his jean's pocket and then made the tea.

From the kitchen he shouted, 'It's mashing, lads. Just need a quick slash.'

He casually shut the back door and went into the hall, looking for the toilet. He knew making a call was too risky, as he anticipated Frame soon getting suspicious and coming looking for him. He could all too easily overhear. His army training had made him memorise Darnley's number and while waiting for the kettle to boil, he had composed a succinct text in his head. He locked the toilet door as he pulled the phone from his pocket, sat on the toilet seat and prayed there was not a security setting applied to the little mobile. He needn't have worried; the phone remained blank – its battery was dead.

Thirty-Three

16:00 That Same Afternoon

I had always hated travelling in a speeding car and doing well over a ton was most definitely speeding. Add to that the incessant whine of the siren and I was finding it almost impossible to concentrate on the conversation. Soon after the second call from our female informant, Tom Corrigan had insisted he should return to his own force area where it now looked more likely the action was going to be. We had barely started to try and convince my senior officers that I should accompany him, when the female caller had rung again about seeing the three men in the Jaguar. Only minutes after that, Northumbria Control informed Tom Corrigan about the officer being run over by the Jag, and then it being discovered burnt out nearby. It was also confirmed that the Jag had contained three men. Ten minutes later, the officer leading the search at Pike's house rang and we learnt the identity of our anonymous female caller.

Debbie Pike had returned home shortly after the copper had been run over and was now under arrest based upon handwritten notes the search had revealed in her underwear drawer, which described many aspects of the crimes under investigation. Despite kicking off and biting the female officer trying to search her, she had eventually calmed down and told the officers how she had been ringing in anonymously. She was also claiming Frame and Keegan had murdered her husband, and seemed desperate to tell all she knew. Her mother had collected her children and she was now on her way to Clifford Street Police Station in Newcastle. Events were moving rapidly and Tom was absolutely correct; we needed to be up there.

We were now within half an hour of the nick where Debbie was being held; keen to hear more about what she was saying. Tom and I were sitting in the back of a marked traffic car, driven by a Class 1 driver who was clearly keen to show us his skills. We were accompanied by Tom's DI, who judging by the way he kept flinching, as our driver made yet another dodgy overtake, was as scared as me. A following traffic car contained DC Beatty and two of his Humberside colleagues. Whatever happened now, both forces needed to work collaboratively. I'd chosen DC Beatty due to his initial contact with Debbie Pike, hoping he could build on their initial rapport when he formally interviewed her.

Before we left Driffield, Tom had organised a covert surveillance operation on *The Blaydon Races*. Forensic teams were examining Debbie's home and the burnt-out Jaguar. We had left ACC Greenhall and the Chief debating the wisdom of calling off the surveillance operation in Humberside. The search for Grantmore had run out of steam, as Debbie Pike's claim that Frame had murdered her husband led most to be convinced he was now with Frame and Keegan.

A heavy agricultural vehicle, travelling at a steady sixty, overtaking a large removal lorry, was blocking our progress up the outside lane of the A1, despite the blue lights and sirens. Tom Corrigan was trying his best to summarise the situation over the racket. This was not solely to make sure we were both fully up to speed with the rapid developments in the case, but also to agree tactics over the next few hours.

'You seem adamant that our third gang member is not this bloke Grantmore. How can you be sure?' he asked for about the fifth time.

'I'm not being defensive, Tom. I know I've cocked up and read him wrong. He's clearly more involved with Frame than he's admitted, and although I can see he'd supply the driver, like he did Emmerson, it's just not his style to take part. I can't be sure... but I'd lay money on it.'

He sat musing on the point when a message came over the car's radio informing him that the three men's army records had been located and were en route to Clifford Street Police Station.

'That should quickly get us some new addresses to search.'

He used the radio, instructing that this was to be a priority.

'And photographs,' I added. 'We get to know what these two bastards look like at last. They're going to have aged a bit and maybe grown their hair... or beards... but it's a start.'

He looked at his watch. 'We need to get the photos circulated to all patrols as soon as possible... and if we're quick... we could get them on the local evening news. We have got to do all we can to stop this crime happening.'

'Seeing their mug shots on the telly might put them off doing the job... too risky for them? But I guess that would be a result too,' I suggested.

"That's not going to happen,' asserted Corrigan, 'they're desperate... they've just run a copper over. They've killed three times and if the lass is right, they're planning to escape the country using the trawler... and kill Grantmore, if he is with them. They're not going to stop now. They're going to carry out whatever it is they're planning, so we've got to get to them first. If we don't, and someone gets hurt and we never used the photos, we'll be crucified.'

He was spot on.

But then he added, 'We've got to use Grantmore's photo as well… for those same reasons.'

'I agree about Frame and Keegan and it's your call… it's your area. But leave out Grantmore's description and photo, as if people see three blokes and one hasn't got a disfigured face and one eye, they might rule them out.'

'On the other hand, if he is with them, he is so distinctive it makes identification easier. With what we have been told, I don't think we've got a choice.'

He was right. We had no choice. Logic kept telling me the third man was Holland but the reality was, I no longer knew. If it was, and he managed to extricate himself from this bloody mess, all the stops would be out to find the third man, who everyone believed was Grantmore. I was fucked whatever happened.

'You're right, Tom. I still don't think he's with them… but do it.'

Tom rang his local contact at Tyne Tees TV to set it up.

While he talked, I seriously considered telling him all about Holland – the truth – so at least we could work out together how the hell to proceed. But I'd never even spoken to the bloke until that week and I had no idea how he would respond. I figured there'd be no way I'd cover up for him if the boot were on the other foot, so I quickly ruled that option out. I thought back to my first vision of Russ Holland catapulting himself at Grantmore in Hull Crown Court and how I manipulated his caution. All this bloody mess just from a simple and honest desire to see justice done. Where the hell did I stand with justice now?

The car sped on.

*

For about the tenth time in as many minutes, I checked my watch. It was still just after 7pm. Despite Holland's insistence that I never try and contact him, I'd tried. But his mobile didn't even ring out. I hoped that Grantmore's TV appearance might just have shocked him into action – but he wasn't answering either. Tyne Tees had been all too eager to carry the story – with photographs and names – of the armed gang believed to be about to commit a robbery somewhere in the Newcastle area that very night. Tom Corrigan had appeared on the programme and appealed for the public to be vigilant, emphasising the dangerous nature of the three men, stressing that no one should approach them but report any suspicions by ringing 999. The full story had also been aired on *Look North* because of the connections to the Humberside area, so the jungle drums would be sounding back in Hull amongst Grantmore's cronies. What the hell would he be making of it all?

DC Beatty and a DS from Corrigan's team had been interviewing Debbie Pike, armed with the notes she had made, for over an hour and I was desperate to know what she had said. I pulled my mobile from my pocket, intending to try both men again but before I could punch out the numbers, it vibrated to show an incoming call. I dared to hope – but the screen showed it was from the incident room in Driffield. It was Tony Ride.

'You sitting down, boss?' He sounded worried. 'Just had a phone call from an immigration officer at King George Dock in Hull who says he saw Grantmore's mug shot on *Look North* tonight and recognised him immediately as a man he checked onto last night's P&O ferry to Amsterdam. He'd actually advised him to have his passport photo changed because of his recent eye and facial injuries. He's checked the manifest and he's right… it was Grantmore. So the news bulletin showing him with Frame and Keegan is bloody wrong.'

I didn't know what to say. I had facilitated his escape by granting him bail. My arguments for doing so had already been rubbished by the Chief – and now he had fled the country. They would hang me out to dry. What did Debbie Pike know about him? What would she add to the story? And we knew there had been three blokes in the car when the copper got run over, so Holland must still be with them.

'Bloody hell, Tony, I've dropped a right bollock there, haven't I? Reckon I'll be in traffic by Monday.' I tried to maintain the Darnley image but Tony Ride would have known that at that moment I was devastated.

He didn't laugh.

'Anyway, get the bloke's statement. We'll track him down eventually. One-eyed, scar-faced Hull pimps are pretty thin on the ground. I did try to persuade Corrigan not to put Grantmore's picture up with the others... least I've been right about something.' I tried to laugh. 'Any more good news?'

'Lots of stuff recovered from Grantmore's house and his two knocking shops... some of it might be relevant. There's a shirt and a towel with what looks like bloodstains... they'll need analysing. Also, another one of his girls that Jo Young interviewed today... Cheryl... has just rung in. She's just seen Frame's photo on the telly and recognises him. Says he was in Cleopatra's last week causing trouble and they had to send for Grantmore. She and the manager Pauline only overheard their conversation but reckon Frame gave Grantmore five grand, and it sounded like Frame had a gun. Jo's back there now, getting statements. With this and the links to Priestley, evidence against Grantmore is growing.'

'That's excellent.' I tried to sound positive but the more the evidence amassed against Grantmore, the worse I looked.

'Any idea of the target at your end, boss? Or where they might be?'

'Not as yet… and the public are now looking for three men, one of whom we've said has facial scars and one eye. We've got addresses for Frame and Keegan now from their army files but there's no one at either house. We're searching them now.'

'What about our anonymous caller? Anything fresh?'

I quickly summarised what extra we knew from the search of her home – the recovered notes and her insistence that Frame and Keegan had killed her husband.

'Still no sign of Morley this end. That's five days now and Pete Granger is going ballistic about it. I think tomorrow we are going to have to step up the search for him.'

Shit. It had been right there in front of me but I'd been focussed elsewhere. The coincidence of the abrupt disappearance of Morley and now his schoolboy nemesis fleeing the country? A bloodstained shirt? At that moment, I felt totally unable to articulate or even accept my fears, so I said nothing. I felt drained and ashamed, floundering in events that were spiralling out of control.

Ridey made some suggestions about what else we could do to locate him, and I could only agree we would take positive steps after tonight's situation was resolved. Trying desperately to gather my thoughts, I told him to keep six officers on duty, until I ordered a stand-down, just in case tonight's events demanded actions resolving in Humberside. I ended the call and slumped in the chair, exhausted and bereft of all ideas.

Before I could regain any equilibrium, DC Beatty appeared at the door of the spare office I'd been using and summoned me to Tom Corrigan's office for a debriefing on the interview with Debbie Pike. Without words, I followed him down the corridor. Tom was sitting behind his desk, which, when compared to mine back in Hull, was remarkably tidy. Graham Beatty's fellow interviewer, a Northumbrian

DS, was sitting on one of three chairs clearly set out for the meeting. Tom indicated the chairs for Graham and me, then asked his DS to update us.

'It's where to start, boss? Basically, she's shit-scared of Frame who she is convinced has murdered her husband Billy Pike, and she's now doing everything she can to make sure he goes to prison. We can't shut her up. As you know, she's even kept notes of what her husband and Frame have said and done. A lot of what she's written we should be able to corroborate. A good example is a note of the blue Jag and its number she says she made this morning when she saw Keegan pick Frame up at her house... we know that's true. But she's also made notes of conversations that we can't ever corroborate... but they are fantastic... and me and Graham believe her.'

DC Beatty was nodding enthusiastically.

Corrigan also nodded. 'Go on.'

The two interviewers grinned at each other and it was obvious that there were some revelations to come.

'Well, the longest set of her notes are the first ones. In them, she describes how Billy broke down and confessed to her that he'd shot Ryan Harrod. What she's written matches what we know, boss... it's got to be genuine.'

Beatty couldn't help but chip in: 'She also describes how Billy told her that Frame shot Emmerson. He wasn't there... Billy wasn't on that job, that's why they used Emmerson... but Keegan told him about it... he saw it... and Frame almost bragged about it.'

All four of us knew that using what Billy had told his wife as evidence in court was fraught with difficulty. He was dead. Billy could never stand in court to be cross-examined – it was what is called hearsay evidence. However, it gave us lots of information to work with and opportunities to corroborate what she said, or saw, with facts, other witnesses and admissions from Frame or Keegan.

The two officers then went over in detail what Debbie Pike had told them about her husband and his two colleagues and what she knew about their crimes. She had described how the men had talked about clothing, money and a weapon hidden on Keegan's trawler. She was adamant that Frame and Keegan had teamed up with a man called Grantmore from Hull, and that the three of them intended to carry out what she assumed was another robbery somewhere in or around Newcastle that night. They believed her when she said that she had no clue about the nature of the crime or where it would take place. To my relief, she had not seen the man Grantmore, or indeed any third man, who she thought was tonight's driver.

By the end of their briefing, we were convinced that we had a star witness and this was a massive step forward. They were confident that she was tough enough to stand up in court and swear to what she knew. However, we all knew her word alone would never be enough, but she had given us lots we should be able to corroborate. *The Blaydon Races* sounded a promising first step and we had that covered.

I waited until they had imparted all they knew before I divulged the embarrassing information I had been given about Grantmore leaving the country. I obviously took no satisfaction at being right about him not being the driver. Tom similarly made no comment about my disastrous decision to grant him bail. Professional – and still mates.

We sent the officers back to continue interviewing Debbie under caution as a suspect, seeking further information, while reassuring her that the police station was the safest place for her until we arrested Frame and Keegan, and that we would endeavour to reunite her with her children as quickly as we could. Tom and I had a brief discussion about whether or not we would ultimately have to charge her with any crimes – a lot would depend on what Frame and Keegan may allege, when and if they gave their side of things. Ideally, we wanted to treat her as a witness, while negating any allegations at a subsequent trial that she was giving false information to save her own neck. But these were decisions for further along the investigation and would need to involve the Crown Prosecution Service. For now, 'keep her sweet and talking' was the instruction, and the two interviewers returned enthusiastically to their task.

After they had left, Tom rose from behind his desk and strolled around his office while I filled him in on the latest news from Humberside. As I told him about the bloodstained shirt and Frame being at Grantmore's parlour with a gun and giving him money, he clenched his fists enthusiastically.

'We'll get them, Matt – I can feel it.'

I knew we would. But at what cost?

Thirty-Four

22:50 That Night

Holland was at the wheel of a Ford Mondeo. Somewhat of a comedown as a getaway car for Frame, but by now the only vehicle to which he had access. The ex-army officer sat at his side, directing him through the Newcastle streets to their target – the Belmont Casino. Frame's succinct and clear briefing had taken place in Stella's bedroom after their steak dinner, while Stella, much to Holland's relief, washed all the pots, thereby removing his fingerprints. Photographs and plans of the premises were studied and precise timings discussed – Frame wanting them in and out within ten minutes, with each man having a precise role. While Holland had absorbed Frame's instructions without comment, Keegan had kept interrupting, asking questions and at times quite obviously disagreeing with the plan. Frame had grown increasingly abrupt, obviously struggling to maintain his temper.

The building tension between the two criminals was having a positive effect on Russ Holland. He now accepted he was on his own and would get no chance to alert Darnley. It would be down to him to disrupt the robbery in some way – and save his own life. He knew Frame had no intention of letting him drive away with five grand. He had no idea how he would extricate himself from this mess but it would certainly be easier with the other two men not acting as a cohesive team. Divide and rule – a tactic he had not used for over twenty years, but one he had once been adept at.

He knew he would not be allocated the sawn-off and sure enough, Frame himself had claimed the weapon, a point clearly not lost on Keegan, who had argued vehemently that he should tote the gun. Russ had little doubt which of the two had executed their other Hull-based driver and decided the fate of Billy Pike. He now knew that Keegan was starting to worry that he too would be facing the same end.

As they pulled into Nun Street and saw the neon sign of the casino a few hundred yards ahead, the flashing blue lights of a police car came into view, moving rapidly towards them. From the rear of the car, Keegan's gasp of fear angered Frame.

'For fuck's sake, calm down.' Gone was the calm, cultured voice.

As the police car sped past, Keegan was almost hyperventilating.

The obvious rift and growing tension between the two ex-mates was widening at the same time that Holland's icy calm was deepening. As he drove, he marvelled at how the intervening years since he had last found himself in such fraught situations were evaporating. The Para's motto *Utrinque Paratus – Ready For Anything* ran through his head. He felt the buzz of exhilaration.

As planned, he pulled into the car park of the Wilko store opposite the casino, from where they could clearly see the main entrance. They each pulled on their gloves. As expected, two security men were in place outside the main doors and luckily there were no queuing customers, allowing an immediate approach. Twenty yards from the front doors, they each pulled down their balaclavas, Frame raised the

317

sawn-off across his chest while Holland and Keegan hefted their baseball bats. The two burly doormen realised far too late what was about to happen and the three robbers bundled them both into the foyer of the building with the threat of the shotgun. Holland strode across the foyer and behind the reception desk, instructing the terrified female employee to lie on the floor. Within thirty seconds, he had taped over her mouth, rolled her onto her stomach and bound her hands to her feet with strong black cable ties. Meanwhile, Frame and Keegan had forced the two guards behind the counter and out of sight of the main doors, and were busy putting them in the same position. His guard silenced and immobilised, Frame hurried to the front doors and locked them using the guards' keys, which he left in the lock. While Keegan finished securing his man, Holland slipped the mobile he had found in the receptionist's pocket into his own.

'Right. Upstairs,' instructed Frame, pushing Keegan ahead of him as he cast a last eye around stage one of his plan.

When Frame had started to outline his plan of robbing a casino while it was in full operation, Holland had been dubious as to how the clientele, let alone the staff, could be controlled. But Frame had done his homework and knew that a wealthy local businessman was hosting his sixtieth birthday party – with his equally wealthy friends – in a private room. This smaller room was well away from the main area and thus the bulk of staff and customers. It was also adjacent to the manager's office and the safe, access to which had been assured. Frame had explained how he had bought off the casino's head of security, an appropriately named Daniel Bent, who would be on duty at the party. As Bent's role was revealed at the briefing, Keegan had exploded in fury, demanding to know what this extra pair of hands was likely to cost them. But almost as the words left his lips, Holland saw that Keegan had realised that this man was to join the list of "disposable assets". Frame had made no comment; just stared at Keegan with almost open contempt.

Holland knew that this final robbery already had a planned death toll of three.

He checked his watch. Less than two minutes had elapsed since they had entered the building as Frame led the way into the party room. He saw a middle-aged man in a smart dark suit nod almost imperceptibly to Frame before striding between the gaming tables towards them.

'What the hell is going on here?' he demanded.

Frame moved to meet him and smashed the butt of the shotgun into the man's forehead. Bent played his part by slumping to the ground, apparently unconscious. Holland and Keegan were prepared for this staged event – as was Bent. This would be his alibi during the subsequent investigation and also serve to immediately subdue the guests with an initial show of violence.

It worked a treat. Some of the male guests made as if to move forward and there were a few female gasps, whimpers and tears, but as Frame moved towards them with his sawn-off swinging, no one screamed, shouted or even spoke.

Stage two completed.

'Everyone… face down on the floor… now. If I see a mobile phone, I will shoot you.' Quietly, but firmly delivered as an order.

He used the sawn-off for emphasis and every single person obeyed, although at different speeds, looking around to see how their friends were complying.

Stage three completed. Less than four minutes elapsed.

Frame turned and nodded towards the manager's office, the instruction to Keegan and Holland to start stage four. Holland moved decisively towards the office and pushed open the door to find the casino manager behind his desk –

and using the landline. He swung the baseball bat, knocking the phone base off the desktop, which ripped the handset from the man's grip. If he had been trying to summon help, Holland was confident that he had not had enough time. As he focussed on disabling the portly manager with cable ties, he realised Keegan had not followed him into the office as planned. He turned back to the gaming room and could see and hear him and Frame arguing.

Stage four was falling apart.

As he rolled the manager to the side, so as to gain access to the safe door, he was amazed to see Frame hand the shotgun to Keegan. Holland's senses kicked into overdrive, as serious fault lines appeared in the plan. Keegan no doubt felt a touch safer with his own finger on the trigger but he was a loose cannon and Frame's focus must now be diverted.

Divide and rule.

Taking on Frame's planned role, Keegan waved a black holdall and screamed, 'Watches, jewellery, wallets and all cash. In the bag.'

He moved towards the first victim.

Frame joined Holland at the safe, using the keys and combination provided by Bent.

Stage four, as amended, back on track with five minutes elapsed.

As he heard Keegan rapidly getting more and more irate with the birthday guests, harrying them to be quicker, Holland fell into role – his old role of twenty years ago. Icily calm and prepared, he remembered his unit's mantra – *Innovate. Adapt. Overcome.* Opportunity was knocking.

Access to the safe was gained quickly and Frame began loading bundles of cash into the holdall that Holland had brought. As he zipped it closed, they could hear a commotion from the gaming room. They re-entered the room and saw Keegan on his knees, struggling to wrest a bracelet from a woman's wrist. The man lying next to her had used the opportunity to try and grab the sawn-off and now all three were engaged in a struggle. Keegan, screaming obscenities, abandoned the quest for the bracelet, desperate to keep control of the firearm. As Frame and Holland moved towards the melee, the shotgun discharged and both instinctively dived for the floor. The noise was deafening in the confined space as shot peppered the ceiling. The two guests ceased their struggle immediately and clasped their arms around their heads in an almost childlike exhibition of terror. Disorientated, Keegan was thrust aside and the sawn-off fell to the carpeted floor with a soft thud.

Opportunity.

Holland quickly rose to his feet and swung his baseball bat at Keegan's head, knocking him sideways, and apparently unconscious, across the woman who had resisted the theft of her diamond bracelet.

But equally quickly, Frame dived for the sawn-off. In a fluid movement, he rolled onto his side and aimed at Holland, who swung the baseball bat, hitting the short barrel as it discharged. Shot peppered Holland's right arm and the baseball bat, which clattered to the floor. Before Frame could react, Holland kicked him in the chest and he fell onto his back, the shotgun now useless. With barely a pause, Holland stamped onto Frame's left leg just below the knee. The snap of the bone was clearly audible. He then repeated the move on his right leg with a similar result. The pursuant screams as he wrestled the gang leader into the position to secure him with cable ties seemed to rouse Keegan.

'You bastard, Long. You're going to get the same as Emmerson and Billy. You are dead!'

He made no effort to even move towards Holland, who stood above Frame, his right arm pouring blood.

Holland realised the adrenaline that had allowed him to use his damaged arm to secure Frame was no longer sufficient, but he needed to ensure Keegan could not escape. In seconds, he came up with a solution that he knew witnesses would describe to the police, enhancing the role he now intended to play. He addressed two of the male guests, who were observing unfolding events.

'You two, sit on this dickhead… citizen's arrest… you'll be heroes.'

Confused by what they were actually witnessing and with obvious trepidation, the two did as he suggested, quickly warming to the task of subduing their earlier tormentor. Two others quickly joined them.

Holland then picked up the holdall of money with his working hand and placed it next to the one partly filled by Keegan.

'I don't want the money or your stuff. Tell the cops that I did this for my mate Billy.'

He walked across the room, pausing in front of Bent, who following the blow to his head had had no trouble remaining slumped against the wall, as he had agreed beforehand with Frame. More of the guests had begun to realise their ordeal was over and were rising from their prone positions.

'Two more volunteers needed over here. This chap was in on the robbery. Tell the cops he supplied the inside information and the safe keys.'

As three men crossed towards Bent, he pulled Keegan's balaclava from off his head and used it to remove any fingerprints from the shotgun he may have left when he had handled it at Stella's. He broke the weapon, placed it back on the floor and then left the room. Downstairs, he removed an overcoat from the cloakroom next to reception and struggled into it, thus hiding his damaged arm and bloodstained overalls. He unlocked the doors and walked off.

Stage five completed – admittedly an improvised version. Innovate. Adapt. Overcome.

Frame's stage six had not been in his briefing. But it was not going to happen anyway. That would have been the torching of the Mondeo after he had been forced onto *The Blaydon Races*, prior to his execution. Holland wanted the Ford found by the police. It contained the plans and photographs removed from Stella's, along with the potential for fingerprints. Not his of course.

He'd only walked a hundred yards when he heard the approaching sirens.

The birthday party was getting into full swing.

Thirty-Five

I sat back in the old and battered, but very comfortable, armchair in the lounge of the Bell in Driffield, contemplating what had been a shattering and stressful, but extremely rewarding, couple of days. All around me, staff from the incident were chatting animatedly, raising random toasts and generally enjoying the successful conclusion of our inquiry. In reality, there was still a hell of a long way to go but tradition dictates that on a major incident at the point of charging someone with the crimes you are investigating, a celebration ensues. Normally, I too would have been in a state of high excitement at this stage, enjoying the vindication of my leadership, but the many loose ends remained personal threats.

Grantmore was still adrift, albeit now tracked by Interpol as entering Spain. Everyone felt positive about finding him – but what would he say when we did?

Morley was still missing. I looked across at Pete Granger, who at this moment seemed as ebullient as the rest, raising his pint towards me as he registered my gaze. Yet only yesterday we had had a heated exchange about when I would find the space to focus the inquiry upon that particular loose end.

But by far my biggest worry was Russ Holland. What a job he had done. He had quite literally delivered Frame and Keegan at the crime scene – on his own. His half of our bargain was way beyond anything I dared hope. But I was now torn between elation that I had planted him with the gang resulting in this success, and dread that his involvement would be discovered because I couldn't deliver my side of the deal – Grantmore.

Minutes after he must have fled the Belmont Casino and I was on my way to the scene with Tom Corrigan, he had rung me. He had uttered only two sentences.

'Three bodies for you, Detective Superintendent. Our business is concluded.'

He gave me no time to respond – which I couldn't have done in any case with Corrigan sat next to me.

Bodies? And three? My blood ran cold – as I'm sure he intended.

Over the next couple of days, I had tried to contact him several times without success. I knew he would be assuming that Grantmore would be facing charges along with Frame and Keegan and that at last his quest for revenge for Lisa was over. What was his reaction going to be when the media failed to mention Grantmore, other than that he was wanted by the police? My initial overwhelming sense of relief that Frame and Keegan had no idea about who Steve Long really was had evaporated. I was incredulous at the ability of the man to act and think on his feet. How he had disabled Frame and Keegan and then planted the notion of him being a friend of Billy Pike's, extracting retribution for his murder. Of course, it didn't fit the scenario of Grantmore providing the driver, and no one apart from me could figure out how to make sense of it all, although Granger must have smelled a rat. There was now an active line of inquiry to TIE (Trace, Implicate or Eliminate) ex-army colleagues of Billy. A total waste of time and resources but what else could I do? To a huge extent, the subterfuge planted by Holland eased the biggest threat to me, but I needed to get hold of him and reassure him we would get Grantmore.

I was interrupted in my reverie as Tony Ride plonked another pint in front of me, sat down and said, 'Sorry I'm late to the party, boss.'

I inwardly groaned. I knew he would not just sit and enjoy a pint but would want to discuss the future direction of the inquiry – checking he was fully on top of things and able to keep his MIR running smoothly. Admirable. Dedicated. But at this precise moment, bloody annoying. I just wanted to continue mulling over the remaining threats to yours truly. However, I knew there'd be no stopping him, so concluded I might find his synopsis useful in my personal deliberations.

Off he went.

'As you know, boss, we had to interview Keegan first, while Frame was in hospital getting potted up.' He smiled broadly. 'Well, he has not shut up. Let's look at the murders first. He says he saw Frame shoot Emmerson. Pike shot Harrod, and Frame forced him to help murder Pike at sea… but he's admitted wielding the murder weapon… a mallet… himself. They threw Pike overboard… along with the gun used to kill Emmerson and Harrod.'

The recovery of that weapon would have been excellent evidence to corroborate Keegan's account, but we still had the strong possibility of proving the bullets recovered from Emmerson and Harrod came from the same gun.

'And what about "Hop-along"?' I asked, grinning.

'Not a single word… not even "no comment".'

'We've got blood spatters on the deck of *The Blaydon Races*, that corroborate Keegan's account. We're hoping they match Pike's DNA… we can use hair samples found in his brush at Debbie Pike's. Then there's her evidence of Frame summoning him to the trawler, seeing him board it… and never seeing him again.'

'How's she holding up… have we heard?'

'They've finished with her for now, but they've put her somewhere safe with her kids. I think they're a bit worried in case Frame's got any mates.'

Tom Corrigan and I had discussed that possibility, so I was glad he was taking this cautious approach. We didn't want anything happening to our star witness.

Ridey kept moving on. 'Now, the robberies… our job first. Keegan fully admits that with Frame and Emmerson. Billy was ill apparently, so Grantmore provided Emmerson as the driver, poor bastard. He describes why Frame shot Emmerson… just as we suspected… the blood. Then we have Beedham's and Cooper's accounts and the Noel Priestley connection… the inside man. And we should get more from Grantmore when we get him… It's all hanging together.'

He paused to gather his thoughts.

'He's also coughed the kidnap and robbery at Ponteland with Frame and Pike and why Pike had to die… same reason.'

'Then there's the recovered money on the trawler as well as the balaclavas and overalls described by Beedham and Cooper. Plus there were plans of the casino job in the recovered Mondeo'

'Debbie Pike's notes and her evidence are brilliant. We've got Billy admitting the killing of Ryan Harrod, as well as odds and sods about the other crimes they've done, then Billy's disappearance and finally Frame and Keegan setting off to meet a third man she still insists is called Grantmore. We need to find this third man… who Keegan says called himself Steve Long. Why the hell didn't he take the money?'

'Like he said at the time, he's a mate of Billy's after revenge… not a crook. Another army lad for sure, he was well handy… Frame will be using crutches for months. We need to find him… he deserves a reward,' I chuckled.

'According to Keegan, he's already helped himself to one… by nicking about thirty grand off the trawler.'

When questioned about the money found hidden on *The Blaydon Races*, Keegan had been adamant the sum we said we'd found was short and had at first claimed the searching officers must have nicked it. Further into the interview, when asked about the mysterious, double-crossing Steve Long, he went ballistic, claiming he must have taken it. As far as he was concerned, Long and Grantmore must have been in it together.

'Then why not nick the cash at the casino? He made a point of showing the witnesses he didn't want it. And we had the trawler under surveillance and according to Keegan, they never let Long… or whoever he is… out of their sight.'

'He reckons Billy must have told him about the cash and he's nicked it before they even met him. He's a right mystery, as Keegan is still insisting Grantmore provided him and they picked him up at Ferrybridge.'

'Guess we'll have to ask him when we find him.' I wanted to change the subject.

Ridey ploughed on. 'Anyway, we've charged both of them jointly with the murders of Emmerson and Pike, the assaults, kidnaps and robbery in Beverley, robbery and kidnap in Ponteland and the casino robbery. It seems the bloke Bent was only in on the casino job. What about the murder of Ryan Harrod, boss? Billy pulled the trigger but do you reckon there's enough for a murder charge for Frame and Keegan?'

I'd been thinking about young Ryan and was keen to discuss with CPS this possibility.

'Pike pulled the trigger and they weren't even there but each knew that gun was loaded and they were committing a violent crime. They shot Emmerson, murdered Pike… it all hangs together as a joint enterprise. I reckon it would stick.'

Then he was off again: 'Lots more work to do to bolster the charges both in terms of witness interviews and forensics, but we're looking good. Keegan has also admitted the Brid job and some other robberies... a couple in Lincolnshire and one in Derbyshire. Plenty of work still to do on them. I think we need a full morning's briefing on Monday to reshape the inquiry. Shall I work tomorrow, boss, to start planning?'

Overtime signs were flashing in his eyes.

'No, we've all had a draining few days. They're charged and going nowhere. Rest day tomorrow.'

'What's your thoughts on Debbie Pike, boss?'

'Tom and I have discussed it and are confident we can treat her as a witness. Okay, she could have told us earlier but she was shit-scared of her husband and Frame. She's done nothing wrong.'

'Just Grantmore to find and fettle then. Keegan has fully implicated him in setting up the Beverley job through the chief exec... and as I say, he's adamant he supplied the driver Steve Long... just as he did Emmerson.'

'All the independent evidence points to it being Billy's mate. We'll concentrate there. But you're right, we need Grantmore. And Morley has to be a priority... I've got a bad feeling that's why Grantmore's run.'

Tony Ride took a swig of his pint. I could tell he had finished for the moment. Satisfied his MIR would be ready for the next phase. I finished my drink then made my way outside to the car park and tried Holland's number again. Nothing.

Three men adrift. Each with secrets. Secrets I needed to keep.

Thirty-Six

The following Monday's briefing had been used to do in detail what Detective Sergeant Ride had done in the pub on the Friday night. The status of the inquiry was dissected and its future direction determined. All of the team up in Newcastle and the bulk of those in Driffield were tasked with those actions that cemented the charges against Frame and Keegan.

We now seemed to have most parts of the jigsaw – and the picture almost made sense. Keegan's admissions, Debbie's account and what the witnesses at the casino had seen all added to what we already knew and provided ninety per cent of the picture. But what about Steve Long? Keegan had stuck to his version of events of picking up the driver provided by Grantmore at Ferrybridge. He insisted Long and Grantmore must have arranged the double-cross. That made sense until you looked at the fact Long left the cash and other booty. He similarly couldn't have got the money off the trawler that Keegan stated was missing. What the witnesses stated he had said at the scene, about revenge for Billy Pike after he attacked Frame and Keegan, made sense of him leaving the spoils.

I let the discussions and theories play out, eventually calling a halt and telling them that Grantmore would clarify matters when we found him – while hoping to God he didn't. Perhaps more hopefully, I expounded the view that it is rare in any large serious crime inquiry for there not to be some unanswered questions. Anomalies are common. There are always pieces of the puzzle missing. It is often the unexplained features of a case that defence tactics tend to crystallise around. I refocussed the team on what we did know; encouraging them to make the case we did have as watertight as possible. I knew that no one but me could possibly know the full and true picture. But I also knew that Grantmore and Peter Granger could work out most of it, and that continued to nag at my confidence.

By now, half of my team were up in Northumbria, working closely with Corrigan's, while we tidied up our outstanding enquiries that focussed on our murder and robbery. I also established a small team in Humberside tasked with finding Grantmore and Morley.

DC Jo Young had been allocated an action she viewed as a complete waste of time, but yet extremely sensitive and difficult – and she'd told Tony Ride as much. The usually easygoing DS rapidly got pissed off and I couldn't help but chuckle as he instructed her to get on with it, making a sarcastic comment about even the boss's "pet" having to do as she was told.

*

As Jo Young drove out to the large house adjacent to Brough Golf Club, her temper did not improve, and now sitting at the breakfast bar in Mrs Marjorie Priestley's somewhat old-fashioned kitchen, as she made her a cup of tea, it was only getting worse.

Marjorie clattered about in the cupboards, hardly concealing her distaste at having yet another police officer in her house.

'How long will I have to wait until I can bury him? He's been dead a week,' she demanded.

Jo kept quiet and continued taking the statement paper out of her briefcase. Her task was to determine if Noel Priestley's wife knew anything about what the girls at the massage parlour had reported about his frequent visits and his association with Grantmore. As far as Jo was concerned, the two women at his parlour had already well and truly stitched Priestley into Grantmore's web and thus identified the inside man who had set up the robbery. For Christ's sake, he'd as good as admitted it in his suicide note. When they found Grantmore, he'd be the source of any corroboration. Why further distress his grieving widow, who surely had no inkling that her husband had been using what were essentially prostitutes? But it was now down to Jo to break it to her. The woman's snotty off-hand manner was at least making her task less upsetting.

'I've got rid of all of his clothes already to the charity shop,' said Marjorie proudly.

Jo's curiosity was roused.

'I've got his car up for sale. I want a smaller one... in white, I think. And as for this tatty old kitchen...'

Jo tested the water. 'How long were you married, Mrs Priestley? It must be so hard for you.'

'Too bloody long.'

With that, the widow turned away from the cupboards to face the somewhat incredulous detective. 'Am I shocking you, love? Sorry... but I couldn't stand the man.'

The two women shared a pot of tea and an open and frank discussion. An hour later, Jo Young headed straight back to the incident room, now in an excellent mood.

*

While Jo Young was busy striking gold, the team tasked with finding Morley were still in the incident room, planning their approach. The consensus at the briefing was that Morley had in some way fallen foul of Grantmore. The optimists favoured the scenario of him being spooked and now lying low. The realists, led by an adamant Pete Granger, thought that Grantmore had killed him. Several of the older more experienced hands were now more than a little pissed off at the young copper's successes – and Darnley's praise – and didn't want to listen to his opinions. They rationalised that he could hardly be right again.

DI Baldwin, who was in charge of this line of inquiry, had decided to start with a detailed examination of the large amount of material seized from the searches of Grantmore's home and businesses the previous week, to see if anything shed any light on Morley's disappearance. Although all the items had been entered in the exhibit store and statements submitted describing where they were found, there had not been time for any detailed assessment as to their worth. They knew about the shirt and the towel with the staining on them and they were clearly priorities. Was it blood? And if so, whose? They were surprised at the amount and variety of stuff that had been seized and knew it would take some time to go through. Baldwin and his team of four detectives now had the property laid out on a desk in the main briefing room. They were just about to start their assessment when Inspector Maggie White, the force Press Relations Officer, entered the room with Richard Wilde.

The charges against Frame and Keegan had come too late for Friday's news, and weekends are never the best days for squeezing the most out of a high-profile local story. But now Darnley wanted maximum coverage and Inspector White was keen to help. All the local and national news outlets were keen to hear more about the sensational developments, arrests and charges. Maggie had been somewhat bemused when Darnley had asked her to invite Richard Wilde, the *Hull Mail's* fledgling crime reporter, to accompany her. But it was no skin off her nose and he'd jumped at the chance. She'd first popped into Darnley's office with Wilde and told him the interviews were arranged and would start in about half an hour, using the incident room as a backdrop. She was surprised not only to hear Darnley offer Wilde a one on one interview and insight into the workings of the MIR, after the others had left, but also of how self-assured the young reporter was in the presence of the senior officer.

DI Baldwin nodded to the PRO and then recognised Wilde as Maggie looked around the MIR for the best spot for Darnley to play host. He realised that a media circus was about to be unleashed.

'You're not bringing the bloody press in here, are you?'

'Afraid so… guess you're going to have to clear this little lot out the way… sorry.'

While this exchange was taking place, Wilde's attention had been drawn to the bagged exhibits on the desk, and a couple of the detectives were growing uncomfortable with his obvious interest, a mistrust of the press being a healthy and intrinsic state in seasoned officers. One of them rose from his seat and with outspread arms, tried to both shield the items from view and usher him away. However, his journalistic instincts had been aroused and he pointed to a camera, clearly visible in its evidence bag, lying amongst the other exhibits.

'Is that Graham Morley's camera?'

All eyes turned to look at the Canon camera with an attached telephoto lens.

'Oh shit,' muttered Granger.

Mally Baldwin asked Wilde, 'What makes you say that?'

Richard Wilde, being very careful about what he said, gave a brief account of his contact with Morley just over a week before and how he had initially coveted his camera while in the café on Spring Bank. Pete Granger told the group that he too could confirm that Morley did indeed use a Canon camera – kicking himself that within the next few minutes he would have spotted the link, if it weren't for the cocky young journalist sticking his nose in.

However, Wilde was able to go further and told the DI the camera model number and make of telephoto lens, which he had seen Morley using. Baldwin examined the exhibit label, and the details matched.

There were excited discussions at the obvious implications.

Maggie White thanked the journalist for his help then led him away for the media briefing, but not before the team had arranged to take a statement from him, after he'd finished the media briefings. He was now a witness in a potential murder inquiry, entirely due to his own investigative journalistic endeavours. He couldn't wait to get back to the office to further impress his bosses – and secure his future.

DI Baldwin rang the photo lab based at Beverley Police Station and arranged for the rapid processing of the film. Getting the stained check shirt and towel found in the same drawer as the camera to the forensic science laboratory was prioritised.

*

It was not until I had finished with the media that Wilde got the chance to quickly tell me about the camera and how he had told DI Baldwin the scant facts of his meeting with Morley in the café, and then near Nicole's. It looked like Pete Granger had been right all along. I was about to discuss with him exactly what he should, and definitely should not, reveal in his witness statement, when Mally interrupted us, keen to brief me about the camera and the action he had taken to get the film in it developed. Not knowing the team had arranged to record his account before he left the MIR, I told Wilde I'd be in touch, and then sat with Mally and Tony Ride to discuss the full ramifications of the discovery and raise a whole new set of actions.

That task completed, I was about to ring Wilde when to my horror I found he was still in the building and in the middle of giving his statement. I was trying to dream up a plausible excuse for interrupting the process, when Jo Young burst into the MIR and insisted on updating me immediately, and in private, with her news.

What a morning. We really were on a roll – but what the hell was Wilde saying? By the time I could get to him, whatever version of his encounter with Morley he had recounted would already bear his signature. I also knew if he'd said too much I'd soon be hearing all about it from DI Baldwin. But I knew Wilde was no idiot and was pretty sure he'd back me up, so I had no choice but to keep my fingers crossed and plough on.

It was obvious we needed another briefing to bring everyone up to speed before they went home. I rang the photo lab and asked how quickly they could develop the film and to contact me as soon as someone from the inquiry could look at the negatives. I then arranged a second briefing for 4pm.

Since Granger was the link to Morley and his photographs, I sent him to view the negatives, as soon as the lab rang me back. When he returned and described their contents to me, he was triumphant; his continual pushing for action to trace Morley vindicated – but his worst fears confirmed. He was also visibly distressed and it was clear that he blamed himself in some way for what had befallen the sad young man.

My guilt was to kick in much later, and I confess I was just elated to have some useable evidence to help us resolve this final element of the case. Here was another chance to boost the momentum of the inquiry – push it to a conclusion – and I needed to choreograph the briefing. Maximum impact.

I decided to go with the contents of the camera first and let Granger describe the series of photographs of Grantmore getting out of a taxi outside Nicole's, and then approaching whoever was taking the photographs – presumably Morley – in an aggressive manner, before attacking them. The photographs clearly showed the location. As I listened with bated breath, DI Baldwin then referred to Wilde's completed statement and read out how Wilde described seeing Morley in that same alley, with the same camera just over a week before. Actions were raised to locate and forensically examine the scene of the attack. We now had a potential crime scene – a murder scene? How could we prove Morley was the actual photographer and Grantmore had stolen the camera directly from him? The same argument from the morning followed – had Morley fled after the attack, or was he dead? The majority now favoured the latter.

Granger looked grim but self-satisfied.

Before we moved on, I asked for Wilde's statement, saying I was keen to read the detail – which I bloody was! How I resisted a quick scan I don't know – but we had to move on.

'Okay, Mally, your team now need to locate Graham Morley... alive or dead. I hate to admit it but my gut feeling is he's dead. So we desperately need Grantmore. He's already looking at serious charges but there's not enough for the murder of Emmerson. He wasn't present and had no way of knowing murder would result from the robbery he facilitated. But if he's killed Morley, we're going to prove it.'

I turned towards Jo Young.

'So, DC Young... tell us where to find him.'

Everyone was gobsmacked when she read out an actual address – a house number and street name in a Spanish village – the whole bloody address. She went no further. We'd agreed to choreograph the event. Investigative velocity.

'Spain. We already knew he'd entered Spain from basic passport checks but this morning, Jo here has unearthed a little gem from the widow of our inside man, Noel Priestley.'

DC Young stood to enjoy her moment in the spotlight.

'Thanks for the opportunity, Sarge.' She grinned at a bemused Tony Ride, savouring her little taste of revenge.

'In a nutshell, she knew full well about her husband's visits to Nicole's and Cleopatra's but never confronted him. She despised him and has done for years. She's actually glad he's dead. I can't explain it but it seems that for her to know all about his shortcomings was just more power to her elbow… just another reason for her to make his life a misery. Anyway, that address I've given you is a small house in a village called Totalan up in the hills, about twenty miles behind Malaga, which the Priestleys have owned for about fifteen years. She occasionally goes there on her own… to get away from him… and about a year ago, one of the Spanish ladies she knows there, asked her who the young woman was who had been staying in her house. To cut a long story short, Mrs Priestley found out it was Janine from one of the parlours. She did nothing, but asked the Spanish neighbour to let her know about any other visitors. Janine's been there twice more since, and so she reckons Janine must have been blackmailing her hubby for free holidays. But now the good news… she got a call yesterday from the Spanish neighbour who told her there's a chap there now… with one eye and terrible facial scars.'

Jo sat down, looking smug.

*

I pulled the car into my drive. It was nearly midnight and I was shattered but exuberant at the same time. The press briefings had gone well and I was so glad that I had decided not to include any mention of the missing Grantmore at this stage. I had agreed with Tom Corrigan and both ACPO teams that we would initially focus only on the good news. My motives at the time were purely to keep the fact that he had fled justice away from Holland, but now I realised that if the media had been given the "wanted" story with accompanying photographs of him, it may just have spooked him to leave where we hoped he was now still in hiding. I had set the wheels in motion with Europol and the Spanish police and had been promised immediate action, and that I would get a phone call within a few hours, one way or the other.

I was still desperately worried about Holland. When I'd read the statement taken from the receptionist at the casino, I realised he must have rung me on the mobile he took from her. I thought briefly about trying it, but judging by how efficient he had been at the casino, I knew he'd have ditched it straight after ringing me. I'd long given up trying his original mobile number. I resolved that I had no option but to call round at his home if the Spanish police did not get Grantmore that night. I needed to explain my position and reassure him – and bloody thank him. I knew that he'd have heard or read the current news and seen that there was no mention of Grantmore being charged alongside Frame and Keegan, and I'd bet my pension he was now thinking I'd done a deal with him. He would be furious and bent on revenge. I knew that until Sean Grantmore was locked up, back in England, charged and in prison, Holland was a continual threat. Looking back, I'm not proud of the fact that all I wanted was to be able to tell the media the next day that Grantmore was in custody and would be extradited on suspicion of serious crimes. I gave not a thought for Graham Morley – I was just obsessed with being able to charge Grantmore with his murder in order to protect myself.

I'd nervously read Wilde's statement at the first chance I got – and it was perfect. It was obvious that he was fully onside and well aware of the implications of what he knew. I found the time to ring him and thank him for his discretion. He was just excited at being so closely involved in a murder inquiry – a key witness – and described his boss's positive reaction to that news. We agreed that if the Spanish police arrested Grantmore that night, he would get it in the paper tomorrow, with a story clearly linking it to the murders and robberies and strongly suggesting Grantmore was suspected of additional serious crimes.

If I could follow that as quickly as possible by media coverage of the charges laid against him, Holland would know I'd kept my side of the bargain. Then I'd never contact him again. His lust for revenge would be fulfilled. I'd be safe.

Thirty-Seven

Three Months Later
Wednesday, 19th May 1999

'The end of a brilliant investigation, Matt,' said the Chief, exuding bonhomie. 'Can we agree that the MIR at Driffield can now go down to skeleton staff?'

I smiled to myself. How times change. I was rehabilitated. Crabbe calling me by my Christian name – and even abbreviated. No more just 'Darnley' – for now at least. Too bloody right after all the good publicity the force – and thus him – had received over the last few months, courtesy of yours truly. I'd even been invited to Strategy Team to finalise my reports – and bask in the glory.

The initial media splurge about the charges levelled against Frame and Keegan, across four police force areas, had quietened, as sub judice applied until their trial started. But the Spanish police did arrest Grantmore that night. I ensured there was immediate publicity. We couldn't name Grantmore, as until he was returned to England and charged, that would be viewed as prejudicing his trial. However, Wilde did me proud. Our carefully worded press release, coming the day after the publicity about Frame and Keegan, would have left Holland in no doubt as to who it was – and that I had fulfilled my part of our deal. He would know his daughter's rapist was soon to face justice.

I still wanted to contact him – I craved total reassurance. I'd driven past his house, even then in an agony of indecision, but it was clearly empty. That unnerved me afresh, and I had made discreet enquiries trying to trace his whereabouts without even a sniff of success. As the weeks passed, I concluded he and Lisa must have opted for a fresh start, somewhere new, and I began to relax.

Grantmore's extradition was expedited and about four weeks after the initial media release, he was charged with the murder of Graham Morley, and jointly with Frame and Keegan with the Beverley and Bridlington robberies. Another blaze of local and national publicity followed.

I was confident that Holland's thirst for revenge would now be slaked.

I never heard from him again.

'Thank you, sir. Skeleton staff it is… a DS and three. I'll keep popping in but we're about done.'

'Are all the searches for Graham Morley's body exhausted?' asked the ACC Ops.

'High-profile media appeals and dozens of interviews with people who knew him have drawn nothing. We've searched a huge area around where Grantmore attacked him, but in truth we have no concrete information about where to focus the search for his body. The public's response has been fantastic… someone vanishing without trace is everyone's worst nightmare. As you know, Grantmore has made "no comment" interviews throughout… his usual approach. My guess is, he's waiting for trial to see if we find the body. If not, he'll admit that he attacked Morley… he can do little else with the photos and Morley's blood on his shirt. But with no body, he can claim he left him alive. However, we may, of course, still find it. But from all we have learnt about him he seems to have been incapable of "disappearing" of his own volition. We can present evidence from those who knew him that make it clear he must be dead. So I'm happy… as are CPS… that the murder charge, although largely circumstantial, will stick. It's actually one hell of a sad but convincing tale. A jury will love it.'

Throughout the numerous interviews with Grantmore, I had waited for him to start making allegations about our various conversations, particularly about him planting my driver and setting up the potential crimes in Hull. But the bombshell never dropped, as he only ever said "no comment". Of course, for him to make allegations about me involved him digging himself in deeper with Frame's planning – so why would he?

Three months on, however, Graham Morley's ghost was quite literally haunting me. I had discovered a conscience. Together, Pete Granger and I had agonised over Morley's disappearance. We both felt partly to blame. It was sadly ironic that the photograph he had taken of the Vectra outside the Silver Cod that had opened up the case would now be used in evidence to help prove his murder. At the trial, PC Granger would describe Morley's obsession with Grantmore, using his file of photos and notes to explain why he was in the alley taking the photographs of the bully who ruined his life. Richard Wilde would appear as a witness, proving Morley had taken photographs of Grantmore from the very alley in which we would state he died. As I'd said to the Chief, this was one hell of a sad yet convincing circumstantial murder case that a jury could believe in. So although Granger and I both badly wanted to find his body, it wasn't just to strengthen the case. We needed to *know*. We felt we owed him that much. There was no one mourning his death. No one needed closure apart from us. I honestly could not believe how sad it made me feel.

I realised I had lapsed into silence, lost in my maudlin thoughts.

Our new Head of CID – Steve Proctor – bailed me out: 'I honestly think we've exhausted all avenues to find him.'

Chief Superintendent Sharples interjected: 'How about finding the third man… the driver on the casino robbery? That's a bloody mystery… he could tell us some useful stuff.'

Steve Proctor again jumped in: 'Our mysterious… and seemingly public-spirited Steve Long. Keegan is still insisting Grantmore supplied him, and it would be great to tie Grantmore into the casino robbery, but at the minute we can't link him.'

'We've run out of options at the minute. We've interviewed nine of Billy's ex-army colleagues who in theory could fit the bill, but to be frank, none even look likely.' I was keen to close off this avenue of debate.

As ever at Strategy Team, someone always wanted to score points, and Paul Jones ACC (Personnel) had a go: 'I bet Billy Pike's wife knows. She seems to be stuck right in the middle of this… but no charges, I understand, Detective Superintendent?' Heavy sarcasm was evident.

Steve Proctor again stepped in: 'I've reviewed all the evidence across the inquiry at Matt's request. There's nothing to show Debbie Pike assisted her husband or the others. She was afraid. She's given valuable evidence. She's done nothing wrong.'

Jones ploughed on: 'For God's sake, she damn well slept with Frame, suspecting he'd murdered her husband.'

He was silenced by the Chief's withering look. I chuckled to myself, wondering how he'd react to the exposé that Richard Wilde was planning after the trials. With my blessing, he'd approached Debbie Pike and come to an agreement to tell her story. He would then syndicate it around the plethora of women's magazines that would lap up the tale of love, sex, crime and violence told by a very pretty woman with plenty of that Geordie charisma. The media would love her. I was already picking up vibes from other contacts in the press that Wilde was highly likely to be snapped up by a national. I knew his loyalty was secure.

I confess Tom Corrigan and I had briefly discussed the idea of the beautiful widow having helped herself to the supposedly missing thirty grand off the trawler; after all, she knew it was there. By some tacit agreement, we never took it further. We didn't want to know. I guess neither of us wanted to blow our star witness out of the water. But if I'm honest, a little bit of me half hoped she had taken the cash – a measure of revenge for what had happened to her husband.

I sensed Paul Jones had not finished. He was shuffling through papers, red in the face and determined to get one over on me, unable to hide his contempt, at me – the dinosaur – for the moment at least, being top dog.

'In my role as head of all personnel issues, I also want to raise the issue of PC Peter Granger and demand to know why no disciplinary proceedings have been taken for the assault… in public… upon Sergeant Knaggs back in January.'

'It was my last action in Professional Standards actually. He was disciplined. I have posted him to Scunthorpe.' Steve Proctor again stepped in.

My old mate Steve Proctor, back in the CID where he belonged. He had been the obvious choice to replace Kingston, who had initially been suspended over the debacle exposed by Richard Wilde. Steve's first job had been to reinvestigate the mysterious death of Keith Donavan at the centre of that affair, and he quickly and easily established that his wife's boyfriend had murdered him. After the charge, Donavan's family renewed their publicity campaign, once again supported by Wilde and the *Hull Daily Mail*, and Kingston, along with his underling, Naylor, was dismissed from the force.

Then when "Wizz" Wilson retired, Steve fulfilled his ambition – Head of CID.

The Chief stepped in: 'I approved the posting. The lad made a mistake. Even the sergeant accepted his role in the sordid affair. Granger's done an excellent job for a young officer. He'll be commended after the trial, I'm sure. To be honest, I was moved to help him when I received a letter from the woman who was almost raped by the gang member who was shot. She was overflowing with the deepest gratitude for all he did for her.'

I chuckled to myself again at how a cooperative Anne Beedham had written the letter at my request and without doubt swayed Crabbe to agree with Steve Proctor's recommendation – over Jones's head.

'Have we got a trial date yet?' asked Jane Greenhall.

'No, ma'am, I expect it'll be about the end of the year, or early next year for the joint charges and the murders of Emmerson and Harrod. But Grantmore will go for a separate trial for the murder of Morley and that will be well into 2000.'

The agenda then moved on into that new millennium and plans to tackle the so-called millennium bug. Plans to tackle bad things that might not even happen.

I had spent the five months since I first saw Russ Holland in Hull Crown Court, planning to prevent bad things happening to me. In so doing, I had "crossed the line" – a legally drawn line. Gone far further over it than I had ever gone before, or ever wanted to go. But planting Holland had worked. No one got hurt that night – other than Frame – and we'd detected three murders. I'd never know if I didn't need to have done it; let's face it, fate just seemed to take over and deliver me good luck at every turn. Somehow, that good luck made me feel morally vindicated. I must have been right. Justice was now going to be served on three evil men. The more time passed, the safer I felt.

Millennium bug? Not for Matt Darnley.

Or was there? My guilt about Morley persisted. Was it my fault he was dead? I had even failed to find his body. He couldn't even be here to see justice delivered for him. I was shocked at how much like Holland I'd become; I had increasingly begun to believe justice wouldn't ease my pain.

Thirty-Eight

I pulled into the car park of Full Sutton Prison and found a space. I felt reluctant to leave the warmth of the Honda, not just because it was bloody freezing outside, but mainly because I have always hated prisons. Having spent my career trying to put people into them, I couldn't help but see them as breeding grounds for criminality and violence. Accepting that while criminals were in there, the public at large were safer, the vast majority came out more effective and committed. Paradoxically, I couldn't help but feel sorry for the inmates in the God-forsaken hellholes. As a detective, I'd often had to visit such places and their "guests" and it always freaked me out. Full Sutton Prison was a category A establishment – only for the most dangerous and high-risk, so I was readying myself for the shock to my delicate system.

I remained in the warm car and reread the letter I had received from Sean Grantmore a couple of weeks previously. He'd asked for a one-to-one meeting, promising me some information. Surely that could only be the location of Graham Morley's body?

Following the usual protocol with such a letter, I had first sent DCs Beatty and Young to see him, but he had refused, repeating that he would only talk to me on my own. Initially, I'd determined not to go, thinking to myself that the next time I would see him would be at his trial. Such thoughts had taken me back to the last time I'd seen him in court when he was acquitted of the rape and Russ Holland had attacked him. That case had also seemed solid – but he had got off. I knew the murder charge was pretty strong but it had the huge deficit of no body, and I couldn't help but have nagging doubts. I tried not to think about what the hell would happen if he were acquitted this time. I had still not seen or heard from Russ Holland. I was letting sleeping dogs lie. But what if Grantmore was acquitted? Would Holland renew his quest for revenge? Would both men speak out? What a bloody nightmare.

But it wasn't just self-interest that drove me to come and see him.

Much stronger was the need to fully complete the investigation, solve the mystery, find the body and thereby, I hoped, assuage my still growing, gnawing guilt. I'd kept in touch with Pete Granger since his posting to Scunthorpe, my intention being to get him into the CID, and I knew he still felt terrible about not having been able to better protect the troubled young man. We both wanted Morley to at long last get his revenge. My guilt was made worse by the reality that it was Morley in effect that had solved the catalogue of crimes, while it was me basking in the glory.

I guessed Grantmore would be after yet another deal. *I'll tell you where the body is if…* He'd just received fifteen years for his part in the Beverley and Bridlington robberies, and seen his accomplices get life with a minimum recommendation of twenty-five years. If convicted of killing Morley, he too was looking at life, with a similar recommendation. He had nothing left to lose. He was desperate. I assumed he was hoping to strengthen his hand in such a deal by threatening me with exposure as a corrupt police officer during his forthcoming trial.

Desperate men with nothing to lose are dangerous and I still had a constant grumble of unease in the pit of my stomach. Grantmore – and this trial – remained my last threat. However, I had rationalised that any allegations he may now throw around would just sound like the fantasies of a man about to get a life sentence. If true, why didn't he say so when he had the chance in interviews?

On any large-scale crime inquiry, the SIO rarely has to make a court appearance. It is the staff working for you that end up as witnesses. It is they that seize exhibits, interview witnesses and suspects. It is they that must promise "to tell the truth, the whole truth and nothing but the truth". It is they that are cross-examined to ensure their story is accurate and honest. I had often thought that very few officers in any complex case actually knew "the whole truth" – they just knew their bit of it. In Regina versus Frame, Keegan and Grantmore, only I knew "the whole truth" and I'd never have to tell it.

So I resolved that there was no more dealing to be done.

As I climbed out of the car, I concentrated on mental images I still held of Graham Morley and how badly I had treated him, and by the time I was at the front gates, about to embark upon the somewhat tortuous security procedures necessary to gain entry, I was almost looking forward to seeing Grantmore's discomfort and enjoying my continuing role in it.

Twenty minutes later, I was being accompanied by a chatty prison officer through a maze of silent institutional corridors towards the small suite of interview rooms that served the wing on which Grantmore was remanded. As we turned yet another corner, I saw there were extensive refurbishments underway in an area that was clearly given over to classrooms and workshops. There was a team of three replastering walls, with another group redecorating an area where the plaster had dried. Up on some low scaffolding were yet more workmen fitting new electric lights.

'Been going on weeks this already,' moaned the warder, 'and more to come. Reckon they're going to be here months.'

'Must be a security nightmare,' I responded.

'The prison was only built in 1987 and it's bloody crumbling already. We've got more workmen than prisoners. They start on the cellblocks soon… *now that will be a bloody nightmare.*'

As if to emphasise the warder's words, another large group of workmen entered the corridor from one of the classrooms up ahead. They were all carrying the tools of their trade and chatting away. As they walked past, we exchanged nods and smiles of acknowledgement. Recognition flared in my brain and I glanced back to see a slim, athletically built man in pale blue overalls doing likewise. Our eyes met.

My bloody nightmare had begun.

Despite the heavy beard, those cold blue eyes were unmistakeable.

It was the restless, resourceful and ruthless Russ Holland.

Quentin Dowse joined the police at eighteen and retired as a Chief Superintendent after thirty years extensive experience that included leading numerous major crime and murder investigations. He holds a Master's Degree in Criminology and has attended the prestigious International Homicide Conference in the USA at which senior investigators share their expertise and knowledge. In 2014 he was approached to work as an 'investigator' during the making of a documentary/ mystery film - The First Film, in which he appears, outlining the results of his enquiries.

This is Quentin's first book – it is entirely fictional.

 Matador